DIRTBAG

A STRANGE TALE

ALDRIC J SAUCIER

ISBN: 0692364137

ISBN 13: 9780692364130

Library of Congress Control Number: 2015930313

Entropy's Espresso,
Superior, Colorado

For Her

CHAPTER 1

———

Long ago, an apocalyptic war left the continents irreparably devastated, forcing the ancients to cover them with the sea. This opened vast, new, fertile lands and effectively tripled the inhabitable surface of the planet. The ancients held the collected oceans behind a structure called simply the Grand Barrier, made of towering, featureless silver pillars untarnished by the passage of time. They loomed like an unlinked fence and held back the unimaginable mass of the sea by means no longer understood or investigated, a magnificent, mysterious permanence from the last great era.

High winds rushing across the surface of the elevated ocean regularly sent a fine mist of water over the edge of the Grand Barrier, depositing substantial amounts of sea salt onto the outlying fields of the small town of Pickle Flats. The prosperous town specialized in making brine, seasonings, and other derivatives of the mineral. Nothing grew in the salt fields, but over the barren landscape hung a perpetual rainbow in the mist that transitioned in color and curvature as the sun traversed the sky. It was a happy town, filled with good jokes, delicious foods, pleasant wind chimes, and people who had a propensity to smile constantly.

The cobblestone streets of Pickle Flats were wide enough for domesticated cars, but none were allowed. The town had a peculiar, hypocritical aversion to certain technologies; many things were banned, though microwave ovens, air conditioning, and salt-refining equipment were permitted. There were few horses, and those that were in town had stylish kilts draped over their backsides. The smiling people of Pickle Flats enjoyed walking; the climate was amiable, and the air carried a pleasing, sweet scent, as if it were always about to rain. If aspects of their lives were unpleasant, they never showed it or acknowledged it beyond a quick sigh followed by a glance skyward at the ever-present rainbow. It was easy to ignore even the most hideous of problems using this technique, and many did so at the sight of Dirtbag.

Dirtbag lay against the side of a building on a street corner as though he had been thrown there some time ago and chosen not to move from the awkward position he had landed in. He was a being sewn into the shape of a man; once he had been someone, but now he was this strange *thing*. His skin had been crafted from a cheap, second-hand denim blanket, which itself had been created from several pairs of well-worn jeans. The indigo dye of the fabrics had faded to a grayish, washed-out-rust color, unevenly peppered with threadbare white blotches, some of which had been haphazardly repaired with duct tape or shoddy patchwork. Upside-down pockets shaped the upper ridge of a frowning brow, with the empty pouches forming his eyes. His mouth was a curved-over slit like that of a sock puppet, filled with flat pebbles for chewing but having the appearance of toothless gums. The top of his head was open, and long, bright-green, wild grass grew out of it like unkempt, eccentric hair, bordered by frayed white strands of denim on either side. He was filled with dirt, which made him lumpy and soft and slightly asymmetrical throughout.

Already his daily cycle was beginning. Every morning he would watch the people cross the street to avoid him as he drank. His denim brow knotted up into a permanent angry scowl, he assailed them with hatred, and their revulsion fueled his unwelcomed, devilish delight. He was surrounded by empty bottles of hard liquor on one side and unopened ones on the other. He sipped from the latest one, not caring what it was. He moved only his arm and his head; the rest of his body had not moved in weeks and was covered with debris. He had fallen into a deep rut and knew it, but he was not ready to emerge from it. He wanted to lie there and see how far into self-hatred and regret he could go. It was as if he had jumped into a pool of murky water that was unexpectedly deeper than he had thought. Instead of clawing back to the surface, he had chosen to sink to the bottom, hoping to push off with his feet when he reached it, but it had been weeks, and still he sank.

There seemed to be endless things he had done worth punishing himself for, regrets that could never be rectified and guilt that gnawed at his dirt guts. He went over the choices he had made in life, how he had thought them right when he made them, and how they had been wrong. He lay there, sipping from his bottle, daydreaming and wishing he could fill the absence of his heart, tormenting himself by remembering whom he loved and how he had treated them. He was a defeated man and every bit the dirtbag he was named after.

The sun had reached its midmorning height, and Dirtbag was working on his second bottle of the day. Across the street he saw the little old man walking alone. The old man frequented the small farmers market every other day, accompanied by his frail wife. The woman had been ailing for quite some time; the right side of her body had been paralyzed, likely by a stroke, and she had a tendency to support her weight on her husband's steady arm. Once the woman had been beautiful, and from the way the old man looked at her, it was clear to Dirtbag that he still saw her that way. But where was she today? Had she died? Dirtbag drank as he contemplated. If she had, why was the old man so happy?

The old man disappeared into the store, leaving Dirtbag to return to his anguish. He gulped too much from his bottle, carelessly dribbling the excess down his chin. He seethed, jealous of the old man. His own life was empty, and he had lost everything.

"Oats alive, Dirt! I've been looking for you for days!" said a charming, noble voice.

A very tall, powerfully built, handsome knight stood over Dirtbag, blocking out the sun. He wore the heavy-plated carbon-fiber armor of the once-illustrious Blitz Knights of the now-defunct order of Warferno, renowned combat specialists. Pearlescent, cobalt blue interlaced with the graphite-black plates of his bulky, silver-trimmed custom suit. Its original majesty was dulled by the scars of old battles and the defaced remains of medals from bygone victories that were subsequently dishonorably removed. He had been the leader of the order and the sole cause of its demise through the disastrous siege of Trucebell, the first known attempt at using excessive barbecuing to bring about surrender. He wore two glossy-black fangs around his neck from the day of the siege, when dragons had descended, attracted by the delicious aromas, and massacred all his men. He had received divorce papers the previous evening from his third wife and had been drinking heavily when the dragons overran his encampment, razing the city encircled with spits of meat.

As Dirtbag looked up at him, the knight's long, golden-blond hair glowed like a halo around his flawless square chin and the cunning smile he had perfected to hide his feelings. The gallant knight kneeled down next to Dirtbag, pushing aside some of the bottles. He shifted his beautiful, flowing hair to one shoulder, removing a dark strand picked up from a recently conquered brunette, and grinned. Dirtbag could see the consequences of his dive into depression in the reflection of the knight's dark-lensed silver-wire aviator sunglasses.

"Well, hello, Tuna Casserole," Dirtbag snarled bitterly. "Took you long enough to find me."

"Whoa, easy on the kindness, Dirt," the knight said. "And it's T.C., remember? Just sound out the little dots, like initials. You know, *tee-cee*."

"You can't hear the dots!"

"I thought you were going to take a walk," T.C. said, immune to Dirtbag's hostility.

"I did…two weeks ago, but then I got tired and sat down."

"Swell. What happened to your button-eyes?" T.C. asked, examining Dirtbag's head with a big, armored hand. "I mean, one's gone, and the other is hanging by a thread."

"Some scumbag bird took it," Dirtbag grumbled. "I think it was mad at me. It was wearing eye shadow…or smoking. Could've been both."

T.C. raised his eyebrows. "You're just going to lie there until you become a one-eyed pile of trash screaming at pedestrians about love?"

"Hey! Who said I was screaming?"

"I mean, just look at you, Dirt. You're just a head and an arm sticking out of the ground, and why's all this money lying around you?"

"People kept throwing it at me so I'd shut up," Dirtbag growled. "I use it to bribe the orphans coming home from school to get me more liquor. I tried asking the kids with parents, but dads started kicking me in the head."

"They tend to do that, Dirt. I mean, there've been some complaints to the sheriff, and now we have to leave town by sunset, or they're going to put you on one of those lists. Oats alive, Dirt, you're lucky I came back when I did. I mean, what's the use of trying to be heroes if the moment you hit a rut you turn unprofessional?"

"I'm really depressed."

"Now, wait just a minute. I've been divorced ten times! Ten times! Oats alive! I mean, that's as bad as…as whatever is worse than kittens exploding."

"She stole my heart."

"OK, and we're going to get it back, right?"

"I don't even know why she stole it. I don't even know if I want it back, either. Sometimes I want to forget those feelings, and I think I'm glad she took it."

"I dunno, Dirt. I got demons screaming at me every second I let my guard down, too. I mean, regrets come at me from every direction, day and night, but isn't that why we do the hero thing?" T.C. shifted his position. "A hero, he doesn't look inward; he looks outward. He can't help himself, so he helps others. That's us, Dirt. We've spent years building up our reputation as heroes. People think we're heroic, and maybe we are—no matter what those court documents allege, right?"

Dirtbag tugged on his buried arm until it came loose from the ground. He combed back his uneven mop of green grass-hair. He looked at his worn denim skin; the coarsely stitched-together fabric held within it the earth that made up his very existence. He couldn't remember being any other way.

"T.C., heroes are certain types of people. We're something else, and I don't know what that is anymore."

"That's bullcookies, Dirt." T.C. smiled. "Nobody knows who we are, and they don't care. We're just the instruments that ease their moments of crisis, something to be thrown away during the good times and sought after in the bad."

"Exactly. I hate that."

"OK, I mean, I feel like we can go either way here, Dirt. We could just start robbing banks, burn the town down, say crass things about their silly rainbow; it could be therapeutic. I can even get out my clippers and shave a few heads."

Dirtbag paused as though seriously considering the supervillain option. He grinned, and then he saw the old man across the street shuffle out of the market, alone but somehow impervious to whatever tragedy had befallen his wife. He found himself envious of the old man's strength. If the old man could hold his sanity together even after losing the love of his life, so could Dirtbag.

"No, T.C., that's not us." He set his bottle down and held out his hand.

T.C. took hold of it, pulling him out of the rubble pile he had become embedded in with uncanny might. Dirtbag dusted himself off. He readjusted the thick canvas strap of a dilapidated courier satchel so that it crossed his body diagonally and hung off his left hip, slightly behind him. He realized something was missing. He dug into the small crater his body had left behind until he found his trusty autopneumatic shotgun. It resembled a short, rectangular, silver pillar, mirroring the design of those that held back the ocean. It was inlaid with stainless-steel piping that connected to a cluster of small canisters beneath the leather-wrapped handgrip. Above the pump handle was a cylinder that forged arrowhead-like diamond projectiles on demand, which he could fire at a velocity comparable to lightning.

Dirtbag cleaned the shotgun off and placed it in the holster on his right leg. It was a weapon he had commissioned with a single purpose in mind: to kill his ex-wife.

T.C. patted Dirtbag on the back, setting free a cloud of filth, and fixed his friend's twisted collar. "Dirt, have you tried getting a hold of Katvanna through your attorney?"

"My attorney won't speak to me anymore. He told me it was a conflict of interest."

"OK, you can be angry. I mean, I would be if my heart was stolen by some hateful witch; just don't be rash, like that time you stole shoes off a sleeping gnome to use as gambling dice."

Dirtbag held the bridge of his brow. "Hey, I gave them back… when he found us." He composed himself. "Maybe I won't completely kill that woman, but I can't pretend she's not who she is. Somehow she was and wasn't always the way she is, and I wish she hadn't been."

T.C. chuckled, shaking his head. "Oats alive, Dirt! Listen to yourself. I mean, you can't let that woman live her life while you just lie down and give up on yours. Trust me; you're just conflicted and angry. I've been there, Dirt. Ten times I've been there. What you need is a drink."

"I have been drinking. It hasn't helped."

"You need a *real* drink, Dirt, something strong enough to turn that grass-hair brown."

Dirtbag let out a long, capitulating breath, and T.C. led him down the street, thrilled they were together again. They turned the corner, and there before them was the old man, walking arm in arm with an attractive young woman; she was a quarter of his age and admiring her new jewelry. She could've been the old man's daughter, but the way she suggestively played with the hair growing out of his wrinkled cauliflower ears revealed she wasn't family. The woman's delighted giggles lit a fire in Dirtbag. "That scumbag!" He pointed.

T.C. was confused at first, but Dirtbag quickly filled him in. "That fossil is never without his sick, old wife. Now she's suddenly gone, and he's parading around with that floozy like he won a prize? His wife is probably buried under the back porch next to her dog he never liked. I'm not certain, but I'm sure enough. I think this calls for a measured response. T.C., get the clippers."

The soft pounding of Dirtbag's soil-filled denim feet charging toward the old man was drowned out by the buzz of T.C.'s hair clippers activating and the screams of watching townsfolk unsure of what was happening or what kind of horrible thing Dirtbag was. Dirtbag tackled the old man to the ground, knocking open his change purse. Six gold tooth fillings rolled out, too small to have come from the mouth of a man. Dirtbag examined one. "Scumbag deluxe!" he shouted, shaking the old man around.

"Wh-what does that even mean?" the old man whined, protecting his face.

"It means you went and put your wife in the ground ahead of time, didn't you? Look at me! You're out spending away what little value you were able to extract out of that old, dry husk on Candy here, aren't you?"

The young woman took a step back. "How'd you know my name, Mister?"

"Get out of here! Your father must be worried sick!" Dirtbag shouted, and she ran.

Dirtbag turned his attention back to the old man. His remaining button-eye dangled disturbingly out of its sunken socket, whipping about wildly as he spoke. "We're going to shave your head, scumbag."

T.C. laughed heroically. "He's got a lot of hair for an old man. I mean, that's like a lion's mane. I better use the zero setting."

The old man whimpered, "I...I suffered for years taking care of her."

Dirtbag's frown tightened. "Well, that's what marriage is: suffering, together. I always thought you were a brave man, a man of endurance, but you were just waiting until she kicked off. Maybe you even sped her along!"

"Y-you don't have any proof; n-nobody does."

"That's true, but hey, you don't seem too broken up about it, and I don't trust a cold heart. If you'd cared, her death would've destroyed you. True love can kill a man when it's lost. But I guess, being a scum-bag, that's something you won't ever understand."

T.C. moved in with the clippers.

CHAPTER 2

———

Dirtbag wearily watched the small shot glass revolve slowly inside the brass microwave behind the counter at Salty, a trendy dive bar on the outskirts of Pickle Flats. A voltaic hot pepper steamed in the middle of an unidentified caramel-colored liquid; every once in a while, a luminescent bubble would boil up to the top of the shot glass and spark. He slouched across the polished bar counter, supporting his head with his hands and listening to the horrid, garbled country music playing from the expensive stereo system. He wondered how it could be so bad. The grizzled bartender tidily wiped the counter at the far end, near where T. C. sat amusing himself by reading the local newspaper. The bartender kept glaring at Dirtbag, irritated the establishment had emptied out upon his arrival.

"There ain't no way!" the bartender said finally, throwing down his rag. "Stranger, Ah served all kinds of messed up thangs, but even Ah got standards. Even a gob-dang ghost squid don't stumble into mah bar with a loose eye."

Dirtbag sat back up, annoyed. "What? What's the problem? Is it the button-eye? Hey, is that it?"

"Take care of that thang! Ah can't have some loose eye flopping around. Gob-dang it, stranger, Ah aim ta serve reputable eats in this establishment! All Ah need is that to hop into a bowl a peanuts, and Ah'd be done in by the county."

Dirtbag casually pulled the hanging button out of his eye socket. The bartender gulped, his face taking on a greenish hue. Dirtbag tossed the threaded button onto the counter, and the bartender quickly cleaned it away with his washrag then immediately walked over to a cast-iron stove and threw the rag into the flames.

The microwave dinged; Dirtbag's drink was ready. The bartender picked up a pair of insulated tongs to serve the steaming-hot shot glass. "Ah'm a setting this drink down here, next to your right-hand glove thang."

Dirtbag grabbed the drink out of the tongs, startling the bartender. "Hey, I'm not blind, moron."

"But you yanked out your gob-dang eye, and they ain't nothang left but deep shadows under that ol', angry scowl. Maybe Ah mighta thought eyes were there from across the room, but if Ah look close, all Ah see is dark pits a hate."

"That's why I sewed those buttons on, so morons like you wouldn't freak out all the time."

"But how can you see with no gob-dang eyes?"

"I'm a big bag of dirt! How do I do anything?"

T.C. folded down the paper he was reading to make sure there wasn't a situation forming. Seeing the bartender's uneasy expression, he quickly said, "Whoa, relax. Dirt's just cursed. I mean, he made some mistakes with his wife, and now he's a living dirt bag. Simple enough."

The bartender sourly accepted the explanation but continued to stare at Dirtbag with a mixture of ire and disgust. Dirtbag tossed the microwaved drink into his mouth, pepper and all. He suddenly shuddered, grabbed his throat, and pounded his fist on the counter. "Yes!" Dirtbag yelled hoarsely. "I felt that! What's this thing called?"

"Ah's call it Oblivion."

"I need another, quick."

The bartender began nervously preparing another drink. "Gobdang, the last time Ah served some stranger two of these creations, he ended up in the hospital in one a them unwakeable conditions where ya grin all the time."

"I would be so lucky." Dirtbag slouched back down onto the counter. "Don't worry. You can't kill me. Dirt can't die."

"Ah ain't never seen a creature like you before."

"A creature?" Dirtbag barked. "Hey! I'm not some mythical foofoo chimera who decided to drop by this pickle-infested cesspool for a visit. I'm a man who's—well—who's going through a difficult time. It's like a midlife crisis with a bunch of other stuff piled on top, a pile of stuff as big as a mountain, and I'm under it, trying to breathe."

The bar's door burst open, and a jubilant wedding party entered, celebrating the recent marriage of two young people. Dirtbag bitterly combed back his grass-hair as the room filled up with smiles. The bartender finished setting up Dirtbag's drink and placed it in the microwave. Dirtbag needed the drink immediately, but he'd have to wait ten minutes for it. He put his head down on the counter.

The party cheered the new couple. Dirtbag held his head tightly and groaned. The groom began to recount the story of how he met his beautiful, young bride, a starry-eyed, corny, exaggerated tale that infuriated Dirtbag. He slammed his hand down on the bar, interrupting their happiness.

"I was like you," Dirtbag snarled menacingly, "giddy and naïve, but a wedding is just a day." He slowly turned around, his appearance shocking them. "Commitment, that's the true test. What you have right now—that's not love."

He suddenly became hesitant to speak any further, but he had already called their attention. He'd told the story he was about to tell many times before, perhaps too many times, but he found a kind of catharsis in telling it, and so he began.

"Once upon a time, there was a man who left behind everything he was and went out into the world to find that one thing he was missing. He was an able warrior with a brilliant mind. In the course of his journey, he saved a small kingdom from ruin, and later that same day he was introduced to that one thing, that one person, that one true love that most people never find but always wish for. She was a princess, small and fair, and they both felt the connection within moments of their first conversation."

Dirtbag closed his pocket-eyes as he continued. "After a year, they married, leaving the kingdom to start their new life together. As they traveled through adversity and moments of tranquility, they forgot who they used to be and escaped into who they'd become. It was a time when things were good, as though that was how it always should've been. They were happy and complete, and they spoke about children. Then one night a team of ruthless goblin mercenaries took her away from him. He was overpowered by their numbers, and never before had he felt so helpless against so many." Dirtbag clenched his denim hands.

"The man tracked the goblins, hunting them down one by one without mercy, until at long last he found where they were holding the princess. She lived but was beyond curing. They had destroyed her, and the man swore such hateful vengeance that within a week he'd slain half the goblin race. As he killed, his princess faded, until he threw down his sword and promised her their final days together would have meaning. He carried her broken body to the point of a great cliff, where the view provided comfort. His anger turned inward with the fear she was leaving him and the guilt that on the night she was taken, so long ago, he had let his guard down, just that once."

Dirtbag exhaled. "For ten days he held her in his arms on the edge of that cliff. He used his body to shelter her, until his back grew rigid like granite and his arms became like stone, and when she died, he let himself die, too. There remains to this day a great boulder on the point of a cliff and, preserved beneath it, a bed of white flowers that can be found nowhere else. *That* is love."

The room was silent. His story had swept away the cheerful mood, and the bride jumped to her feet, livid. "What a stupid tale," she spat out. "That had nothing to do with me!"

"Were you homeschooled?" Dirtbag growled.

"Ugh! You sound just like my father!"

"I can't imagine any daughter of mine growing up to be such a selfish ignoramus. The world is about more than just you. You may not think so today, but never forget tomorrow will be for everyone."

The groom pushed a table aside and threw a fancy white glove at Dirtbag. "Foul creature! How dare you disgrace my newly beloved! I challenge thee to a duel."

T.C. snickered and folded up his newspaper. "Look, kid," he said. "Do you want to die? I mean, the burden of youth is making it safely through the young-and-dumb phase without being too stupid, right?"

Dirtbag picked up the thrown glove, tossed it in the air, and blasted it with his shotgun. A transparent diamond blade stuck the glove against the bar's wall, just high enough to be out of reach. Dirtbag pumped the shotgun, loading a new blade into the barrel. A flame ignited inside the cylinder as the shotgun began forging more ammunition. Dirtbag laid the shotgun across his lap threateningly. "Get out," he told the wedding party evenly. "Go somewhere else, read a book, volunteer, spay a cat, and stay out of trouble. If I hear otherwise, you might wake up one night to find me in your house."

The wedding party rushed out of the bar, knocking over chairs and tables in their haste. The door closed behind them, and the micro-wave dinged. The bartender looked at the mess left behind, dismayed. "Gob-dang bag of dirt, you just cost me a bushel of business."

Dirtbag unzipped his chest, reached inside, and tossed a sizable bag of gold on the counter. "I'm the only customer you need. You keep those things coming. I have to leave town before sunset anyway."

The bartender gave Dirtbag his beverage, plainly displeased. He grudgingly collected the gold and began preparing another round.

T.C. sat down next to Dirtbag and ordered one of what his friend was having.

Dirtbag sipped his drink, wincing at the strength of the liquid. "Hey, don't give me that look, T.C."

"OK, then don't give me the same old excuses, Dirt. I mean, other people have a right to be happy."

"When we're out having adventures, I don't dwell on it that much, and it doesn't get to me, but when I slow down, the past catches up, and you know it tears me apart inside."

"I get it; you're angry at me." T.C. folded his hands guiltily. "I mean, I admit I could've returned sooner. I really could've, had I just known, but I must've visited every woman who would have me on the way back. I just don't have those opportunities when"—he glanced at the bartender—"when my horse is around."

"You spent the last two weeks working the countryside, while I sat here trying to drink myself to death?"

"Trust me. I was drinking, too, Dirt," T.C. assured. "Besides, the blacksmith said it would take just a couple weeks, and it's been about a couple of weeks, so it should be ready soon. Then we can go find somewhere we can do good, or as good as good gets with us."

"It had better be worth it; you can't be a knight without a sword."

The bar door abruptly opened. A pair of bright-red snakeskin cowboy boots clumped in. Dirtbag and T.C. turned around and were simultaneously startled by the sight of the man. He wore a brown, salt-dusted, wide-brimmed cowboy hat, chain-mail chaps over sienna dungarees, and a leather vest adorned with an extravagant sheriff's badge. The sheriff's face was entirely buried under two huge, bushy eyebrows interwoven with a gigantic, shaggy walrus mustache. When the sheriff spoke, the hairy mustache split apart like theater curtains, revealing gold-capped teeth to the listening audience. The giant brows furrowed, and a loud, gruff voice marred by salt inhalation spoke, accompanied by the sudden smell of fried chicken. "You, uh, fine fellas have caused quite a ruckus."

Dirtbag sipped his drink. "We're just passing through, Sheriff."

"That so? I heard all about you, Dirtbag, and, uh, I gotta say, you certainly don't live up to your highfalutin whizbang-do reputation."

"Well, I'm in a rut at the moment, and you haven't seen me in action yet. It'll blow your mind right out your ears."

"Do tell. I was about to, uh, turn a blind eye to your most recent of indiscretions, given your obvious impairment, being intoxicated dirt and all, but insulting my daughter on her wedding night? That demands answering."

T.C. hit Dirtbag in the back of the head, causing him to spill his drink on the floor. The liquid burned a hole straight through to the ground. "Sheriff"—T.C. worked up his most charming smile—"we'll be happy to leave town right away, and we'll even pay restitution to make up for our rude behavior. I'll just get out my checkbook here—"

"A check? Do I look like a fool to you?"

T.C. stepped in front of Dirtbag to prevent him from answering. "Now, wait just a minute," T.C. said. "You see, this is a magic checkbook. I mean, money will appear in your hand as soon as I give it to you."

"Do tell. Why are you wearing sunglasses indoors? You, uh, hiding those eyes so I can't detect your fraudulence?"

"Whoa, that's a big word for a——"

"For a what?" The sheriff's brows formed angry arches that raised his hat up a notch.

"I'm just cursed," T.C. explained. "Actually, I've got quite a few curses, at least one from each ex-wife, and there were ten of those. I wear sunglasses because my eyes can be frightening, I mean, to some people."

The sheriff started to unsheathe his sword. "Take 'em off, nice and slow."

T.C. carefully removed his sunglasses, keeping his eyes closed as he did. After they were off, he slowly raised his lids. His eyes were pupilless and glowed a deep blood red.

The sheriff jumped back and drew his sword. "Them's a demon eyes if I ever saw!"

"It's *supposed* to keep him from charming the ladies," Dirtbag grumbled, stepping off his barstool.

"Fraudulation almighty! Burning lies from a pair of disreputable drunkards if I ever heard it!" The sheriff pointed his sword at Dirtbag. "You can't even walk sober!"

"Hey, I can't get drunk. My dirt innards neutralize the alcohol in minutes. That's why I try to keep a constant flow. I walk this way because I don't have any knees. See? My leg can swing both ways."

"Fella, that be the way a demon walks, with the reversed hoof step of a goat. I can't allow some fraudulatin' drunk demons to roam free accosting, uh, upstanding members of the community. It's high time I introduce you drunkards to a cell."

Dirtbag and T.C. looked at one another and agreed to go to jail.

CHAPTER 3

The sheriff had incarcerated Dirtbag and T.C. in the substation at the center of town, which was arguably completely counterproductive since they had been asked to leave by the end of the day and had almost left. Dirtbag paced the small jail cell, alternating between clenching his fists and stiffly clasping his grass-topped denim head as he struggled to tame unseen forces. His erratic movements gradually lessened as he emerged from his emotional rut, a process made easier thanks in large part to the presence of T.C.

A beat-up, filthy jukebox in the corner of the cell blinked off and then on when T.C. kicked it after it refused to accept his selection. The old vinyl record it had decided to play scratched loudly as it started. "Oats alive!" he shouted, kicking it again. T.C. shook his armored fist at the machine in a threatening manner and adjusted his sunglasses, flicking his hair as though the entire matter were beneath him. "Did you see what we were charged with? Dirtbaggery! I mean, can you believe it?"

"I thought that sheriff had a sense of humor, and then I saw he accused me of being the anti*crisp*, whatever that means. Probably some pickle law," Dirtbag groaned. "These theme towns are the worst. I'm not even sure how I ended up here."

"At least it's not as bad as Haggis-shire." T.C. shuddered, remembering. "It's a shame, actually. My taxidermist lived out there, though he was never very good at getting the paper work done on time. I mean, he always just rounded up for some reason. He told me to get an accountant, and I told him I don't kidnap royalty."

Dirtbag rubbed his denim hand over his face, but words escaped him. The jukebox short-circuited and began playing the record neither of them had chosen, backward. The singer's voice grew deeper as the speed slowed, and T.C. told Dirtbag how it reminded him of an obese, sick ox that had been a cousin four times removed from one of his wives, though how that was even possible was never explained to him, and he'd been pressured to never ask.

"At least it has rhythm," T.C. said, snapping his fingers to the horrid sound. He took his bulky boots off to avoid trampling Dirtbag's feet in the small space they shared. "I once broke out into a dance during a divorce hearing. I mean, she was taking everything, but she couldn't take my moves."

Dirtbag smirked. "Speaking of which, show me some of those new ones you picked up."

"I'm about to," T.C. said as he stretched and loosened his body. "OK. Take your foot, and put it like this." T.C. moved his leg out.

"Like this?"

"Just like that. Now twist to the left, and step back to the right. Put it all together."

"I think I got it."

"You do! You do! And you have your own style, too, Dirt."

"Where'd you learn this again?"

"There's a women's college a few miles from here."

They both danced to the beat of the dysfunctional jukebox inside the dimly lit, cramped concrete jail cell. It was late, and the sheriff had gone home hours earlier, leaving them alone in the empty substation. He had interviewed them until he was thoroughly disturbed by their answers, and they had enthusiastically consented to spend a few days behind bars for having shaved the old man's head, who, as it turned out, was the brother-in-law of the mayor of Pickle Flats. They were reminded that the whereabouts of the old man's wife was a job for local law enforcement and not highfalutin vigilantes. The sheriff knew they were capable of escaping, but given their generally heroic track record, he trusted they would honor their sentencing.

"Hey! Watch this!" Dirtbag performed a series of flexuous dance moves, made possible by his lack of bone. "How does it look?"

"Whoa, you can call that the dirt seizure," T.C. suggested as he danced into the center of the cell to show off some smooth moves. "It helps to have a few of these you can work into your melee combo. I mean, people see you have some moves, and they start talking. That's how you go from being that guy to that legend, right?" A static shock stung him in the foot, and then another got him in the other foot. He jumped up on a cheap folding table, knocking over the house of cards they'd built.

Dirtbag grinned. "Hey, that's what you get for spinning around on a shag carpet in silk socks."

"OK and how come you're not getting shocked?"

"Because I keep touching the metal bars to discharge it."

"I thought that was just some new-age style you were developing."

"Why don't you try dancing over there on that big stain that's all matted down with crust?"

"I dunno, Dirt; that looks like a camel spilled its bladder over there."

The jukebox coughed out a puff of blue smoke and died, ending their dancing. The cell was uncomfortably silent. T.C. stepped back into his boots and began buckling up the numerous straps that held on the multiple layers of plate armor. When he finished, he kneeled down to examine the shag carpet.

"This used to be a nice hide," he said, petting the carpet. "One of my wives—actually, I think it might've been the Great Thighlossus—had a carpet-pillar farm. This was before she joined that book club and turned goth on me. Anyway, these critters were huge and docile, like cows, I mean, they looked like overstuffed pillows pushed together. You had to watch them all the time, because if they got too close to one another, all that rubbing would build up so much static electricity they'd just burst into flames."

"*She* liked carpet-pillars," Dirtbag said, his mind drifting. "Back then I couldn't afford them, and we were always on the move, fleeing Katvanna's wrath. All my money went to the Guild of Attorneys to keep her off our backs. All of it."

"Now, wait just a minute, Dirt. She was happy when you had nothing. She accepted you as you were. That's true love, right? For most women, every man has to be in line to be king, and if you don't become king, they hate you for it. Then, for some reason, they just settle for some unemployed vampire who owns a motorcycle."

Dirtbag wasn't listening. His face contorted as if his memories were stabbing him. "All the places we liked, the way we met, the time we had together, all of it is so embroiled in pain that it kills me inside to remember her. I'm not even sure I want my heart back. I don't know what will happen to me when the love inside it tries to fill me up again." Dirtbag clutched his chest. He sat down and asked if he could have a few minutes.

As T.C. watched his friend recover, he quietly swore never to leave him alone for so long again.

CHAPTER 4

———

A soft, golden-papaya hue inundated the cramped jail cell, casting a morning glow over the tensely held playing cards of the two occupants. The game was called Gerrymander, a game of ever-changing rules that Dirtbag and T.C. swore to never play again after each and every time they played it. All the face cards were used as betting chips, and the wager was always for the various rules of the game. Whichever player won the hand had the right to change the particular rule wagered, and the longer the game was played, the more convoluted and entangled it became. It was a game for sharp minds, a battle of wits with the potential for a psychotic breakdown.

T.C. confidently turned over his card, the ace of anchors, the fifty-third card of a deck that, legend told, appeared out of thin air as a result of a mathematical improbability brought on by excessive paradoxical rule changes. Dirtbag grinned. He knew T.C. had taken the card out of his boot, and he knew T.C. knew he knew, but he enjoyed the challenge. Dirtbag stared at his own hand; he had two ace-of-anchor cards he'd collected from their previous games, and he couldn't wait to turn the tables on T.C. He was about to make his move when, at the jail-cell window, they heard a horse snort.

"Muffin!" T.C. said happily.

Muffin poked her snout in through the bars and dropped a green apple on the floor as a present. She was a frumpy, carnation-pink horse sporting pearl-studded pierced ears and long, strawberry-blond hair braided with baby-blue ribbons. She whinnied at T.C., desperate for his attention.

"Good girl!" T.C. told her, rubbing her nose. She pulled away for a moment and then delivered an envelope sealed with a kiss into his hand. T.C. opened it. "It's from the blacksmith," he said, reading the note inside. "He's finished with my sword." Muffin disappeared outside again.

"He? What kind of blacksmith seals a letter that way?"

"Whoa, he says he upgraded Muffin, too, for free!"

"Upgraded?" Dirtbag combed back his grass-hair, anticipating insanity. "Exactly how do you upgrade a unicorn?"

A mechanical clattering came from outside. A chainsaw engine revved up, and Muffin's pink unicorn ears expelled white exhaust. T.C. looked out the window and waved and yelled at Muffin. "Whoa, there! Easy girl! Easy, We're fine; we worked out a deal. Everything is fine." The chainsaw throttled down and turned off. Muffin neighed. T.C. turned away from the window with a disturbed grin. "She just thought we were trapped, Dirt."

Dirtbag slowly nodded, acknowledging, but not fully accepting, Muffin's transformation. "Hey, I guess it wasn't enough to have that pink unicorn running through our battles stabbing people with her horn, breaking the hearts of little girls the world over. No, we can do better than that; we can make it so they never sleep again."

Dirtbag looked out the window to confirm it was as bad as he suspected it to be, but it was far worse. "Well, at least it's not another tattoo. What are we going to call her now? A uni-saw?"

"I mean, before she was just a horse I was in love with; now she's an asset. Do you think that chainsaw runs off of apples?"

Dirtbag held the bridge of his brow and sighed. "If we had really been trapped in here," he said, "I could've squeezed through the bars or even used science to make explosives out of this terrible shag carpet. Colors that loud could blow out the entire side of a building."

"You should watch it with the *s* word, Dirt. You don't want another mob to tie you to a stake. I mean, like when you set that giant parsnip on fire, the one that old man spent six years growing, just because he said it was magical."

"Those farmers only beat me with shovels for an hour before they gave up trying. I just told jokes the whole time. That was the most pathetic farmers market I've ever been to. They didn't even have pecan pie. And, for the record, science grew that thing." Dirtbag frowned. "That's not the issue here, is it? Your unicorn has a chainsaw on its head. A chainsaw!"

A white dove suddenly flew in through the window and landed on the table. It kicked a few playing cards off as it waddled around. Dirtbag and T.C. looked at each other. The dove's body appeared to be made of folded flat angles.

"Looks like it's made of paper," T.C. said, slowly approaching the bird, being careful not to spook it.

The dove watched them both with unblinking eyes that appeared to have been crudely scribbled onto it. Then, without warning, it charged toward Dirtbag, unfolding itself midflight into a greeting card embossed with gold-leaf designs and fancy silver lettering. The card landed in Dirtbag's hand with a gentle coo.

"What is it?" T.C. asked.

Dirtbag opened the card, closed it angrily, and then reopened it. He read it again and again, his anger growing until he tore the card apart, leaving a small cloud of down feathers floating in the air. He grabbed his head and groaned. "It was a wedding invitation from Katvanna," he growled. "She's getting remarried, and she's going to use my stolen heart to do it, since I broke hers. She's goading me to stop her, because she knows I can't find her."

"I knew she was powerful, but I didn't know she could animate papercraft."

"She can't; few can"—Dirtbag had an epiphany—"which means she hired some scumbag who could, and that means we can find that guy and make him talk."

"Swell. We should've looked over that bird for clues before you killed it."

"You're right; I didn't used to be this angry." Dirtbag squatted down to pick through the paper down feathers. "I doubt whoever conjured this thing up autographed it."

"I dunno, Dirt. If I spent all day folding paper into life-size pigeons, I'd sign my name where people could see it. I mean, that's craftsmanship."

"Odds are this is some lunatic wizard whose brain is spinning around in his head, completely out of control, and that's dangerous, like a merry-go-round run by insurance salesmen."

T.C. raised his eyebrows. "OK. Was there at least a date for the wedding?"

"I think it said 'soon,' which, knowing her and how much she likes to keep people waiting, could mean in a few weeks or months from now."

"This is her first new husband since you, right?"

"I'm going to try and make it her last, too...probably some poor sap that has something she wants."

"Like a shoe salesman?"

Dirtbag withheld a retort. "One thing's for sure"—he glanced into the empty substation—"we can't wait around here any longer."

"Just say the word, Dirt." T.C. clenched his armored fists, ready to wreck up the place.

"Let's try some diplomacy this time. Maybe we can work something out."

T.C. let out a deep breath and placed his hand on Dirtbag's shoulder. "My friend, we're divorced men; we know nothing of diplomacy."

"Hey! It takes *two* countries to go to war."

They heard a commotion outside in the street. At first it sounded like a few people shouting. Then they heard a window break and people begin to scream. Muffin stomped her hooves, agitated by whatever she was seeing. T.C. tried to get a look, but the window was small, and Muffin's head blocked the view.

"Why is she afraid?" Dirtbag snarled. "She has a chainsaw on her head!"

"Hear that, Dirt? It sounds like the town is under attack."

A woman screamed for somebody to save her babies.

"That's the sound of opportunity, T.C. Either that sheriff is going to come through the door and ask us to take care of the problem or the problem is going to inadvertently break the jail wide open. Then we can set a fire and start a rumor that we're dead, but this time it'll work."

The mayhem outside grew louder. Dirtbag passed the time by ripping up chunks of the shag carpet and rolling them up into phony corpses to cover their escape. The crackling sound of fire raging began to echo in the streets. T.C. rubbed Muffin's nose to keep her calm. An explosion thumped close by, shaking the substation. The front door flung open, and the hairy, brow-stached sheriff ran in, accompanied by a fat man wearing a gigantic plastic top hat with a slightly off-center jade pickle embedded in it. They were singed and wild-eyed with panic.

"You must save the town!" the fat man pleaded.

"I don't hear a *please*," Dirtbag griped.

"But—but you're him, the Dirtbag! And you, the blond swordsman!" the fat man blathered. "You're the same heroes who slayed the vile magma-worm that plagued the resort village of Geyserknoll, aren't you?"

Dirtbag threw the half-made carpet corpse on the floor and folded his arms. "You know, that story is not as heroic as people make it out to be. Sure we killed that thing after it ate those tourist kids, but it turned out their famous hot springs were powered by heat from its hidden lair. I think the whole village filed for bankruptcy afterward."

The man in the top hat only heard what he wanted to hear. "Honorable sir, I am the mayor of Pickle Flats, Qucumberlin. Sheriff Rexer and I, we—well—sir, we beg you to save our humble town from destruction."

Dirtbag turned to T.C. and silently mouthed the names he'd just heard. T.C. shrugged and encouragingly motioned for him to remember to be heroic. Dirtbag looked over the mayor and inaudibly muttered something about who was stupider, the politician or the people who'd elected him. "We'll save the town," he curtly grumbled.

The mayor squealed with joy. The sheriff immediately protested the mayor's intentions. "Them's a couple a burned-out, highfalutin demons. Heroes? Uh, in name only. Couple a fraudulent, disreputable drunkards if I ever saw!"

"There are a few conditions," Dirtbag told them, knowing he had the upper hand. "T.C., give them our card."

T.C. handed them an oversized business card printed with fill-in-the-blank talking points the press could copy word for word detailing their heroism, a waiver exonerating them from all liability, and a clause that retroactively granted them immunity from prosecution. The sheriff almost threw down his hat while reading it, and the mayor anxiously ate through half a bag of roasted, salted almonds before he reached the last paragraph. Somebody outside shouted that the animal shelter had caught fire and the Pickle Exchange had been overrun by the evil menace.

"Trust me," T.C. said with a charming grin, "we're not perfect, but we'll get the job done."

The mayor agreed to their terms and ordered them released.

"One more thing," Dirtbag said. "I need one of those Oblivion drinks that the Salty bartender makes, and I want *you* to get it." He pointed at the mayor.

"Me?" the mayor stammered as a distant explosion rumbled through the floor and people shrieked. He reached in his bag for an almond to chew on, but the bag was empty.

"Better make that a double," Dirtbag growled.

The mayor frantically looked at the sheriff, saw no sympathy, and ran out the door to get the drink. The sheriff nervously searched through his many keys, trying to find the right one to open the cell door. T.C. stepped up to the door, grabbed it with both hands, and tore it off its hinges. The sheriff was furious over the damage.

"I think that was metal fatigue." T.C. smiled, setting the door to one side.

"Here, take this, and say nice things." Dirtbag gave the sheriff a handful of gold coins.

"Fraudulation almighty!" the sheriff shouted.

Dirtbag retrieved his shotgun from the evidence locker and looked at T.C. "Well, this will be interesting, since you don't have your sword."

T.C. hardened his armored hands into fists. "Divorce has made the body strong, Dirt."

"And the mind?"

"Thirsty."

They stepped outside into the whirlwind of fire and screaming townsfolk, poised to handle whatever the situation was. The sheriff stayed within the doorway, watching. Dirtbag and T.C. assessed the chaos before them. Towering flames were consuming buildings under a shimmering rainbow sky. People were running in every direction, covered with razor-thin cuts, but there didn't seem to be any fatalities.

"What are those things? Square-headed ninjas?" T.C. asked as he watched a blocky humanoid creature leap through the air with a strange lightness, as if it weighed nothing. Another ninja ran past them. "Whoa, that guy's karate pajamas look like they were drawn on by talentless kindergarteners, and just look at those weird knife-blade hands. And purple? I've never fought purple ninjas before, Dirt. I mean, I don't even know what they like to eat."

"Let's get a sample." Dirtbag pumped his shotgun and fired at the nearest one. The diamond blade tore right through the purple, square-shaped body of the ninja with a loud rip and left a jagged hole. The ninja hissed with anger and rushed at him. "Zombie ninjas?" Dirtbag asked calmly. "Again?"

"I don't see them trying to eat anyone, Dirt." T.C. intercepted the attacking ninja with a one-handed choke hold, but his firm grip unintentionally crushed its square neck with a hollow crunch. "It's made of paper!" He dropped it. "Paper ninjas!"

The crushed ninja jumped to its feet and lunged at T.C., slashing at his face with sharp paper-blade hands. Dirtbag grabbed the ninja, bent it in half, and then crumpled it up into a big, twitching ball. "Flimsy," Dirtbag noted, using his shotgun to staple it to the side of the substation. "Just like the dove."

"Oats alive! Papercrafted ninja assassins!" T.C. said excitedly. "It's genius...unless it's raining...then I guess you could use wax paper. But then, that's noisy." A ninja glided overhead. "They're using the updrafts from all the fires to leap around. I mean, if we could just find a fire hose, we could soak them."

"Look around, T.C." Dirtbag gestured to the bucket brigades trying to put out the burning buildings. "This is the sticks. We need something else, something unexpected."

Muffin whinnied as she galloped around the corner to meet up with them. She nuzzled T.C. affectionately, her chainsaw-horn idling contentedly.

The sheriff gasped and pointed at the pink unicorn. "That filly ain't right! It—uh, it has a rump like a woman!"

"Whoa, that's because Muffin *is* a woman," T.C. said, giving her a quick kiss. "Or at least she used to be. My last wife caught me having an affair with the stable maid. She cursed Muffin, and here we are. Muffin's still my one and only. Isn't that right?" Muffin made some agreeable sounds and wagged her tail twice.

"Fella, you can see her shame!"

"Then just stop looking!"

The mayor called out to them for help as he ran past flipping ninjas and fiery explosions carrying a small tray with a shot glass chock-full of voltaic hot peppers on it. He carefully kept a hand hovering over the sparking drink to prevent any flying debris from ruining its contents. He called out for help again, scared and exhausted. Dirtbag and T.C. just watched him, curious if a politician so clearly allergic to exercise would actually succeed.

The mayor stumbled over his own feet a few times but finally made it. He handed Dirtbag the warm shot glass and fell over onto his back, wheezing, his face covered in paper cuts. Dirtbag downed the drink at once; his body twisted to one side, arched forward like a crescent moon, and shook off the effects with a final jolt. "I think that did it," he said, throwing the empty glass into a nearby fire.

"Save town?" the mayor wheezed. "Save Pickles!"

"Sure." Dirtbag stretched, pounding his chest to work through some indigestion from the concoction he'd swallowed. He reached under Muffin's saddle and retrieved a roll of garbage bags and a box of crayons. "I told you these things would come in handy, T.C."

"I thought we didn't do autographs anymore, Dirt."

Dirtbag opened the box of crayons and held one up in the air so that the ninjas could see. Loud, excited whispers came from every direction. Dirtbag returned the crayon and closed the box. "Well, they're as vain as real ninjas, which means we can lure them to us with the promise of fixing up their scribbled-on faces."

"That's a great idea! I mean, some of those things don't even have eyebrows."

Dirtbag frowned at T.C. "I don't either. Implying something?"

"Here, let me try." T.C. removed an orange crayon from the box, waved it high enough that all the ninjas took notice, and fed it to Muffin, who thought it was a carrot. The ninjas howled with anger and began swarming around them to attack. T.C. took out a pink crayon and told Muffin it was peppermint flavor. Muffin's ears twitched, and she happily chomped on the crayon.

"You're a cruel man," Dirtbag said, shaking his head. "She'll believe anything you tell her."

"I dunno, Dirt. Remember the way you described the world to that blind man?"

"Hey, if I had told him the way the world really is, he would've killed himself."

"Save the town!" the mayor screamed from the ground.

"We're on it," Dirtbag yelled back. "We're professionals; we know what we're doing."

"Sometimes," T.C. said.

"Well, most of the time," Dirtbag admitted.

T.C. fed Muffin a handful of crayons and tucked the remaining ones under her saddle. The ninjas glided in to steal the drawing tools. T.C. whispered into Muffin's ears a plan he'd just thought up. She grunted and took off running. The papercraft ninjas leapt to stop her, hissing threateningly, but these were imitation ninjas, far less dangerous than real ninjas, and it quickly became clear that whoever had created them should have taken the time to fold brains inside their empty heads. Over the next three hours, Muffin chased down the ninjas with her buzzing chainsaw, trampling them in the streets, where Dirtbag and T.C. tore their crippled bodies apart one by one, stuffing them into garbage bags then tying the bags closed with double knots. Detecting resistance, the arsonist ninjas tried to mount a counterattack with fire bombs, but Dirtbag simply shot them with their explosives in hand and watched them burn.

With the ninjas distracted, the townsfolk were able to get the fires under control, depriving the papercrafted creatures of updrafts to ride. Muffin coordinated with Dirtbag to round up the grounded ninjas, which, although easily defeated, had invaded the town in surprisingly large numbers. Luckily the town's obsession with pickles meant there were barrels full of them everywhere. Dirtbag threw the wet cucumbers at the ninjas and dunked them in brine every chance he had.

T.C. herded a large group into the town hall, corralling them inside the confined space of the mayor's office, where they couldn't escape his fury. The mayor was outraged when his custom-made, pickle-patterned desk chair exploded out of his office window and onto the street below. Dirtbag convinced the mayor sacrificing his own office helped make him a hero to the people; he shared their pain now. The mayor liked that idea.

As the crisis ended, more people came out from hiding to help douse the remaining fires. They picked up the scattered garbage bags and dragged them into a mountainous pile. The bags twitched and hissed. Muffin polished off the remaining crayons as she watched Dirtbag and T.C. give interviews to overexcited reporters who'd never had anything other than pickles to write about.

By sundown, the townsfolk had built a sizable victory bonfire using the splintered remains of the mayor's pickle-patterned office furniture, and the entire town turned out to celebrate the strange heroes who had saved them. Muffin tossed the first twitching garbage bag into the fire. The people applauded her, and she blushed. Then T.C. threw three bags in at once. The people hailed his strength, and he saluted them. Finally, Dirtbag tried to throw five bags into the inferno and failed. The people laughed at his overzealousness, and he could barely contain how much he despised them. They burned all the bags except one, which Dirtbag kept.

The mayor thanked them, the sheriff presented them honorary certificates, and the people cheered. Dirtbag endured a procession of well-wishers, his actual ambivalence toward the proceedings overlooked by their feverish revelry. T.C. graciously accepted a custom-tailored plaid kilt for Muffin—long enough to hide her shame—taking care not to mock their values.

The sun sank beneath the horizon, and the townsfolk served a great feast. From a corner that gradually became hidden in shadow, the heroes watched the people dance and sing into the night. Dirtbag drank bitterly. "This is a farce," he growled. "These cowards could've saved themselves. Those ninjas were made of paper!"

T.C. fiddled with his half-eaten, brined pork chop. "Sometimes, Dirt, people just want someone else to save them."

"You know, when you put a person on a pedestal like this, you invite abuse."

The mayor called his people together to give a grand speech that ended in some hastily arranged fireworks. While the entire town was preoccupied, Dirtbag and T.C. broke into the central bank and stole only a single gold coin, which they knew would be dismissed as an accounting error. They did it because they could. As the people fell to sleep, feeling content and safe, the duo quietly slipped out of town and disappeared into the moonless night.

CHAPTER 5

———

Dirtbag sat still under a tepid cerulean-blue sky, his sullen face revealing nothing of what tormented him. They were memories without feeling, thoughts inhabited by phantoms, instances of happiness that seemed distant, as though he should question if they even happened, but they had. He thought at first of a living room, and they were reading together, but then he was with her in a kitchen, and she was singing. He couldn't remember her voice. They'd shared a secluded stone cottage at the peak of an orchard-filled valley. In the evening he would observe the stars, using an ancient telescope he'd built from blueprints he had found somewhere. He would show her his discoveries, and she would lean close to see, tickling his skin with her soft hair. Later they would lie under the stars in each other's arms, snuggling beneath blankets she had sewn. They were happy, and that was how things should have remained. "But you're gone," Dirtbag said, allowing the fantasy to pass.

A scrap of paper scribbled with purple markings crawled through the grass, blindly groping for an escape route. Dirtbag picked it up and placed it onto a stack of crumpled sheets under a heavy stone. He reached inside the garbage bag and pulled out another piece of the papercraft ninja. It was time-consuming to carefully unfold the intricately layered paper. The paper moved much less now than it had during the night. The power that had given it life was fading away.

T.C. lifted his head out of the crystal-clear stream they had stopped at and threw back his wet, lengthy blond hair. He squirted a small amount of conditioner into his armored hand and worked it onto his scalp. Dirtbag watched with disdain the effort T.C. went through to keep his hair so good-looking. "Does the eighth bottle really make a difference?" Dirtbag ridiculed.

"This one has those magical herbs that will add an aura of allure."

"Magic?" scoffed Dirtbag. "Don't you see that algae bloom downstream? That wasn't there this morning. Look at that thing; I think it's growing an eye. Did you even check the ingredients on that bottle?"

"You're just jealous the only conditioner for your hair comes out of the backside of an animal. I mean, I think that's something Muffin can help you with."

They both looked over at Muffin, sleeping on her back under the shady side of a tree, her legs pointed skyward. A gentle breeze caused the tree to sway, disturbing her slumber. She snorted loudly and passed gas, causing her kilt to fall open. Dirtbag scooted farther away from the horse, dragging his paper with him.

"She really was a sight to behold when I met her," T.C. reminisced.

"I'm sure they all were."

"Trust me, Dirt. You should always pursue young women, because once they stop growing up, they start growing out—out of the clothes they used to wear, out of the interests you shared, out of the perfume you liked, out of that long hair you could run your fingers through, and, eventually, out of their minds."

"So you just trade them in every few years? And that's what love is to you?"

"Women always make it sound so wonderful and endearing to grow old together, but it's just never that way. I mean, you wake up one day next to a total stranger, and then you meet someone else who reminds you of all the things she used to be."

Dirtbag grew restless as thoughts concerning her invaded him: the quirks that had made him smile and the mutuality they had shared, all suddenly vivid. He wanted to give up and live inside his mind, but he knew it was something she wouldn't have accepted. He swallowed his thoughts back into the empty space where his heart should have been. He unfolded the last piece of paper; it was blank. "Well, none of these had any kind of markings on them."

T.C. rinsed his hair in the stream, clouding the water with green, glowing foam that flowed down into the thickening algae bloom. The algae glared at them with its bloodshot eye. T.C. sat down next to Dirtbag, brushing out his beauteous hair. "What about that invitation? Did it say anything else? I mean, did it say who she was going to marry?"

Dirtbag regretted tearing it up so impulsively. "Do you know what it really said? It said she had found her own true love, that I was cordially invited to witness the culmination of her new happiness, and that she'd personally commissioned a special flowerpot I could sit in for the occasion. Then she wrote out '*bwah ha ha ha.*'" He folded the shredded papers up and put them in his satchel. "She actually wrote that out."

"Oats alive, Dirt. I would've ripped that apart, too."

"She knows I can't rest until I get my heart back and that I'm tired of living. I'm old and worn out."

"Whoa, is your life really that bad?"

"Are you blind to what is going on with me?"

"No, I'm not. I mean, I can see you're hurting. Oats alive, I hurt inside, too, Dirt, more—much more—than I'm willing to admit. Every divorce I got was bigger and more hateful than the last, but did I stop living? Nope. I just moved on and found myself a better wife."

"And how's that working out?"

"OK, I'm between wives right now, and that's always a difficult time for me."

"You're hopeless."

"Yeah, I'm a romantic."

A horrible belching noise moaned from downstream. A large, gelatinous green blob crawled onto the shore, gnashing its toothless mouth in a threatening manner.

"There's your conditioner," Dirtbag said as the blob began to inch toward them.

T.C. put two fingers in his mouth and whistled. Muffin woke up midsnore, confused. T.C. pointed at the blob. "Get 'em, girl!"

Muffin's chainsaw clattered to life; she galloped to the streamside and cut the blob apart. She calmly began to eat the remnants, and as she did, her mane took on a bright, golden sheen. T.C. sauntered over to her. He pulled her kilt back down to hide her shame and whispered sweetly into her ear. Dirtbag had never heard a unicorn giggle that way before.

CHAPTER 6

———

The blacksmith's shop sat at the lowest point of a deep basaltic canyon where intersecting tectonic plates had torn open a volcanic fissure along the rocky foundation. Stifling waste heat and particulate soot, by-products from the act of blacksmithing, were trapped within the canyon under a permanent cloud of suspended ash, creating a toxic greenhouse effect. The ground was black, covered in small abrasive rocks, and lit by still-glowing fallen embers, as though a night sky full of stars had been haphazardly spread across the ground. The few trees that remained had a polished, fossilized appearance, their bark having been worn down over time by the fine, gritty pollutants in the air. The inferno contained within the shop's thick-pitted metal walls beamed out of half-closed vents and windows. Suspended above was an obnoxious blue-neon sign showing an animated hammer striking a gold anvil; with each hit, sparks flew in the air, illuminating a calligraphic name in bright red: "Bistro."

The incessant baritone pounding of metalwork being forged inside the shop reverberated under the thick canopy of air, producing an industrious, overlapping thunder. A single winding road, made of surplus metal ingots, led down into the canyon and to the shop. Two figures appeared out of the dark, hanging cloud of ash, dancing their way down into the cauldron, with a chainsaw-horned pink unicorn trotting not far behind.

"What are you listening to?" T.C. asked as he strutted, snapping his fingers.

"Rock 'n' roll," said Dirtbag, twisting and turning left to right. "You?"

"Disco."

The music existed only in their heads. The two of them danced silently, not the least bit concerned about how they appeared. At some point on the way to the blacksmith, they had both run out of things to talk about. T.C. was not well-read on interesting topics, and Dirtbag was tired of reminiscing about old adventures they had shared. That was when the dancing had begun. The two of them danced down the road to the shop, up the short path to the front door, and right inside, heading straight to the customer-service counter. They compared dance moves, oblivious to everything around them.

"Whoa, that's pretty good, Dirt. Let me see if I can do that without dislocating my foot," T.C. said, trying to recreate the maneuver.

"Wait." Dirtbag looked around. "Hey, we're there! Or here, wherever this is. How'd you find this guy again?"

"He was recommended by the friend of a brother of a girl I knew, whose husband found out I had an affair with her and commissioned this exquisite armor I'm wearing to bribe me into marrying her twin sister, who had a superfluous nipple on her neck, which was just awkward. I mean, that was the first time I used a twin-sized mattress for the purpose its name implies. Tempers flared, words were said, one thing led to another, and now I can't ever take this armor off, except for the boots and my codpiece."

"How fortunate," Dirtbag sneered.

"Trust me; you only need two things to be successful in the bedroom: traction and action."

Had Dirtbag had any eyes, they would have been rolling up into his head at that moment.

The duo stood there snapping their fingers and spinning around, seemingly writhing out of control. "Well, should we stop dancing?" Dirtbag asked.

"Heh heh. If ya want to walk out of here, yeah, ya should," a huge mountain of a man said suddenly from the open front door. He was carrying a hefty brown paper bag full of delicious-smelling hoagie sandwiches. The man pointed to the large, well-used steel mallet hanging from his belt. "If I can forge metal with that thing, ya can bet I can pound the urge to dance right out of ya screaming little bodies." They stopped dancing immediately. "Ya blasted horse-thing better wait outside, too."

"Whoa, horse-thing?" T.C. said. "That's Muffin, remember? I mean, you put that chainsaw on her head not more than a week ago."

"Oh, oh, that's right, heh. I watched ya go and make out with that horse-thing. Must've slipped my mind, like those other traumatic life experiences I try to forget. It stays outside; got it?" He spoke with a booming, deep voice that sometimes grew louder when the ringing in his ears changed pitch. "I'm the master blacksmith. Some people call me Scooter, heh heh, and those people usually wind up dead, so ya better call me Bistro."

Bistro quickly reached for his hammer. T.C. and Dirtbag jumped back. Bistro laughed at them and patted it. He opened the brown paper bag, gave Muffin a fresh green apple, and shooed her outside with a firm slap on the behind. He stepped inside the shop with a sharp click of his shoe.

Dirtbag looked down to see what had made that noise and quietly gasped. "Why are you wearing high heels?"

"Heh heh. The more important question is, how did I find them in my size?"

"No, nothing is more important than knowing why a blacksmith wears high heels."

Bistro clicked his way around the counter and set the bag of sandwiches down next to an ash-covered cash register. "Heh heh. Let me ask ya, does my appearance bother ya?"

Bistro seemed to be a man-shaped rock elemental, with arms as thick as five-hundred-year-old oak trees, and was covered in singed body hair that stuck out of his rocky hide like quills on a porcupine. His beard was a waterfall of molten iron that had become encased in cut glass. Two horns protruded from his stony forehead as though they had been carved out of it. It was unclear if he had once been a man and evolved into this form or if he was something else altogether. He bent over until he was eye level to Dirtbag. "Heh! So, ya want to know why I wear the high heels?" Bistro let out a hardy, mocking laugh. "Because I can run in them! Let me tell ya, if a guy like me comes running after ya with a sledgehammer, wearing a pair of six-inch-stiletto-heeled red pumps, ya gonna need some new underpants, because whatever ya wearing won't survive the complete psychological collapse of ya mind's ability to control ya tiny bowels."

"Bistro"—T.C. made the motions of introduction—"this is my good friend Dirtbag."

"Heh. Dirtbag, eh? And ya're Tuna Hole, right?"

"That's Tuna Casserole, but you can just call me T.C."

"Heh, well, ya arrived just in time. Fact is, I'm going out of business sometime today." Bistro leaned forward, his good eye leading the way, examining Dirtbag's appearance. "And where do ya come from, Grasspants?"

"Outer space," Dirtbag answered sarcastically.

"Heh heh. All right then, and how 'bout some lunch, Mr. Spaceweed? Are ya hungry?"

"Whoa, we can't just sit around and hang out," T.C. said, trying to expedite things. "I mean, Dirtbag's got to find his ex and crash her wedding."

"She stole my heart," Dirtbag explained.

Bistro folded his arms around his massive stonelike chest. "So, it's an adventure, eh? Heh. I remember when my first husband pulled a knife on me. We were out golfing. I tell ya, when they try to kill ya, that's when ya know it's love. Don't worry; I'll take good care of ya guys. After all, us girls have to stick together, don't we?"

Dirtbag slowly turned to T.C., his denim face full of accusation, and T.C. instinctively opened his mouth to defend, but all that emerged was a faint whine, like that of a deflating balloon.

CHAPTER 7

Bistro entertained Dirtbag and T.C. with sordid tales about operating a multigenerational business over a volcano as they sat around an enormous, anvil-shaped table inside the air-conditioned and asbestos-stucco-covered break room of the blacksmith shop. They ate hoagies the size of baby manatees, the sandwiches overflowing with assorted sodium-infused luncheon meats, shredded lettuce, grilled tomatoes, and gluey, low-fat mayo; they used crooked, homemade forks and knives of polished steel. Bistro was such a big man that each sandwich he ate was entirely consumed in two forkfuls. He'd reach into the bag for another without ever breaking conversation, but increasingly he seemed distracted by the window, leaving them with the impression that something bad was coming and Bistro knew what it was.

"Oh, the shop's been fully automated for three years now," Bistro yelled over the noise of his own openmouthed chewing. "I kept that bunch of young men around because they were pretty to look at." He pointed at a group portrait on the wall. "They did a good job keeping the place neat, but, heh, now look at it."

The anvil table was covered in a thick coating of iron filings and rust. Bistro had been unable to find plates and explained that he suspected his staff had taken off with them after he'd abruptly fired everyone the day before. He suggested they eat the sandwiches inside out, like avocados, to avoid ingesting anything lethal. The screeching of Bistro's metal knife cutting across the wrought-iron anvil table-top was drowned out by his booming voice. "My blasted father, rest his rotten soul, crafted the royal wedding armor for the great King Immaculmedes, right here in this room. That armor had a built-in chastity lock. The king's new wife went and lost the key on their wedding night in an alcohol-fueled game of high-stakes poker. Heh heh. The week before that, Crog Wolter, 'the Black Knight,' took my virginity on this very anvil." Bistro laughed, nearly choking on his food. "Let me tell ya, that man had some big, sweaty hands."

Dirtbag lost his appetite and pushed the sandwich aside. "You know, the work you did on Muffin is psychotically impressive. Transforming a unicorn into a nightmare, that's no easy feat."

"Muffin?" Bistro asked, confused.

"My horse," T.C. interjected.

"Oh, oh, right. Heh." Bistro looked over his shoulder through the door to make sure the pink varmint hadn't come back inside and then turned to the window and glanced farther afield for a second. "I've never seen a horse-thing dressed in a miniskirt like that; I hope the two of ya aren't engaging in anything unnatural with that animal."

"I don't even have privates," Dirtbag disclosed, trying to avert questions about the unicorn and its relationship with T.C.

"No blasted privates?" Bistro shouted, appalled.

"I'm made of dirt."

"But ya eat. Where does it all go?"

"Well, I compost the food, and it becomes more dirt."

"Heh. That explains just about nothing," Bistro barked. "And what about that weapon on ya leg? Can ya explain that?"

"That's my autopneumatic shotgun."

"Pneumatic? Heh heh. That sounds scientific."

T.C. gave Dirtbag a hard look that asked him not to say anything further, but Bistro witnessed the obvious eye contact and smirked at them. "Heh! What kind of blacksmith would I be if I didn't study science?"

"Most people don't react well to scientific thinking," Dirtbag said. "A mob of alchemists once chased me down and beat me with their pestles because I told them not to put grapefruit juice in their antacid tablets."

"Whoa, you did a little more than that, Dirt," T.C. reminded.

"Hey! It's common courtesy to have a pedicure before you parade your feet around in public wearing sandals! I had intended to trim their yellow claws down to a respectable length, but the only tool I had on me at the time was a pair of pliers."

"Oh, nothing will get ya point across faster than fear," Bistro chuckled, leaning back against the wall to pick at his granite teeth with a sawed-off unicorn horn. "Heh heh, there's no real distinction between science and magic," he said as his teeth turned a shade whiter. "It could be that all magic is actually science or all science is actually magic; it's hard to tell, because in our world they meet in the middle and kind of blur together. Let me tell ya, most people don't care how a thing works, as long as it works."

"That's right," T.C. agreed, somewhat distracted. A familiar straw-berry-vanilla odor emanating from the sawed-off horn confirmed it belonged to Muffin. "I mean, nobody cares how microwaves work; they just want to know how to farm them."

"Yeah. They're a regular cash crop, too. Pluck them right out of the ground like a potato, but didn't ya ever wonder how they get new features? Ya can't breed a blasted popcorn button! Somebody out there knows something about scientific discovery, and they aren't tell-ing anybody that they know. It's probably for the best, too; ya put the understanding of science in the wrong hands, and it's war. Then, after the war, ya got these things that can't be controlled roaming around."

"Dragons." T.C. sighed.

"Oh, there are worse things than dragons out there." Bistro pushed the unicorn horn into his mouth and chewed it up. "Heh. You ever heard of mechanized temporal distension? It's when a minute turns into an hour through artificial means. The Guild of Attorneys cracked some secret of the ancients that allows their offices to exist in a slower time than the rest of the world. Yeah, ya can be in there arguing with ya blasted ex for hours, but outside, only a few minutes will pass. That's how they stay so rich; they can take dozens of clients each day and charge for weeks of work. It's not magic—it's science. And when you know something about science, you'll find it easy to take advantage of the ignorant."

"That's what my attorney said about practicing law," T.C. grumbled, "right after I gave up fighting my exes in court. I just started telling them to take it all. The wife wants my record collection? Just take it. I told her I have them all memorized in my head. That's when she tried to sue me for half my brain. I mean, my attorney decided to prove to the judge that I was too stupid to remember music, which he did by submitting to the court how much I was paying him. Then, to add to that humiliation, the Guild started invoicing me for things instead of money. I mean, that's how my attorney got my yacht."

"Heh heh, it's hard to picture you sailing."

"I get that a lot."

"Hey, let him have the boat." Dirtbag grinned. "It's a lot easier to hide money anyway."

Bistro shook his head. "Let me tell ya, ya can't hide money from ya ex. That gets them motivated to find other ways to hurt ya, and that's when ya get cursed. They make one of those pilgrimages to the Island of Vindictagos, seeking the help of the Dark Witches of Hatred. Fortunately for me, the worst one of them all, the high-elf sorceress Katvanna, went and quit for some reason, right before my ex found out he wasn't getting squat out of me. Heh. That blasted Katvanna, I never heard of any woman so absolutely evil."

Dirtbag combed back his grass-hair, mortified. "She wasn't always that way. I wouldn't have married her otherwise."

"Holy matrimony!" Bistro exclaimed. "You married that witch?"

"Well, it's complicated."

"Oh, it always is, that blasted love."

"I can't make up for anything she's done," Dirtbag conceded, "but I intend to do something about it."

"Heh. I heard that woman tiled her guest bathroom with stolen gravestones, and when she visited downtown Los Chronos, she made the dogs meow like cats, and you know how dogs can't keep quiet. That city once made the finest watches of all the nine regions; now it's the most annoying place on the planet."

"When was this?" Dirtbag asked. "I'm trying to find her."

"Let me tell ya, ya're never gonna find her. The last place she stopped by, she turned all the witnesses into pizzas, and they were eaten by wild animals. She can't even be prosecuted for it. No evidence. Heh. Do something about it?" Bistro scoffed. "Ya're her husband; some people would say ya're partially responsible!" Bistro glanced out the window as if he saw something in the distance. "I take it that shotgun was made to fight her?"

"That's the plan." Dirtbag pulled the shotgun out of the holster on his leg and showed it to Bistro. "It's a hybrid weapon that uses both what we know now and what the ancients knew then. I bought the schematics at a yard sale; the guy had no idea what he had."

Bistro gestured to ask if he could hold it. Dirtbag brazenly handed it over, seemingly not the least bit concerned.

"Heh. The design appears to have goblin tech all through it."

"It was made by a goblin weaponsmith."

"Must've been the last of his kind."

"Must've been," Dirtbag said coldly.

Bistro looked into the dark, empty pockets that were Dirtbag's eyes, and Dirtbag sat there, unpierceable and blithely audacious.

Bistro chuckled. "I've made a powerful weapon for T.C. It may be the most powerful sword I ever forged, heh, if not the most ridiculous." He glared at T.C. then turned back to Dirtbag. "This shotgun, I can perfect it, if ya allow me. I also have some armor from a canceled order that might fit ya. It's light, too, made of a leather-titanium composite I created myself. The client backed out of paying for it. Since I'm going out of business anyway, I'd like to give it to ya, for free."

"What if your client changes his mind?" Dirtbag asked.

"Oh, he won't be doing that. Heh heh. He's dead. I gave him the hammer. Made fun of my shoes." Bistro sat back, proud of himself. "News of my crime has already reached his father, General Bloodblivion."

"Oats alive!" T.C. yelped. "You murdered Lord Impaler? I mean, are you mad? This place will be razed to the ground by the general's army!"

"Heh. It's like I said, I'm going out of business today." Bistro stood up and cleared off the table, pushing the leftovers onto the floor. "Let me tell ya, life is about choices; ya mind makes good ones, ya heart makes bad ones, and an uncontrolled temper makes rash ones. If ya gonna take a life without reason, ya should expect to have yas taken without cause."

"Bistro," Dirtbag confessed. "I think I'm going to kill Katvanna."

"Heh. A lot of people would like to see that happen. She's an evil, dangerous woman." He peered out the window. "This weapon is good, but ya gonna need more of an edge to face that witch, and, let me tell ya, I can give ya one."

The light in the distance flickered; dark forms were approaching through the ash cloud. Bistro watched coolly, accepting the coming assault. "This has been a long time coming. I used to think I could avoid the consequences, but when ya do one thing, suddenly it's easy to do another. Heh. I knew it was either going to be these guys or the Guild of Attorneys."

"You murdered your lawyer, too?" T.C. said with shocked admiration.

"Yeah, I folded him right up into his crocodile suitcase next to his little plea bargain. Heh heh, then I left, bought some sandwiches, and came back here. But before I left, I took this." Bistro held out a device that looked like a taxicab meter. "This is how they slow time. Ya just pull the red flag down, and it starts ticking away at the speed of time ya set with that knob. Let me tell ya, with this thing, I'll have plenty of time to work on that shotgun, prepare that armor, and engineer a way of getting us out of here."

"Whoa, what about my sword?"

"Heh heh, that must've slipped my mind—there's only an entire army marching down the road. But don't worry; it's done. Oh, it's done."

T.C. was ecstatic. "If things turn ugly, Dirt and I have a lot of experience fighting armies."

"Well, bad experiences," Dirtbag said, looking out the window.

By then they could hear the distant clanking of soldiers marching in armor. The army was filling the canyon wall to wall to prevent escape. The trio of besieged men heard the faraway jet turbine roar of a dragon landing, followed by a curious mechanical whirling noise. Bistro turned toward them. "Have you two ever fought a Gatling-Dragon?"

"What kind of dragon is that?" T.C. asked.

"Heh," Bistro replied nervously.

CHAPTER 8

———

Dirtbag watched an ominous black mass of marching shadows pour onto the winding, ingot-paved road that led to the defenseless blacksmith shop, choking off what little light there had been under the deep canyon's stagnant volcanic-ash cloud. The People's Ultimatum Army, as General Bloodblivion had named it, was a merciless force that operated on the principle of overkill to ensure victory. They were trained executioners under the command of an overeducated, geriatric despot who sought to rid the world of those who affronted his narrow definition of common decency.

Dirtbag cupped his hand next to where an ear should've been on his head. A car horn honked in the distance. "They might have a couple of weaponized Cadillacs in the back and"—a deep swishing sound emerged over the ambient thunder of the blacksmith shop—"probably a street sweeper." Dirtbag looked at Bistro, concerned. "I think they mean to clean up the place."

"Heh. A clean sweep? I'm honored." Bistro chuckled.

"Well, you're going to be dead if you don't get in there," Dirtbag told him.

"Oats alive!" T.C. said, watching the approaching army. "Stop wasting time, Bistro!"

"Oh, relax; time is the least of our worries." He pulled the red flag down on the time meter, walked out of the break room into his personal workshop, and then immediately returned, looking positively exhausted. He polished some smudges off Dirtbag's shotgun and handed it back to him. If he'd made any changes to it, they weren't apparent at first glance. "Angle it in the light," Bistro told him.

Dirtbag moved the shotgun around, and some intriguing extra mechanical details materialized. He could feel the new additions with his hand, but he could only see them when he held the shotgun at specific viewpoints.

"That's mirage ore," Bistro said boastfully. "Yeah, that will keep other people from using ya new capabilities by hiding them in plain sight. Make sure ya test out those settings before ya use them. Don't worry; I kept the labels on the dial simple. They're all pretty much self-explanatory."

A terrifying, concussive roar echoed through the canyon as a blazing volley of fiery, bullet-filled dragon's breath ripped apart the stony ground outside the shop. Muffin whinnied and rushed inside the break room. T.C. calmed her with a quick kiss, forgetting that Bistro might be disturbed by the sight.

Outside the window, in the ashen darkness, was a kind of dragon neither T.C. nor Dirtbag had seen before. Dragons were known to be mechanical creatures of ancient origin that projected fire and could hover in place using the multiple jet turbines contained within their wings. The cornered trio could just make out the silhouette of this unfamiliar Gatling-Dragon in the dim light. It was four times the size of a normal dragon, was heavily armored, and had numerous lit-up eyes. Inside its glowing open maw were three triangular, multibarreled rotary cannons that spun out bolts of searing, armor-piercing lead. Its unnerving howl reminded them of metal buckling.

"Heh heh. Focus on me. Don't worry about that thing," Bistro said as he set a bundle of armor on the table. "Dirtbag, this is the armor I made for the late Lord Impaler. It's light, maneuverable, and able to resist most projectiles, notwithstanding harsh words."

"Hey, I don't have any use for this. I'm a big bag of dirt."

"Oh, I think ya do. Let me tell ya, I saw the way ya walk. Ya body has no support, because ya have no bones. This armor will sort of act like an exoskeleton. Ya can still move as fluidly as ya do now, but ya'll have added rigidity, so ya won't look like ya walking drunk all the time."

Dirtbag opened the bundle of armor to examine it. The texture of the pieces resembled leatherized tree bark, with veins of silver titanium filling the fissures between the bumpy notches. He held the armor up to himself, pretending not to be excited. The armor complemented his rusty, worn denim skin as though it had been destined to be a part of him from its initial conception.

"And finally, heh, this is it, Tuna." Bistro placed a thick blanket on the table. He carefully unwrapped it, revealing a beautifully handcrafted scabbard. "When ya came to me with this project, heh, I thought it couldn't be done, but sure enough, the formula was there in that ancient goblin-metallurgy text ya found. It's too bad ya only had the one page; a man can spend a lifetime trying to rediscover these ancient materials."

"Sometimes they rediscover you," T.C. said, pointing at his dragon-tooth necklace.

"Heh, when ya see that shiny, glossy-black metal on an adversary, ya best kiss ya precious tenders good-bye. That's the lightest, strongest, most durable material on the planet. Nobody knows how the ancients made it, but they used it as armor on all their blasted war machines. Metalworkers like me can only repurpose what's lying around, and let me tell ya, there's a lot of it. This weapon might be the closest I ever get to reproducing that evil blackness. Could be the next-best thing."

Bistro unsheathed the sword. T.C. carefully picked up the hefty claymore with both hands. It had a sleek, royal-purple cross guard at the base of the blade and a black leather grip with a pommel at the end, shaped like an iron fist clutching spiked brass knuckles. The blade was a flawless shard of golden amber, as transparent as glass, which appeared to glow when it caught the light. Positioned within the amber blade, along the center edge, at equal distances, were ten wedding rings, one from each failed marriage.

"It's warm to the touch," T.C. said.

"Heh heh. That's hate radiating off it."

T.C. swung the sword a short distance then tested the balance with one hand. "It's perfect. I'm going to call it: The Amber Blade of Divorce."

Dirtbag covered his face in embarrassment. T.C. laughed. "I mean, what do you think will happen if I stab somebody with this?"

"Heh! They'll probably cry, scream, feel crushing despair, stuff like that," Bistro guessed. "Ya need to be careful; that's no ordinary sword. A tiny cut could completely ruin somebody's life forever."

"I can't wait!"

"Oh, I should tell ya that some faults developed during production, faults that are unique to its design."

"Like what?"

"On the first of every month ya should probably keep it sheathed; in fact, don't use it at all on those days. If ya do, the rings in the blade will absorb any currency that comes near it and send it to ya ex-wives. It's some kind of alimony vortex. Let me tell ya, I watched that thing empty out my wallet from across the room."

"Oats alive!" T.C. said, thrilled with the sword.

"Oats? Alive? What does that even mean?"

"He's cursed," Dirtbag explained. "He used to have a filthy mouth. He shot off at an in-law postdivorce, and now if he says a bad word, any bad word, his lips will catch on fire."

"Gives a whole new meaning to curse words, doesn't it?" T.C. chuckled, playing with his new sword.

The room shook, deep-thumping bullet fire tore through the sky, and the neon sign above the shop crashed to the ground outside the break-room window. The marching army was coming into view, their white-skull-painted helmets gleaming under the falling embers of volcanic ash. The Gatling-Dragon loomed overhead, hidden in the dark clouds; only the grinding roar of its turbine-powered wings gave away how close it was. Suddenly, a feedback-laden loudspeaker crackled from within the ranks of the advancing troops. "Bistro the Blacksmith, you have five minutes to come out with your hands up or face annihilation. Don't make us come in there!"

Bistro busted open the break-room window with his steel mallet. "Get stuffed!" he shouted, laughing as he did. "Let me tell ya, I'm flattered, ladies, but I can't go to all ya proms at once, so why don't ya girls go home and fold up ya grannies' filthy panties. Oh, and Lord Impaler was a blasted, wart-faced pig who smelled like cheap bacon when I set his screaming body on fire. The customer-service counter is open, and I'm ready to hear grievances with my complaint hammer. Heh! So come on in, ya cowards! Try my salad bar!"

"Whoa!" T.C. said, shocked. "That's The People's Ultimatum Army, and those people just gave you an ultimatum. You know what that means, right?"

"Yeah, well, I have to lure them in closer so I can blow them up," Bistro said matter-of-factly.

Dirtbag and T.C. stared at him blankly, in need of an explanation.

"I know it seemed like an instant passed by a few moments ago when I stepped into my workshop," Bistro began, "but I spent days in there preparing for this. I jury-rigged a bomb using a basket full of hot rocks called plutonium."

"You kept plutonium in a basket!" Dirtbag was appalled. "What did you use to refine it, a blender?"

"Now, wait just a minute," T.C. said, confused. "I mean, what kind of bomb uses hot rocks?"

"Heh. A fission bomb," Bistro grinned. "Yeah, I dug up a rough draft of it last year when I was out disposing of my therapist. At first glance, I thought it'd be perfect for duck hunting."

"We have to be miles away from a fission explosion!" Dirtbag warned, checking the open window to see where the soldiers were. "I hope you have a good escape plan, Bistro."

"Oh, that's the best part." Bistro kicked open the door to his workshop. "I also built my own flying machine!"

Bistro's workshop was unusually organized for a man with his level of insanity. At the rear of the shop was a great crucible filled with bright-orange, boiling metal. Beneath it was a pool of molten lava regulated by stone-carved pipes and valves. The fission bomb, a copper, football-shaped device covered in cogs, pistons, and naked sticks of dynamite, rested on a table under a fireproof tarp on the left side of the room, near the lava. On the right was the flying machine, a balloon gondola with two pairs of massive, white eagle wings attached to the top in place of the balloon. The wings were folded into resting positions aligned with each corner of the gondola.

"Are those wings made of paper?" Dirtbag asked.

"Yeah, this crazy old wizard commissioned me to make him some belt, and then he paid me with this amazing paper. Ya can fold it into anything, and it will come to life. It took a few tries, but I made these wings and glued them to this basket."

"Whoa! Did you say you glued them?" T.C. cringed. Muffin neighed behind him. "It's OK, baby," he reassured her.

Dirtbag examined the still-damp glue. "Why don't we just use that time meter thing to walk right out of here?"

"Heh heh, because I used it in the bomb," Bistro said as he rushed around the shop tossing his belongings into a steamer trunk he carelessly dragged behind him. "Yeah, when this bomb goes off, it's going to be a slow-rolling detonation meant to prolong agony for as long as possible. The whole canyon is going to become a gigantic, radioactive microwave...unless I carried that five wrong. Heh, in my excitement, I accidentally used all the clocks I had for the plutonium implosion mechanism, so now the only way I can set it off is with an old-fashioned fuse."

"I see," Dirtbag said, measuring the fuse line with his hands. "I think you might want to make this a little longer. Have you ever seen a fission explosion?"

Bistro didn't answer, but the nervous excitement on his face told Dirtbag that he hadn't. The shop rattled as flaming bullets ripped holes through the ceiling. The loudspeaker outside yelled they only had one minute left to surrender before the building was stormed. The soldiers began beating their axes against their metal shields to dissuade resistance.

"Everyone into the flying machine!" Bistro shouted, tossing his overstuffed steamer trunk inside the gondola. "Heh. Try not to tear the paper getting in."

They heaved Muffin into the basket, and she moved to one side, trying to appear dainty, but she was just too large to ignore. Dirtbag and T.C. climbed on top of her so that there was enough room for Bistro. The paper wings seemed to sense their urgency and stretched out in unison, readying for flight.

"Impressive material," Dirtbag said, comparing the wings with a scrap of the papercraft ninja from his satchel. "I think I'd like to meet this wizard."

"Oh, I'll show you where to find him," Bistro laughed, "if we make it."

The soldiers began to assault the building. Bistro slammed the workshop door closed and locked it. He activated the time meter then lit the end of the fuse with a match. He needed to open the skylight and ran across the shop to flip a small switch. He tripped while running back to the flying machine and fell headfirst into the basket.

The wings began flapping. A gust of wind whipped up within the shop as the flying machine took off. The wind blew the bomb fuse into the pool of lava, where the length of it was incinerated.

"That's bad, right?" T.C. asked.

The bomb exploded.

CHAPTER 9

T.C. stared at the corpse of Muffin, his face stoic but not entirely apathetic. Her big brown eyes were rolled back into her head, exposing their white edges, full of fear. Her pink tongue hung motionless out of a relaxed mouth, as if frozen in the middle of a hearty laugh. This dead unicorn had been, at one time, a vibrant young woman. Behind him, the sky still rumbled from the explosion of the fission bomb, and the world was silent, as though every living thing that witnessed the detonation had collectively gasped in horror.

The lime-green mushroom cloud was finally beginning to dissipate into the upper atmosphere. Bistro explained that it was being carried away from them and moving toward the farmlands recently annexed by General Bloodblivion, who would be furious. That was, if he'd survived.

Bistro looked at his creation with deep satisfaction. "Oh, it's more beautiful than I could've ever imagined."

"Death should never be called beautiful," Dirtbag said bitterly, standing beside him.

The time meter had slowed the detonation of the bomb down enough for the gondola to ride the initial shock wave right out of the canyon. The flying machine had then tumbled out of control through the sky, wings on fire, until it struck a rocky outcropping at the top of a faraway hill. Muffin's body took the entire impact of the crash, saving all their lives. The charred paper wings lay across her broken body, hiding the extent of her fatal injuries from view.

Dirtbag turned from watching the mushroom cloud. He had left T.C. alone long enough and gingerly approached him. "How do you feel?"

"It's strange," T.C. said. "I feel the same way I do after I get a divorce."

"Sad?"

"No. Relieved." T.C. was quiet and then sighed. "I ruined her life, Dirt. I mean, we had that one night together, and it was great, but when I woke up the next morning, she'd been turned into a unicorn and the wife had filled the barn with the finest attorneys in all the land. At first it was fun. I think we both thought we'd find a way to turn her back into a woman and we'd live happily ever after. But that never happened. I used to be able to look in her eyes and see a young girl aching to escape. Then one day that was gone, and all I could see were the same dull eyes every horse has. Who Muffin was died a long time ago; this was just some poor horse I liked making out with." He kneeled down and cut off a long braid of blond hair from Muffin's mane and wrapped it around his wrist, where he could see it and remember her.

Bistro came over to see what they were staring at; he scratched his head. "Heh heh. It's gonna to take all day to bury that mess."

"Well," Dirtbag said, "I saw a ditch behind that tree. It would be a lot quicker to drag the whole thing over there."

"Yeah." T.C. nodded. "That just about fits my emotional investment in it."

They pushed the gondola into the ditch, tipping it over. Muffin rolled out, already purplish and puffy, with her legs sticking straight up. The ditch wasn't as deep as it appeared, so they went about trying to find rocks to bury her under. About an hour later, they had filled the ditch with assorted stones, but Muffin was still not completely covered up.

"She's gone to a better place," Bistro announced after a few minutes, but none of them were completely sure of that.

They sat in the sun resting and watched the residual mushroom cloud as it drifted away, dissolving into the sky. Dirtbag unbundled the leather armor and started to put it on. Bistro showed him how the various parts cleverly overlapped to provide protection without restricting his movement.

"Heh, there!" Bistro said. "Ya don't look like a rag doll anymore."

T.C. knocked on the leather armor. "Can you still do the dirt seizure?"

Dirtbag did the dance. T.C. laughed, and Dirtbag smiled. "Hey, how do I look?"

"Like you're breaking all your bones, Dirt," T.C. replied. "I mean, with that armor on you walk so normally nobody will suspect you can move like that."

"Good. I like being underestimated."

At the base of the hill was an overgrown brick road. They made their way down to it and began walking. Bistro dragged his overstuffed steamer trunk behind him. The sun began to set as they went. Eventually they came to a fork in the road. "Heh, I'm headed this way," Bistro said, pointing down one road. "Oh, the wizard who made the paper is over that way"—he pointed in the opposite direction—"a few miles through that little forest."

T.C. looked into the foreboding woods. A pack of wolves howled, and then a pack of bears roared, followed immediately by the sound of bears eating wolves.

"Swell," T.C. said. "Now, are you going to give us a name, or do we have to guess?"

"Let's see…yeah, I think his name was Donny Brooke."

"Are you kidding me? That's a terrible name," Dirtbag remarked. "Well, at least we'll have something in common."

"Watch what ya say around him. He's got a bit of a temper." Bistro smirked. "Be sure to thank him for saving our lives."

"Actually, I think you deserve that thanks, Bistro." T.C. bowed politely.

"Oh, ya're not thanking me for making that bomb, are ya? Heh, I hope not. Yesterday only a high wizard or sorceress could unleash destruction of that magnitude, and today, thanks to me, anybody can do it in their garage. Let me tell ya, with that explosion, kings and generals are gonna be searching for me, ready to pay mountains of gold just to have me in their arsenals. Yeah, they'll pay me a fortune to do what I just did to anyone they don't agree with."

"Whoa, wait a second," T.C. said. "You plan to sell your mass murder to the highest bidder? That's sick!"

"That's capitalism! Heh heh. Moreover, if I don't sell out, I'll be hunted down and forced to work for someone anyway. Selling out affords me protection and funding to further my creativity as an artist."

Dirtbag rubbed his face. "Well, I've heard enough. It was nice to meet you. Good luck with everything. Let's get out of here, T.C."

T.C. stepped in front of Bistro and leaned as far back as his spine would allow.

"What's that supposed to be?" Bistro asked.

"That's an unbow. I'm just taking back my respect."

"Heh! I never asked for ya respect in the first place!" Bistro spun around on the toes of his red high heels and began walking away from them. He disappeared into the fading light, accompanied by the steady, heavy clicking of his questionable shoes.

"Did we just make a new enemy, Dirt?"

"No, he was just one of those people you encounter that never cultivated a soul," Dirtbag growled. "You'd be surprised how many people are alive but incapable of living."

"How do you want to handle this Donny Brooke guy?"

"Well, I have no problem beating up an old man." They chuckled, relishing their blatant hypocrisy.

They camped near the edge of the woods after the sun had set. In the distance a strange glow lingered in the sky over where the bomb had exploded, and it remained there throughout the night.

CHAPTER 10

———

Donny Brooke, the wizard, opened the door to his humble cottage in the middle of a secluded, angelic forest clearing. The rising sun lit up specks of dew that had settled on his front yard as if a thousand diamonds had emerged overnight. Little birds with puffed-up feathers encircled him with song. He greeted them all with a warm smile. "Lah la la la lah!" he sang in a raspy, unharmonious voice, hoarse from years of screaming.

The old wizard stretched out his arms and wished the world a jolly good morning. He picked up a bag of animal feed and strolled down through his peaceful garden to a small pond. As he walked, flowers bloomed, honeybees stirred, and a young deer appeared from the bushes. The wizard opened the sack of feed and pulled out a handful of golden powder. He spread it onto the ground, and the creatures fed. The deer approached him cautiously. He held some feed in his hand, and it accepted the offer. After a few moments, the deer had eaten enough, and it turned toward the pond to view its reflection, but it did not drink, because it, and everything else surrounding the wizard, was made of folded paper.

Donny Brooke wore a lavish purple-velvet robe complemented by a white feather boa around his neck. Hidden beneath the shadow of a matching purple traditional wizard hat was a pair of weathered, craggy eyes framed by a long, well-manicured, faded copper-red beard.

He approached an alabaster pedestal in the middle of his garden. On it was a thick, leather-bound spell book. He opened the book and chanted several spells that pushed the potential rain clouds in the sky far away from his creations. He cast another spell, and from a shelf by the pond arose more animals out of a flattened stack of paper. The papers fluttered into the air, folding themselves into a giraffe, a rhino, three tortoises, and six ninjas, all of them crudely decorated with crayon scribbles. The ninjas bowed before the wizard and rushed through the cottage door to prepare breakfast for their master. Soon the scent of eggs frying and black coffee brewing wafted through the air.

Dirtbag and T.C. discreetly assessed the wizard from the edge of the woods near the cottage. They watched as he opened the doors of a small shed and pulled out a large vat. He briefly disappeared inside the building, made some loud noises, and reappeared with long pieces of wood and a roll of thin wire mesh. He fitted the wood together like a picture frame, using wooden pins to hold the sections. He stretched the roll of wire mesh across the frame to make a canvas. He took the lid off the large vat, reached inside, and pulled out a handful of wood-pulp slurry, which he then spread slowly across the mesh.

"Now he's making paper," Dirtbag said in a low voice, observing the wizard from behind a tree. "We should attack him before he has his first cup of coffee, while he's still groggy."

T.C. watched the wizard as he bumbled about. The old man did not appear particularly threatening. "I dunno, Dirt. There's something about that name, Donny Brooke. I mean, I know I've heard it somewhere before."

"Hey, look at that guy; he's probably retired and crazy. He folds paper ninjas, T.C. What, are you afraid of a paper cut?"

"Trust me, Dirt. Old wizards like this relic are the most dangerous kind of wizard. They hide their true powers with deception, just like my ex-wife. The way I see it, we need to keep him from going for his staff."

"Well, what if he doesn't have a staff? Remember the wizard who summoned that tobacco hydra using a 'magical' sitar?"

"Thanks for bringing that disaster up." T.C. rubbed his nose under his sunglasses as the disturbing memory flashed through his mind. "OK, maybe he doesn't have a staff."

They saw the old wizard forget what he was doing for a second.

"Aw, he's just some dumb, old man," Dirtbag said, feeling confident. "I bet I can push him down and hog-tie him with that stupid boa he's wearing."

"Trust me, Dirt. Old men are evil. Inside, he's full of applesauce and rage. One just feeds off the other in an endless circle."

"It's called retirement," Dirtbag said, not really listening. "I guess he could have a file cabinet full of ninjas hidden somewhere."

"I can just tear those apart with my bare hands, Dirt. Those paper things aren't the problem. I mean, look at that guy." He grimaced as the wizard sang a horribly off-key song to himself. "Doesn't he look suspicious to you?"

"We're overthinking this. How many old men have we beaten up?"

"What? Whoa, we always had a cause. I mean, we can't just—"

"Can't just what? He attacked a town with those ninjas and likely sent that wedding invitation to me...or knows who did. He's a grade-A scumbag deluxe, T.C. He's probably got kidnapped orphans in his basement making toothbrushes out of badger hair."

The wizard lazily worked the canvas, yawning. Dirtbag stepped out into the clearing. "This is how a professional does it, T.C.," he whispered.

Dirtbag made his way across the yard while T.C. watched from their hiding spot. As a being made of soil, Dirtbag's presence was less detectable by wizards than a normal man's. He blended in with the earth, and his soft feet moved silently across the ground. The wizard appeared to be blissfully unaware of Dirtbag as he approached the old man from the rear, arms raised with clenched, leather-armored fists, ready to strike. A twig snapped.

"You'd better be my coffee, Brother," the wizard said suddenly in an explosion of anger, "or, so help me, the volcanic fury of my size-twenty-two boots will erupt and stomp your worthless carcass so hard into the ground the entire planet will be knocked off its axis!"

Donny Brooke spun around, throwing off his robe in a thunder-ous explosion of electric-guitar riffs and excessive fireworks. The wizard's body rippled with veiny muscles upon muscles and a deep bronze tan. He wore spandex pants with the word *Doomsday* stenciled in gold over a purple lightning pattern that faded to black midthigh. Around his waist was a heavy, gold championship belt covered with platinum skulls. He wore the unmistakable high-laced boots of a professional wrestler.

"You made the biggest mistake of your short life, Brother!" he shouted, pumping his arms repeatedly, growing larger as he did. "You entered the arena! Challenged the unstoppable machine! When I'm done with you, Brother, I'm going to mulch my garden with your crippled body and grow hot peppers between your sitt'n' cheeks! Beg for death, you big bag of trash!"

Dirtbag looked back toward T.C., finding the entire spectacle humorous. He boldly threw a punch into the face of the muscular wizard. The bees suddenly stopped buzzing, the birds stopped singing, and the deer darted for cover. Donny Brooke bent his broken, bloody nose back into place with a loud crunch. He snapped his fingers, and the blood disappeared. His breathing increased, like a locomotive getting ready to leave the station, as he pointed a white-taped finger at Dirtbag. The wizard's mouth spoke words, but his voice made incoherent grunts of rage, like a bull about to break out of its pen at a rodeo.

"Oats alive!" T.C. shouted, "I know who that is! That's Donny Brooke, 'The Doomsday Machine'! Get out of there, Dirt! Run!"

"It's all show," Dirtbag snickered. "Wrestling is fake, scientific fact."

A fist flew into Dirtbag's face, flipping him head over heels across half the lawn, landing him onto the front porch of the cottage. The punch had hit Dirtbag so hard all the dirt in his head had shifted around the point of impact, making a crater. He squeezed the sides of his head together to push it back into shape. Donny Brooke was already barreling across the lawn like a runaway boulder rumbling down a mountain. Dirtbag scrambled to his feet and ran.

"You can't escape the all-seeing eyes of the Machine, Brother!" the muscled wizard furiously screamed, chasing after Dirtbag. "I'm going to tear your soul right out of your body and spread it on my toast for breakfast. You hear me, Brother? You fell into a fault line during an earthquake, magnitude—extinction! I'm going to crush you like a tidal wave of annihilation crashing down from space! Total destruction! All that will be left is what I scrape off my size-twenty-two boots, Brother!"

Dirtbag dove through the nearest cottage window, and Donny Brooke ran straight through the adjacent stone wall as if it wasn't even there. He grabbed the kitchen table Dirtbag was hiding under and splintered it with his hands. He flexed his arms, screaming strange noises; his eyes grew large as his muscle mass increased to inhuman proportions. Dirtbag had never seen anything like it. He ran from the room.

"You've ignited the inexhaustible combustion of pure manpower, Brother!" Donny Brooke roared. "I'm going to use the leftover rags of your body to scrub my bathroom!"

T.C. bolted from the woods with his sword drawn, his every step driven by concern for his friend. He could hear Donny Brooke screaming inside the cottage. He heard Dirtbag fire his shotgun twice. There was a momentary silence; then the cottage shook, and furniture began blasting out the windows. Dirtbag rode a thrown couch out to the front yard. T.C. caught up with him to see if he was injured.

"And you call *me* rash," Dirtbag shouted to T.C., peeling himself off the broken couch.

"Did you shoot him?"

"He was too fast. I missed and shot a photo album, and that didn't go over very well."

They heard the front door of the cottage creak. The wizard slowly walked out, took off his pointy hat, put on a purple bandanna covered in gold skulls, and leisurely slurped his cup of piping-hot black coffee. "The Machine's granting you a temporary reprieve, so you can say farewell to your existence," the wizard said, lifting his head high, his eyes wide open. "You can't escape the tornado of pain once you enter the cathedral of carnage. Bow down, and beg the Machine for forgiveness before his coffee is finished and the door to oblivion reopens."

"We need to think of something quick," Dirtbag said, watching the wizard sprinkle protein powder into his beverage. "You saw what this guy did *without* his morning coffee."

"Wasn't the original plan to basically mug a poor, old man?"

"Hey, I never put it that way, but pretty much."

"OK, maybe it's not too late for diplomacy." T.C. stood up on the couch, presenting his most charming smile. "Excuse me, sir? Mr. All-Powerful Doomsday Machine? I think we started off on the wrong foot."

"Brother, the only foot we need to talk about is the one contained within my preferred head-kicking boot that's already ramping up to launch your brain right out your mouth." The wizard sipped some more of his coffee. "Unless you meant the other foot in the other boot that is preparing to shoot straight up your prune cave."

"Whoa, now, wait just a minute. 'Prune cave'?" T.C. looked at Dirtbag as he repeated the term. He opened his arms in a gesture of goodwill to Donny Brooke. "We came here because my good friend Dirt was sent a villainous wedding invitation from his ex-wife in the form of a papercraft dove. We just thought that maybe you made it or know who did and that we could find out who commissioned it and where she is."

"That, Brother"—the wizard pointed at them both with one hand while crushing his empty cup of coffee in the other—"is how my morning should've started. You could've said, 'Good morning, Unstoppable Machine of Endless Pain. Blah blah blah, my ex.' Then I could've said, 'Why, yes, I can help you. Come inside for a delicious cup of coffee.' That's not how it happened, is it, Brother? You didn't recognize the Doomsday Machine, the ultimate weapon of biological destruction, and you stepped into the arena. You mistook this old body for a weakling. I'm the last innocent old man you're going to terrorize! When I'm done pulverizing justice into your bodies, the only thing left will be a fine mist on my lawn that I'll personally hose off after enjoying a pitcher of tea!"

"Hey, innocent is a bit of a stretch," Dirtbag scoffed. "You sent a bunch of paper ninjas into that town full of pickle-obsessed morons."

"And just who are you?"

"I'm Dirtbag."

"So, you're the *heroes* who tore them up?" The wizard threw the scraps of his crushed coffee cup aside. "I'm going to teach you a lesson, Dirtbag, you and your pretty friend. That town of gutless cowards has sworn allegiance to that dictator General Bloodblivion. They arrange for their daughters to marry his men, even name bar drinks in his honor. Those spineless weaklings deserve to be punished, Brother."

"Their daughters?" Dirtbag said quietly. He clenched his denim hands tightly. "Hey, I'm tired of fighting wars for other people!" he yelled. "It never ends! There's always the next tyrant waiting to seize power the moment you turn your back, and there's always that group of people ready to support him. I'm sick of it. I've got my own problems to deal with—problems I've left alone for too long. Whatever is happening around here is none of my business."

"Brother, a true hero can't be selectively heroic; you have to take on every injustice that comes your way!"

"Hey! We can't rescue the whole world!"

"Only a coward would say that!" Donny Brooke leapt off the porch in an attempt to tackle Dirtbag. Dirtbag rolled out of the way, turned, and fired two shots, which the wizard swatted away like harmless insects. Dirtbag angled the shotgun so he could read the secret new dial hidden by the mirage ore. He set it to the first mode he saw: "Afterburner."

Donny Brooke's knuckles began cracking by themselves as he slowly approached Dirtbag. "You're facing the most powerful, indestructible force on the planet!" the wizard screamed. "There's water, air, earth, fire, and the Doomsday Machine, Brother! In two seconds I'm going to fly over there and slam your body down so hard your vital organs are going to leap out to save themselves. The coming brutalization will be so utterly apocalyptic, Earth itself may very well explode into cosmic dust!"

"Bullcookies!" T.C. shouted, trying to draw the wizard's attention. "I've been through ten divorce proceedings. I mean, I've heard worse from exes under oath. You'll have to try harder than that to hurt my feelings."

"You'll die alone," Donny Brooke said coldly.

The comment hit T.C. with such fearful truth that he reacted as if he had been gored. He lifted his sword and charged madly at the wizard, swinging hard. Donny Brooke caught the amber blade between the fingers of his weaker left hand, a veteran combat move of such skill that it was clear he was toying with T.C., but the follow-up move, a twist of the fingers meant to break the blade of the sword, failed to work. T.C. yanked the sword away, cutting the wizard's fingers. Donny Brooke stared at his hand briefly, curious, and then pulled back his arm to punch T.C.

Dirtbag took aim and fired the special "Afterburner" shot; a red ember hit Donny Brooke in the back, engulfing him in superheated flames.

The wizard flexed his arms into a front double-biceps pose and blew the fire off his body with one breath. The wound to his hand was healed with a snap of his fingers. He put his hands on his hips and chuckled, appearing confidently invincible, assuring them they had no chance whatsoever of defeating him.

"The animals, Dirt!" T.C. shouted. "Set them on fire!"

"Nooo!" shouted Donny Brooke, leaping to intercept Dirtbag before he could attack. The wizard swung a thunder-cracking punch at Dirtbag, intended to knock the shotgun out of his hands, but Dirtbag leaned back, bending himself in half, a maneuver no human being could make. Donny Brooke missed and seemed shocked that he had.

T.C. rushed in from the right and cut into the wizard's arm as he ran past. Donny Brooke turned and punched T.C. in the back with such force that the knight was sent soaring across the lawn and through the open front door of the cottage, where the paper ninjas stood watching.

Dirtbag unfolded his body and fired shots continually at Donny Brooke, retreating as he did to keep the Doomsday Machine out of reach. The wizard slapped each shot away, not particularly bothered by small cuts or bursts of flame, and moved quickly to close the gap between himself and Dirtbag. Donny Brooke lunged at Dirtbag, grabbed him by his grass-hair, and threw him to the ground. He flicked the shotgun out of Dirtbag's hand, reached down, and tore the armored chest plate off the denim man. He punched a crater into Dirtbag's face, then stood up, lifted a *Doomsday*-stenciled leg, and began to stomp Dirtbag's unprotected torso until his dirt innards were lumpy and pushed far out of place. Dirtbag rolled over, clutching his body, not in pain but in shock.

T.C. ran out of the cottage, his face covered in paper cuts. He saw Dirtbag on the ground, horribly injured, and using all his might, he quickly hurled his sword through the air at the wizard. Donny Brooke turned in time to catch the blade with his hand, but it sliced through his grip and pierced deep into his body. The wizard fell to one knee with a painful exhale. "That pain!" Donny Brooke shouted, feeling the effects of the wedding rings within the Amber Blade of Divorce. "I can't block it out! It's like I'm dying inside, Brother!"

"Multiply that by ten, and you have my life!" T.C. shouted, dashing over to the scene. He punched Donny Brooke in the face. The wizard shook it off, surprised that a mere swordsman was so physically strong. T.C. kicked the blade deeper into the weakened wizard, causing him to cough up a spat of blood.

"And to think," T.C. snarled, "Bistro wanted us to thank you for saving our lives."

"Bistro? The arms dealer?" Donny Brooke sneered between painful winces. "Brother, that man is a full-blown homicidal maniac! He made this thing, didn't he?" The wizard looked down at the sword sticking out of him. "This is the most punishing weapon I've ever experienced; it's a tool of pure evil."

Donny Brooke fell to one hand. T.C. foolishly turned away to see how Dirtbag was doing. The wizard suddenly swept T.C. off his feet and held him in a bear hug, head butting him again and again until T.C. lost consciousness. Donny Brooke tossed T.C.'s limp carcass aside and pulled the sword out from his own body. With a snap of his fingers, his injuries were instantaneously healed. He turned his attention to Dirtbag, who was now huddled under the thrown couch, clutching his misshapen guts as if he had been cut open. Donny Brooke threw the sword away with a chuckle.

"Pathetic!" He kicked the couch over, exposing Dirtbag.

"What kind of wizard are you?" Dirtbag asked nervously.

"That's probably the smartest thing I've heard come out of your mouth." Donny Brooke squatted down next to Dirtbag. "I hate to shatter your preconceived notions about what a wizard is, Brother, but I don't have a staff. I have this"—he pointed at his championship belt—"which, by the way, was not made by Bistro. I know he likes to say otherwise, but he only engraved the name of my last competitor, who, I might add, recently ceased to exist."

"I don't care." Dirtbag gritted his teeth. "I have my own problems."

"Brother, you should be thrilled that you faced the Doomsday Machine and lived. The Machine is a heavyweight magic grappler, champion level. Everyone knows a magic grappler uses physicality to cast spells. There is no escape once these volcanic hands of total annihilation grab hold. I built my body, trained my mind, and fortified my diet, and now I'm unbeatable. The Machine crushes all contenders, Brother!" He sighed, calming down a little. "I only papercraft on the side. I do wedding invitations, birthdays, graduations, craft fairs, whatever pays the bills."

"It's your hobby?" Dirtbag said in disbelief.

"I'm not answering questions, Brother; I'm asking them! It's time for the headlock of truth!" He grabbed Dirtbag and stuffed his dirt-filled head under a big bronze arm; his massive biceps flexed like expanding rocks, squishing Dirtbag's neck. "Comfy?"

"Not really," Dirtbag said, wiggling a little but not fighting it.

"Why is it so important to find your ex-wife?"

"She stole my heart," Dirtbag said, relaxing within the inescapable grasp.

The wizard rubbed his beard, thinking. "Well, that is some significant motivation, Brother, but it doesn't excuse your actions. This land is a festering powder keg on the verge of total detonation. People have had it with Bloodblivion, and frankly, so have I. Something has to be done about that man. There's a war coming, a big one. If you're not going to help these lands, then you should be thrown out of them."

"Hey, all I want to know is where my ex-wife is."

"Aren't you two divorced?"

"It's complicated; but I guess we are." Dirtbag hung limply. "I left her for another woman I met, a young princess. It was true love."

"But this other woman, she died, didn't she, Brother?" the wizard said, peering into Dirtbag's soul.

"She did, and I never left her."

"So, your ex-wife stole your heart for revenge?"

"Who knows? She was never the same after she found out that I had loved that girl so much more than her. She hated me because I chose to die with that girl."

"That's not all, though, is it, Brother? You abandoned your family, your child, for that other woman, didn't you? You really are a dirtbag."

"I know. My life is a mess right now."

Donny Brooke dropped Dirtbag and stood up, dusting off his spandex pants. "The Machine never reveals the identity or intentions of his clients, especially to losers, Brother. By tradition, any man who challenges the supremacy of a wizard and is defeated cannot simply walk away, not without a penalty." Donny Brooke grinned. "But I think I can make your punishment work for both of us."

"Wait." Dirtbag crouched, holding his lumpy insides together. "What would've happened if we'd won?"

"I would have owed you a favor, Brother."

The wizard picked Dirtbag up with one hand and flipped the couch right side up with the other. He patted Dirtbag on the head, chuckling as he set him down. He dragged T.C. over by his armored foot and placed the unconscious knight on the couch next to Dirtbag. Donny Brooke gathered their belongings together then made some poses as he prepared to pass judgment on them. "You, Dirtbag, and you…" Donny Brooke frowned at T.C. "What's his name?"

"Tuna Casserole."

The wizard closed his eyes and let out a long groan. "Brother, that is the worst name a man can possibly have."

"It's a curse from one of his ex-wives," Dirtbag said. "Whatever his real name was, he's permanently forgotten it, and so has everyone he's ever known."

"No man is beyond redemption, Brother." Donny Brooke took a deep breath and pointed a finger at them. "Tuna Casserole and Dirtbag, you've challenged the Doomsday Machine and utterly failed. The usual punishment is annihilation; your punishment is banishment to the unending lands of Melpomene. I think you'll find that is where *heroes* like you belong."

The papercrafted animals dragged over a large, fresh sheet of paper. Donny Brooke kneeled down and began folding, laughing mischievously with each crease he made.

CHAPTER 11

———

Gentle, steady fluttering wings lifted a giant, undecorated papercraft moth and its cargo, a smashed couch, high above an endless ivory desert. The ground below was a moonscape of deep craters, a battlefield nature seemed unable or unwilling to erode away. Littered across the scarred earth were the glossy-black skeletal remains of massive, ancient war machines, unblemished by the passage of time and long since stripped of anything useful but still intimidating and nightmarish to behold. They were enablers of death, sponsored by the bilateral hatred of a disconnected history no longer remembered, testaments to the inability of humankind to resolve even the most basic of differences, and further proof that the greatest problems facing individuals are those that are created by themselves.

"Whoa! Are you blooming?" T.C. asked Dirtbag, holding on to the flying couch as it sailed over the desert.

"I haven't been drinking enough," Dirtbag told T.C. as he began to uproot flower buds poking through the threadbare blotches of his denim skin. Drinking alcohol kept things from growing inside him, and there were things that wanted to grow, things from the past. A few buds were beginning to open into white flowers, the kind that only grew in one other place. "It's her again."

"I've never been in love like that," T.C. said, watching Dirtbag drop the flower buds onto the arid land below. "I mean, not like the way you were with that girl."

"You must've felt like that about one of your wives."

"I loved them all, Dirt," T.C. said, thinking. "Just not the way you tell it."

"Well, maybe I've told it too many times. It was so long ago I can't even remember much about her other than what I felt, and even that is vague without my heart."

"Vague. That's how I feel about Muffin." T.C. paused dramatically. "I miss that pink horse. I loved that horse like a man should love a woman. I mean, OK, it was wrong to love a unicorn that way, but she was so kind to me," T.C. whined. "And her hair smelled like fresh strawberries. Poor Muffin!" he sniffed. "I can still hear her laugh; it was so contagious."

Dirtbag scowled at him. Muffin had been a burden for as long as he had known T.C. Dirtbag listened to T.C. recount the few good times with Muffin, joking about the mountain of bad, all the while sporting his trademark charming grin, but it barely disguised some unrelated, unspoken, deep, churning misery within the knight. They were friends, but there were always those things deep inside they could never share with one another. Dirtbag opened up his satchel and pulled out an unlabeled silver bottle of rum and gulped down half of it. The remaining flowers withered and fell off his body. T.C. motioned for Dirtbag to hand him the bottle.

"It's really bitter," Dirtbag warned.

"So's my life."

Dirtbag groaned. "Hey, don't drop it!" he shouted. "That's a gift from Donny Brooke."

"Are you sure we should be drinking this, Dirt?" T.C. asked, drinking it anyway. "I mean, what if it's cursed?"

"Are you kidding me? Look at us; we can't get any more cursed." Dirtbag watched T.C. take another long drink, smacking his lips from the bitterness, then drink again. As T.C. leaned his head back, the wind lifted his long blond hair. Dirtbag suddenly pointed at T.C. "Hey! That's a dent!" he said.

"Where?" T.C. felt around until he discovered an indentation adjacent to his forehead. "Swell."

"There is a dent in your head, T.C. A dent!"

"Trust me; I'm fine. That's just another curse."

"I thought you told me all of them."

"Not all of them, just the ones that mattered. I mean, I had ten wives, Dirt. I can't keep track of all their hatred." He drank. "OK, look, Dirt. I'm hollow."

"Hollow? But how does that work?"

"I dunno; how does being made of dirt work?"

"I see your point."

"Do you? You don't even have eyes." T.C. drank again. "Oats alive! I'm empty inside, Dirt. I've been this way since before we met. I don't dent easily, but I do dent; without this armor, I'd be dead. Don't worry; I mean, I'm tough." He clunked the rum bottle on his forehead. "I'm not going to suddenly implode."

"Why don't you wear a helmet?"

"That would cramp my style. Besides, those things just don't work with sunglasses."

"I'm surprised Donny Brooke didn't knock those off."

"I'm always prepared, Dirt." T.C. pulled his hair back to reveal duct tape behind his ears, holding his sunglasses to his head. "I mean, women have small hands, but they slap hard." He chugged the bottle, trying to finish it off, and almost choked on the deluge of liquid. "I can't believe this thing is still full!"

"It's an enchanted rum bottle. It will never run out, no matter how much we drink."

"Are you sure this was a gift? I mean, how can we practice moderation if it never runs dry?"

"Simple." Dirtbag took the bottle from him, corked it, and put it back in his satchel.

T.C. slouched down on the couch, comfortably inebriated. He took out his hair clippers and changed the attachment, converting it into an electric shaver. He buzzed his face until it was smooth again.

Dirtbag stretched, checking his insides; everything seemed settled back into place. He picked up the chest piece Donny Brooke had torn off. He put it on and used the armor to mold his torso back into shape, tying the leather-titanium plates together with the remaining unbroken straps. It no longer fit properly. He asked T.C. to help him fix it and handed T.C. the duct tape. They used half the roll. When T.C. had finished, the look on his face was easy for Dirtbag to read. "Hey, I don't care how bad this looks," Dirtbag quipped.

"Actually, I didn't think you could look much worse, Dirt."

"Thanks."

They sprawled out on the flying couch, watching the land pass beneath them. T.C. looked up at the steady beating wings of the faceless paper moth. "So he just read your mind and then made this thing?"

"Then he handed me the rum as a consolation prize and snapped his fingers to put me to sleep so he could enjoy his breakfast in peace. He told me I couldn't be knocked out because I didn't have a brain."

"Trust me, Dirt. You have to have a brain; I mean, you're smarter than me, which I know is not really a compliment to either of us, but let's pretend it is."

"He also said that if we returned to the Northern Terpsichore lands before two years had passed, he'd find us and perform the six-fingered clamp of total obliteration."

"Six fingered? Is that a two-handed technique?"

"Do you really want to find out?"

"Nah."T.C. sighed, blowing his breath out through his lips lazily.

The moth flew quietly over the cratered desert. The towering husks of the ancient war machines soon faded behind them, and the sun passed its apex into the afternoon. Dirtbag slumped; bored, he searched his satchel for his playing cards, but they had been left behind in the jail cell. Neither of them knew where they were going or how far away they were from being there.

"It's just too quiet," T.C. said. "I feel like something is about to happen, something bad."

"That's anxiety. Relax. Think of something else."

"Like what?"

"Well, like a ham sandwich."

"Yeah,"T.C. said with a grin. "On some soft rye bread with a little mayo."

"Or horseradish sauce."

"Horse rash?"T.C. said, remembering. "Muffin had that once."

Suddenly the sky exploded with antiaircraft fire. Thunderous, black bursts of shrapnel detonated around them, shredding the couch's upholstery. They held on to the bucking couch as the moth took evasive action through the storm of cannon fire. It was impossible to see where it was coming from; the land below seemed to be a featureless, white glare expanding to the horizon in every direction.

The moth squealed.

"Oats alive!" T.C. shouted. "We're hit!"

And they fell.

CHAPTER 12

———

Dirtbag pulled his scruffy head out of the ethereal white sand, shaking the fine grit from his green grass-hair. He coughed up a sizable rock and let out a long, deep breath. Behind him, not far away, the paper-craft moth lay on its back, dead, its legs curling up into black cords as fire consumed it. The crash landing had thrown them off the couch on impact. He looked around for T.C. and heard a low groan nearby. Dirtbag climbed over a dune in the direction of the sound, searching for his friend.

"Uhhh. It's like a swarm of wasps just flew into my pants," T.C. said, trying to lift himself off the cactus he was straddling.

"Well, how did you manage that?" Dirtbag asked, helping him down, mentioning as he did that there wasn't another cactus around for miles. "Did you ever think that maybe you're unlucky?"

T.C. pulled a couple of cactus needles out from between his legs. "But I *am* lucky. See? No penetration."

"Hey, that must be a first for you," Dirtbag sneered.

They climbed back over the dune to where the couch had landed. They picked up their scattered things, reequipping themselves with weapons. Dirtbag held his hands up to the afternoon sun in order to see what direction they had been traveling.

"I can't believe we got shot down. What kind of scumbag shoots down a moth?"

"The way I see it," T.C. said, noticing they had no water, "Donny Brooke sent us out here on purpose. To die."

"He did say he was sending us where we belonged." Dirtbag clenched his fists. "We weren't flying over the desert; we were flying into it. That's why he gave us this never-ending bottle of rum."

"Swell. Do you want to add him to the revenge list?"

"No, I threw that away last year when I had to start keeping track of more than one page." Dirtbag looked out onto the vast expanse of sand. "As long as we're careful, we can make it out of here."

T.C. noticed something sparkling on the upended couch. He pulled off a seat cushion, and a pile of loose change fell to the ground.

"Oats alive!" he said, leaning down to scoop the coins up with his hands. The sound of loose change jingling resonated across the empty, still wilderness.

"Hey, we have plenty of money," Dirtbag reminded T.C. while he watched the horizon warily. "We have to get out of here before whoever shot us down comes looking."

T.C. pulled the other cushion off the couch with a loud rip; more change rolled out onto the ground in a chorus of metallic notes. He gathered up the coins, shaking them in his hands to sift out the sand. The noise carried far, and in the distance something awoke. A diesel engine turned over with a garish snarl, revving from somewhere unseen in the barren wasteland. Dirtbag drew his shotgun, listening to the guttural engine idle, but it was hard to hear with T.C. sifting the loose change. Then he suddenly put the two together and grabbed T.C.'s hands. "Stop!"

T.C. heard the engine, too. He dropped the coins to the ground and unsheathed his sword. The engine sound started moving, shifting gears roughly as it did.

"What is that, Dirt? I mean, it sounds like somebody buried an overturned lawn mower."

"Haven't you read about the machines that live in the desert? It was in all the papers."

"News is for entertainment, Dirt, not information." He chuckled, but this made Dirtbag angry. T.C. straightened up. "Besides, cars need lots of lush grassaline to eat. Did you know Mustangs can commute together in herds of as many as forty cars?"

"That's not a Mustang; that's a diesel engine, and only one type of creature has an engine like that *and* is attracted to the sound of loose change."

"Oats alive," T.C. said, growing pale. "You mean a bus-worm is out there?"

"Exactly. It's got to be a big one, too; otherwise we wouldn't hear it while it's underground."

"Wait," T.C. said, hushing his voice. "Listen. It's close."

The growl of the diesel engine suddenly rose to the top of the sand dune in front of them. They stepped back, but it was too late. The front of the bus-worm burst out of the dune in a ruction of buzzing, bright headlights and blaring horn that knocked them down as it sped past in a roar of black exhaust. They scrambled behind the couch. The bus-worm circled around the dune, picking up speed, and barreled right at them. They ducked, and it leapt overhead. Dirtbag counted three segments; it was a biarticulated bus, the longest and angriest kind of bus-worm. The bus-worm made a sharp turn, rolling the rear sections over. The internal lights within the coach flickered, and through the windows they could see the decomposed remains of the unfortunate passengers it had consumed over its lifetime being thrown about inside.

"Once you get on the bus," Dirtbag said grimly, "you never get off."

The bus-worm snaked over a shallow slope, aiming its headlights at Dirtbag and T.C. The destination sign lit up with the perplexing words, "New Jersey," accompanied by a deep, hollow cry reminiscent of a funeral bell tolling.

"Oats alive! Oats alive!" T.C. shouted, watching the huge, thunderous beast gain speed. "Let's get out of here!"

They moved as quickly as they could through the sand, with the bus-worm stalking after them and revving its engine menacingly. The bus-worm gently goosed the throttle, gliding effortlessly across the desert as though it was on pavement. Dirtbag and T.C. rapidly became exhausted from trying to run across the piles of loose granules. The bus-worm pulled up alongside the broken couch, opened its front side doors, and gobbled up the furniture in two swift bites. Dirtbag began searching the settings on the shotgun's dial for ideas.

"Maybe you can throw your sword at it, T.C."

"No way. I mean, if it's like any other animal, it will blindly flee from the pain. That thing would probably dive deep under the sand and die, and that would be the end of my sword. I'm not even sure if the Amber Blade will work on animals. I mean, do they get divorces? Why don't I try slashing the tires instead?" The bus-worm belched heavy, black exhaust. "If I just had a good-sized potato."

Dirtbag turned the dial on his shotgun, considering which mode to use. Some of the settings on the dial seemed appropriate, while others had names he was apprehensive to try. He admitted he should have tested them out beforehand. He settled on "Electrocity" and took aim.

The bus charged toward them, its horn honking wildly, but before Dirtbag could fire, several pineapples and a pomegranate were flung underneath the creature. The bus-worm exploded into a fireball; its horn sang out a spine-chilling death note from its gutted, burning hulk. It slowly cruised past Dirtbag and T.C., horn blaring, on fire, over a dune and off into the unending tract of desolation.

"Hey, is someone throwing fruit? That explodes?" Dirtbag asked. T.C. pointed toward the dune over which the fruit had been thrown. Dirtbag nodded, and they began cautiously climbing it.

"Fruit doesn't normally just explode," T.C. whispered. "I mean, unless it's a bunch of apricots with mayonnaise. Actually, that combination blew up one of my marriages."

They neared the top of the dune, but they saw nothing behind it except footprints. Dirtbag and T.C. decided to follow the tracks and soon realized that the trail was leading back to where they had started. Dirtbag sighed. They had been outflanked. He abruptly spun around. Three masked bandits stood watching them. The bandits wore long, hooded trench coats that faded in and out of visibility, making them shimmer like heat haze. All three bandits reached into their coats and pulled out bananas, which they pointed at Dirtbag and T.C. like guns.

"Bananas?" T.C. mocked. "We're in trouble now, Dirt."

One of the bandits aimed a banana at the cactus T.C. had landed on and fired a shot, blowing the cactus apart. Three more bandits emerged from a nearby heat haze, surrounding Dirtbag and T.C. They motioned for the two to put their hands up. Dirtbag steadfastly refused, ready to shoot them all, but when the bandits unmasked and were revealed to be fair-skinned young women, he reconsidered. He slowly set the shotgun down.

"What are you doing?" T.C. demanded. "They're armed with bananas."

"Well, maybe we shouldn't be so hasty this time. Maybe these womenfolk can tell us where we are and the best way to get out of here."

"These are desert sirens armed with bananas, Dirt. It's a kinky combination I don't trust."

"Hey, for once, please try not to be you," Dirtbag said, irritated.

T.C. grumbled, noticeably slighted by the comment, and reluctantly lowered his sword. "OK," T.C. said impatiently. "Now what?"

"Take us to your leader," Dirtbag announced boldly.

"Yes." T.C. smiled glibly. "Take us to the top banana."

A woman fired a shot in the air and jammed her banana gun into T.C.'s ribs. She stomped her foot down and pointed for him to get walking. He made kissy faces toward her. She stuffed the still-smoking banana gun in his mouth and cocked the trigger. She whistled, and twenty more banana-gun-wielding young women appeared out of the shimmering wilderness. He promptly agreed to do anything she asked.

CHAPTER 13

———

T.C. listened to the automated, steam-driven pipe organ squeeze out a cover of an ancient guitar solo; he was astonished that such a feat was possible using the antiquated instrument. He had been working in the cathedral-like greenhouse for the past three days, following their capture. Dirtbag was occupied elsewhere; he was deep inside the secret lab of their host, the eccentric mad scientist Doctor Swinebaum, assisting the doctor with clandestine experiments.

The greenhouse and its connected buildings had been constructed inside the skeletal remains of a derelict, ancient war machine. The strange, glossy-black metal alloy of the armored bones was impervious to the relentless heat of the sun, making it ideal for shelter. From the outside, it appeared to be a large, menacing wreck slowly being consumed by the surrounding arid, white desert. Sharp-edged, aggressive architecture warned away would-be explorers. However, inside the monolithic structure, the air was moist and cool, and the sweet scent of plants was everywhere. It was a private oasis, locked up not just from the desert but from the rest of the world, in a perfectly controlled environment of complete artificiality.

The arched central pavilion of the compound resembled a colossal rib cage. The ceiling was covered with a kaleidoscope of mirrors that angled the harsh sunlight through filters to lessen its intensity to a soothing, plant-friendly glow. The internal layout of the pavilion shared many similarities with the expected design of a real cathedral, but the space normally devoted to pews had been converted into rows of interconnected cubicles. Everything was grown in small batches separated by thick, transparent, blast-proof plastic walls. The weaponization of fruit and vegetable seeds took place within the secret lab, which could only be entered through a large, rather noticeable vault door at the far end of the pavilion that was partially covered by a red, polka-dotted shower curtain.

T.C. moved about the growing weapons using a small spray bottle to spritz water on any plant that looked thirsty. His long, golden-blond hair was tucked up into a teal-colored hairnet, and he had managed to find a lab coat large enough to fit over his irremovable, bulky armor. Beautiful, very friendly, young co-eds performed all the labor within the facility. They communicated with various tones of giggles or head-nodding yips but never spoke and seemed incapable of doing so. The girls all had strange ears that resembled colorful, soft flower petals at the very tips where normal ears rounded off.

Doctor Swinebaum was a brilliant, if highly paranoid, man. He had shot down their moth, believing it was a spy beast sent by various state-sponsored agents of espionage intent on stealing his latest creations. He never elaborated on how he had turned purple mangosteen fruit into flak ammunition. Swinebaum had spent most of his life designing weapons, and the weaponization of food was to be the culmination of his long-held belief that the best defense against tyranny was combining a balanced diet with freely available firearms.

Luckily, Dirtbag and T.C.'s reputation had preceded them, and upon meeting Dirtbag, the doctor quickly turned the discussion to researching the mysterious properties of his dirt innards. Doctor Swinebaum was disturbingly fascinated with the possibility of creating soldiers made entirely out of fruits and vegetables that could be grown in the comfort of anyone's backyard. Dirtbag expressed a mutual interest in learning more about his own dirt body and agreed to temporarily donate his time to the scientific effort, at least until he figured out a way to leave the desert.

For T.C., this meant being put to work tending to the latest crop of weapons and, on occasion, tending to the pretty ladies working beside him. "At least I'm not in court," he chuckled to himself as he sprayed a small buffalo berry shrub. The plant snorted at him, and he paused to frown at it.

A lovely, violet-eared brunette wearing a cardigan lab coat and lensless prescription eyeglasses pranced over with a clipboard to inspect his work. T.C. watched as she jotted down a few happy faces and stars with her bright-blue pencil. He gave her his best sultry grin and implied positions of debauchery, using nonsensical gestures with his hands to illustrate. She was receptive and sheepishly yipped in the same airy manner as the other girls. She turned and "accidentally" dropped her pencil on the floor, covering her mouth with deliberate surprise.

"Oats alive," T.C. faux gasped, playing along.

He watched her slowly bend over to pick it up, her tight, bright-yellow miniskirt riding up the backs of her thighs all the way to the base of her round bum as she stretched. Bent all the way over, she turned to make sure he was watching. His gaze melted over her body, and she laughed flirtatiously at him. Dirtbag suddenly hit T.C. in the back of the head, knocking his hairnet out of place.

"Whoa, that's not cool, Dirt. I was having a moment there," T.C. complained, turning around to reveal he'd grown out his facial hair. "When did you get released?"

"Are you kidding me?" Dirtbag barked.

"It's called a balbo; I mean, this fertilizer is great for hair. All natural, too. Just dab it on, but only a little, or it could turn wild, like a llama. The girls love it." T.C. winked one of his glowing red eyes from behind his sunglasses. The girl in the yellow skirt sprang up to her feet with a distracting bounce, tugging her skirt down with a suggestive twist. "She reminds me of the ex-wife who was a gymnast; we used to fulfill our obligations in the trunk at the foot of the bed. Actually, I herniated a disc in my lower back trying to keep her happy." He let out a painful laugh. "She left me because I couldn't bend over backward for her."

"This Swinebaum guy tied me down to a slab and screamed at me about Katvanna for an *entire* day," Dirtbag recounted. "Didn't you hear all that profanity?"

"That's a strange experiment," T.C. said, not really listening.

"What's going on with you?" Dirtbag questioned. "Wait, hold on a second."

Dirtbag asked if the young woman would excuse the two of them. She played with the pencil in her mouth and stared longingly at T.C., clearly trying to convince him to overrule the request. T.C. kindly shooed her away. She pouted her lips with a huff and reluctantly left the two of them alone.

Dirtbag watched her sway her hips out of the cubicle, distrustful of her motives. He turned to T.C., whose attention had left the room with the girl. Dirtbag knocked the spray bottle out of T.C.'s hands.

"OK! Easy there, Dirt," T.C. objected, picking up the bottle.

"I thought you said you were going to be on your very best behavior."

"Now, wait just a minute, Dirt," T.C. whined. "I mean, look at them, pretty and perfect and…supple."

"They're plants!" Dirtbag pointed. "All of them!"

"Don't worry; I don't tell them anything."

"Not plants, you fool. *Plants!* Swinebaum grows them out of gigantic pods. They're made of soybeans and quinoa."

"Aren't all healthy girls?"

"Hey, you're not listening; I hatched two of them the other day, and he's not growing them for medicinal purposes. I told him if he wants soldiers, this is not the way to go, but he's convinced he's only two years away from screening out eye rolling. He kept talking about some calendar he wants to shoot—and who knows what he actually means."

T.C. looked about cautiously. "Have you noticed Swinebaum's got this whole cult-of-personality thing going on around here, too? I mean, how many self-portraits does a man need anyway? Who has time for all those poses?" T.C. gestured toward a life-size portrait hanging above the door to the pavilion. It was of a stout, pale man with wild, bushy, carrot-orange hair and a matching neck beard; he was sitting on a pile of dead leopards in an orchard full of white deer. "The worst one is over the toilet in my room. I got that guy smiling behind me with his mouth wide open while I'm shooting out five-star vapor. Oats alive! I've never eaten so much tofu in my life."

Dirtbag rubbed his denim hands together, agitated. "He kept trying to grow a rutabaga in my armpit, and I allowed it in the interest of scientific discovery, but that was before the screaming and wild accusations. I managed to work out a deal as a lab assistant. Don't ask where that rutabaga finally took root, but he's got it now, right on his desk. Hey! Pay attention. My lunch break's only ten minutes."

T.C. stroked his balbo-styled chin. "You should grow a beard, too, Dirt," he suggested. "Transplant some of that grass from your head onto your face. I mean, you could grow it out real long, like some crazy whaler captain."

"Hey!" Dirtbag shook his head. "You need to stay away from the girls. Got it?"

"It's OK, Dirt. We've only shared a few showers together. No big deal." T.C. grinned, unable to hide his guilt. "OK, there were a couple back massages…and then a front…and one or two times the soap slipped, and you know how that can end up places."

"You better be careful. Swinebaum is insane."

"Turning a bean burrito into an explosive device does seem extreme…or ironic. I guess it just depends on how you look at it."

"We have to assume that we're under constant surveillance."

They both looked around slowly, eyeing with suspicion the women taking care of the plants in adjacent cubicles.

T.C. nodded and then carelessly asked, "So how's our escape plan going?"

Dirtbag threw up his arms in dismay at T.C.'s disregard of the warning, furiously running his hands back and forth through his long grass-hair. "Great!" he said, giving up with a sigh. "I've gotten together almost everything we need, and I finally have access to the map room."

"So where are we?"

"Well, I've only had a quick look, but it appears we're lucky Swinebaum shot us down, because we were flying into the middle of nowhere, straight toward a bus-worm depot."

"Swell. Would you mind if I mailed a burrito to Donny Brooke? He'd never expect a snack attack."

"No. Don't do anything. Keep your hands off the girls, and please, please, don't put a banana down your pants again. You saw what happened to that poor girl who imitated you."

"That's not my fault. She didn't have the safety on."

"Hey, I only need one more day in the lab to gather supplies. Then we can finally leave this crazy place."

"Today's Wednesday, right?"

"Last time I checked."

"OK, let's plan to burn this place down Friday morning then. You just give me a wink, and I'll start setting fires. Wait, you *can* wink, right?"

An alarm bell sounded suddenly. The lab's vault door swung open, and Doctor Swinebaum ran out from behind the shower curtain like a rookie quarterback taking the field for a championship game. Dirtbag and T.C. watched as he sprinted the length of the entire pavilion with his lab coat flapping behind him like a cape. The alarm bell shut off, and the only remaining sound was the running footsteps and heavy breathing of Swinebaum making his way toward them. As he neared, he slowed down, fixing his manic hair with a bent comb missing half its teeth. He popped a breath mint in his mouth and tried to look calm. He entered the small cubicle they were standing in, with a grin that no one in the world would trust.

"Ah! I zhought ve could do lunch, *ja?*" he said in his fretful, low-toned, unusual accent that seemed prone to sudden shouting. "I am free at ze moment; are you?" He casually aimed a banana at them.

"I dunno, Doc," T.C. said, unfazed by the banana, staring at the girls watching them. "I mean, I better hit the showers first to freshen them up—I mean, me. I should freshen up."

"Ve are havink lunch in ze arboretum, immediately! Ve can go together, *ja?*" Swinebaum motioned with the banana for them to start walking. "Come now; I insist."

"Is that thing even ripe enough to shoot?" Dirtbag asked, emboldened by the presence of T.C. and pointing out how green the banana gun was. "And look at it; it's crooked."

"He's right, Doc. You're swinging to the left there," T.C. said.

"I assure you it contains ze vigor of a veapon duple its size," Swinebaum replied, exasperated. He snapped his fingers, and two co-eds came into the cubicle, armed with Dirtbag's shotgun and T.C.'s Amber Blade of Divorce.

"Whoa, a five-way? Somebody's going to have to share,"T.C. said excitedly, pulling off the hairnet. The co-eds giggled, further irritating Swinebaum. "I'm not sure I can even be harmed by that sword," T.C. declared. "I mean, it's filled with my pain."

"It is time ve discussed Katvanna. I zink over lunch, ja?" Swinebaum persisted.

"I'm going to make you eat your shoe, scumbag." Dirtbag said, having had enough. Bistro had remade the safety on his shotgun with mirage ore, and it was unlikely the co-eds had figured out how to operate it.

"Just some advice, Doc: I wouldn't talk so much while we chow down. You're liable to choke."T.C. pantomimed simultaneously choking someone with one hand while continuing to eat, undeterred, with his other hand. "I mean, you know how dangerous food can be."

"Indeed I do." Swinebaum cocked the banana. "Shall ve proceed?"

"I give; let's do lunch, scumbag," Dirtbag grumbled.

They walked as a group across the pavilion floor into a long, well-lit hall lined with portraits of Swinebaum, which seemed to be arranged in order of increasing absurdity. Swinebaum kept smiling as they went. Dirtbag returned a self-assured bravado, causing beads of nervous sweat to appear on the mad scientist's forehead. Two co-eds skipped ahead to open the thick glass doors of the arboretum.

"Please sit!" Swinebaum gestured toward a picnic table covered with an obnoxious flower-patterned cloth. "Immediately!" They unhurriedly sat.

The arboretum had a luscious cut-grass floor surrounded by custom-made library-style bookshelves of fine dark wood. Overgrown vines of exotic flowers obscured many of the old leather-bound books sitting on the shelves. Sand-worn skylights projected soft white light over the picnic table in the middle of the room. Four co-eds dressed like cheerleaders pushed a hidden bookshelf door open, ripping apart some of the vines, and carried out a gold king's throne that had been reupholstered in furry cowhide.

"My mother-in-law had one of those," T.C. whispered to Dirtbag as they watched. "I don't remember which one; I mean, they all kind of looked the same: big and hairy, like Sasquatches wearing aprons."

"Silence!" Swinebaum shouted, sitting down on his throne at the head of the table, still holding the banana. He motioned for the girls to continue. They dragged out a large barbecue grill and a couple plates full of marinated tofu kabobs to cook. "You *verbrechers* plan to burn *mein* house down zis Friday mornink!" he screamed at them, slamming his banana-free hand on the furry armrest.

"Sue me." T.C. folded his arms. "There are always other options. I mean, I could just reach across this table and pull out your teeth with my bare hands."

"He's really good with his hands," Dirtbag added.

"Zat vill not be necessary." Swinebaum gently set the banana down and cautiously ordered their weapons returned. "Please! Let zus resolve our problems viz diplomatic conversation, ja?"

"We're divorced men," Dirtbag said, scratching his denim neck. "Diplomacy is not really our thing."

T.C. watched the girls struggle to figure out how to light the grill. He smirked at their futile efforts. "Look, Doc, just what makes you think we're going to burn this place down?"

Swinebaum threw a stack of papers on the table. "I have ze transcripts!" he shouted, then reached in his lab coat and clicked a button. One of the bookshelf walls slid open, ripping more vines apart, and a co-ed stenographer rolled out, wearing a frilly maid outfit. She was frantically typing away. He clicked the button again, she rolled back in, and the wall slid shut. "I have surveillance raisins hidden zroughout mein residence!"

T.C. looked at Dirtbag and mouthed, "We've got to get out of here." Dirtbag nodded in agreement.

Swinebaum leaned forward, trying to hear them. "Satisfactory arrangements can be made zat are agreeable to all parties, ja?" Swinebaum said, darting his eyes back and forth between Dirtbag and T.C. "I suspect mein name reached your ears before ve met, ja? Perhaps in academic circles? Have you heard of me? You must be familiar viz science. Katvanna vould have little interest in you if you vere not."

"She understood the true nature of the world. We had that in common," Dirtbag acknowledged. "I've been thinking about all those things you said; the flashes of incoherent anger and rage. You dated her, didn't you? She has that effect on men, especially morons."

"Vhat?" Swinebaum screamed.

"OK, I remember now, I *have* heard of you, but it was your name and this other word." T.C. rubbed his balbo. "What was that other word, Dirt?"

"Crazy-insane-egomaniac-who-likes-to-turn-bananas-into-hand-guns," Dirtbag said.

"Zat is not one vord!" Swinebaum shouted. He held his hand over his face, calming himself. "Zis vould go much easier viz tasty food. Vhere is ze food?" He turned to see the co-eds still struggling to figure out how to light up the barbecue. They had resorted to reading the manual. "Vhere have I erred?" Swinebaum groaned.

T.C. raised his hands in a nonthreatening manner. "Say, Doc, let me help them with that."

"You have helped yourself to zem enough!" Swinebaum yelled. "You have been touching zeir onions!"

"Whoa, I only went as far as their tomatoes. I swear."

"Don't do that," Dirtbag said.

"What?"

"Swear," Dirtbag growled. "Of course you touched their onions. You can't be left alone in a room with young women."

"I just—I mean, I really love women, Dirt," he reasoned. "All of them."

"That's not love."

"Not this again," T.C. said, annoyed.

"Remember Muffin?" Dirtbag lectured.

"I'm trying to move on; why won't you?"

Swinebaum nervously watched them argue. "In ze interest of friendship, I vill allow you to help ze girls cook," Swinebaum said loudly, "but on ze condition zat you are a gentleman. *Verstanden?*"

"Trust me, Doc." T.C. smiled. "I'm always gentle with the ladies."

"Make sure you remember that it's the grill we need turned on," Dirtbag told him.

T.C. sprang to his feet and walked into the arms of the struggling co-eds, speaking softly to them and assuring them he understood their troubles, even though he had no idea what they were yet. They surrounded him, snuggling up to his big, armored body, making needy, low yipping sounds. They handed him the barbecue-grill manual; it was full of easy-to-understand, colorful pictures, like a children's storybook. Keeping two girls under each arm, he managed to ignite the grill using a sudden thrust of his armored abdomen. The girls cheered and placed a chef's hat on his head. Then they began dancing.

Swinebaum became enraged by all the attention his beloved creations were giving T.C. and began reaching for the banana. Dirtbag drew the madman's attention with some timely throat clearing. "You said, repeatedly, that Katvanna wronged you in some way. Well, me, too. I think that the two of us, being sort-of men of kind-of science, can work something out where you tell me what's bugging you and I don't accelerate my foot into your mouth."

"It is quite simple; you are destroying yourself pursuink her," Swinebaum said.

"Maybe so, but it'll be worth it in the end."

"A curious zing for you to say." Swinebaum folded his hands. "Ze more I studied your dirt, ze more I realized zat it vas merely dirt from a grave zat somehow became a man."

"She stole my heart, scumbag, and I'm going to get it back."

"Ah! By killing her, ja?"

"I haven't decided."

"You realize zat vhatever you are now cannot be cured, and it cannot be fixed. You are like a piece of ze earth zat has come to life; an elemental force zat has absorbed a human soul. You are dead. You vill never know rest, and you vill never again feel ze vay you vonce did."

"What do you know about feelings?" Dirtbag retorted, unconvinced. "You hide out in this bunker of yours surrounded by self-aggrandizing portraits, growing companionship like it was a crop."

"Ah! But ve have so much more in common zan you zink. I met Katvanna long before you did, vhen she vas just twenty-six."

"She's always been 'twenty-six,'" Dirtbag griped. "Your point being?"

"After her I could love no other. I tried to find love again, but my zoughts vere always of her. She vas a goddess, and in her absence I slowly self-destructed. In a desperate act to regain mein sanity, I took mein heart out and crushed it. I vas left free of her but empty. As viz all zings, science solved ze problem."

Swinebaum unbuttoned his shirt and opened the collar. In the middle of his pale chest was a brass door. He opened it, and inside, where his heart was supposed to be, was a gold pocket watch. He reached in his chest and pulled the watch out of its velvet-lined box. It was connected to his body by a silver chain; he wound the watch then carefully placed it back inside his chest and closed the door.

"You see, I filled zat space viz somezink else. Zis mechanism makes it easier to reason, rationally, vizout ze pain of loss. Zis can save you from Katvanna…and from yourself."

"Whoa, Dirt, he's actually got a ticker," T.C. ribbed.

Dirtbag scowled intensely at Swinebaum. "This place, it looks like a sanctuary, but it's really a prison. You thought you'd never love again and locked yourself away from the risk of trying. You've been export-ing your self-hatred as weapons, fueling other people's torment like some kind of passive-aggressive anarchist, just so you can take com-fort that you're not the only one suffering. Hey, I admit my heart car-ries a lot of pain, but it also carries a lot of joy, and I want it back, all of it. You gave up, and that solves nothing. I should know. That thing in your chest? That's a pitiful placebo for the stinging bite of existence. You're pathetic."

Swinebaum was pale with shock. "And you are a simpleton. You fail to realize zat you are your own problem." His face twitched. "Ask yourself zis; vhy do you pursue your heart, because you *need* it, or because you *vant* it? It is mathematically impossible to defeat Kat-vanna. You have no chance of victory. No hope of overcomink her great power. You can't accept zat fact, because you don't like it. I offered you a vay out. Zat offer has now passed. You are already dead. Consider zat perhaps she can make better use of a heart zan you."

Dirtbag pounded his fist down on the table, startling Swinebaum. He took in a deep breath, as if preparing to scream at the mad scientist, and then left the room. T.C. tossed his chef's hat aside and ran after Dirtbag, leaving the girls behind. They heard Swinebaum begin to weep and hastened their pace down the portrait-lined hall. The co-eds followed but made no effort to stop them as they broke into the map room to steal what they needed for the desert. The girls giggled and flirted the same way they had when the two of them first arrived, but now the behavior felt unsettling; the girls were the reflections of a man driven insane by heartbreak.

CHAPTER 14

———

At sunset, the desert proved that even in the midst of isolated despair, in that space where life did not flourish due to that noisy, ancient thing called radiation, there could be stunning beauty that comforted lost souls. The sun was touching the horizon, scattering its light across the windswept sky, a pink lavender spilling over a fading deep orange, the peaks of the white dunes burning bright like hot coals beneath it, and every shadow between them resembled a cavernous pit filled with glimmering flecks of grain.

Dirtbag and T.C. stumbled awkwardly in the direction of Canopus, the second-brightest star in the sky. Ancient legend told that the brightest star in the sky, Sirius, had once inexplicably changed location overnight and was no longer trusted. The explanation of why the cosmic event occurred had been lost over time, like most ancient knowledge, and only the condensed version of its betrayal remained. T.C. passed the enchanted bottle of rum back to Dirtbag. This would be their second night in the desert.

The sun gave way to a waning, gibbous moon that lit the white sand with a faint, soft blue light. Dirtbag tapped the half-empty bottle against his leather-armored leg, listening to the pitch change as the rum refilled, and watched the sky fully embrace the night. The great band of the Milky Way galaxy glowed overhead. Behind it, another galaxy, called Andromeda, spiraled toward it on a multibillion-year collision course long prophesized by the ancients, an inevitable cataclysm that would permanently turn the two galaxies into one, as though the universe did not understand the concept of divorce.

"Doot deet doo deet da doo," warbled T.C. lazily with rum-wet lips.

"The inmates sang that where I was committed," Dirtbag mentioned as he drank.

"I forgot about that, Dirt," T.C. said. "It just popped in my head. I mean, you were only in there a day before I broke you out."

"Hey, I saw guys in diapers talking to spoons." Dirtbag gave the bottle back to T.C. "Next time, if there ever is one, flirt with the girls after I'm rescued."

"I mean, they were nurses, Dirt." T.C. guzzled down a large amount of rum. "They did serve a nice rhubarb pudding though, right?"

"Let's not talk about food," Dirtbag growled. The bag of fruits and vegetables they'd taken from the lab had exploded under the heat of the sun the day before.

"I think we can defeat Katvanna," T.C. said, breaking his promise to drop the subject. "We just need to find a good wishing well." T.C. offered Dirtbag the bottle.

"Hey, I wish away my problems all the time." Dirtbag took a long drink. "See? Just like that." He returned the bottle to T.C. "Here, make a wish."

They shuffled over a steep dune. T.C. lifted his sunglasses for a moment to light up a suspicious shadow with the glow from his red eyes. Nothing was there. Dirtbag checked the map to make sure they weren't lost. The desert was vast, and they were depressed, which meant that even if they were making good time crossing it, it felt like they were getting nowhere.

"Whoa! There's a kitchen over there!" T.C. shook his intoxicated head to make sure what he was seeing was real.

"Don't fall apart on me, T.C." Dirtbag said, putting the map away.

"I see a sandwich!" T.C. pointed and took off running into the night.

Dirtbag chased after him and kicked the back of T.C.'s knee, causing him to fall. T.C. grabbed Dirtbag's leg as he fell, and they tumbled down a dune, sliding to a stop a few feet away from the mysterious kitchen.

"Why'd you do that, Dirt?"

"Are you kidding me? Only sober heroes run toward danger; the drunk ones yell at it from a distance." Dirtbag dragged him behind a small rock. "Give me that bottle. We need to clear our heads. That only takes a few minutes for me, so you need to get started now. We don't even know what that is." Dirtbag corked the rum bottle and put it away.

T.C. squinted his eyes slowly, nodding in agreement. "OK." He tried to focus. "A kitchen in the desert is pretty weird. I mean, it could be some kind of deadly sandwich siren that lures hungry wanderers to a dinner table of doom."

"Or it could just be a sandwich in the desert."

"Now, wait just a minute; what if it only exists because we're looking at it—like if a tree barks in a forest and nobody is around to hear it, is it a dog?"

Dirtbag covered his face with his hand and slowly tugged on his grass-hair. "Well, do you want to sit here and incoherently philosophize, or do you want to apply the scientific method?"

"Whoa! You want to blow up that sandwich? We don't even know what kind it is. I mean, if it's olive loaf, OK, but I mean"—T.C.'s gaze mellowed—"what if it's a lady sandwich?"

Dirtbag sighed. "Let's go take a look."

The kitchen was a gaudy, orange, L-shaped laminated countertop with a glowing blue refrigerator at one end and a gleaming white stove at the other. Rosy-brown cabinets accented with a bright-yellow posy design clashed horrendously with the lime-colored, hex-patterned, faux-porcelain linoleum floor. Dirtbag and T.C. were forced to momentarily shield their eyes from the hideous sight as they approached. In front of the countertop, next to the fridge, was a circular table covered in a white linen cloth with a crocheted wedding-ring pattern. Sitting in the middle of the table was a plain paper plate with a good-sized sandwich on it. Next to the sandwich was a handwritten note with the message, "Do not eat the universe."

"No chairs," Dirtbag said inquisitively as he stepped into the small kitchen.

T.C. opened the fridge. "There's nothing in here but condiments."

They looked inside all the cabinets and the stove, but everything else was empty. They cautiously approached the sandwich. The grain-specked white bread was mouthwateringly fresh, with a thick, fluffy, sponge-cake quality. As they neared it, a breeze blew toward them, carrying a delicious aroma. A variety of meats were stacked between the bread, under lettuce and tomato slices that glistened with drop-lets of their own juices. The meats appeared to be deli-sliced hickory-smoked, honey-touched chicken; spiral-cut peppered Black Forest ham; and perfectly sliced bourbon-glazed, seasoned rotisserie tur-key breast. All the ingredients smelled as if they had been cooked up barely five minutes ago.

"It's just beautiful, Dirt," T.C. said, his stomach growling.

"It's a sandwich…in a kitchen…in the middle of the desert. Don't touch it."

T.C. picked up the note and read it. "'Do not eat the universe'?"

"Don't get any ideas."

"But can a sandwich as amazing as this truly be bad?"

"You know it is!" Dirtbag warned.

T.C. gently poked the top of the sandwich with his finger. They heard thunder in the distance, but nothing else happened.

"See? What's there to worry about?" T.C. reached out and pinched off a small piece of the bread, igniting a catastrophe. The sky shook, the desert shifted, stars blinked out, and a deep, rumbling quake tore a bottomless fissure in the earth next to the kitchen. Dirtbag scowled at T.C.

Suddenly the ground beneath them lurched five feet up, knocking them off-balance. They fell onto the table, catapulting the sandwich into the air over their heads. It struck the edge of the laminated countertop and exploded apart, sending sandwich layers in every direction. The kitchen spun, turning upside down then right side up. Time moved forward, backward, and, at one point, diagonally. The world around them detonated into a collection of rocks and gaseous clouds that were indirectly connected or not connected at all. The kitchen became a floating island in the middle of a universe now engulfed in complete chaos.

"Congratulations!" Dirtbag screamed, pointing accusingly at T.C. "You've destroyed the universe!"

"What do you mean I've destroyed it? My ex-wife said it takes two people to destroy something nice," T.C. argued. "Of course, when she said that she was going through our photo album with a carving knife."

"Look at that!" Dirtbag motioned toward a cloud of wailing people being sucked into a tumbling volcano. "How do we fix that? Huh?"

"I dunno, Dirt. Maybe we better contact my attorney."

"He's dead! The whole world just blew up, T.C.!"

"OK, but there's always a bright side to things. I mean, we just saved a lot of time in the area of revenge. We just got everyone all at once."

"Hey, you're right. Now we can take a vacation."

"Yeah!"

"To where, T.C.? It's all gone."

"It's not gone. It's just spread around." T.C. gestured to different sections of floating destruction. "See, there's some over here and some more right there. We can jump down to that lake and go fishing."

"How can you take this so lightly?"

"I dunno. What do you want me to do, freak out? I've been divorced ten times, Dirt. I've seen stuff like this before, I mean, in my mind."

"Wasn't it just yesterday we talked about being better men? And now you've gone and blown up the whole world." Dirtbag took out the enchanted bottle of rum and had a long drink. "When that volcano comes around again, I'm jumping in."

A cosmic doorway suddenly opened next to the stove. White light poured out of the opening, and a transparent, bright-magenta, squid-like monster thing floated into the kitchen. It looked around and screamed hysterically, holding up its many tentacles.

"I can see its brain!" T.C. shouted, drawing his sword.

"Well, at least it has one," Dirtbag sneered sarcastically. He held up his denim hands. "We mean you no harm," he announced to the monster.

"Unless, of course," T.C. said, "you're evil; then you're dead. I mean, we have a stove here."

"Squeee!" the glowing squid said, waving at them, the broken kitchen table, and the scattered remains of the sandwich.

"Is that your name? Squeee?" T.C. asked. "What are you? Where do you come from?"

"Squeee!" the squid responded.

"This thing smells like mint, Dirt." T.C. sniffed near the squid. "It's clearing my sinuses."

"Let's try one question at a time," Dirtbag said, struggling to remain calm. "Do you know what's going on?"

"Squeee!" the squid said again.

"We don't have time for this!" Dirtbag pulled out his shotgun, set the dial for "Frequent Flier," and blew the squid away. It was hurled off the kitchen island, squealing, tentacles convulsing wildly, spinning out of control, straight into the orbiting volcano, where it shattered into fragments of flaming glass-like shards.

"That's just superduper, Dirt," T.C. said, putting his sword away. "That just buttered both sides of my bread."

"Hey, I know that seemed rash, but did you see the crazed look in its eyes?"

"Oats alive! You lied to that thing, Dirt! You told it we meant no harm, and then you shot it!"

"It wasn't a lie when I first said it," Dirtbag tried to explain. "It became a lie later."

"My ex said the same thing when I found three centaurs under our bed."

"Three?"

"It was a big bed, Dirt, king-sized," T.C. reminisced. "I mean, just don't ever hire a centaur to give your wife riding lessons."

The cosmic doorway suddenly opened again. A larger squid-like monster thing with an angry expression floated out. "Hoh! You killed my brother!" the squid shouted telepathically in a high-pitched, rapid-fire voice.

"Whoa! This one's got two brains!" T.C. said excitedly.

"Hey!" Dirtbag aimed his shotgun at the new squid. "We didn't know what that thing was or that it was anyone's brother; it just appeared and started making weird noises."

"You barbaric ignoramoids! That sandwich you destroyed is the embodiment of the entire known universe!"

"Bullcookies! That sandwich is here"—T.C. pointed at the mess on the floor—"and all that is out there."

"Ugh! If I tried to explain, your puny, incompetent minds would only interpret the intricate complexities as an obnoxious squeee sound!" the squid shouted.

"Hey, if I shoot you, will a monster with three brains appear?" Dirtbag asked threateningly.

The squid scooted away, visibly disturbed by Dirtbag's appearance. It frowned. "Uh, ugly autonomous sod, do you want to fix this insanity and continue with your lives as they were, or do you want to spend eternity in this kitchen?"

"Well, let's see…we have endless booze, plenty to watch, and if your kind is edible and delicious, I guess I'd have to think about it."

"I dunno, Dirt. Eventually we're going to run out of condiments."

Dirtbag holstered his shotgun. "Maybe I would like to fix this, but we can't trust a talking monster unless we get some answers."

"Pffft! Fine," the squid snorted. "But, oh, we have to be quick; reality hangs in the balance and stuff."

"Of course it does." Dirtbag folded his arms. "So, what are you?"

"Oh! Oh! A magical beast that lives between universes!" the squid taunted.

"Don't get fresh with me, scumbag!" Dirtbag threatened.

"It's minty fresh already, Dirt." T.C. reminded.

Dirtbag glared at T.C., silently telling him to muzzle it. He continued. "What is it that you do between universes?"

"Hmmm, I guess the closest equivalent is janitorial work."

"Why would the universe be in the form of a sandwich?"

"Oh, pass! Pffft! That's too difficult to explain."

"Well, then why was the universe left unattended, on a table?"

"Uh, you'd have to ask my brother…oh, but that's right, you can't, because he's dead!"

"Hey! There's more than one volcano out there to fall into."

"Hoh! If you kill me, you'll commit yourselves to a lifetime of chaos."

"You've never been married, have you?" T.C. peeled some of the universe off his boot. "OK, monster, you got a name?"

"Ugh! It's too difficult to express in your primitive language."

"Try me." T.C. folded his arms, waiting.

"Quag-Blwahzah-Fuphom-Keeguha-Chewagah-Vutshoot-Jiffysl-noobah-Kobana-Arama."

"That's not even a word! I mean, that's just a bunch of sounds thrown together!" T.C. complained. "Now I'm mad. So I'm naming you. Your name is now Toasty Shoe."

"Oh pffft," the squid groaned. "I just want to fix this universe before my shows start."

"And just how do we do that, Toasty Shoe?"

"Hoh! You can start by picking up that sandwich!"

"Hey, why don't you do it, scumbag?" Dirtbag growled. "With all those arms, it would take you half the time."

"Oh! Oh! If I do it, you won't learn a lesson. Now get to it, but be careful. That's your whole universe lying on the floor."

Dirtbag and T.C. grumbled as they picked up the scattered parts of the sandwich and set them on the countertop. They fitted the ripped slices of meat back together and picked off the filth one granule at a time. A tomato had slid under the fridge; they broke a stick off a passing tree to fish it out, but unfortunately, the tomato didn't survive the effort. With the tomato destroyed, the squid began to panic. T.C. suggested that they just substitute it with ketchup from the fridge.

"Hoh! But it won't be the same!" the squid shrieked.

"It'll be close enough," T.C. reasoned. "I mean, ketchup is still tomato, right?"

Dirtbag examined the glass ketchup bottle, reading the ingredients. "Do we really want to add high-fructose corn syrup to the composition of the universe?"

"There's other stuff in there, too, Dirt," T.C. said, reassembling the sandwich. "Besides, adding a little more flavor to the universe just might turn out to be a good thing."

Dirtbag glanced at the squid; the squid shook its head-like mantle part, refuting that idea.

"Don't put too much of that stuff on there," Dirtbag advised. "Try to approximate the same volume as the tomato."

"I'm making the sandwich here, Dirt! What are you, my wife? Trust me; everything is going to be just fine."

As the sandwich came together, the universe around them reformed. The land returned to where it belonged, the people returned to their homes, and the stars returned to the sky. They arranged each layer carefully under the nagging direction of the glowing squid, until all that remained was the ketchup. The three gathered closer to the sandwich to observe the procedure.

"Oh! Oh! Make sure you shake the bottle first!" the squid blurted out nervously.

"Oats alive, Toasty Shoe! I'm a divorced man! Do you know how many sandwiches I've made? I've got this; just relax," T.C. said, unscrewing the top of the ketchup bottle.

"Not too much, now," Dirtbag said, simultaneously watching the ketchup coming out of the bottle and the world around them.

T.C. waited patiently for the viscosity of the ketchup to ease. The condiment slowly flowed out of the bottle and onto the bread. T.C. made a small circle about the size of the demolished tomato and filled it in. He quickly pulled the bottle away. Ever so gently, he set the bread back onto the sandwich. Thunder sounded around them, and the world seemed fully restored. Dirtbag pointed at the pinch of bread that was still missing. They searched the kitchen and found it on the floor between the stove and countertop. T.C. blew the fuzz off of it and gently pushed it back into the bread.

He pressed the pieces together to join them, and then at last they were done.

"From chaos to sanity, all in a day's work," T.C. said, dusting his hands off. He turned to Dirtbag. "This has to be the biggest reversal of fortune of our lives."

Dirtbag watched as the squid floated around the desert inspecting different things. It began to laugh, but it was not a happy laugh; it was a cackle that was borderline nervous breakdown. The squid floated back to the kitchen.

"Hey, is everything all right?" Dirtbag asked.

"Hoh! It's mostly the same...oh, close enough; in fact, I doubt anyone will notice the difference or even care."

"But it's not the same, is it?"

"Oh, pffft! It's just minor details." The squid's eyes darted about franticly.

T.C. put his hands on his hips, irritated. "Look, we did the best we could under very difficult circumstances. We saved the whole universe; I mean, I think a thank-you is in order."

"Pffft! Thank you? Hoh! You're joking, right? You really have no idea what you've done, do you?"

Dirtbag walked around the desert. Everything appeared to be back to normal. He returned to the kitchen. "Well, I can't see any difference," he said.

"Oh! Oh! Of course *you* can't," the squid snorted. "Before, you didn't have a chance, but now, now you've changed things! You've altered the laws of probability."

"And now we have a chance?" T.C. asked, confused.

"Pffft!" the squid replied, giggling hysterically.

The sandwich, the squid, and the kitchen suddenly disappeared into a flash of white light, leaving Dirtbag and T.C. standing on an empty concrete foundation. Dirtbag drank some rum. A gentle night-time breeze blew across the sand, carrying the delicious scent of freshly made assorted meats. T.C.'s stomach growled.

CHAPTER 15

The desert flowed down into lowlands, where it ended abruptly. The barren white sand and lush blades of short, mossy grass confronted each other in a natural stalemate of opposing forces that created a distinct line between the two environments. The air grew fragrant with the scent of plants as Dirtbag and T.C. descended into the rolling hills. Breathtaking varieties of flowers covered jagged rocks jutting up through the dark earth, their sharp edges long worn away by erosion. By midmorning the sky had become a light gray and a summery rain was falling. It was pleasant to feel, but it tasted salty and reminded T.C. of tears.

The falling rain ran off Dirtbag's waterproof armor; however, his grass-hair and dirt body drank it up. He felt himself grow increasingly heavier as they walked, until his body's thirst had been quenched. The arid climate of the desert had dried him out inside, and he hadn't noticed until now. He wondered if he eventually would have turned to dust and crumbled without regular sips from the rum bottle.

They pushed through the pouring rain, neither of them complaining as the accumulated sand and grime were washed away. A sudden cloudburst made it difficult to see very far ahead, so they stooped down and followed the road of loose gravel, unconcerned about where it was leading them. The road turned into carefully laid stonework, and they knew a town was near. Through the storm, a hilltop came into view, and on it was the silhouette of a small municipality. Dirtbag took out the stolen map to see what it was. He managed to read the name "Aloftden" before the map disintegrated in his hands under the heavy rain.

As they neared Aloftden, light broke through the clouds, and the rain let up. The warming rays of the sun gently dried the water on the buildings as fast as it had fallen. Shop doors reopened, cafés set out tables, and, somewhere, a street musician began to expertly play his guitar while singing completely off-key.

Dirtbag whisked the rain from his grass-hair and caught an eye-opening whiff. "Is this entire town brewing coffee? All at once?"

T.C. breathed in deeply as he brushed his long, blond locks. "Whoa. This place is great!" He shook out his well-groomed hair and walked around. A group of hyperactive kids sped by, howling and laughing. "See those hooks up there, Dirt? On top of the roofs? And those weird chimneys? This is one of those traveling towns. When they get tired of living somewhere, they just attach hot-air balloons, fill them up, and sail away."

"Well, it doesn't look like these people have gone anywhere for a long time," Dirtbag said, nudging a pile of sediment that had built up around the base of a bakery. "Maybe they've had it with the rest of the world."

A little old lady unlocked the front door to the homely *Bon Vivant* bakery and opened the windows. The gentle, sugary, irresistible aroma of freshly fried doughnuts filled the vicinity outside the shop.

Without another word, Dirtbag and T.C. walked into the bakery and walked out with a box of assorted lard-fried, powdered confections.

"Well, that was an interesting conversation," Dirtbag said, scratching his head. "I don't think that woman was hard of hearing; I think she just enjoyed screaming at us for some reason."

T.C. bit into a doughnut and immediately sat down. Dirtbag asked if they were awful. T.C. only handed him the box. Dirtbag tried one and sat down, too. Each bite was like eating a warm cloud of love. They sat outside the bakery and quietly ate, each of them escaping into the sweet affection the delicate treats offered. By the third doughnut, the pleasant feeling had disappeared and had been replaced by a horrid, clogged-artery heaviness. They threw the rest of the box away and swore to never buy such evil things again.

"OK, now I need some coffee," T.C. hacked, trying to clear his throat of phlegm.

"Why don't you try breathing deeply? Coffee air this potent is probably loaded with atomized caffeine," Dirtbag encouraged. They inhaled together.

"This isn't working," T.C. coughed. "Those doughnuts left my mouth coated like a pan of butter. I mean, I don't want to breathe coffee, Dirt; I want to drink it."

"Want some rum instead?" Dirtbag offered, smearing powdered sugar across his face as he drank.

"Nah. I'm tired of drinking that," T.C. said. "It's a rum bottle that never runs dry. That's the curse, Dirt. The more you drink, the less you want; only there's always more."

"That's the curse of all alcohol," Dirtbag responded as he scrutinized the choices for coffee that surrounded them. It seemed even the rats in the sewer were brewing up a fresh cup. "How about we buy some coffee from that scumbag over there?"

T.C. eyed the pathetic-looking barista operating a street-cart-mounted coffee-making contraption. The barista wore a half-unbuttoned black silk shirt and thick, dark-red corduroy pants. Copper wires ran across his clothing into a belt-buckle battery. A neon lightning bolt hung under the red-and-white parasol of the cart. Beneath it was a sign. T.C. read it aloud: "'Super Conducted Coffee'?" He laughed. "I mean, we've got to try that, Dirt."

Dirtbag groaned.

The barista was just beginning to brew a fresh batch of coffee when they walked up. He poured beans onto a copper plate, pushed the bulbous end of an electric resonance transformer over them, wound up a generator, and zapped the coffee beans with several bolts of lightning, until they smoked. The charred beans were swept off the plate and placed whole into a large copper steam pot covered with pipes. The barista closed the pot and turned some valves, and it began to thump and rumble.

"Oats alive!" T.C. shouted at the barista. "You just burnt the flavor right out of those beans!"

"Hey, how much for a cup of that trash?" Dirtbag demanded.

"'Tis free, traveler. 'Tis free," the barista replied in a blissful tone.

"I bet it's free; that thing is better suited for cremating small animals," Dirtbag criticized, blowing powdered sugar off his face as he spoke.

"It's free coffee, Dirt. Relax."

The barista watched Dirtbag and T.C. with a half-raised eyebrow, evidently impervious to insults. His hair appeared to be permanently charged with static electricity, and his eyes were red, as though he had not slept for days. He had a metal bolt, with a copper clamp attached, sticking out of the base of his skull. It was connected to the belt-buckle battery by wire. The barista softly clasped his hands together with a content, otherworldly smile.

"This blessed drink is offered by my parish, the Holy Church of Electric Lightning, to provide heathens with illuminating mental revelations," the barista evangelized. "Do you believe that lightning is a creation of man, whose blessed development costs were covered by the divine venture capitalist called God, and that His Electric Holiness Father Raygun is the selected chairperson prophet of everlasting polarity who will bridge the gap between positive and negative?"

"If it's free, I'll believe whatever you say, scumbag," Dirtbag growled.

The barista opened a spigot on the copper steam pot, and coffee sprayed out of it horizontally. The barista caught enough of it to fill two Styrofoam cups. The rest of it landed on a stray cat, which took off running, knocking over a garbage can. The barista blessed the coffee with an incantation of lightning and electricity noises—"Take this coffee, heathens; may it illuminate your consciousness. Ka-boom, ba-zap"—and handed the cups to Dirtbag and T.C.

Dirtbag yanked the coffee out of the barista's hand. "Hey, it better do something after that performance. The only thing you didn't do was a backflip onto a wooden stake," Dirtbag said, taking a sip. The flavor was vile, and his head jerked back as if he'd been punched in the face. "Are you kidding me? This tastes like elephant dysentery!"

"It can't be that bad." T.C. took a sip. His face scrunched up from the bitterness, and he shuddered. "Oats alive! This is terrible. It's like you just replaced the water with embalming fluid—not that I've ever drunk that," he quickly corrected, "now or at any time in the past."

"'Tis perfect then, heathen strangers. It has been made as ordained by His Holiness Father Raygun. Ka-boom ba-zap."

"Father Raygun, eh?" Dirtbag snorted. "Is he the leader of your cult that can't even make a cup of coffee?"

"You humble me with your ignorance, heathen. The will of Father Raygun and the Church of Electric Lightning strikes with the holy randomness of lightning, unexpected and awe-inspiring." The barista reached behind his cart and pulled out a book with an aluminum-foil cover. "'Tis written here, in the *Holy Conductive Book of Raygunomics*. Perhaps I can interest you in a stress test?"

Dirtbag threw his coffee on the ground. "You know, science and religion don't go together for a reason. One is about discovering what's true about the world around us, and the other is about making up explanations to excuse your own blatant stupidity. Science has a way of being conveniently obvious, while faith is as convoluted as you want to make it, so that only the most devout can claim to understand whatever it is."

"His electric blessings be upon you. Ba-zap zap zap." The barista bowed.

Dirtbag slid his hand down his face in disgust and walked away. T.C. tossed his coffee and followed.

"OK, so science is about truth?" T.C. wondered aloud. "I thought it was just about blowing stuff up."

"Well, it can be. In fact"—Dirtbag grinned—"I have a lot of faith in that aspect."

They saw an espresso shop and stopped in, only to discover that it was also a music store. They bought two vanilla lattes that had been allegedly harmonized by a cello. Outside the shop T.C. sipped his beverage and reacted with bitter revulsion. "Oats alive! How can everyone in this town be making coffee and none of it be any good?"

"Did you see that the cellist had a bolt in her head, too? And her shoes were mismatched." Dirtbag drank his coffee. He made a sour face. "You know, maybe people here just don't have any taste."

Down the street was a small tent-covered bazaar. There were two rows of merchants selling vaguely sorted goods. There were piles of books on one table, piles of clothes on the other, and buckets full of knickknacks. Dirtbag and T.C. moved through the merchants, haphazardly picking through the items, not really looking for anything in particular. T.C. drank his horrible coffee, reacting the same way each time. "If you want anything, Dirt, I can write a magic check."

"I still can't believe you successfully hide money from the Guild of Attorneys. You should introduce me to your guy."

"Can't. He's dead. I mean, it was a long time ago, Dirt, a pretty dark period of my life, too. It had to be secret and stay secret; he was kind of rude, anyway."

"Aren't those checks admissible in court?"

"Nah. They disappear when the recipient receives the money. They're untraceable; that's the way he set it up. Plus any check I'm forced to write to the Guild will automatically bounce the money back into the secret location I keep it in after a few days. Trust me; I'm covered."

Dirtbag suddenly stopped. He walked up to a pile of books on sale and read the titles, frowning. He picked up some clothes, and then thumbed through a collection of old records. He recognized everything. "Hey! This is all my stuff!" he said, shocked and slightly saddened. "Katvanna must've cleaned house. This is practically everything I owned during our marriage." He set his belongings down. "I forgot I had so many things. I wonder how they all ended up here."

"Should I run my sword through these defenseless merchants to get some answers?"

"Why don't I ask nicely instead?"

All the merchants bore the same blissful expression as the barista. Dirtbag and T.C. picked out one that looked more alert than the others, and Dirtbag menacingly walked behind the tableful of goods. The merchant dropped his coffee and backed up against the tent wall, terrified. He threw money at Dirtbag, begging him not to eat his soul. Dirtbag picked the merchant up by the collar of his half-buttoned, blue polyester shirt.

"Listen up, muttonchops! Where did you get all of this stuff?"

"These fell from yonder sky. Bless the electric discharge! Ba-zap zap!"

Dirtbag shook the merchant, spun him around a few times, and roughed up his hair. T.C. sipped his coffee, enjoying the show. Another merchant approached them and asked what they were doing. T.C. explained they were trying a newly developed stress test, making sure to end his lie with a few lightning sounds. The second merchant believed him and left.

"From the sky?" Dirtbag snarled at the first merchant, resuming his interrogation.

"Aye, heathen, from an upside-down flying castle that came to pass, these were pushed out, like droppings from a bird. All together they fell that morning, and I gathered them up, made them right for buying, and there they be. Electric blessing be upon you. Ka-boom ba-zap."

"Well, when did this"—Dirtbag scoffed—"upside-down flying castle fly over?"

"Not more than four months ago, heathen."

Dirtbag let go of the merchant, dropping him to the ground. He turned to T.C., thinking. "I wonder why she held on to my things for so long. I've been dead for years."

T.C. drank his coffee. "It could be she got rid of them when she met her new man, the shoe salesman."

"How did she even get an upside-down flying castle?"

"Trust me. Every guy has his thing to get the ladies excited. Some guys have it down their pants, and other guys have it in their wallets. This guy has a castle that flies, and that sure beats a motorcycle."

The muttonchopped merchant told them that if they weren't going to buy anything, he'd have to ask them to leave. They stared at him until he slunk away.

"Hey, did you notice that guy also had a bolt in the back of his head?"

"I try not to let things like that bother me, Dirt. I mean, it takes all kinds, right?"

Dirtbag picked through his long-forgotten past and sighed. "This is all junk to me now. The most valuable things in life tend to be intangible; I wish I had realized that earlier."

"Whoa, Dirt, don't start digging a rut. We've got a clue to a new direction. We're going to find that castle and burn it down, maybe even with your ex-wife inside! I mean, I haven't seen such a clear path to destruction since I got drunk inside that glass factory." He threw his coffee down a gutter. A cat shrieked. "We should celebrate!"

"I don't know which is aggravating me more, Katvanna or those awful doughnuts." Dirtbag rubbed his burning guts. "Maybe we should get some real food first and then figure out how we can track down some crazy flying castle."

"That's the spirit! Let's really spoil ourselves!" T.C. clapped enthu- siastically. "Now, I'll pay, but you buy. You just keep pretending to pull bags of gold magically out of your chest. The Guild of Attorneys has spies everywhere, and as far as they and the exes know, I'm broke."

A pied falconet landed on an awning behind them. It was small and looked determined—with a white chest; onyx-colored back, head, and talons; and sharp, jet-black wings adorned with stripes of white. Its dark-blue eyes blinked, metallic-purple eye shadow catch- ing the light, and it lit a cigarette. The scent of rose petals and cloves filled the air.

CHAPTER 16

———

Dirtbag looked over the indecipherable, leather-bound menu of the prestigious *Le Meilleur Restaurant de la Ville*, trying to appear sophisticated and at ease while straining over the meaning of the vineyard-inspired hieroglyphics before him. Both he and T.C. had stopped by a posh boutique on the way there to purchase ostentatious monocles and clip-on tuxedo bow ties so they blended in better with the other stuck-up dining patrons. Dirtbag was initially barred from entering because he was made of denim, which was against the dress code, but was admitted after he produced a sizable bag of gold coins. He adjusted the fancy monocle wedged under his scowling brow. Wearing it only drew attention to the fact that he had no eyes.

"I should've bought a mask instead," he lamented.

T.C. concentrated on reading the menu's unfamiliar, fancy language. His golden monocle was tactfully duct-taped over his silver-wire aviator sunglasses in a manner he hoped was respectable. "The way I see it, Dirt, you go through these phases where you suddenly care about your appearance."

"Hey, being dirt-filled denim doesn't mean I'm dirty. That's just a stereotype."

"I have the same problem. I mean, just because I'm a blond doesn't mean I'm stupid, right?"

Dirtbag's monocle popped out; he made up an excuse about it not fitting properly and pushed it back into place. He could hear the snooty customers whispering unkind things around them.

The restaurant was small and covered wall to wall with obnoxious art. There were eleven tables; each was adjacent to a window with an unobstructed view of the town below. The restaurant had been built on top of the clock tower above Aloftden City Hall and used the clock's machinery to slowly revolve the floor. While the steady ticking of the mechanism couldn't be heard, its faint vibration could be seen in the perpetual ripples of every drink served.

A large, open kitchen sat in the middle of the restaurant. It was filled with two dozen cooks preparing elaborate food under the direction of the renowned executive chef Cram Bury, who was a bearded, screaming phantasm of hatred that, according to Dirtbag, should be stuffed headfirst into a broiling oven. Casual conversations within the restaurant were frequently interrupted by the cooks shouting, "Yes, chef!" in unison, which was often followed by repeated whip cracks and quiet sobbing. An unmanned, cheap electronic keyboard, playing its demo song in a loop, provided the ambient music.

"Hmm," T.C. said. "OK, I think I'll have the *Merde Pas Cher*."

"Do you even know what that means?"

"It sounds fancy. Plus it costs more than an hour with my attorney. That's good enough for me. Take a chance, Dirt. I mean, the odds are in our favor now, right?"

"Well, by that logic, I'll have the *Corbeille à Chaud.*"

"What's that?"

"I'll find out when it gets here." Dirtbag glanced across the room to see what other guests had on their plates. "And judging from what those scumbags are having, it's probably a piece of something covered in sauce."

T.C. waved his hand in the air to call the waitress over. She was a cute redhead dressed in a midnight-blue skirt, a black apron, and a nice jade-green shirt that matched her eyes. She was the only waitress in the restaurant and was constantly dashing between tables, frantically doing her best to please everyone. She picked up a basket of fresh breadsticks on her way to them. When she arrived, T.C. put on his most charming smile and ordered for himself and his friend, making sure to address the waitress by her name: Caley. The girl was so overworked she barely noticed. Caley sped away, and T.C. remarked that she had a tear along the seam on the back of her black nylon stockings. "I should help her out of those," he said, ogling at her fondly.

"No, you should leave her alone."

"That girl deserves some loving, Dirt, some quality me time."

"Hey, you can't invade the life of every woman you desire. She's pretty—I'll give you that—but receiving a generous tip is going to mean more to her than screaming out your name, Tuna Casserole."

T.C. hated his full name. "I'm just trying to stockpile memories for when I'm old and nonfunctional…or dysfunctional. I could end up both."

"You know, that's a pretty selfish perspective; think about her side."

T.C. peered over at the sheathed, wedding-ring-filled Amber Blade of Divorce sitting at the end of the table then at the blond braid of Muffin's hair he wore around his wrist. "You're right," he said. "I don't have anything else to say about it either…I mean, other than you're right."

They sat together gazing out the window, eating breadsticks, and watching the town circle below. They finished a basket, and Caley dropped off some more.

T.C. sat back, getting comfortable in his seat. "OK, so now you're not sure if you want to kill Katvanna?"

"Maybe."

"You've talked about revenge since forever, Dirt."

"I don't know why she has to be the way she is."

"Love can make people do crazy things. What if she's just possessive, Dirt? I mean, one ex, we started off holding hands, and by the end she was chaining me to the bed every night."

Dirtbag chewed slowly, thinking. "I'm not sure if we ever truly loved one another. Maybe we just said we did. Things happen, and you wake up one day with responsibilities, just like what happened with you and Muffin. I did my best to make her happy, but it fell apart and became a mess."

A flash of lightning from outside the window distracted them. They scanned the horizon to see where it had struck. A second bolt tore through the clear blue sky. It shot from the ground up somewhere in the distance. Caley returned to their table with instruction booklets, hand drawn by Cram Bury, that told them how to properly eat their meals.

"Just how tough is the meat here?" asked T.C., holding up his dining hatchet.

"Welp, His Majesty doesn't approve of knives being used on his food," Caley informed them.

"His Majesty?" T.C. mocked, flipping through the instruction booklet. "OK, what happens if I choose to ignore these instructions?"

"He's been known to whip disobedient customers before." She shrugged. "Yup, and I wouldn't push him today; he's overdue for a new battery."

"New battery? From the Church of Electric Lightning?"

"Ba-zap." She winked and pulled back her hair to show them the metal bolt implanted into the base of her skull.

"You have one of those, too?" Dirtbag snarled.

"Yup, Father Raygun came up with these thingies. They turn bad feelings into uplifting tingling; it keeps me emotionally balanced. It even helps His Majesty control his temper, too." There was a loud crack of the whip from the kitchen. "I couldn't live without it, not with the divorce. Yup, it certainly helped me accept that my hubby has moved on."

"Why would anyone leave you?" T.C. probed. "I mean, you're beautiful."

"I'm also thirty. He had a thing about age; he said I had lines." Caley's lips trembled. "I tried so hard!" she cried out, collapsing in a burst of uncontrolled sobs. T.C. seemed taken aback by her pain. Caley quickly reached behind her apron for the battery connected to her bolt by a wire and rotated a numbered knob on it to the highest numeral. She suddenly stood up straight with a jolt, breathing a sigh of relief. She stared at her hands with a curious smirk. "Huh, I can barely feel them."

Cram Bury shouted from the kitchen that tables were waiting to be serviced.

"Welp, can I get you two anything else?" Caley said confidently, her face still moist from tears.

"Uh, yeah," Dirtbag said, gesturing out the window. "We saw some lightning outside. I take it that's from the church?"

"Yup! Father Raygun is consulting with the divine investors so he can write the next edition of the *Raymanac*; that's his almanac. He writes all his prophecies for the year in it. He's a blessed man."

"Hey, an almanac!" Dirtbag's brow shot up. "He must watch the sky pretty closely then?"

Caley nodded happily. Cram Bury yelled at her again, and she rushed off to tend to other tables, walking strangely, as though her feet were asleep.

Dirtbag's mind was immediately lost in thought. "Well, I doubt this Father Raygun could've missed a castle flying past his church. We're going to have to meet this guy."

T.C. nodded, preoccupied by the sight of Caley hurrying around the little restaurant. He saw Cram Bury pull her aside for a moment to scream an etiquette lesson into her ear. "That's bullcookies, Dirt." T.C. pointed.

Dirtbag watched Caley get back to work, her emotions dampened entirely by the device she wore. She stumbled over her own numb feet and broke a plate. Cram Bury flew into a rage and raced out of the kitchen with his whip. The patrons casually turned up their battery knobs as they watched the proceedings, detaching themselves entirely from compassion. Cram Bury grabbed Caley by the arm and slapped her around. She laughed out loud, as if he were tickling her, even as a drop of blood ran down her nose from the brutality of the beating. Cram Bury punched her hard, knocking the poor waitress to her knees.

"I'm docking your pay, you inefficient cur!" Cram Bury screamed at the top of his lungs.

"Hey! What is with you people?" Dirtbag yelled at the customers emotionlessly witnessing the assault. "You don't have to feel to care!" He stood up, shotgun in hand. "Get away from her, you scumbag!" he threatened Cram Bury.

"Mind your own business, heathen!" Cram Bury replied, yanking Caley by her hair. He raised his hand to thrash her with his whip.

"Oats alive!" T.C. shouted, drawing his sword from the table. "How dare you strike that woman! She was just doing the best she could!"

T.C. leapt out of his seat and charged into the fray. He seized Cram Bury by the back of his head and threw him to the floor, knocking loose the wire to his bolt. T.C. stomped the whip out of the chef's hand, pinning his arm to the floor beneath a boot, and plunged the amber blade through Cram Bury's bicep, purposely avoiding the artery. T.C. now understood that the secret of the Amber Blade of Divorce was in the unique pain it delivered. It was an unending excruciation that wouldn't kill but would make the recipient wish for death.

Cram Bury struggled with his uninjured arm to reattach the wire to the back of his neck. T.C. pummeled him and tore the battery off his belt, throwing it across the room. "You can't escape this pain! I won't let you!" T.C. worked the blade in deeper, but the chef didn't scream. Instead he quietly snickered through the agony. T.C. stepped away, disturbed. "Not even ten divorces can reach this monster, Dirt."

Cram Bury rolled under a nearby table, clutching his bloody arm. The patrons continued to drink and eat while this was going on, watching without a care. Dirtbag searched through the settings on the shotgun for options. As he did, he kept an eye on the cooks in the kitchen, but they seemed content with being blissful spectators. Every setting on the shotgun seemed inappropriate to the situation. "Let's grab the girl and get out of here," he said finally.

"Should we burn the place down?"

"No, I don't think these people would even notice."

Outside, T.C. sat down on the steps of Aloftden City Hall, holding Caley in his big arms, and he gently removed the copper clamp from her neck bolt. She shuddered from her injuries and softly wept. He rocked her back and forth, reassuringly stroking her hair.

"It's OK to hurt," he said. "It doesn't feel good, but trust me, it's OK."

T.C. tended to Caley as though he had loved her all his life. Her face was bruised, and her shirt had been ripped in two places. People passed them by as they sat, and if the onlookers saw anything that made them feel uncomfortable, they turned up the knobs on their batteries to tune it out of their lives.

Dirtbag kneeled down beside the two of them, completely exasperated. "These people are totally disconnected."

"I mean, who isn't these days, Dirt?" T.C. sighed, his gentle manner drawing out a shy smile from Caley as he held her.

"I'm sorry," she muttered quietly.

"Hey, don't be," Dirtbag said. He let out a frustrated growl. "So Father Raygun put that thing on you?"

"It was great at first," she admitted. "A little comfort when I needed it, but after the divorce, I just started liking it better when I didn't have to feel anything at all."

"I numb my pain with drinking"—Dirtbag threw away his monocle—"probably too much or maybe not enough; it's hard to say. What

I do know is that when I drink, it has consequences." He examined Caley's bolt; it had been surgically implanted and was irremovable. "If I could turn off my pain, consequence-free, I don't think I could call myself alive. My pain is a burden, but it's also there for a reason. Without it, I'd be living in perpetual denial."

"Yup, that's what it feels like," said Caley, "and after a while, it's all you know."

"Well, all that's behind you now." Dirtbag helped her to her feet. "I'm not sure what T.C. and I are going to do about all this, but you're going to leave town and start a new life."

"I want to. I do, but I can't afford to just get up and go."

"Here." Dirtbag handed her a large bag of gold. "Change your life."

Caley opened the bag and squealed. "Ka-boom! Ba-zap! Oh, thank you so much!" She hugged them one at a time.

T.C. held on to her a little longer than he should have. "Look, uh, Caley, I don't know what makes you happy, but I mean, I'm really good with my hands...never had any complaints."

"Oh, are you a chef, too?" she asked innocently.

"No," Dirtbag said, mortified. "He's a gentleman—we both are—and now it's time to start your new life. Be careful out there, and I don't know if you're on good terms with your dad, but I'm sure he'd like to hear from you."

Caley hugged them both again. They watched as she walked down the street, made a left, and entered a shoe store. They looked at each other. "She's just self-medicating," T.C. assured. "Trust me."

Dirtbag vigorously rubbed his face. "Well, how about some coffee? I'm sure if we buy enough of it, these numbskulls will tell us exactly where we can find this Church of Electric Scumbags."

A few hours later, after visiting half the shops in town and purchasing coffee from every single one, they had collected enough information to put together detailed directions to the Church of Electric Lightning. Cram Bury never pressed any charges, and no one ever spoke to them about what they had done. The restaurant was bustling when they passed by on their way out. They walked down the gravel road once more, this time with a destination.

"OK, what's the plan, Dirt?" T.C. asked.

"Find this church and burn it to the ground. Question whoever survives."

"That's my favorite kind of plan, the kind with no thought put into it."

The sun was setting, and they decided to camp discreetly near the church in order to surprise the parishioners in the morning. As they began to blithely dance down the road, fueled by an excessive amount of caffeine, neither of them felt compelled to have a second glance at what they were leaving behind, but had they, they would have seen the pied falconet following high above.

CHAPTER 17

The surprise attack was not going well. A cannonade of booming thunderclaps tore through the well-manicured landscaping from the top of a towering spire of polished aluminum ringed with gigantic copper heat-sink fins, shaking the very foundation of the Church of Electric Lightning. Father Raygun returned to his public-address system's broadcast booth, hidden somewhere inside the fortress-like church, and ordered his followers to prepare the lightning cannon for another volley to smite the heathen trespassers. Then he picked up his screaming, never-ending sermon where he had left off just before the cannon fired. The lawn was a battlefield of deep, smoking trenches, ripped into the earth by blasts of lightning, and the strewn bodies of unconscious, devoted followers wearing half-unbuttoned, fancy dress shirts. Dirtbag poked his head up from one of the trenches, shaking his fist in defiance at the lunatic inside the church. Father Raygun's rant grew even more intense, and his words began piling together into unintelligible garble.

"OK, now he's mad, Dirt," T.C. said, standing up with his sword in hand. He swept a chunk of singed sod off his shoulder and threw back his unscathed, magnificent hair, allowing it to catch the rising sun. "Next time we should try attacking after dinner, at the end of the day, when people are tired. I mean, I just don't think mornings are good for us."

"Do you hear that?" Dirtbag asked him. Behind the whir of the massive electric generator powering up within the church were chanting voices. "It's 'ka-boom ba-zap' again, and it's faster than last time, like they're juiced up on espresso."

"Swell. We've been out here so long they've already had breakfast."

"Hey, any second those doors are going to fly open, and another dozen people are going to run out here with plastic forks and rubber mallets."

T.C. chuckled uneasily. "I just can't keep punching people in the head, Dirt. I mean, I'm going to end up giving somebody brain damage."

"These people are frying their central nervous systems with batteries! A concussion is the least of their problems; in fact, it might actually be beneficial. Think of it as knocking them out of their complacency."

"My punches are actually healing them?" T.C. liked that idea. "Do you think it's possible I can beat a sense of style into them, too?"

"Anything is worth a shot."

"All those open shirts. I mean, sure, it works for the girls, but the guys…does wearing that many gold chains really make you more of a man?"

Dirtbag looked over the battleground of smoking trenches and scattered bodies. The lightning cannon's generator clunked as it shifted into a higher gear to top off the capacitors for firing. Father Raygun's voice seemed on the verge of skipping words altogether in favor of continuous screaming.

"Let's run over to that open area on the left." Dirtbag pointed to the pristine flower beds and meticulously cut hedgerows. "That way they won't fry anyone we've knocked out."

"Whoa! Do you think they'd do that?"

"Hey! Listen to that guy! He's talking about doorknobs coming out of people's eyes! Raygun is completely out of his mind!"

"In the bad way, Dirt?"

"Is there any other?"

"I dunno, women sometimes——"

Loud metal clangs echoed from within the church's spire as circuit breakers switched back into position. A low-level electric hum began building in the air; it quickly escalated into a high-pitched, crackling buzz. The lightning cannon was mounted at the top of the spire, having a similar design to an enormous optical astronomy telescope, but it was heavily modified to contain multiple copper coils, tightly wrapped around stacks of polished metal spheres and rare earth magnets. Heat shimmered off the spheres from the buildup of energy. A rectangular rod at the tip conducted the discharge into a single beam of superheated plasma.

"We need to get over there!" Dirtbag shouted, leaping out of the trench.

Father Raygun continued to incoherently scream his corporate message of holy electric repentance as Dirtbag pulled T.C. out of the trench. They ran across the lawn, trampling shrubs and kicking flowers out of the way. The lightning cannon noisily clanked gears, and the entire spire began to rotate, following their movement. Father Raygun's voice went silent; then he gave the order, and the cannon fired.

"Get down!" T.C. yelled, throwing Dirtbag behind him.

The air sizzled, and a distinct burnt-ozone odor wafted into T.C.'s nostrils a split-second before the lightning bolt was released from the cannon. It arced across the lawn like a stream of water from a sprinkler, a blinding, purple-tinted light that bore through the atmosphere to connect with the ground, throwing up chunks of flaming terrain in a series of successive pops. It burned a deep line into the earth as the spire rotated, dragging the beam across the land at a pace faster than any man could outrun. T.C. dug his feet into the ground and swung the Amber Blade of Divorce at the coming beam, intercepting it in a blazing flash. The sword repelled the energy back into the beam and turned white hot. The unexpected resistance set off the breakers within the church, instantly cutting off power. T.C. dropped the glowing-hot blade on the ground, where it burnt the grass around it. He rubbed his armored hands.

"I can't believe that actually worked," he said, watching the sword cool, the embedded wedding rings still glowing brightly. "I mean, it must have some hidden aspect of rejection built in."

Dirtbag looked at the smoldering sword. "That thing is as impressive as it is disturbing."

The lightning cannon's generator began to whir again. Dirtbag cycled through the settings on his shotgun. They heard the sound of overly caffeinated, chanting zealots gathering behind the heavy mahogany church doors. "I'm going to use the 'Special Delivery' setting before he can send more people out."

"OK. But, I mean, do you know what that'll do?"

"It's the only setting with a warning label, so I hope it does something spectacular. I think we've shown too much restraint."

"Are we still trying to be better men?"

"Well, we haven't killed anyone yet."

Dirtbag pumped the shotgun, took aim at the lightning cannon, and fired. A single, yellow, arrowhead-like projectile launched from the barrel and penetrated the spire. They heard Father Raygun scream a series of expletives. The spire cracked open, the cannon shattered into pieces, and the entire upper half of the church exploded skyward, sending flaming debris several miles up. Dirtbag and T.C. ran in separate directions to dodge the falling chunks of burning structural remains, casually reemerging out of the settling dust cloud moments later, dancing in an intimidating manner they had practiced the night before and finishing with a triumphant pose, touting their victory.

"That's science in action." Dirtbag picked a metal shard out of his grass-hair. "You try something, even though you're not quite sure how it will turn out, there's a result, and now you know."

"We can just say it was magic though, right? I mean, if anyone asks."

They heard Father Raygun shouting from within the church—no longer over the speaker. The front door unlocked and slowly creaked open. A white flag, draped over a charred metal rod, popped out and timidly waved.

"I think he wants to talk, Dirt," T.C. chuckled.

"I guess that means we have to try diplomacy," Dirtbag growled, holstering his shotgun.

"Swell. I mean, the last time I had a disagreement with a minister, it involved some tooth extraction." T.C. sheathed the cooled amber blade. "I thought he sang much better afterward."

"I'm so mad right now." Dirtbag watched as a man appeared from behind the church door. "If this scumbag can't hold a conversation, I'm putting my fist in his mouth and going with head nods."

Father Raygun, a skinny beanstalk of a man with straight, static-charged white hair, walked toward them in a peculiar rhythm of two steps followed by a nervous hop. He wore a black silk shirt, gold corduroy pants, yellow rubber gloves, and black, knee-high, rubber wading boots. He was covered with copper wires connecting batteries to a bolt in the back of his head. He was followed by a delighted barista, possibly his mother, who was dressed in similar clothing and carrying a sky-blue, plastic coffeepot with matching mugs.

"Beware of the electric albino," T.C. whispered.

Raygun stopped just in front of them. The barista poured coffee into one of the mugs and handed it to Raygun, who drank the entire thing immediately and then began staring at Dirtbag and T.C. Not knowing how to react to this man, they stared right back. The fires of the exploded lightning cannon simmered around them, and followers of the church worked diligently to douse the flames. Five long minutes passed as the trio stared. A small breeze blew dust behind T.C.'s sunglasses, and he was forced to blink, but Dirtbag was still in it. He stared harder at the pale man, grinning mischievously, and finally the man flinched.

"That's not fair, man!" Father Raygun bellyached in a whiny, unhurried but oddly intelligent manner of speaking. "C'mon; you don't even have eyes!"

"Hey! You oversized, anemic asparagus!" Dirtbag responded loudly, startling Raygun. "You lost, so shut up!"

"That's not cool, man!"

"Didn't I tell you to shut up, scumbag?"

"Wait," T.C. said. "He has to talk, Dirt. I mean, we can't do the diplomacy thing if he doesn't."

Dirtbag reluctantly agreed. "My name's Dirtbag, and this is T.C. We came here to liberate these people from your cult of numbskull bolts and bad coffee."

"And I'm Father Raygun," he chimed sardonically. "Just look what you two did to my front yard, man! C'mon; where's the respect?"

"Yeah, we get that a lot." T.C. smirked.

Raygun paced back and forth, trying to calm himself down. "Just what do you guys think you're doing? Huh?"

"Righting all the wrongs in the world," Dirtbag declared.

"Really? Just how do you determine that, man? What's your basis for that reasoning? C'mon! Are you people crazy?"

"You're the one who's crazy, scumbag," Dirtbag snarled. "We're here to save these people from your crazy."

Raygun put his hands on his hips and glared at them. He sent the barista away. Once the woman was out of earshot, Raygun's posture relaxed. "It's all an act," he whispered.

"What?" Dirtbag barked.

"Can we...can we take a walk?"

T.C. loudly assured the frail man his stick body would be broken in half at the first hint of treachery. He illustrated with a karate-chop gesture. The pale man smiled nervously. Dirtbag and T.C. followed Raygun away from his congregation and around the side of the church, where a path led through a small peach-tree orchard. Once they had walked halfway in, Raygun turned to them and confessed. "I'm not crazy," he told them calmly.

Dirtbag frowned. "And what about all that garbage you were yelling?"

"C'mon, man; that's a bunch of scripted nonsense I read when guys like you show up."

"Like us?"

"Cheah! Man, you two really live up to your reputation. You—you destroyed more in an hour than the last invading army did in two days. Had I known it was you guys attacking, I probably would've just surrendered. Shoot. Man, the dry cleaning alone—"

"If you have something to tell us, scumbag, then you had better get it out of your mouth."

"Not…not everyone in the world is strong enough to handle difficult times," Raygun began plainly, "and I don't mean trivial pain, man. I'm talking about the kind that devastates a human being and changes a person forever. The death of a wife or…uh…uh, a child or discovering you're terminally ill. Man, some people escape into drink and self-destruction, other people into empty relationships that only compound their problems, cheah, and the worst afflicted end their own lives. So, I made this thing"—he pointed to the bolt in his head—"because I lost my family. Man! I needed something, anything, to help me ease that pain. When it worked for me, I thought it could work for others, too, and before I knew it, I had a full-blown church of followers."

"Are you telling me you're exploiting these people's desperation, scumbag?"

"No! Man! No!" Raygun panicked. "C'mon, man, relax. We do a lot of good here," he defended. "We take care of the sick, bury the unwanted, and I keep those guys who are just looking for doctrine busy with research for my new almanac. I wrapped this phony, magical religion stuff around science to gain acceptance. C'mon; you know how people are; it's easier to believe in something than to understand a thing. Cheah. Then you guys come along and…uh…uh, blow up my tax breaks like bad accountants. Those flowers were vanilla orchids, man! There goes our next batch of wafer cookies. For no reason, man. Some heroes you are, shoot."

Dirtbag combed back his grass-hair, irritated. "Hey, we had a very good reason: pain is life; you can't take that away from people without consequences."

"Why? Why not? Huh?"

"Because that's cheating," T.C. said. "The way I see it, I've been through gut-wrenching times in my life, times I just don't even want to remember, but I made it, and I'm stronger because of it. Life is not easy. I mean, it's about figuring things out as you go and doing the best you can, and there'll be pain along the way, but that's OK."

"C'mon, man. Obviously not everyone agrees with you, or I wouldn't have people lining up at my door. I don't put a bolt into just anybody; you have to be at the end of your rope. Do you even know what that feels like, man? When you have nothing left, nothing at all, and you just want to sit down and die?"

"I know what that feels like," Dirtbag said bitterly, "because that's exactly what I did."

"I dunno, Dirt; we'd be foolish to expect sincerity from some numbskull," T.C. said skeptically. "I mean, how do you explain those books your people hock, *Raygunomics?*"

Raygun almost pulled his hair out with frustration. "C'mon, man; do you know how much it costs to operate a lightning cannon?"

"Just why do you have a lightning cannon anyway?"

"For the supernatural razzle-dazzle, man. But every now and then some nut shows up with an army. Shoot. Either it's some factoid they disagree with in the almanac or they're freaked out about seeing a head bolt that offers more relief in a minute than a lifetime of prayer. We...we're always under the threat of persecution; a lot of people hate the truth, man, and...uh...uh, truth is what science provides."

T.C. looked at Dirtbag.

"Well," Dirtbag said, "I don't disagree with you, but what brought T.C. and I here was what we saw in town. People used your device to tune out even the slightest thing that caused them discomfort. They're all disconnected and numb."

"C'mon; I never said my invention was perfect. The dial is there to provide people with a choice, man. They can feel as much or as little as they want. Obviously, the problem is not with my bolts; it's with the people themselves. It's an issue of morality, man, and that's a social problem that can't be easily fixed…" Raygun drifted off, thinking about it for a moment. "Sure, I can take away the pain, but I can't make people change who they are. They have to want to do that themselves. You know what I mean, man?"

T.C. took out his checkbook. "OK. How much for the damages?"

Raygun grinned as he led them out of the orchard and back onto the front lawn. "Don't worry about it; we—we're loaded, man. There's a ton of money in religion. The real question is how can Father Raygun help you?"

Dirtbag was amused by his offer. "We're looking for an upside-down flying castle."

Raygun's eyes grew intense. "Ba-zap! Man! Ba-zap! We were attacked only four months ago by one of those things. Man, some glowing guy in a business suit jumped out and tried to tear the lightning cannon right off the roof with his bare hands. Fortunately, his old lady started screaming at him to get back inside and pick up the wet towels he'd left on the bathroom floor. I cover the whole incident in my upcoming autobiography: *The Raygunator*. The cover is going to be rubber; you know, nonconductive. Cheah." He pushed his nervous hands into his pants pockets and moved a scorched piece of metal around with his toe. "Don't worry about the damage. I have insurance. I'll just say it was an act of magic and collect a fat settlement. Sure, you blew it up, but man, I got a ton of data out of it. Wait until you see the next one. Science is all about iteration, man."

"That it is," Dirtbag said, rubbing the back of his denim neck. "Well, we're on a mission, and I'm not sure what kind it is, but I can pretty much guarantee you what we have in store for that castle isn't covered by any insurance."

"Right on. I'll show you where that thing went, no problem— whatever you need, whatever it takes to get the two of you on your way and off my lawn, man." Raygun waved over the waiting barista. "Coffee?"

The barista passed around coffee mugs, and they all drank together. Dirtbag and T.C. almost doubled over from the horrific taste. "This stuff is putrid." Dirtbag hacked.

"What? C'mon, man. It's an acquired taste, like marriage: the first gulp is bitter and hard to swallow, but then after a while, there's that sweet aftertaste, but you have to stick with it to get to it. You know what I mean?"

Dirtbag was flabbergasted and was about to respond when T.C. urgently motioned for them to look at a tree on the edge of the church's property.

"Is that bird smoking a cigarette?" he asked.

"I hope not, man," Raygun said, enjoying his coffee. "Those things can give you cancer."

The bird glared at them with its dark-blue eyes, as if it had been listening and was annoyed. It abruptly took flight. Dirtbag watched it soar from view with great suspicion.

CHAPTER 18

———

Dirtbag and T.C. stumbled along the gravel road, lurching forward like overloaded carts on broken wheels, passing the rum bottle back and forth as they maundered. They paused to caustically yell at a tortoise trying to cross the road, eventually blaming it for everything and then heaving it back into the woods from which it came. They were between towns and between adventures. It was at these times that their fortitude deteriorated, consumed by old feelings that crept out from those dark places busy minds forget, and the ever-looming cloud of depression took hold, strangling their self-worth. They had stayed in successively worsening lodging over the past three days, descending from a cheap, run-down motel to a barn and, at their lowest point, a discarded cardboard box. It didn't matter as long as it was near a bar.

They wandered down the road like vagrants, unaware of how much time was passing but knowing well enough they should keep moving. Dirtbag wearily checked the compass Father Raygun had given him to make sure they were still headed in the right direction. They were. He looked up and saw a noodle stand at the top of the next hill.

"Hey, T.C.," his voice croaked, "let's get some breakfast from that boat up ahead."

"Whoa, what's a boat doing on the road?" T.C. said softly, squinting and rubbing his uncharacteristically disheveled face, his balbo having overgrown into an uneven beard. "The sun is just too high for breakfast, Dirt. I mean, this is going to have to be lunch."

An invigorating breeze carried the delicious scent of food their way. They picked up the pace to the noodle stand. The feeble old man who ran the stand welcomed them to sit on the long bench in front of the boat. The stand had no wheels, and it was unclear just how the boat had arrived there. The old man stood behind a small counter on an elevated platform, his frail body remarkably energetic, cooking up a feast as if expecting to be busy that day, even though there was no one around for miles. The old man hummed to himself, handing them washcloths to clean their hands.

"Hello, boys! Nice to see you!" the old man said in a friendly, raspy voice that sounded conspicuously like a squeaky door with a slight lisp. "Don't look so surprised. I'm your new pal, Flea. I've been waiting for you."

"Uh, you have?" T.C. groggily inquired. "Have we met?"

"It's not like you boys practice discretion, he-he-he. You two are like a traveling traumatic event. Everybody's heard of you. People lump you in the same category as sewer foot and chipmunk pox. You're a plague. You may save the day, but then you spend the week drinking away your heroism, until people get fed up and run you out of town."

"Oats alive! It's easy to judge us for doing something about the world's problems from the position of doing nothing, you...you fiend. I mean, your name is Flea, right? And I have a big boot, OK?" T.C. warned rudely.

Flea pulled out a wooden school ruler from behind the counter and hit T.C. on the hand.

"Ow!" T.C. recoiled. "I felt that right through my armor."

Dirtbag chuckled. Flea hit him on the hand, too.

"I'm made of dirt; that doesn't bother me," Dirtbag smirked.

Flea thrust the ruler into Dirtbag's mouth and shook it around. Dirtbag grabbed it out. "Hey! Watch it! That's not nice!" he said, irritated.

"What makes you think I'm trying to be nice? The only reason I'm here is because you degenerates pay people with big sacks of gold. I want to retire, but I never saved. A common dilemma with only two choices: find you boys or start pimping chickens. Pretty easy decision if you ask me, he-he-he," Flea chattered, handing them menus. "I know it's easier for you two to make enemies than friends, but just this once, try to be gentlemen."

Dirtbag and T.C. exchanged puzzled glances but were too drained to care. The menu was packed with hundreds of things to choose from. Dirtbag set the menu down, unable to decide. "I'm really hungry," he told Flea. "I'll take whatever you think you make best."

"You know, I'll just have the same," T.C. said.

"The easy way out, eh? What happened to the great captain of the Blitz Knights? The leader of Warferno? A man renowned for his unconventional strategy and planning? You saved Trucebell with your quick thinking, and now you ask me, Flea, to decide for you? I couldn't even plan my own retirement!"

"That was a long time ago"—T.C. fiddled with his dragon teeth—"and I've never considered what happened there a victory."

"You carry that pain like it happened yesterday. You, too, dirt man. Divorce doesn't mean you die. Life goes on."

"The name's Dirtbag, and life simply does not go on."

"I follow the gossip column in the *Daily Scrag*." Flea giggled. "You and Katvanna are like opposing magnetic forces. They say when the two of you eventually come together again, it's predicted the entire world will end."

"Magnetism doesn't work that way. Besides, T.C. and I already ended the world once, and everything worked out just fine." Dirtbag examined an unfamiliar perforated red jar sitting between the salt and pepper shakers. "Is this granulated ketchup?"

"What else would it be?" Flea served them two cups of mint tea.

"Mint?" T.C. curled his lip up. "When I smell mint, I think squid."

"That's an interesting association." Flea frowned, curious. "When you got that dent, did it affect your olfactory nerves?"

"My old factory works just fine," T.C. said, still foggy. His stomach growled. "I'm about ready to start throwing gold at that tree over there, to see if I can pay it enough to grow apples, if you don't get going cooking something."

"You both want the same thing? Fine. I'll make you my miracle noodles."

"Do they have special powers?" Dirtbag asked, cynically.

"No. But it's a miracle I'm still alive to serve them, he-he-he." Flea stared at the dent in T.C.'s head as he started chopping vegetables. "You want a bandanna or something to put over that? It's kind of distracting."

T.C. had allowed his usually well-groomed hair to turn tangled and wild. When it was in place, the dent in his head was barely noticeable. He pulled out his brush—he paused to stare at a jumble of Muffin's hair still entwined in the plastic teeth—and then began combing out his knots. Flea saw his efforts and set a mirror on the counter in front of him.

"Oats alive! I look bad," T.C. said, angling his face so that he could see the growth of his beard. He took out his hair clippers to shave it off.

Dirtbag leaned over, gazed into the mirror, and was disgusted with what he saw. "Well, I can't fix that," he snarled, annoyed.

T.C. shaved his face and suddenly grimaced at a group of gray hairs on his chin. "Swell. I'm showing my age," he complained, shaving the hairs off. "I'm at the end of my prime, Dirt. I should be settled with a family. I never even made the time to have kids. I mean, I guess I never let that happen."

Dirtbag put his head down on the counter and groaned.

"These lines on my face run deep, Dirt," T.C. said, staring into the mirror as he cleaned himself up. "They used to only show up when I smiled or made a face; now they're there all the time, just like scars, from the good times, the bad, the weird, everything. My whole life is on my face."

Dirtbag looked up. "Hey, how do you think I feel?"

"But I was pretty," T.C. reminisced bitterly. "There was this one time, with the first wife, where I chaperoned a slumber party for my then niece. I mean, one girl brought over a suitcase full of makeup, and I let them do my hair and nails. It was fun." He started to grin, but the lines became more pronounced as he did, and he stopped. "I really loved my first wife, Dirt. If we had had a son, I mean, as a father, I would've taught him how to be a man—a good man. But if we had had a daughter, I realize now, she would have taught me how to be a better man." He stared down the road. "I don't know why I destroyed what we had, but I feel like there's just not enough time to find that again. Every time I met my next wife, I always thought she'd be the one, the last one, the one I could grow old with, but it never worked out like that."

Dirtbag squirmed in his seat and sipped the tea. "You know, when you fall in love, real love, you ruin each other," Dirtbag told him, "and it's never the same afterward. It's something different, and that either works or it doesn't, but if it does, it's because it works for the both of you."

T.C. finished fixing himself up, Flea hid the mirror away, and T.C. turned to Dirtbag, throwing back his restored luscious hair to display his clean-shaven face. "How do I look?"

Dirtbag sighed. "Gorgeous."

"How much like an old man do I look?"

"Do you want to look young?"

T.C. thought it over. "Nah," he said. "I dunno what I want any-more."

Dirtbag grumbled. "You do know. It's in there, even if you can't quite grasp it. Don't dismiss aspiration outright. That's a bad habit to get into, and we already have plenty of those."

Flea served them two bowls of hot miracle noodles, each tweaked with personalized ingredients, and it enlivened them inside as they ate. When they had finished, they paid Flea two giant bags of gold. He cried for joy, and they watched as he enthusiastically burned down his noodle stand. The oddly colored green smoke carried for miles. The three cheerfully parted ways. A half hour down the road, Dirtbag and T.C. were once again passing the bottle of rum between them.

CHAPTER 19

———

Dirtbag and T.C. found themselves in a thousand-year-old forest, lying facedown next to a stream in a ditch by the road, hungover. Sunlight cascaded through the thick, towering redwood trees, lighting their resting place in a pleasant, yellow jasmine radiance. They had walked through the night, drinking from the enchanted rum bottle until they were belligerent and angry. They could only remember random incidents of what had transpired, and none of them made much sense. They had chased a farmer into his house and demanded a stick of butter from him. Then they had left before he could give them anything, wandering through the forest until they happened upon a clearing where sheep were resting. They had shaven at least one of the animals, and T.C. had stuffed the cut wool down his pants. The rest was a blur of talking loudly at various objects or people or each other.

"I overdid it," Dirtbag said, holding his head.

"Whoa," T.C. groaned woozily. "You passed out, too? I thought you couldn't get that drunk, Dirt."

"I drank so much my body became saturated," Dirtbag grumbled, "just like overwatering a houseplant."

T.C. rolled over onto his back, his nose red and his face pale. "Is that a bag of potatoes?" he asked.

"Looks like it," Dirtbag said, poking the sack sitting next to him.

"That bird's back, Dirt," T.C. mentioned, noticing a lit cigarette under the shadow of a tree branch close by. "I think it's following us."

"I know," Dirtbag told him. "She's been tailing us for days now."

"How do you know it's a she?"

"She's wearing makeup."

"Oh." T.C. tried to see if that was true, but the bird was too far away.

The pied falconet abruptly darted out from her hiding spot above them, yawping, apparently chastising them for what they'd done. Dirtbag lethargically waved for the bird to leave them alone, and it flew off, quietly fuming. T.C. pushed himself down the ditch toward the stream with his legs, until his head was submerged under the cool, clean water. He stayed that way for two minutes before sitting up. Dirtbag dragged himself to the stream and rolled his body in. The water soaked into him, forcing the rum out. After a few minutes, he felt completely refreshed. He helped T.C. to his feet.

"I'm tired of walking, Dirt," T.C. sighed, setting free a field mouse that had become trapped in his boot.

Dirtbag checked the compass against the position of the sun, scratching his head. "Well, we're still going in the right direction."

"Oats alive!" T.C. growled. "We'll never catch up with a flying castle at this rate. We should get some horses, or maybe we can tame a wild car."

"Hey, I'm in no hurry to find her. Are you?"

T.C. brushed out his wet hair. "Yeah, I shouldn't be complaining," he said, thinking. "I mean, Katvanna could just destroy us with a word, right?"

"Exactly, she knows the language of the ancients. She might be the only person in the world who does, too. There's nothing else like it or more dangerous. She also knows we're coming; she invited me, which probably means she plans to kill me, I'm guessing for her entertainment at the reception, so the wedding might be held up until we arrive anyway."

"I can't wait to meet this woman," T.C. said sarcastically. He lifted his sunglasses to rub his glowing red eyes and yawned. He started walking.

Dirtbag scowled at him. "At least take the wool out of your pants."

"OK, but what about those potatoes?"

"Well, what about them?" Dirtbag said, leaving them behind.

They followed the stream deep into the woods to a grain mill, drawn by the scent of baking bread. They bought two warm loaves from the skittish baker, unsure if they had run into him during the night. As the sun rose, they felt better.

"What a night," T.C. exhaled, picking at the bread as they walked through the forest.

"I don't think I can do that again," Dirtbag said.

"That was a pretty bad one, Dirt. I've been feeling low ever since we got that compass. You think it's cursed?"

"That's dread. Don't let it bother you." Dirtbag threw some crust away. "Inevitability can be a heavy burden, but if you put it in the right perspective, it can be a relief, as long as you can accept the waiting outcome."

"Now, wait just a minute. You make it sound like we don't have a chance, but we do, remember? The squid said so. I mean, when this is all done, we can take a vacation, find some cute psychiatrists, and—"

"No. When this is finally over and I have my heart again, I'm going back. I want to finally lay myself to rest." Dirtbag tossed his half-eaten loaf away. "It's what I've always wanted, T.C."

T.C. looked at Dirtbag, troubled by what he heard but silent.

A sudden, deep-toned, whining thunder echoed from the sky. They stepped out into a clearing, an untouched, flower-laden acreage, and watched as a white cloud soared out of the glare of the sun like an ominous tentacle stretching forth to capture prey. It arced downward, banking sharply, growing in size as it approached. As it came closer, they could see a giant, sinister shadow with beating wings at its tip. Each oscillation caused the cloud enveloping the menace to swirl strangely around the vortices it created. The cloud slowed to hover above them; jet turbines in the wings dispersed the vaporous fog, kicking up a strong wind that brought with it the terrible, metal-buckling howl of a dragon. Its glowing motorized maw opened wide, and three triangular, multibarreled rotary cannons pushed forward out of its throat. Dirtbag grabbed T.C., and they ran into the woods to protect themselves from the ancient war machine.

"No greenwood can hide you from me, loathly mongrels!" General Bloodblivion roared from the back of the Gatling-Dragon. "Come forth, and accept your moment of expiry!"

CHAPTER 20

———

The Gatling-Dragon hovered before Dirtbag and T.C., expelling searing-hot exhaust from its many jet turbines, which were spread across a wingspan of at least six hundred feet. Its peculiar anatomy was made up of layer upon layer of gunmetal plate armor over a protruding, glossy-black skeletal structure that vibrated from the stress of containing the inferno within. Its movements were smooth and precise, refined beyond even the most fluid biological creatures, and utterly alien in their artificial exactness. Every bend of its body caused armor plates to separate, revealing an internal assortment of superheated spinning clockwork gears and machinery that resembled hydraulic pistons in place of muscles. Sharpened blades covered the end of its long mace tail, and it flung sparks off its scythe-like talons, sharpening them in anticipation for battle. Its razor-toothed mouth held the weapons of its namesake inside a heavily armored head dotted with eight burning-white, unblinking eyes, like that of a spider. It paced the edge of the forest as if seeking to draw them out; its patience was a reflection of its master's wishes, because a thing such as this, created for no other purpose than war, could on a whim easily flatten anything in its path.

Dirtbag and T.C. watched the nightmarish Gatling-Dragon from behind the trunk of the largest tree they could find, weapons in hand. The very presence of the creature bombarded the area with a gut-shaking, low-pitched, thunderous rumble.

"Well, how do we fight that thing, T.C.?" Dirtbag asked.

"OK, I know it looks bad. I mean, I've never seen a Gatling-Dragon up close, and this thing's got to be bigger than any dragon I've fought before, but on the other hand, it's been broken in and has a rider, which could be something we can leverage."

"And Bloodblivion?"

"Now, are we sure that's him?"

"Are you kidding me? Look at that guy."

General Bloodblivion sat atop the Gatling-Dragon in a metal saddle welded to a plate of spinal armor fastened between the beating wings. He wore a formfitting, blood-red skull mask over half his aged face, and it barely covered his extensive radiation burns. His scalp was missing chunks of his long white hair, and as they watched, strands were periodically liberated from his head by the turbulence of the jet turbines around him. Even in his obvious terminal state, he was a fortress of a man, dressed in multifaceted, blood-red, heavy armor that had been etched head-to-toe with the names and places of those who he had conquered, crudely carved in by his own claw-like hands. His history of unbound aggression was reflected by the many sections of bolted-on polished steel that had been used to patch horrendous battle damage throughout his body. He turned the Gatling-Dragon to face them. He'd known where they were the entire time.

"Do not defer that which is now preordained!" he roared, his voice somehow artificially amplified through his armor. "Tomorrow is lost, for your demise is forthcoming. There will be no mercy. None at all."

Bloodblivion snapped the reins of the Gatling-Dragon, and its rotary cannons ignited, spitting out a torrent of screaming bullet fire that tore through the forest, splintering hundreds of trees in one deafening sweep.

Dirtbag and T.C. dove behind knotty roots, hunkering down under the stream of bullets, unsure how to begin a counterattack. General Bloodblivion's sadistic laugh bellowed over the percussive impacts of still-falling trees and smoldering remains.

T.C. rolled out of the way of a tumbling tree and clambered over to Dirtbag, using the burning stumps for cover.

Bloodblivion coughed hard and wiped a glob of black blood from the corner of his mouth. "With my own eyes did I observe the loss of my army, my reign, and my life under a cloud of fiery bane, whereat I swore that they who were accountable would be found and slain by my hand alone," his seething voiced boomed. "Hear this! There will be no mercy! There is no escape!"

Bloodblivion pulled out a bloodstained leather sack from behind his saddle, reached inside it, and threw something into the forest. Dirtbag and T.C. watched the object bounce over a fallen tree, roll down a splintered branch, and land at their feet. It was Bistro's decapitated head. T.C. kicked it away. "Oats alive! If he's been tracking us the whole time, what about all the people we've met, Dirt?"

"He's a single-minded despot bent on revenge who doesn't have the time or the manpower to search for us. We've been betrayed."

"Bistro did have it coming to him, but I mean, I liked some of those people. Like that waitress, the redhead—I can't believe I've forgotten her name already."

"The most likely answer is Flea signaled him. That scumbag knew too much. Our drinking made us complacent."

"We were sloppy, Dirt. We should've—"

"There are a lot of things we should've done better. But we can't fix the past, T.C. You should know that by now."

"The squid lied, Dirt. The odds have turned against us."

"Nonsense. Statistically, improbable things happen all the time. We can do this. Tyrants are not, and have never been, invincible."

Dirtbag flipped through the settings on his shotgun's dial until he came to "Special Delivery." T.C. gripped the Amber Blade of Divorce tightly.

"OK, OK, this won't be easy, Dirt."

"Hey, it's never easy, and there's not much use talking about it."

T.C. swallowed his fear. "Let's divide up the work."

"Well, I guess I'll take the dragon," Dirtbag said, pumping his shotgun.

"Bullcookies, I'm a knight, Dirt. I should take that."

"No, a knight should fight a knight. I'm dirt; having holes punched in me by bullets won't kill me. Plus, I don't burn that well."

T.C. touched the dragon teeth hanging around his neck anxiously. "Dragons can do a lot worse than making you burn, Dirt. At Trucebell, my men, I mean, they were one hundred against three of these things, and it was over pretty quick."

"We've killed monsters as bad as this a dozen times before."

"You're right. I mean, I just have to remember what I've learned since back then: feeling fear is OK; just don't let it get to you."

"Exactly. And since nobody is around to witness this, forget honor. Do whatever you have to do to get the job done. We'll gloss over the unsavory parts later."

"Already victorious, Dirt?"

"We won't get very far planning for defeat."

"Swell. So how should we begin?"

"I'll start."

T.C. groaned, girding himself. "I hate guys like this."

"Me, too."

"Ready, Dirt?"

"Not really."

"Me neither."

Dirtbag leaned out from behind the burning tree stump; the sky had grown dark with smoke. He fired at the Gatling-Dragon. The dragon tried to dodge the shot but was too large to avoid being hit. The leading edge of its wing exploded apart, sending red-hot metal turbine fragments everywhere. Bloodblivion wrestled with the reins to land the dragon. Dirtbag took aim and fired again. The shot landed near Bloodblivion, and the force of the explosion knocked him out of his saddle. The dragon bucked in pain and crashed to the ground, nearly trampling Bloodblivion beneath its piercing claws.

"There will be no mercy!" the general shouted as he picked up his sword and drew it from its protective scabbard. A luminous, transparent green blade emerged, accompanied by an intimidating howl of anguish. It was a soul blade, one of two known to exist, capable of extracting the essence of living things in the course of a killing blow, and Bloodblivion had filled it to capacity with his many victims. It was said that the memories of those it absorbed could be viewed through the blade, uncovering every secret and preserving the final thoughts of a slain enemy at the moment of death.

Dirtbag hauled himself over a splintered, fallen tree and chased after the injured Gatling-Dragon even as it writhed in pain. T.C. paused for a second, holding the Amber Blade of Divorce to his head and allowing a bead of sweat to run down the leading edge. The ten wedding rings inside the blade glowed. He took a deep breath and charged into battle.

Bloodblivion saw Dirtbag running after the dragon; he rushed to intercept him and prevent further use of the shotgun—a weapon that might be capable of killing his fearsome pet. T.C. shouted to get the general's attention and put all his weight behind his first strike. Bloodblivion turned in time to parry the attack. Their swords clashed together, discharging a halo of competing energies around the warriors. Bloodblivion was quick and powerful, but T.C. was seasoned from fighting many types of creatures and opponents. He knew how to turn Bloodblivion's assaults against him, dodging, sidestepping, blocking, and when there was an opening, he struck hard. He was scared of this insane man and the weapon he possessed, but he remained calm and wore his enemy down.

Dirtbag could hear the Gatling-Dragon's mechanical body clanking through the settling dust cloud it had kicked up. Red embers glinted within the cloud from the damaged wing, but he couldn't tell which way it was facing. A scythe claw lashed out of the cloud. Dirtbag fell backward to dodge it. The dragon surged forward, jumping on top of him. It held him down and bit into his torso. The razor teeth punctured his leather-titanium armor, and the dragon shook him, mauling his body. Dirtbag could feel his seams tearing and aimed the shotgun at the uninjured wing. He fired another "Special Delivery" round. Immediately, a piece of the dragon's body exploded off. It dropped Dirtbag, wailing in pain, and, in a panic, tried to fly away. As it beat its wings, parts began falling off, and Dirtbag watched as the already-wounded appendages failed catastrophically midflight in an explosion of broken gears and ruptured pistons. The beast called out to its master for help as it plummeted to the ground.

Bloodblivion turned his attention to the crying dragon for only a second. Seeing the opening, T.C. stabbed the Amber Blade of Divorce between sections of the general's patched-over armor, sending his sword through the weakened layers and into unprotected flesh. Bloodblivion kicked T.C. to the ground, furious. The blade had penetrated deep into his chest, and he lacked the strength to pull it out. T.C. brazenly lunged to finish the job, but Bloodblivion punched hard, knocking him away. Then, quickly, Bloodblivion kneeled down, placed one foot on the cross guard of the sword, as if it were a shovel spade, and, with all his might, stood up, yanking the blade from his body in a deluge of his own irradiated black blood. He weakly kicked the weapon aside, clutching his chest, but remained resolute, ever the specter of villainy.

Dirtbag crouched behind a smoking tree stump, unable to see exactly where the Gatling-Dragon was among the brightly illuminated debris it had shed and the cinders of the burning forest. Without warning, the head of the dragon accelerated out of a wall of smoke, rotary cannons spinning. It blasted bullets across the ground, their spray chewing through everything in their path, including Dirtbag. He was blown along the ground with the other debris, like a leaf being fanned by a strong wind. He dove behind a boulder and took a roll of duct tape out from his satchel. His body was full of holes. Only his armor was holding him together. He taped up as much as he could while the Gatling-Dragon advanced.

Dirtbag leapt from his boulder refuge just as the dragon's mace tail smashed it to rubble. He cycled through random settings on the shotgun, firing at the dragon repeatedly. He turned its tail to ice and fractured it with a bolt of lightning and then blew off a quarter of the armored head with another "Special Delivery." The Gatling-Dragon reared up on its hind legs, making a terrible grinding sound as it opened its chest, and a massive, human-skull-shaped rotary cannon pushed out from its fiery core. The chest cannon spun up, but instead of firing bullets, it sprayed molten metal over the fallen trees surrounding Dirtbag, cutting off every possible route of escape.

Bloodblivion coughed up black blood, distracted as he watched the Gatling-Dragon turn the tide. The injury T.C. had struck, combined with his own dying body, had already defeated him. Though he would die, he refused to yield. He would punish them.

T.C. rose to his feet behind the general, having recovered his sword during his opponent's reckless inattention, raring to continue. He threw a rock toward Bloodblivion's left and struck viciously on the right with the Amber Blade of Divorce. The general was too cunning for such a trick and met T.C.'s sword with his own. T.C. twisted around and tore the skull mask from Bloodblivion's face, taking with it a layer of necrotized flesh. Bloodblivion was unfazed and grabbed T.C. by the throat. T.C. dug his foot in the ground and swung his sword upward, cleaving through the lightly protected armpit and maiming the general's arm, releasing himself from the choking grip. Bloodblivion glared at his ruined arm and grew enraged. The general charged forth in a ferocious, single-handed onslaught, his every move committed to dealing a deathblow.

T.C. met the attack head on with equal vigor. Their swords violently collided again and again, but as the Amber Blade of Divorce glowed brighter, the soul blade began to crack, and with one final swing, T.C. shattered Bloodblivion's sword, releasing its tormented energy. The general fell, and before he could utter a final damnation, T.C. beheaded him. He kicked the severed head across the battlefield, impaling it on a burning tree branch.

T.C. stared at the glowing wedding rings within the amber blade. "Love is a powerful thing," he said, cleaning the blade of black blood. "Thanks, ladies."

On the other side of the clearing, Dirtbag had run out of duct tape. His tattered denim body was barely holding together, and he was unable to react as fast as he had earlier. Bullet fire tore through the log he'd hidden behind, breaking apart his duct-tape bandaging. He was leaking clods of dark-brown dirt, lots of them, and that had never happened before. He was focused on refilling himself when, unexpectedly, the Gatling-Dragon howled. Dirtbag looked over to see the mangled corpse of General Bloodblivion on the ground and T.C. running to the rescue. The dragon went wild with grief over its slain master. It knocked the pulverized log out of the way and pressed its open jaw up against Dirtbag, spinning up the cannons. Dirtbag tried to fire his shotgun, but his arm could no longer support its weight. The dragon attacked at point-blank range. The barrage of bullets shredded Dirtbag's body, and he lost an arm. The dragon sliced off a dirt-filled leg with a scythe-like talon and cruelly watched as Dirtbag tried to crawl away. The dragon fired again, throwing the ragged denim man against a rock, and that was when Dirtbag realized, to his shock, he no longer had enough dirt inside to move.

"No!" T.C. yelled, running as fast as he could toward his friend. The distance between them was vast, and his quickness was hampered by the inconvenience of fatigue.

The Gatling-Dragon slowly stalked Dirtbag, knowing the half-empty, threadbare sack of dirt was helpless. T.C. shouted at him. Dirtbag looked over. A moat of molten metal blocked T.C.'s path. Dirtbag watched the rotary cannons spin up once more and was hurled through the air by the volley of bullets. He landed without limbs, his body wrecked.

Suddenly, the pied falconet appeared over the battlefield. She dived down from the sky, and as she did, she transformed in a flash of black light and feathers. A black-cloaked, pale young woman landed on her feet next to Dirtbag. She stood between him and the dragon, protecting him. The Gatling-Dragon spun up its cannons to fire, but the young woman held up her hand and, with one word, obliterated the dragon into ashes. She fell to her knees over Dirtbag, holding him.

"Dad!" she screamed hysterically. "Dad!"

"Dad?" T.C. said.

Dirtbag stirred in her arms.

"Dad!" she said happily. "How do you feel?"

"Old," Dirtbag whispered. "Worn out."

"Don't worry, Dad; I can sew." And she hugged him.

CHAPTER 21

———

Heavy rain fell outside of the Sarsaparilla Pizza Parlor Pub and Grill, a cozy establishment that had been built out of an old two-story-cabin boardinghouse. Inside, the tacky, rustic decor created a feeling of comforting warmth augmented by the gentle ambient heat emanating off the authentic brick oven in the kitchen. The wind fitfully whipped rain against the windows like handfuls of thrown pebbles. The unexpected storm had cut the usual lunch crowd in half, but it was a necessary rain, needed to put out the forest fire ignited by the Gatling-Dragon. Dirtbag's daughter had summoned the downpour shortly after her father was put together enough to walk. The atypical party of three sat in a crescent booth, with torn green cushions, around a cheap, wooden table, far away from the battlefield.

"Dad, T.C.'s staring at me again," Dirtbag's daughter said, annoyed, as she carefully reworked her stitching on his neck.

Dirtbag held still for her, sporting a wide grin on his face. "He doesn't mean you any harm, Loranna," he assured her.

"Gah! Don't call me that!"

"Well, that's your name."

"I hate that name so much; it sounds like Mom's name."

"Loranna is a very attractive name for a young woman," T.C. observed.

"Call me Rai. It's short for Rainelle," Rai said defiantly.

"Swell. Because you can ask the sky to rain and it does, right?" T.C. ribbed. "What's with the changing into a bird thing? Why didn't you just get yourself a driver's license? Then we'd have a car, and you wouldn't have to wear that crazy costume."

Rai gritted her teeth behind her purple-painted lips, irked. She was pale, not white, but a soft shade of corn silk, with bobbed, deftly styled black hair. A glowing strand of bright turquoise weaved through a length that hung over the right side of her face, which she had a habit of tucking behind her ornately pierced elfin ear. She wore a black leather bodysuit with ventilation slits strategically cut into it; knee-high, loose-fitting, black leather boots; a short but respectable pleated black leather skirt decorated with mottled black-and-white falcon feathers; and a close-fitting, cropped black leather top that left her shoulders exposed, helping to promote her cleavage. She kept most of herself concealed under a long, hooded black cloak, but that still didn't stop T.C. from staring at the crumpled pack of cigarettes tucked between her petite breasts.

Rai took a needle out of her mouth to lecture T.C. "I think more men should study art. Men tend to express their apprecia-tion of beauty sexually. They have to sleep with what they find beautiful; they don't understand how to appreciate things that are pleasing to the eye without desire. It's all right to look at me because you like what you see, but don't let me catch you desiring me, or you'll wish you hadn't." She narrowed her eyes at him and held her hand up like she did with the dragon. She snickered. "Just don't be a dirty old man, T.C.! Think of me as the daughter you never had."

This statement wounded T.C. inside, but he maintained his usual grin. "Whoa, you're just full of fire, aren't you? OK, so Dirt, he's my friend. Since you're his daughter, we're probably going to be spending a lot of time together—doing things and stuff—adventures, I mean." His rambling couldn't disguise his candor. "I've never had a daughter or any kids—that I know of."

A loud rip of duct tape interrupted his train of thought. "That… that just looks really bad, Dirt. You look like you're wearing a stained-glass window," he remarked, watching Dirtbag repair his mangled armor using glossy-black scraps of metal that had been blown off the Gatling-Dragon. "I mean, I'm sure we can find another blacksmith to help fix that."

"No," Dirtbag replied sharply. "No more blacksmiths, ever. These dragon bits are tough and light. That's as good a replacement as anything, and I don't care how bad it looks."

The peppy waitress arrived with their pizza and set it in the middle of the unvarnished table, passing around the cherry colas they had ordered. Rai finished up her work on Dirtbag, biting off the end of her thread. "There," she said in her small but feisty voice. "All done."

Dirtbag set the roll of duct tape aside and felt his neck to check her work. He was impressed by her skill. She told him she had sewn her entire outfit all by herself. Then, unexpectedly, she snuggled up next to him for a hug, and he was taken aback by her impromptu affection. "Hey! I…I thought you hated me," he said, gingerly patting her back.

"I did, Dad, for a long time," she sighed. "But when I got older and I fell in love for the first time on my own, I found out how difficult it is. It's complicated and confusing. You know true love when you find it, and it's always at the worst time, and it can turn your whole life upside down. I guess I just started to understand why you left. And… Mom's crazy."

"I'm sorry I wasn't there for you," Dirtbag said, combing through her hair with a denim hand. "I know saying that doesn't make up for anything."

"I went through some really bad times, Dad," she told him. "I learned everything the hard way, the wrong way."

"Well, didn't Katvanna take care of you?"

"Mom and I had a big disagreement, and she kicked me out when I was fifteen."

"What? Why would she do that?"

"Dad," Rai said, sitting up nervously. "I'm gay."

"Well, that changes nothing. You're still my daughter," Dirtbag said, softening his standard frown. "As long as you remember to use a condom."

"Dad!" she shouted, her face red with embarrassment. "It doesn't work that way."

"I like girls, too," T.C. said with a chuckle. "I've been married ten times."

"Oh?" Rai said skeptically. "And did you kidnap them?"

"No," T.C. replied, irritated. "I'm just good with my hands."

Rai was reviled. "Gah! Who is this goon with the sunglasses, Dad? What's his deal? He's got nicer hair than I do, and that's a problem, because I'm a girl."

"Now, wait just a minute. I don't color my hair or smoke, for starters," T.C. defended.

"Hey! Let's not fight." Dirtbag scowled at the two of them. "I haven't seen Loranna—Rai, for most of her life."

"Oats alive! You could've told me you had a daughter, Dirt!" T.C. grumbled. "I can't believe it never came up with all we've been through together."

"Are you kidding me? Look at the way you are with young women!"

T.C. slumped down in his seat, stung. Dirtbag offered him a slice of pizza. T.C. accepted it and began chewing. Rai pulled her hood over her head, covering her dark-blue eyes in shadow. Her hood had an unusual shape that vaguely resembled the feathery crest of a pied falconet. She sipped her soda and picked at her slice of pizza.

"Eat something; don't just peck at your food," Dirtbag told her. He paused. "That's not what I meant."

"I like being a bird, all right?" Rai said, quietly eating a little piece of cheese.

"You can't live off cigarettes alone," T.C. lightly chided.

"Gah! I get it, all right?" she said loudly. "Smoking is bad for you. These are herbal cigarettes. Yeah, I know they're bad, too, but if I want to smoke them, it's my choice. I don't need to be reminded of it. I don't do it all the time. Oh, just leave me alone."

"I don't think anyone can be considered alive without at least one bad habit," Dirtbag conceded. "I'm just glad you found us when you did."

"What took you so long to get here anyway? All you had to do was follow the wedding invitation I sent." Rai spoke as though she expected them to know what she was talking about.

"You mean that paper pigeon? *You* sent that?" Dirtbag thought for a moment. "I got mad and tore it apart and then decided to beat up the guy who made it, but that didn't exactly work out so well."

"You tore it up? I spent three days folding that thing—most of it—but, really? Oh, I knew you'd make this difficult somehow. At least Donny Brooke made sure you two got where the bird was supposed to lead you. I left a bunch of clues for you guys to follow the whole way, and you missed half of them."

"We're men, Rai; if you needed our help, you should've just asked us directly," T.C. rationalized. "I mean, clues? Half the time I don't know what I'm doing wrong anyway, until I get that look. Like the one you're giving me right now."

"Gah…" Rai rolled her eyes. She let out a long breath. "I guess I never thought you guys would spend so much time drinking and fooling around."

"It's called procrastination." Dirtbag combed back his grass-hair. "It's what you do when you're depressed."

T.C. was unfazed by the confession; he'd accepted their condition long ago. "Just how did you meet Donny Brooke, 'The Doomsday Machine'?"

Rai fidgeted a little. "Um, I used to date his daughter. He always said I was a bad influence, but we parted on good terms, and she even came to my wedding."

Dirtbag looked at her, stunned. "You got married?"

"Yeah, Dad." She smirked. "Her name was Jyn, but it didn't work out, so we got a divorce. I know, right? I guess it kind of runs in the family."

"You've lived your whole life without me."

"Don't worry, Dad. You didn't miss much. I'm still figuring out who I am."

"I've got bad news for you, kid," T.C. said, distancing himself from his initial attraction to her. "You may never fully understand who you are. Trust me; I've been working on that my whole life."

"So how did you meet my dad?"

"Our attorneys share the same office," he chuckled.

Dirtbag let out an uncomfortable breath and folded his hands together. "Loranna—" he began.

"Rai," she interrupted.

"Pumpkin," he continued. "Many years ago, Katvanna, your mother, my wife, came to where I was resting—"

"Where you killed yourself holding that girl?"

"Yes," Dirtbag groaned awkwardly.

"And she stole your heart? Yeah, I know, Dad. I wrote the invitation." Rai grinned mischievously. "What'd she do, chip it out of that big rock you turned into?"

"She's a powerful sorceress. Who knows?"

"Have you heard about this guy she met?"

"Rai, don't play games with us," T.C. advised. "We're angry old men, divorced and bitter. I mean, we've been trying to hit bottom for years, and it's a deep well. Trust me; there's nothing you can say that's going to shock us. Just start talking, and get it out there. Just fill us in."

Rai sipped her soda, trying to figure out where to begin. "So, do you remember how Mom was always kind of borderline? Well, when you married that princess, she crossed over. She went super evil, and, in a way, it was pretty cool for a while. She taught me all kinds of spells in the ancient tongue, all the secret words. But when you do those things—like cast a talking hemorrhoid plague on a city or make it so rats yodel—those kinds of things attract certain types of people. She dated some real freaks; I remember one guy even owned a comic-book shop. I know, right? This other guy was a chef, and I thought, cool, but then I found out he only cooked people. That's why I went vegan for a while. Then, this other time, she was having an affair with my English teacher; he dissed her new shoes, and she turned his feet into hooves. I was so embarrassed."

T.C. looked at Dirtbag and shook his head.

"She was great when I first met her," Dirtbag insisted, "though that wore off rather quickly."

"Because she changed, didn't she, Dirt?" T.C. inferred. "I don't know why they do that."

"Wait. What? They?" Rai questioned.

"I mean, change isn't always bad—as long as it's good." T.C. said hastily.

Dirtbag rubbed his face. "Pumpkin, one of the reasons we've been procrastinating is because if I find Katvanna, I think I'm going to kill her. She's gone too far."

"That's right, Rai." T.C. beamed. "Daddy's going to kill Mommy."

Rai laughed excitedly. Dirtbag and T.C. exchanged a worried glance. "I'm totally on board with that, Dad." She tried to lessen her glee. "I don't hate her—she is my mom—but I guess when you grow up, you go from idolizing your parents to seeing them as who they really are…And she's so sick and twisted these days."

"Hey, I don't know if I'm *actually* going to kill her." Dirtbag walked back his intentions. "Maybe I'll just find a nice switch and whip her good."

"Oh, I doubt you'll be doing that with her fancy fiancé around. He's from outer space. Don't forget, Dad, since you're legally dead now, she can marry whoever she wants."

"Rai," T.C. said, taking another wedge of pizza, "why don't you just tell us everything you know about this guy in the shortest, most attention-holding manner possible."

"She met a guy from space; he's a star, like the kind up in the sky. His name is Van Slice."

"Van Slice?" T.C. repeated. "Swell. I mean, why not Prince Bread?"

"Gah! I know, right? So he's an astrophysicist attorney. He understands how the sky works and handles cosmic litigations that threaten the laws of physics and stuff. He's big-time. He has attack-toos, tattoos that can come off his arms and attack people. He also wears this business suit of armor and can control gravity...I think because he's a star. He's a complete slimeball. He and Mom fell for each other instantly; they're both super evil, and they like doing evil things together, but he can't marry her, because he doesn't have an earth-heart. I think that's why Mom stole yours, Dad. Oh, he also has this spaceship that looks like an upside-down flying castle, and he owns a motorcycle."

Dirtbag and T.C. sat quietly, taking it all in.

"OK, this guy owns a spaceship and a motorcycle?" T.C. finally said, massaging his temples. "I mean, the odds of that must be *astronomical*, right?" he snickered bitterly. "Never trust a squid!" he declared, sitting back. Rai glanced at Dirtbag, confused. "Oats alive!" T.C. shouted. He called the waitress over. "What's the strongest drink you have?"

The waitress thought. "Homemade moonshine distilled from cough syrup and antifreeze."

"Bring me one of those."

"Sure thing, hon. I'll get the waiver."

Dirtbag cleared his throat and shifted in his seat. "Just how did she meet a guy from outer space?"

"Oh! I heard it was at this black magic orgy; he—"

"That's all. That's it. Don't tell me any more, because it doesn't matter," Dirtbag said, holding up his hands to stop her.

"So he's a space attorney?" T.C. asked, trying to follow. "And he's a star?"

Rai nodded, picking a little more off her pizza. "And he glows."

"All over?"

"No, he only glows from the inside out. You know, his eyes, ears, mouth, and fingernails. The rest looks normal, but he's really tan. It doesn't look natural, like he bathed in gold caramel. He might glow other places, too, but I try not to think about that."

"Whoa, there's a full-moon joke in there somewhere," T.C. quipped.

"Anything else, Pumpkin?" Dirtbag asked.

"He said he's from Sirius."

The waitress set a large jug on the table, along with a straw. T.C. signed the waiver. He picked up the straw. "Since when are these made of wood?"

"Uh, since always," Rai said.

"It's commonplace, like ketchup sauce on pizza." Dirtbag gave T.C. a look.

"Sirius! See!" T.C. promptly continued, sipping from the jug of moonshine with the wooden straw. "The ancients were right. That star can't be trusted!"

"Katvanna can't take my heart and give it to some scumbag attorney from space," Dirtbag growled, growing angry. "I can't believe I have to deal with this! I guess it's what I deserve for leaving her the way I did. I was a terrible, selfish husband; I should've just stuck with that witch and died early of a heart attack."

"That's awful!" Rai cringed.

"Don't worry, Pumpkin; I would've somehow made it to at least your first wedding, but after that, dead. As quick as I could go, too."

"That's not funny. You're all I've got left, Dad."

Dirtbag's eyeless, denim-pocket gaze looked at her as caringly as an eyeless, denim-pocket gaze could. He let a long breath out. "How are we going to hunt down my ex and some scumbag from space with an upside-down flying castle before they destroy the world?"

T.C. and Rai looked confused. "Dirt, what makes you think they're going to destroy the world?" T.C. asked.

"Didn't you say that?" Dirtbag looked at Rai.

She shook her head. "It's all right, Dad. Heroes don't always have to save the world; sometimes, it's just, you know, personal."

"Well, that's true, but let's pretend that we need to save the world anyway. I think more people will help us if we tell them that than if we say I'm trying to stop my ex-wife from being happy."

T.C. hiccupped. "I dunno, it depends. Nobody wants to see their ex happy. I mean, the divorce rate is like fifty-five or seventy percent or whatever; that's a lot of angry people out there who can help us." T.C. waved his hand in front of his face to make sure he wasn't going blind.

Dirtbag groaned. "We still need to find her."

"I know where she is, Dad," Rai confessed. "Gah! I know my whole trail-of-bread-crumbs thing totally failed, and I guess, in a way, it was a stupid idea, but I was just afraid to talk to you, Dad. I wasn't sure how you'd react. You seemed so angry."

Dirtbag swallowed. "I am angry, Pumpkin, but it's not your fault."

"Dirt's a good man," T.C. slurred. "Or whatever he is. He's got nice, earthy breath. Trust me, the fresher the breath, the greater the subterfuge. I mean, when you think about it, mint in itself is a lie." T.C. blew out an intoxicated sigh. "I'm just really tired of walking."

Rai thought for a second. "I know where some Mustangs are; maybe we could wrangle one."

"As long as the seats are leather. It's like I told my ex: I don't do vinyl." T.C.'s head suddenly hit the table with a thud. He had completely passed out. Dirtbag and Rai sat in uncomfortable silence for a minute.

"Would you like some ice cream?" Dirtbag sheepishly asked her. He sighed. He didn't know his own daughter anymore.

"I'm too old for that, Dad," she said with regret that so much time had passed. "I'm not a little girl anymore. I'm all grown up."

"I can see that." He pushed his soda around. "Well, here we are. What do normal people do? Normal families, I mean?"

She didn't know any normal people, and neither did Dirtbag, so they sat there as the rain poured outside. She scooted closer to him. He put his arm around her, and for the moment, everything was all right; they were together.

CHAPTER 22

———

Rai yawped cautiously as she soared through the bright, cornflower-blue, cloudless sky. She circled high above Dirtbag and T.C. as they crawled through the tall, citrine-hued prairie grass to the edge of an uneven cliff that overlooked a flourishing valley where a herd of Mustangs congregated. They watched as the vibrantly colored Mustangs raced up and down a straightaway, tearing up the sod, honking their horns excitedly, and revving their noisy engines. No other land animals were as fast as these beasts. Capturing a wild one was very difficult and extraordinarily dangerous.

"Grassaline," Dirtbag said. "The whole valley is covered with it. No wonder the herd is so large."

T.C. covered his mouth and nose with a thick rag to filter out the toxic fumes permeating the air. "Whoa, my eyes." He coughed. "We can't risk using weapons or spells. I mean, we don't want to spark a fire down there, right?"

The Mustangs ran circles around each other, rode on two wheels, and spun doughnuts into the oily grassaline, until, at last, the stallion, a souped-up Mustang Boss, cruised through the herd, bringing them to order. The stallion was old and scuffed, with dark, burgundy-tinted windows. Rust had taken hold around his chrome wheel wells, and his once-magnificent coat of midnight-black paint had begun to oxidize. He was a boisterous twelve cylinder, and it sounded as though he'd lost his muffler years ago, possibly during a mating duel. The stallion's imposing growl reverberated through the valley, warning away competitors. The herd settled into grazing the hydrocarbon-enriched grassaline, not the least bit aware they were being studied.

"OK, Dirt, what color should we get?"

"I don't care about the color; I care about not getting run over," Dirtbag said, watching the Mustangs peacefully graze. "We'll never catch a V-8; we'll have to focus on the V-6s."

"A convertible will be easier to get into."

"Well, I see only two of those. The yellow one keeps speeding up and down the cliff face with its high beams on; it could be diseased. The red one looks docile enough, and it's moving in our direction. If we can get to it while the stallion is on the other end, we might have a chance."

T.C. chuckled nervously. "You ever done this before, Dirt?"

"No, you?"

"I saw it done at a rodeo once. Three clowns died."

Rai flew over, swooping low, calling to them. T.C. looked at Dirtbag, confused. "Do you even know what she's saying?"

Dirtbag waved animatedly to get Rai's attention and pointed sternly to the ground. Rai landed, transforming into a young woman in a flash of black light and feathers. "Didn't you guys hear me?" she asked.

"Hey, all I heard were crazy bird noises," Dirtbag griped.

Rai folded her arms, frustrated. "Gah! Fine! I was saying that I think we should go after that red convertible."

"We were thinking the same thing, Pumpkin."T.C. grinned.

"No. I'm sorry, T.C. No. Only Dad can call me Pumpkin, all right? You have to stick with Rai, or miss, or Your Highness."

"Swell. She's all yours, Dirt; I'll just wait over here, like a complete stranger."

Dirtbag rubbed his face. "Your Highness?"

Rai narrowed her eyes. "I don't want him to call me Pumpkin, Dad; it's weird."

T.C. walked back over with a smirk. "I'm just kidding, Rai; it's just so easy to get a reaction out of you."

"Dad!"

"Hey, you two." Dirtbag combed back his grass-hair, aggravated. He looked at them both, his staunch gaze challenging them to behave. "Let's hear the big plan, Rai."

She reached into her little black leather purse and handed some items to Dirtbag. "All right. The only way to tame a Mustang, or any car for that matter, is to make an ignition key. This is a blank key I borrowed from Van Slice, along with a few of his prized locksmithing tools. I'll go harass the stallion so it'll follow me, and then, Dad, you jump into the front seat of the convertible and start making a key while T.C. distracts it."

"That's a fantastic plan," T.C. ridiculed. "I don't even have a lasso. Me and Dirt are just going to run down there into that herd of wild cars? I mean, have you ever heard of reckless endangerment?"

"Pumpkin?" Dirtbag asked, ignoring T.C. "How are you going to harass that stallion?"

"I'm a bird, Dad. I'm going to, you know, drop on it."

"That's dignified," T.C. jeered.

Rai rolled her eyes. "Gah! Do you have to be so difficult?"

"That's just part of my charm." T.C. grinned, enjoying annoying her. "I mean, first you hate it, and then you can't get enough."

"Gross! Have it your way, you big goon," she said, not actually annoyed in the least. "So, you'll need these." She handed T.C. earplugs. "Dad? Do you want any?" She held out her palm in offering.

"I don't have ears, Pumpkin."

"Ew. But how do you hear?"

"In stereo, mostly."

"He's dirt," T.C. chuckled. "I'm hollow, and you turn into a bird. I mean, we all have things we have to live with. I just hope you're not too stopped up from all that cheese."

"Oh, I'm sure your charm could loosen up any woman," Rai scorned and flew away.

T.C. turned to Dirtbag after she was out of earshot. "Are you sure we can trust her, Dirt? We only met her yesterday."

Dirtbag watched his daughter fly off into the sky as a pied falconet. "Hey, I don't completely trust anyone, but she hasn't done anything yet that would make me not trust her, and you saw what she did to that dragon."

"I did, and I mean, that's the problem. If she really is that powerful, why does she need us? I feel like she's planned out our whole journey already. Why doesn't she just fly down there and vaporize that stallion?"

"Well, that would be excessively cruel, don't you think? Those Mustangs are just living their lives. They're not war machines, and she doesn't seem like the hateful type."

"But why does she need us, Dirt?"

"You know, sometimes the only person you can turn to who won't judge you for what you've done is a parent. Good parents—not the bad ones like her wicked mother. If she has no one left in her life to turn to but me, her dirtbag father, she must be in a lot of trouble. She probably doesn't trust us either."

They stared down into the valley of feeding Mustangs. T.C. sighed, thinking. "OK, how should we do this? Should we surprise it?"

"Maybe I should dance," Dirtbag said sarcastically.

"Yeah...that just might work."

The red Mustang convertible's engine idled quietly as it tore large clumps of grassaline from the ground with its mouth. It chewed slowly, oblivious that Dirtbag and T.C. were crawling toward it from behind the overgrown bushes near the base of the cliff. The Mustang moved closer to them, lured by a patch of newly sprouted grassaline. Suddenly, Dirtbag sprang out and did the dirt seizure. The Mustang recoiled in fright, and its horn beeped frantically. T.C. threw himself on the hood to muffle the sound. The Mustang shifted into reverse, trying to buck him off. The doors flapped open and closed in a commotion of sound and panic that immediately drew the attention of the old stallion. Dirtbag circled the bucking car, trying to find a moment he could jump inside it, inadvertently getting too close. The Mustang charged him. The front bumper hit Dirtbag in the legs, sending him tumbling over T.C., across the windshield, and into the backseat.

"Screee!" yelled Rai from above the advancing Mustang Boss stallion. She really needed a cigarette to help her relax, but there was no time; the stallion was speeding toward the red Mustang, and the rest of the herd was stampeding out of the valley, led by the alpha mare. Rai dove down in front of the stallion, intent on making a delivery, and the result was spectacular. The stallion had been traveling so fast that when she struck, her effort streaked across the entire hood, covering the precious last remaining patch of unoxidized, youthful midnight-black paint with filth. She flew away, yawping out a laugh that filled the stallion with insane rage. It turned and chased after her.

Dirtbag sat up in the backseat; he touched his neck, realizing he'd popped a stitch. "Hey! T.C.! Are you good?"

T.C. held tightly to the front of the red Mustang as it spun, bucked, and kicked. His long hair whipped about like a flag in the wind. "I just finished duct-taping my hand down, Dirt; there's no way I'm coming off," he shouted over the roaring V-6. "But we better hurry; I mean, her engine's getting really hot. We don't want her to overheat."

Dirtbag tossed himself into the driver's seat and slid under the steering wheel, wedging his body beneath the dashboard. He started fitting the ignition key, filing the teeth as fast as he could. The Mustang did a 360 on two wheels; the radio turned on and assaulted him with deep bass thumps that shook the roots of his grass-hair. The doors periodically opened and slammed shut as the car sped around, trying to knock them off. Half the air vents were heating him up, while the other half ran ice-cold air conditioning across his hands. He felt the Mustang sail through the air and land with a loud bang, bucking wildly as it skidded through the tall grassaline. T.C. yelled out from the hood that he was still OK but had accidentally swallowed a vole.

Rai dodged a tire iron thrown from the stallion's trunk. The stallion chased her from one end of the valley to the other. She made sure to keep it away from the red Mustang. The angry Mustang Boss flexed its hood and shot out a venomous stream of hot motor oil. She avoided it with a barrel roll and glanced behind her to mock the old car with a flippant squawk, but when she turned back around a tree was directly in front of her. She rammed into it and fell to the ground, transforming back into a young woman. She sat with her knees together in a bed of dandelions, holding her head, surrounded by mottled feathers and parachuting seeds. The stallion was right behind her. She turned to face it, angry, and held up her hand, but just as it was about to reach her, she took flight. The old Mustang's brakes locked up, and it struck the tree with a damaging crunch. Rai landed beside it as a human, concerned that it was hurt.

Dirtbag tried pushing the key into the ignition; it almost fit. He filed a tooth down a little more and pushed it in again. Success! He scrambled into the driver's seat and buckled himself in. He carefully put his foot on the brake and turned the ignition; the Mustang shuddered and then grew calmer. Dirtbag turned the stereo off. He slowed the car down, speaking to it softly as he petted the dashboard, reassuring it that everything was fine.

T.C. cut his hand free of the duct tape and climbed into the passenger seat. His hair was a mess. "Oats alive, that was a chore," he said, taking out his hairbrush.

"What's she doing over there?" Dirtbag wondered aloud, watching his daughter.

Rai gently touched the crushed, soiled hood of the old Mustang and whispered a word. The hood creaked and popped back into shape, spotless. The stallion slowly backed up from the tree and gingerly moved close to Rai's leg, its V-12 purring, thanking her for her kindness. When Dirtbag drove the red Mustang over to pick her up, the stallion reacted aggressively. She caressed it and explained they needed the Mustang. The reason did not entirely sit well with the machine, but after a hood-to-hood good-bye nuzzle with the convertible, the stallion cruised away in the direction the herd had fled, stopping briefly to honk farewell. T.C. got into the back, and Rai took his place in the passenger seat. She looked saddened that they were taking the red Mustang away from its home.

"That's life, Pumpkin," Dirtbag said, patting her head. "Right and wrong, those are just things we will into being to make ourselves feel better. Life is gray; you can only do what you hope is best."

"I mean, it's not like we could've walked up to that beast and just made friends with it some other way," T.C. said, cleaning dirt off his sunglasses. "It's a wild animal. It was doing what it felt had to be done, and I guess it realized we were, too."

A few tears rolled down Rai's cheeks. Dirtbag and T.C. looked at each other for guidance, but there was none to be shared. They both inched closer to Rai, trying to be supportive.

"I'm all right," she insisted.

"But you look upset, Pumpkin," Dirtbag said.

"My life is a mess, Dad, and I just want everything to work out."

"Well, things typically don't work out on their own; you have to go do something about it and make it happen, make it better."

"Dad, I have to tell you something." She looked up with tears in her eyes. "Mom took my heart, too."

"I—I didn't realize, Pumpkin. You seem so full of emotion."

"I know…It's been weird without my heart. I guess, in a way, it's confusing to care and to know that I care—to know it in my mind—and have that other half, my heart, missing. I want to say I feel things, but they're not the same. It's all dull; nothing is bright and sharp, like I've forgotten the details. It hurts, Dad, in a really strange way."

Dirtbag looked at T.C. again, but all T.C. could do was encourage him to hug his daughter, because there was nothing that could really be said. Dirtbag put his arm around Rai and held her close.

"She said I didn't deserve it because of the way I am," Rai whimpered. Dirtbag's grip on her tightened. "Dad, you're squeezing me!"

"Sorry, Pumpkin, it's just, your mother…" He let go of her and tried to breathe out his anger. "Tell me what I need to know; don't sit there, keeping secrets."

"You promise you won't be mad?"

"I'm mad already."

"After you left, Mom destroyed her heart to increase her powers. So now, in order to marry Van Slice, she needs a pair of hearts, and after I found out what she did to you and told her she was wrong, she decided to just take mine, too. I don't think they even love each other; it's more like an alliance."

"Why did you marry this woman again?" T.C. asked, confused.

"I know, right?" Rai said.

Dirtbag wrestled with his temper. "She wasn't like this when we first met; in fact, she was great. She changed after we had Rai. I can't believe how bad she's gotten. How can she live without a heart? I can't stand the absence of mine, and I can't believe she destroyed hers for even more power than she already had. How egotistical can a person be?"

T.C. threw back his restored hair. "Anyone up for a cheeseburger?"

Dirtbag and Rai looked back at T.C., speechless.

"OK, I mean, I've been through ten divorces. I have all kinds of curses. Sure, a lot of it's my fault—maybe all of it's my fault, but when life gets you down, the best way to ride through those tough times is to bury yourself in the warm embrace of a cheeseburger. A burger can't blame you; it can't hate you or yell threats against your manhood. All it can be is delicious."

"Cool," Rai said with a sniff. The Mustang's glove box suddenly popped open, and inside was a box of tissues.

CHAPTER 23

The red Mustang convertible bounded over the top of a hill, hanging for a moment in the air with its wheels spinning and then landing with a thud on the paved road, kicking up a cloud of dust. The engine revved enthusiastically with a cheerful whinny. T.C. picked up his spilled tub of vinegar-soaked garlic french fries from his lap, a task made easier by the peculiar absence of ketchup as a condiment. It may have been too soon to let the Mustang drive by itself, but it was following the road and they were making good time. He leisurely dug out another wrapped cheeseburger from a large white paper bag with a blue castle logo on the side. The Mustang leapt over another hilltop. The landing knocked the unopened burger out of his hand, and the subsequent full-throttle acceleration sent the sandwich tumbling under the driver's seat, beyond his reach.

"Well, are you going to get that?" Dirtbag asked with his mouth full of food.

"It'll work itself out; trust me. I mean, I'm not going to tear apart this car just to dig out a burger, especially when there are more in the bag. Besides, look how happy the Mustang is." T.C. held on tight to the door handle as the car took a sharp corner without slowing down, wheels squealing with delight. "What do you think, Rai?"

Rai was spread out in the backseat, lying on her back, watching the clouds in the sky pass by as she slowly ate her cheeseburger. The sun shone down on her black clothing, and she soaked up its warm embrace. Her bootless, pale feet dangled over the side of the Mustang, feeling the air as it rushed between her toes.

"Rai?" T.C. repeated, glancing in the rearview mirror. "Whoa, neon-orange nail polish? That's the last color I'd expect of someone who wears so much black."

Rai sat up, hiding her feet. "So? What color are *your* toenails, T.C.? Probably a dark-yellow-fungus mustard with a smell like a yogurt factory that went out of business."

"*Hey!*" Dirtbag snarled. "I'm trying to eat here."

"But he started it," Rai protested.

"Did not!" T.C. responded instinctually. "OK, maybe I did, or did I? Forget it. There's no use arguing with women."

"Oh, you can argue with me, but you're wrong," Rai reasoned.

"See what I mean, Dirt?"

Rai wrinkled her nose up in disdain. Dirtbag finished his cheeseburger and tossed the paper wrapper out the window. Rai was horrified and started talking about the environment. Dirtbag just nodded. "I hope we're heading in the right direction," he said, changing the subject.

"What? Well, we are," Rai said positively. "This road will take us all the way to the sea, where my ex lives."

"Uh oh," T.C. groaned.

"Jyn is really nice; she is. She's a mechanical engineer. She knows cars, and she can make them fly by adding dragon parts."

"Oats alive!" T.C. declared. "I've fought both dragons and exes, and those are not forces to take lightly. The last time I asked an ex for a favor the sky turned black and the dead started shooting out of their graves claiming I owed back taxes. And see these?" He showed her the dragon teeth around his neck. "I pulled them out with my bare hands. I'm sure you can imagine how I ended up in a dragon's mouth."

"You were making out with it?" Rai sneered.

T.C. threw a handful of french fries at her; she squeaked and dodged the attack. Dirtbag prevented any further escalation by sternly holding up his hand between them. "T.C. does have a point," Dirtbag granted.

"But I'm not you guys. Jyn and I didn't have a war. It—well—I guess it wasn't meant to be, and we both knew it." Rai sipped her chocolate milk shake. "But she's always been there for me when I needed her, as long as I've asked nicely."

"The last time I asked 'nicely' I had to see a doctor about a crab claw growing out of—someplace, and—" T.C. shook his head and groaned. "OK, look, why don't you just fly on ahead and smooth things over before we get there?" he suggested.

"Because it's a long way. I'm nervous enough already with the whole Mom thing, and I guess…I feel safer with you guys."

Dirtbag's brow arched skeptically. "Pumpkin, you blew up a dragon; nobody is going to mess with you."

"Gah! Dad! I'm feeling really vulnerable inside, all right? I can do things, but I don't want to do them alone, you know? I'm kind of scared."

"Pumpkin, look, T.C. and I are both degenerate, hypocritical scumbags," Dirtbag admitted.

"So? I'm not perfect either, Dad."

"Hey, did you hear what I said? I'm not called Dirtbag just for being dirt in a bag. T.C. and I have tried to be heroes, and sometimes we are, but most of the time our good intentions get engulfed by that gray area I told you about."

She was quiet for a moment. "Dad, what is T.C. short for?" she asked.

"Tuna Casserole," T.C. answered. "I poisoned my ex-wife's father with one because I found out he beat her when she was young. I mean, I think that was the first and last time I actually cooked a casserole, too. Turned out she loved her father more than she hated him, so I got divorced and cursed, and here I am."

"But that's terrible; it sounds like you tried to do the right thing, I guess, in a way."

"Sometimes what's right is a matter of perspective." T.C. exhaled. "It's like your father said: life is gray."

Dirtbag handed T.C. the rum bottle, and he took a long drink from it.

"Uh, any chance I can get some of that?" Rai asked.

"I dunno," T.C. said. "What do you think, Dirt?"

"No," Dirtbag replied immediately, "she already smokes."

Rai leaned forward and snatched the bottle out of T.C.'s grasp. Dirtbag tried to grab it back, but his greasy denim hands couldn't get a grip. Rai gulped down a mouthful. "Gah! Nasty! This stuff is so gross!" She made a sour face. "It's unbearably bitter."

"Well, after a while you get used to it," Dirtbag said, taking the bottle away from her. "That's why you shouldn't drink it. When you stop tasting how bad it is, you'll start feeling the way we do: indifferent." He took a drink, corked the bottle, and put it away. He looked at Rai and sighed. "You should've told me what Katvanna did earlier."

"I know…but I couldn't dump all my problems on you at once. I wasn't sure if you were the same."

"Hey, I'm not the same; I'm a big bag of dirt!"

"If that's what you want to believe, then fine. But I watched you guys for days, and you're still my dad. Even if you're dirt, I still see you in there."

T.C. snapped a look at Dirtbag and handed him a gold coin.

"Wait! What just happened?" Rai frowned.

"Dirt and I had a little bet."

"You made a bet over my feelings?" she asked, disgusted.

Dirtbag and T.C. chuckled.

"Don't laugh! That's awful!"

"Hey, hold on." Dirtbag forced a straight face. "We're not laughing at you; we just like your reaction."

"You what? Did you two really have a bet, or did T.C. just hand you that coin for no reason?"

The Mustang suddenly jammed on its brakes, throwing them forward as it skidded to a stop. Rai picked herself up off the floor of the backseat. T.C. pried his face out of the driver's side air vent, gingerly touching the strange grid mark it left on his forehead. Dirtbag calmly plucked a fry off the dashboard, blew some filth off it, and ate it. He was the only one wearing a seat belt. "Great." He chewed. "It's a troll booth."

The Mustang whinnied.

"A troll what?" Rai said, picking fries out of her hair.

In the middle of the road was a moss-covered castle turret with a large, rectangular window and a huge oak-log gate arm blocking their way. A door on the side of the turret slammed open, and a tall, morbidly obese, wart-covered green creature stepped out wearing a crisp white dress shirt, a black tie, and pleated, black chain-mail dress pants. He produced a clipboard crammed to its breaking point with multicolored official documents and began writing down a description of the Mustang.

"So we pay the toll, and that's it?" Rai asked.

T.C. rubbed his head. "It's just not that easy, Rai. Trolls are very procedural. That clipboard he's holding is admissible in court and could be used against me by one of my exes or the Guild of Attorneys to request an audit, and I'm not sure I can withstand one of those."

"All right, so what do we do?"

"We just have to lie our way through. We're broke, we stole this food, the Mustang was a gift—things like that, just as long as he hears enough to fill up his paper work with gibberish that can't be used against us. I mean, the more confusing we are, the better."

"Well, that shouldn't be a problem," Dirtbag said. "You and I are unfaithful men, so understandably we are practiced liars, and Rai, well, she's a woman, so lying comes naturally."

"Dad!" she objected.

T.C. chuckled. "Trust me; he meant that with the utmost respect for your skill."

"Gah!" Rai leaned back, coyly turning away so they couldn't see her smile.

The troll casually walked up to the side of the Mustang, scribbling away details, flipping between different colored forms to check regulations, and eyeing them suspiciously. He paused for a moment;

something was missing. He reached in his pocket, pulled out his Troll Collection Agency badge, and clipped it to his belt. The badge was circular, with an etching of a bridge showering money onto a troll in an office cubicle beneath it. A name was inscribed on the front. It read: "Bill."

"And what's wrong with *him?*" Bill barked in a voice that sounded like someone belching through a cardboard tube. They smirked but were careful not to laugh at him. Bill asked again, pointing at Dirtbag.

"We're a family," T.C. said, choosing his words carefully. "I'm Uncle Tuna, and that's Grandpa Jeans. As you can see, he's old as dirt, and that's my brother's adopted daughter, Birdy. She's one of those special-needs kids."

"What?" Rai whispered furiously.

"Hey, it's my birthday tomorrow!" Dirtbag said loudly, hunching over to appear feeble. "I'm getting a hernia. A hernia! The doc said it was a surprise, but I have to wait until after the marathon for the operation. He's a dentist."

Bill scribbled across his clipboard, trying to keep up, holding his pen the same way a child holds a crayon. He waddled around the Mustang. "And what's the carbon footprint of this vehicle?" he demanded.

"I think it's a size twelve wide," T.C. told him confidently.

"Uh-huh, size twelve tires?"

"Actually, those aren't tires; they're sandals. You see we're just on our way to the lake."

"And which lake would that be?"

"The big lake, the ocean. We heard cucumbers are plentiful out that way."

"And do you plan on fishing?"

"We plan to eat rocks; Birdy needs to put on a little weight, so she doesn't blow away in the winter."

"And how will you get over the barrier wall?"

"Now, wait just a minute. We're not going all the way there; we're just going to get close enough to catch the salty mist that blows off the top, so we can flavor our drinks."

"Yay, margaritas for everyone," Rai cheered sarcastically.

"That's one of her special needs." Dirtbag glanced at her. "She also needs to be quiet."

Rai folded her arms.

Bill nodded, flipping through his forms, writing feverishly.

"Special needs, uh-huh," Bill said. "And Grandpa Jeans has no eyes?"

"He has a great smile," T.C. assured, "but we're trying to get that fixed. I mean, he only recently learned how to play the piano backward using golf clubs and a kazoo."

"And can you explain that mess of fries in the front seat?"

"Those just grew out of the air conditioner when we tuned the radio to the frequency of desire. All they need is a little ketchup."

Bill abruptly stopped writing and put his hands on his fat hips. "Ketchup on fries? You think you're really fooling me, huh?" he said, disgusted. "Nobody wants to pay taxes or tolls, but they all want the roads to not have potholes and be free of vampires. Those services cost money. Uh-huh, uh-huh, and I can't let you pass without paying something. You have to pay."

"Anything?" Rai asked. T.C. cringed and braced himself.

"Something!" Bill repeated.

"We don't have any money"—she fluttered her eyelashes at him, not very convincingly, but she was trying—"but I could pay you with a kiss."

"Uh-huh," Bill sputtered, adjusting his tie uncomfortably. "I suppose that would be acceptable, but it would have to be off the record, of course."

"Oh!" Rai gasped. "But what about the roads?"

"Uh, I'll just overcharge the next guy."

"Come over here." Rai smiled daintily, luring him next to the car, melting the big troll's heart. "I'm a little shy, so you have to close your eyes, all right?"

Bill closed his eyes; she put two fingers together, licked the tips, and tapped the troll's cheek while making a kissing sound. Bill's lids opened, his eyes rolled up, and he grinned bashfully. He tore the half-filled-out forms from his clipboard and handed them to her, completely love struck. The oak gate arm swung open. Rai urged T.C. to get going while they had the chance.

As they sped away, Dirtbag turned around and gave Rai the gold coin. "You deserve it, Pumpkin," he told her. "You turned out all right. You're smart and clever and brave."

Rai took the coin and put it in her purse, not revealing how much it meant to her to hear her father say that.

CHAPTER 24

———

Dirtbag sat slumped on the concrete curb of Argyle's Essential Accoutrements and Assorted Appliances, a hardware store, sipping coffee from a plastic bag with a wooden straw. He had told the pimply know-it-all manager they were out of coffee cups and had been promptly handed the bag to hold his beverage. Rai and T.C. were busy unpacking a brand-new, six-foot-long lumberjack chainsaw from its box. They had pulled over just outside of Cogcinnati for a break before entering the city. Traffic was sparse. Occasionally the natural serenity of the landscape was interrupted by people stopping in to use the restrooms; otherwise it was quiet.

Dirtbag absent-mindedly picked at his worn-out, heavily patched denim skin, methodically searching for white flowers that might be growing just below the surface. He watched his daughter with profound guilt from having not been there for her, and there were those other things, things that could never be fixed, only missed. His picking seemed rhythmic, almost mechanical, as though he were restitching the same torn seams over and over again.

"I see you thinking, Dirt. Don't let yourself fall into a rut," T.C. advised.

"Don't dwell, Dad; it's not healthy." Rai tucked her hair behind her ears.

Dirtbag scowled at them but knew they were right. "Give me a couple minutes to put my thoughts away."

"Dad, are you drinking out of a bag?" Rai asked, her nose wrinkling.

"It's coffee, Pumpkin. The worst part is it's not that bad."

He looked at Rai, his daughter, and smiled. She saw but pretended she hadn't. T.C. directed her to pay attention as they lifted the chainsaw out of its box and gently set it on top of the Mustang's hood. The car snorted nervously, unsure of what was going on. Rai stood beside the chainsaw with her hands on her hips, disapproving. T.C. waved for her to step closer. "OK, Rai, can you do it or not?" he asked.

"Yeah, but it feels wrong, like really wrong."

"You see that?" T.C. pointed down the road at the expansive, writhing metropolis before them. Buildings were shifting and moving as if in a state of constant transformation. "That's the machine city of Cogcinnati, one of the largest cities on the planet. The entire city is just one gigantic mechanism, home to about fifteen million people. I always wanted to see that place. I mean, there's a café in there called Schmousse that serves butterscotch marshmallow pie." He paused to think about the pie. "But we don't have time for that, do we?"

"I know…" Rai sighed, also thinking about the pie. "The last I heard, Mom was getting married at the start of the next lunar eclipse, and I think that's pretty soon."

"Hmm," T.C. said, flipping through an advanced copy of the pocket edition of Father Raygun's almanac, the *Raymanac*. "That's just two weeks from now, if this book is accurate. It certainly has enough coupons in it. I mean, how much cheese can a man eat?"

Dirtbag walked over, drinking from his bag of coffee and feeling better. "Well," he said with his usual growl, "it should only take a day to speed through Cogcinnati with a chainsaw on the hood. People will be diving out of our way, fleeing for their lives, instead of ignoring yet another car horn."

"But, Dad, couldn't we…oh, I don't know…"

"Pumpkin, what do you have against putting a chainsaw on a Mustang anyway? I thought you liked heavy metal?"

"Gah! Just because I wear black doesn't mean I listen to that stuff, all right?"

"Well, what do you like then?"

"Boy bands," she said guiltily.

"Oats alive!" T.C. snarled.

Rai frowned. "This car is a living creature; you guys can't just attach a chainsaw to it."

Dirtbag and T.C. looked at each other; both remembered Muffin and grinned for a moment before the memory of her sudden, tragic end caused the grins to fade. T.C. angled the chainsaw's blade to sit forty-five degrees off the front edge of the hood.

"OK, Rai, let's make it happen."

Rai mumbled discontentedly as she placed her hands on both the Mustang and the chainsaw. She petted the hood gently and whispered to the car in a language it understood. "Vah-room. Vroom," she said soothingly.

"That's just bullcookies," T.C. scoffed.

"Oh? Is it? Excuse me, Tuna; do you speak car? Are you an empowered, magical being that can destroy dragons with a single word?"

"Now, wait just a minute; I can make a grilled cheese sandwich on any surface."

"Yeah right. The only thing you ever cooked up was that toxic casserole!"

"I cook…things. I mean, OK, I'm a divorced man, but I can cook stuff and things."

Dirtbag ran his hand over his face. Rai snickered and closed her eyes to concentrate. She whispered an ancient incantation. The chainsaw sank into the hood of the Mustang, fusing it to the car. A red ignition button, with the silhouette of a chainsaw on it, popped up on the dashboard next to the air-conditioner knob. Rai stepped back, both pleased with her work and disgusted at what she'd created. "Yay, that looks completely disturbing. Oh, and it's removable, just so you know."

T.C. stared at the blasphemous combination in awe. "I dub thee Sawstang," he said, slowly petting the car. The Sawstang throttled its engine, starting up the chainsaw. The chainsaw revved loudly in tune with the engine. People that had been standing around outside of the hardware store, watching, quickly fled, fearful of what might happen next.

"Hey, are you sure that's the biggest one they had?" Dirtbag ridiculed.

"What matters is it's loud and looks insane," T.C. said, stuffing the box it came in into a nearby plastic trash can, breaking the lid. "I mean, nobody is going to stand in the way of this, unless they're crazy, and then that's their problem."

Rai scooped a bale of grassaline into the Sawstang's mouth. It reacted happily and methodically chewed the food. The V-6 engine suddenly began to knock and bang.

"Pumpkin, did you get the premium plus?" Dirtbag asked, listening to the engine thump.

"Yeah!" Rai insisted.

"Hey! Is that a new pack of cigarettes between your, your"—Dirtbag became flustered—"your tomatoes?"

"My *tomatoes*? Dad!" She stomped her foot. "I don't have any pockets, you know."

"Well, what do you keep in that little purse of yours?"

"Woman things. You know, things women need to be women."

Dirtbag scowled at the answer, unwilling to probe further. The car banged and shook. T.C. stroked the hood, trying to calm the beast. Her tires dug into the ground, the metal body flexed and strained, and suddenly there was a loud crunch. The engine rattled, struggling to keep running, but as it struggled, it became stronger and stronger, until the sound of a powerful V-8 roared to life.

"Oats alive!" T.C. shouted. "She's older than we thought! She just grew her second set of cylinders!" He leaned down and hugged the Sawstang, kissing it lovingly. The car purred under him, revving louder than ever before. "Oh, my baby!" he cooed.

"Hey, make sure you keep that platonic," Dirtbag warned. "Don't traumatize that car."

"Gah!" Rai said, disgusted. She turned to her father. "See, Dad? I spent the money on premium plus."

"But what about those cigarettes?"

"I stole them," she said matter-of-factly.

Dirtbag gripped a handful of his grass-hair. "Why would you do that? I may not have been around when you were growing up, but I'm here now, and my daughter does not need to steal. Go back in there, tell them what you did, and pay for them." He handed her more than enough money to do so, irritated that she had done such a thing.

"Fine, but what if they want to press charges?"

"Are you kidding me? You tell them that if they don't accept your apology, their store might catch fire."

"Dad!" Rai said, horrified.

"Go in there and apologize," Dirtbag said sternly. "Do it because it's the right thing to do for these people. They're just trying to earn a living."

"But if you burn the store down, they won't have any jobs."

"Well, you'd better hope they accept your apology then."

Rai folded her arms, giving him a look that seemed to question his authority. Dirtbag stared back at her, unmoved. She narrowed her eyes, outwardly immune to his gaze. He slowly, ever so carefully began to smile, and she had to bite her lower lip to maintain her air of defiance without cracking up. She turned and went into the store.

"Don't worry, Dirt," T.C. assured. "I've seen far worse parenting. I mean, your ex-wife for example."

"I hate being such a hypocrite," Dirtbag grumbled.

"The way I see it, we've only stolen things from people that deserved it. That doesn't make it right, but it's less wrong. I think."

Dirtbag shot a bewildered look at T.C. He took out the compass Father Raygun had given him and checked their position. T.C. fed the last of the grassaline to the Sawstang and walked over to view the compass. He looked around to make sure Rai was still inside. "You don't trust her?" he asked, a little too loudly.

"Half of her did come from Katvanna." Dirtbag exhaled.

"She seems like a good kid. She's a little rough around the edges but no worse than either of us."

"Well, she's leading us in the right direction so far." Dirtbag closed the compass. "Which either proves she *is* a good kid or that we're walking into a trap—a trap she might not even know about."

"A surprise trap? Those are the best kind, Dirt," T.C. said in a falsely cheerful voice. "I remember one time an ex invited me over for dinner; she told me she wanted to call the whole divorce off. I get over there and, 'Surprise!' The judge, my attorney, and all three of hers were running court transcripts through the karaoke machine. I mean, I used to say, 'uh,' a lot."

Dirtbag supped a bit more coffee through the wooden straw. He looked at it, dissatisfied. "This should be plastic. I keep getting this mild birch aftertaste."

T.C. chuckled. "Flavors do seem more abundant now, don't they? My mouth gets excited just thinking about the possibilities. I mean, if this is the extent of—"

Rai suddenly walked up to them, fuming. "So, he accepted my apology but then kept the change," she said, miffed.

"What do you mean he kept it?" Dirtbag inquired. "You didn't take anything else, did you?"

"I thought about it."

"Now, wait just a minute," T.C. said, getting mad. "I mean, are you saying that after you apologized and paid for what you took, this guy then basically stole your money?"

"I know, right?" Rai told them. "I suppose, in a way, it's fair, but it wasn't very cool."

"No, that wasn't cool at all. Was it, Dirt?"

"Let's…" Dirtbag thought it over, finishing his bag of coffee. "Let's drive the Sawstang through the store."

T.C. smirked, nodding. Rai half laughed, not taking them seriously. But they were.

CHAPTER 25

T.C. checked the Sawstang's rearview mirror to see how many more police cars had joined the pursuit. The screaming, hood-mounted chainsaw roared over the frequent honking of its horn, forcing well-dressed, fancy-shoe-wearing pedestrians to somersault out of the way in a flurry of fist shaking and choice words.

The Sawstang rocketed the three sought-after adventurers through downtown Cogcinnati, a city famous for constantly changing shape. The Department of Transformation choreographed the movement of buildings and streets into configurations that optimized the daily grind of the city's inhabitants, accounting for weather and holidays. There was no standard layout, and no one had attempted to print a map in years. To make matters worse, the perimeter of the city expanded during the summer to open more space for parks and swimming pools. It was a colossal, organic metropolitan labyrinth, and there was simply no time to go around.

An off-ramp mechanically lowered on their left, with a dozen of Cogcinnati's finest speeding down from the elevated highway to intercept the wanted Sawstang. T.C. turned sharply, jumped a curb, and blasted into a public park filled with people on their lunch breaks.

"I just can't believe Schmousse didn't have that pie!" he complained. "Who eats candied haggis?"

"Pumpkin, put your head down for a second," Dirtbag said from the passenger seat, aiming his shotgun at their pursuers.

"Don't mess up my hair, Dad!" Rai squealed, ducking down.

Dirtbag fired at the ground behind them, turning it to ice. Three police cars spun out of control into a hot-dog stand. Another six slammed on their brakes, smashing together in a pile. T.C. held the horn down as he drove. The Sawstang ripped across a picnic blanket and knocked over a barbecue grill, ruining a family outing. The father chucked a jar of pickles at them but missed. Rai lifted her head a little. She rode in the backseat, with her nails dug deep into the leather cushioning.

"You guys are crazy!" she kept repeating over and over again.

"Pumpkin, you can fly away anytime if it bothers you that much," Dirtbag said, shooting out the base of a tree with a "Lightning Bolt" round. The tree fell over behind them, forcing the pursuant police cars the wrong way down a one-way street.

"What's the matter, Rai? Is it your hair?" T.C. shouted back to her as he turned the Sawstang onto Central Avenue, an eight-lane thoroughfare. "We're making great time. I mean, we even stopped for pie. Didn't you like your mint-crème mousse with the chocolate drizzle?"

"It fell out of the car! Oh, or I guess it was hurled out…into the street."

"Swell. I liked that mint; it didn't say squid," T.C. said. "Don't worry, Rai. We'll just circle back around."

"No, it's gone," Dirtbag told them, firing again over the side of his door. "We have to get out of here. They must have the entire police force after us."

"I know, right? We only plowed through a hardware store, a museum, and that restaurant that refused to seat us," Rai said sarcastically. "That's hardly grounds for arrest."

"Hey, denim is who I am. I'm not going to bow to some dress code," Dirtbag growled. "Those people were bigots, no matter how good their tenderloin was."

"Usually local law enforcement isn't this organized," T.C. said, jerking the wheel hard to avoid a woman pushing a stroller. The woman shrieked at them and threw her gourmet latte. T.C. caught the latte in his hand and drank it down as he drove, nearly gagging from how bitter it was. He tossed the empty cup into a passing trash can. "Did you see that, Rai? I care about the environment."

They heard a high-pitched yelp as the Sawstang thumped over something. A man holding a leash screamed from behind them. T.C. cringed and hit the gas.

"Did you just run over a little dog?" Rai gasped, trying to see what had happened in the quickly fading distance. "That's awful! How can we call ourselves heroes after that?"

"That could've been a rat. I mean, those things can get pretty big in the city," T.C. insisted, glancing in the rearview mirror, his attention elsewhere. "Oats alive! Those cars are fast! They're right behind us again. They must be using some kind of high-octane grass."

Dirtbag fired another ice shot at the road, sending the cars behind them on a catastrophic detour through the city aquarium. A half dozen freed sharks slid across the street and into the sewer system.

"They look like Mustangs that were specially bred for policing, probably all males with oversized engines and pent-up frustrations," Dirtbag speculated, pumping his shotgun. "Hey, at least they don't have bus-worms."

"I mean, why not?" T.C. asked. "They have everything else, Dirt. Even the roads are machines."

As if on cue, warning whistles blew above them and the road-way they were on suddenly began to transform. The pavement split open, revealing giant, nickel-plated cogs. The buildings disconnected and pulled back from the street. Pedestrians hopped onto the moving structures like they were casually boarding a train. The road clanked upward, joining with another road to form an on-ramp.

"They're trying to funnel us back downtown," Dirtbag said, watching for an alternate route. He glanced behind him and saw Rai wasn't there. "Stop!" he yelled. "Rai's missing!"

The Sawstang screeched to a halt at the base of the clanking on-ramp.

"OK, don't panic," T.C. said. "Let's think. Where was the last place we saw her?"

"In the car!" Dirtbag shouted. "That's it! I'm going to make her wear a bell!"

"Screee!" a pied falconet called from overhead, soaring down into the car. It transformed into Rai in a flash of black light and feathers. "What's wrong, Dad?" she asked.

"OK, OK, hold on," T.C. said, staring at the string-tied pastry box she was holding. "You went all the way back to Schmousse?"

"And I healed that little dog you squashed."

"Pumpkin"—Dirtbag was flabbergasted—"how did you find the time to do all that?"

"Gah! I'm a woman, Dad; I was multitasking, all right?"

Dirtbag stared at her in disbelief. "Well, did you get anything for us?"

"Yeah, I did, but you're not having it unless the two of you make an effort to not be so completely irredeemable."

"Bribery? That's just like a woman," T.C. grumbled. "I mean, the next thing you know, she'll be grading us on a point system." He jammed down the accelerator.

The Sawstang neighed and sprinted up the transforming on-ramp. The road-changing mechanism sacrificed haste for precision, having been designed for regulating congestion within the city, not for high-speed pursuits. The on-ramp was slowly swinging around to connect with the main highway, lowering to meet up with a waiting battalion of furious police officers. The Sawstang barreled around the corner and launched off the unconnected end, sailing over the highway below.

"Oats alive! She's a natural flier!" T.C. boasted proudly as they glided through the air. He glanced behind him; the chasing police cars were being rerouted after them, but it would take a few minutes to move another bypass into position. He chuckled and then looked ahead. "Whoa! Everyone veer to the right, or we'll hit that elementary school!"

They leaned; the car's trajectory changed slightly, missing a building full of cheering children, who were too enthralled by the spectacle to realize the danger they'd been in. The Sawstang crashed through the metal roof of a warehouse and landed in the middle of a fish market. The red convertible revved its chainsaw angrily, and the fishmongers ran for their lives.

Rai squeaked from the backseat; a giant, headless bluefin tuna had landed in her lap. "It's dead!" she cried. "Eww! It stinks! It stinks!"

"Whoa!" T.C. smiled. "Just hold on, Rai. I can make us a casserole."

Rai gritted her teeth. "Get it off me!" she snapped.

Dirtbag hopped out of the Sawstang and helped pull the giant fish off Rai even as police sirens neared. T.C. popped the trunk open, and Dirtbag stuffed the tuna inside. T.C. mentioned that it would spoil without ice, so Dirtbag shot the fish with an ice round, flash freezing it, and closed the trunk. He jumped back in the car and turned to Rai. "Better now, Pumpkin?" he asked, unable to hide his amusement.

"I'm sorry about the women-bribery crack earlier," T.C. jumped in. "I mean, bitterness just wells up inside me like a spring of lemons."

Rai smelled her hands and shook them as she shuddered from the stench. "Ew! Gross! Gah! This is so nasty! I should've flown ahead like you said!"

"Nah." T.C. reached back and vigorously rubbed her head, messing up her hair. "We like having you around."

"Do you? Are you sure?" She fixed her hair using her uncontaminated wrists. "Because I guess, in a way, I feel like I'm only encouraging you guys to be even worse than you normally are, since I can always say a word and *poof*."

"Hey, that's not true." Dirtbag grinned. "Pumpkin, we're always this bad; we thrive on making questionable—"

"Interesting," T.C. corrected.

"—choices," Dirtbag continued. "If anything, you inspire us to do better."

"Yay, I inspire you," she sneered cynically. "I hope that fish tastes better than it smells. The whole backseat stinks now."

"Don't you have a spell or something you can do, Pumpkin?" Dirtbag asked.

Rai thought about it and spoke a few ancient words. Ice cubes from the fishmonger stalls gathered above them then instantly turned into fragrant wild flowers and dropped into the car, filling the Sawstang up.

"Oats alive," T.C. said, spitting out some petals. "We're a parade float!"

A fishmonger started bawling at them that they were stealing his livelihood. T.C. put the Sawstang into drive, but Rai gave Dirtbag a look. They waited while Dirtbag quickly negotiated the highest price possible for the tuna and paid the man. They sped through the market and back onto the street, trailing flower petals behind them.

"Happy?" Dirtbag asked her.

"I need a bath!" Rai replied, frustrated.

"Would that be a birdbath?" T.C. chuckled.

Dirtbag hit T.C. in the back of the head, misaligning the knight's hair. "Don't look at me! Watch the road, and don't hit any more dogs!" Dirtbag demanded, pointing at the windshield.

"I never aimed for it, Dirt," T.C. defended, returning his magnificent blond mane to shape with a quick headshake. "It wanted to die. I mean, did you see that horrible sweater it was wearing? In this heat? I figured it was just asking us for a favor."

"Oh, I know, right?" Rai huffed. "But it's fine. I think more than anything the police are mad about the art museum."

"Now, wait just a minute. That wasn't art; that was garbage," T.C. said, speeding through a sidewalk café. Tableware clattered over the hood, accompanied by the profanity-laced shouts of the sophisticated patrons. "Besides, pottery is nonflammable, right?"

"Any scumbag can paint a canvas red and call it *Summer Roses*," Dirtbag growled while throwing out handfuls of flower petals from his seat, "but only 'artists' can come up with enough hyperbole to convince people that their complete lack of talent is actually talent."

Rai giggled. "I told you I went to art school, didn't I, Dad?"

"I never meant to insult you, Pumpkin, but—"

"What? No, I'm not insulted. You're right." She smirked. "Not about all artists, but you'd be surprised how far hyperbole can get you."

T.C. nodded. "Yeah, my attorney said the same thing about my ex-wife."

"Which one?" Rai asked.

"They all run together, Rai, like a marathon of hate."

The Sawstang turned a corner, scaring a flock of pigeons, who took off into the air and showered them with droppings. Rai squawked at the birds, lecturing them in their native dialect, but the mess had been made.

Ahead of the Sawstang, the police were barricading the exit out of Cogcinnati, organizing one last attempt to prevent the fugitives from escaping. T.C. reached under the dashboard and tickled the Sawstang in a sensitive area, causing it to lurch; it tilted to one side, driving on two wheels. With the chainsaw buzzing, flower petals spilling, and pigeon droppings running, none of the police officers wanted to go near the Sawstang. They threw down their hats as it squeezed past the blockade and out of their jurisdiction. Dirtbag yelled an apology and tossed them a bag of gold to cover the damages, but they were so enraged they threw it back at him, striking him in the head.

CHAPTER 26

———

Dirtbag stood, looking relaxed, behind the candy-apple-red enamel counter inside the empty, stainless-steel, pill-shaped diner. He was wearing a checkered apron and a matching chef's hat. He pressed a spatula down on a tuna-melt sandwich, browning it on the shiny grill in front of him. When the edges had turned a crispy golden orange, he flipped it over and pressed again, until the coloring was uniform. A freshly showered Rai sat at the counter, her hair wrapped up in a towel turban, as she nibbled on the buttery, toasted bread of her tuna melt. Rain poured down on the prefabricated metal roof, creating an odd, metallic white noise that hung in the air. T.C. sat at a booth by the window—his hair also wrapped up in a towel turban—laughing.

Outside, a group of dwarves dressed in baseball jerseys was struggling to wash an angry, bucking Sawstang amid a thunderous storm. The dwarves ran a rest area called "The Shortstop"—a name that had elicited much controversy and several lawsuits—next to a small road not far from the highway that led to Cogcinnati. The dwarves had bought the land cheap, ahead of a proposed bypass, but construction for the new route was far behind schedule, bogged down by environmentalists. Apparently, the highly endangered glass squirrel, a creature no one had seen in ten years, inhabited the nearby woods. No official survey had been taken to verify that the squirrel lived there; it was assumed to be alive based on the amount of broken glass continually found in the forest. The close proximity of six rowdy pubs and a community college had been dismissed as mere coincidence. With their business plans imploding, the dwarves were drowning in debt and desperate to please any customers that happened upon their out-of-the-way, poorly located establishment, even if this meant scrubbing down a chainsaw-wielding Mustang in the middle of a downpour.

"Just look at them go! Woo!" T.C. laughed, his mouth full of food. "I mean, look how fast those little legs move!"

Dirtbag served up the last tuna melt, sliding it onto a plate stacked high with sandwiches. They had rented the entire diner from the dwarves for just a few coins; so few customers came to The Shortstop it was hardly ever used. The dwarves kept it clean and prepared for the day the bypass would, hopefully, finally come through.

T.C. leaned against the window, watching the dwarves dive for cover as the Sawstang burned a doughnut in front of the service station. He laughed again.

"That's awful," Rai said with a shameful grin, driven in part by T.C.'s joy. She ate a little more of her sandwich and fiddled with the Schmousse box, peeking inside it.

"Whoa! The bearded one just flew into the woods!" T.C. pounded the table as he laughed. "Don't worry, Rai. I'm going to leave them a tip so big they'll be able to relocate this whole place." He watched the dwarves wrestle with the car and chuckled again with a sigh. He walked over to the counter and picked up a couple more tuna melts.

"These are great, Dirt! I can still make us a casserole. I mean, there's just enough fish left over in the fridge."

"Hey, the only casserole you ever made killed somebody," Dirtbag snarled. "Who knows what would happen if you made another?"

T.C. reluctantly agreed. "I mean, too bad a squid didn't jump in the car. I could've made us some battered calamari rings. Trust me; I can fry like the wind, Dirt. You can fry mint, right?"

Rai wrinkled her nose. "What is it with you and mint anyway?"

"There was this squid in the desert with two brains, and I had to make it a sandwich—"

"Is that some kind of thing?" Rai recoiled. "Because if it is, don't include me in it."

"It really happened—at least I'm pretty sure it did." T.C. returned his attention to the circus outdoors. He doubled over laughing, almost choking on his food as a dwarf was cartwheeled headfirst into a stack of tires. "The car," he giggled. "It's on a roll!"

"If they see you laughing like that, they're going to get mad," Dirtbag cautioned.

T.C. stepped away from the window and sat down at the counter next to Rai. She pushed away her tuna melt and pulled a brand-new mint-crème mousse out of the pastry box to console herself. "How can you even laugh about that?" she asked, shielding her dessert from potential weird comments.

"I dunno, Rai." T.C.'s smile faded. He thought about it as he ate. "I remember times when I just wanted to curl up and not exist. I mean, I wanted to go to sleep and never have to wake up again to face the world. It was right after my first wife left me. I loved that woman...Those were dark times, but I kept going. I kept getting up because I knew I had to. Nobody just exists; if they do, they're wasting their lives. I mean, living isn't easy, but I believe destiny isn't given to you. You create it, every single day."

"That's a little grandiose, don't you think?" Rai observed, eating her dessert.

T.C. shrugged, taking a bite of his sandwich. "I like to remind myself that things could be worse. They could always be worse."

They each stared off into a separate corner of the diner, considering how much worse things could be and might very well get. It wasn't very uplifting. Dirtbag handed Rai another tuna melt. "Why don't you try eating one more, Pumpkin?" he urged. "You're just a little thing, and I want you to be strong."

She refused the sandwich. "I am strong, Dad. We all are." She looked at them and saw they didn't quite understand. "I know I look small, but I've studied, and a lot of our perceptions about health are just echoes from the past when the ancients lived. The ancients were smart, but they weren't as strong as us. I guess, from the way it sounded, it was like they didn't even live as long as we do."

"It's debatable if I'm even alive, Pumpkin," Dirtbag growled, having a sandwich.

"Of course you're alive, Dad. You're standing right in front of me. We just like to think that we live the same way as the ancients, and we don't. I guess it's more like we're just very resilient."

T.C. took the last tuna melt off the plate. "Is that why you made dessert your dinner, Rai, because you're resilient?"

"No. I just wanted to eat it more," she shyly admitted. "But think about it, T.C. How old are you?"

T.C. looked uncertain. "Let's see. I mean, I think the last birthday I celebrated by number was in my late forties. I just stopped keeping track after that, and, uh, well, I just lied about it from then on. I mean, my life has been up and down, this way and that, and often months and years just mush together."

"You don't know how old you are?" Dirtbag criticized.

"Do you, Dirt?"

"Well"—he thought hard—"I don't keep track either; it was never that important."

Rai leaned back alongside the counter. "T.C., you've been divorced ten times, and you talk about each of those marriages like they lasted for years, and if you add that up, that's a whole lot of life you've lived."

"Am I really that old?" T.C. said, thinking about it, stunned.

"Interesting." Dirtbag mulled it over. "So the ancients lived much shorter lives than us but almost destroyed the planet? If that's true, it would make sense that their legacy might be hardier descendants."

T.C. shifted restlessly in his seat. "Where did all the time go?" he lamented.

"Into memory," Dirtbag said quietly.

Rai opened the pastry box from Schmousse and took out two slices of butterscotch marshmallow pie. "Oats alive!" T.C. excitedly gasped. "They told us they were out, Rai."

"No," she sang. "They told us they hadn't made it yet, so when I went back, I got some." She happily watched as her father and T.C. enjoyed the slices of pie.

"Here, I want to show you something," she said. Rai opened her tiny purse and pulled out a small painted portrait of Katvanna. It seemed slightly larger than what should be able to fit in the little handbag. She turned the portrait to face them. A fair-skinned woman with purple-colored eyes; glowing, whitish light-blue hair; pointy elfin ears; and a mischievous, soft pink smirk stared at them. T.C. almost fell off his stool at the sight of her.

"I know, right?" Rai grinned. "Say what you will about my mom, but she's a beautiful woman. This is pretty recent, too. Mom commissioned some pictures for the wedding, and I took this one while nobody was looking."

"You stole it?" Dirtbag admonished.

"Yes, I guess I did, all right? I thought you two might want to see what she looks like, especially T.C., who's never met her before."

"All part of the plan, eh?" Dirtbag teased.

"That woman!" T.C. said, completely breathless and pointing at the picture. "That's Katvanna?"

"Hey, are you all right?" Dirtbag asked.

"Oats alive! I—I remember her…"T.C. stammered. "From a long time ago—I mean, I had her…I mean, she had me…" T.C. held his head. "Dirt, she's the woman who ruined my first marriage, the only marriage that ever worked, and she ruined it."

"Gah! You did my mom?" Rai said, horrified. "There's a word for that, T.C."

"Hey, that's a word we won't be using, right, Pumpkin?" Dirtbag stated sternly.

"Oh no! *No!* Was this before she met you, Dad?" Rai began to hyperventilate. "Dad, is Tuna Casserole my real father?"

"No! No! No!" both Dirtbag and T.C. denied, waving their hands.

"OK, Rai, all this really means," T.C. began, articulating his speech with gestures, "is that before, I mean, things were complicated, but now, things are really complicated. OK? Before, I was just helping Dirt on his quest to get his heart back, doing the hero thing, or trying. Then you came along, and I'm helping you, too, but now—now it's personal, superduper personal."

"But you're not my father, right?"

Dirtbag placed his hand down on Rai's wrist and reassured her. "You're *my* daughter," he told her firmly. He patted her arm, trying to figure out what to say next. He knew she was his; she was why he had had to marry Katvanna. Her conception had been an accident, and he had sworn he would never reveal that fact to her. "You were ours from the beginning, and you were born into our arms well after we were married. Your mother was a different person back then, and I loved her."

Rai took a deep breath and relaxed.

T.C. looked insulted that Rai would react so strongly over the possibility she was his daughter. "I'm not that bad, am I, Rai?" he asked her.

"Uh…no, of course not, T.C. It's just…well, it would've been weird and really awkward." She fidgeted. "Just how did Mom ruin your marriage?"

"Are you sure you guys want to know?"

"Well," Dirtbag said warily, "I'd like to know, but try to clean it up for Rai."

T.C. motioned for the rum bottle. Dirtbag took it out of his satchel, and they began drinking. T.C. recounted how Katvanna had seduced him three years into his first marriage. He explained that he was unable to resist her incredible, unearthly charm and how every day their rendezvous became riskier until finally they were caught.

"OK, so there I was, hot dog in the bun, standing there, holding her legs wide open in the air on top of my mother-in-law's chest of drawers, which had been handed down for twelve generations, with Kathy—that's what she called herself—wearing my wife's old wedding dress that I had torn open in a fit of wild passion, when the door opened and the wife walked in with her sister."

Rai stared at T.C., thoroughly captivated and, at times, visibly disgusted by what she heard. Dirtbag drank heavily from the rum bottle as he listened, not at all fazed by the story. Katvanna had been a wicked, vicious person when he first met her, but she had a way of being good when she wanted to be. She put aside her past and settled down with him to care for Rai. They were happy for a while, but it didn't last, and as she grew increasingly hostile, he took on greater, longer-lasting, more dangerous quests that took him far from home. He had never meant to leave Rai behind. He watched his daughter style her dry hair, listening to T.C. with morbid curiosity.

"Then what happened?" Rai asked.

T.C. scooped up some more pie with a fork and washed it down with rum. Despite his casual manner of retelling the past, it was tearing him apart inside. "She told them to join in! The wife called the palace guards, her sister pulled a knife and tried to cut something off I wanted to keep, and I was run out of the kingdom wearing only a bed sheet. I spent years in litigation. I've never been able to be faithful since. I mean, I try. I really try, but I've never found anything like what I had with my first wife, and I ruined that."

The rain softened outside, and they paused to take in the gentle cadence.

"She ruined it, T.C., not you." Dirtbag took off the chef's hat and combed back his grass-hair. "There were times Katvanna could be kind, when she was amazing; then there were times when she was so ruthlessly hateful I couldn't stand being around her. It always worried me how much pleasure it gave her to hurt people. She enjoyed being feared."

Rai held out her hand for the rum bottle; T.C. checked with Dirt-bag, who nodded his approval. She took a long drink, wincing from the bitter taste. "Dad,"—she wiped her mouth—"just what *is* wrong with Mom?"

"Pumpkin"—Dirtbag exhaled—"I think your mother is a full-blown psychopath who desires happiness but not in the way we know it."

Rai passed the bottle to T.C.

"Trust me; we're not the only lives she's ruined. I mean, we just happen to be the closest connected. She's a monster," T.C. said. He passed the bottle back to Rai.

"I know…" She flinched as she drank. "But are we really going to kill her? Is that the right thing to do?"

Dirtbag took the bottle for a gulp. "We'll find out when we get there."

And they continued to drink well into the night.

CHAPTER 27

———

Rai came to, rolling her slumping head back and forth between her shoulders as if she had been trying to unconsciously wake herself out of an incapacitating delirium. People were talking around her; the room was blurry and reeked of cheap coffee and stale doughnuts. She shook her head to fight the malaise and desperately tried to find her strength. Her head was pounding with steady, deep thumps she could feel throughout her entire body. She was sweating and a mess. As she fought to gain focus, she suddenly realized that she was tied to a chair, with the worst hangover she had ever experienced, and somebody was kicking her ankle.

She yanked at her restraints. The ropes felt unusually tough, as though they had special properties that dampened her strength, and she couldn't break free. She panicked; she didn't even know where she was or what was happening, but she resisted the urge to shout a destructive word, lest she kill scores of innocent people. Moreover, her mouth was gagged with something rubbery, held in by duct tape. She gnawed on it, and it squeaked. It was a dog's chew toy. Someone kicked her ankle again, and she glared at her attacker. It was Dirtbag. He was gagged and tied, too, and T.C. was as well, in the next chair over. She noticed the chew toys in their mouths were stained and tattered. Used? She freaked. Were the toys even clean?

"Squeak squeaky!" Dirtbag said, working the chew toy.

"Squeak?" she demanded.

Dirtbag shrugged his shoulders and squeaked softly, trying to calm her down.

The last thing she could remember was drinking rum in the diner. They kept sharing bitter memories, growing more depressed as they did, and somehow the only solution had been to increase their intake of alcohol. Then it hit her. She'd participated in one of Dirtbag and T.C.'s alcohol-driven benders. Her eyes widened as she struggled to remember what they'd done, but there were only disjointed fragments. They had gone to a village, danced through a municipal garden, threatened some vegetables that were too suggestive, and then taken those vegetables to a midnight wake. She remembered being chased by torch-bearing villagers and laughing at them. Somehow, they'd allowed themselves to be arrested and infuriated a judge by speaking in rhymes. They had found his anger hilarious, but the last straw was when T.C. made a grilled cheese sandwich in the middle of the courtroom. They were sentenced to something, and now they were in this strange place.

It was a beige meeting room with rows of folding chairs lined up before a small, plywood stage. The floor was covered with a gray carpet marred with the black spots of ground-in discarded bubble gum. The room's fluorescent lights were turned off, allowing the sun outside to illuminate the space through large windows. As far as Rai could tell, she, Dirtbag, and T.C. were the only people in the room gagged and tied to their chairs. She saw a dozing old farmer dressed in overalls, a guy with greased-back hair wearing a bathrobe, and a seven-foot-tall, boorish, nose-picking amazon who wore a polyester skirt so high up on her body it could have been mistaken for a shirt. The other chairs were occupied by a sleepy looking wizard, a burned-out, filthy blacksmith with his hand down his pants, and an unshaven man in a grubby bunny suit who openly drank from a brown paper bag.

T.C. squeaked his chew toy and threw back his hair as he endeavored to revive himself. Dirtbag surveyed the room by turning his boneless neck around to look directly behind him. Neither Dirtbag nor T.C. were alarmed about their situation; they seemed to be interested in where they were and almost excited to see what would happen next. Rai stomped her feet. They both squeaked at her, but she had no idea what they were trying to say. She sighed and attempted to relax.

A clock chimed, and two armed knight deputies walked into the room escorting a woman wearing a long, flowing, lavender silk robe. She slowly made her way between the chairs, eyeing everyone in attendance suspiciously and carrying a freshly cut green switch. She whipped the sleepy wizard so hard on the head that his pointed hat fell off, and she confiscated the bunny's brown paper bag. She stepped on the stage and cracked the switch against her hand, startling everyone to attention. With the room awake, she strode behind a small podium, tilted her head to one side, and smiled.

"Welcome, addicts," the woman began, speaking in a forgiving, overly sympathetic, self-righteous manner. "We tend to think of our problems as belonging to the individual, but they do not. We live in a community where each of us bears responsibility. Substance abuse is a plague we can cure together, by bonding our hearts, by bonding our minds, and by accepting that pain shared is pain that can be endured, that through sharing, we can lead better lives individually and as valued members of the community. Our journey together is only sixteen steps, but each step embraces love, and—"

T.C. screamed through his gag. He bit the chew toy in half and started bouncing up and down in his chair. "Fooo!" he shouted.

Dirtbag tried assuring him they could survive this, but his squeaks went unheard.

"Phuuuuk uutt!"T.C. screamed through the scraps of his gag.

Sparks began igniting off his lips. He continued to scream until his lips caught fire, burning through the duct tape. His mouth free, T.C. unleashed a torrent of profanity so offensive two people passed out and the amazon darted from the room, crying in horror. T.C. spat fire onto the ropes tied around his ankles, weakening them. The lavender-robed woman rushed over and started beating his head with the switch, messing up his hair. The deputies pulled their swords. T.C. broke free of the ropes then crushed the chair in his hands and threw the pieces at them. He picked up Dirtbag's chair and ripped it apart. Again he screamed the most offensive profanity anyone in the room had ever heard, causing windows to shatter and minds to warp. The farmer jumped up and grabbed his chest in an apparent heart attack; the deputies rushed to aid him.

"OK! Let's go!"T.C. screamed with his lips on fire. He picked up Rai and put her under his arm; she squeaked at him to untie her. He laughed and held his hand up in the air. "It's the first of the month, ladies! Payday! Olly olly free alimony! Come and get it!"

They heard a crash in the adjacent room. A locked evidence trunk burst through the wall, and out of it exploded the Amber Blade of Divorce. The sheathed sword flew into T.C.'s hand; he attached the scabbard to his belt and pulled the blade out. Coins from all over the room flew out of purses and wallets and into the ten glowing gold wedding rings within the blade. He swung the sword around his head, screaming madly as it absorbed all the money in the room in a tornado of currency.

"Mmmff!" Rai kicked and squealed, demanding to be cut loose as people fled from the room, holding their ears.

T.C. cackled like a madman and released another deluge of shocking curse words that shook the very foundation of the building. "Yeah!" he yelled. "Times two!"

"Hey, hold on, Pumpkin; let me get our stuff," Dirtbag said, digging through the exploded remains of the trunk. He found her purse, her cloak, and his shotgun and satchel.

The lavender-robed woman continued to beat on T.C. with her switch. T.C. sheathed his sword, grabbed the woman by her waist, and pulled her toward him for a big, sloppy, burning kiss. She ran shrieking into the hallway and promptly threw up. T.C. set Rai down and split the chair she was in apart with his bare hands; she plopped onto the floor. She tore off her gag and immediately said an ancient word that lifted her haze. "Dad! T.C.'s lost it!" She cringed, looking at him.

"No, I haven't!" T.C. replied. "I mean, is this the face of a maniac?" He picked up a vending machine with one hand and threw it into the doorway, blocking any reinforcements. "Trust me, Rai," T.C. shouted through flaming lips. "Ladies love a man who can channel his emotions constructively!"

"Oh! I know, right? And you're so good with your hands," she mocked.

"And don't you people forget it!"T.C. barked, shaking his armored fists. "I haven't even used my kicking foot yet; I just need a volunteer."

Dirtbag grabbed Rai and dragged her over to a window shattered by T.C.'s profanity. "Pumpkin, fly outside and find the Sawstang. It's probably impounded close by," Dirtbag told her. "Here, take the key."

"I'm on it, Dad." She smirked, taking flight as a pied falconet in a flash of black light and feathers.

Dirtbag grabbed T.C.'s head and smothered his burning lips with a cool denim hand. He held his hand there until T.C. nodded that it was out. "I think I may have gone too far, Dirt," he said, looking around at the cowering people. "I'm pretty sure I just destroyed Rai's expectations, too."

"Are you kidding me? How did we even end up here? We did pay those dwarves last night, didn't we?"

"Oats alive, I don't know what happened,"T.C. said, stumbling to one side and holding his head. "Whoa. We need to cut back on drinking, Dirt. I mean, we need to do something else when we feel low, like play cards or bake cupcakes."

"Well, cupcakes would be more rewarding."

"I just hope I haven't permanently hosed our reputation."

"I think we did that a long time ago." Dirtbag twisted his body, forcing out enough rum from his inner dirt to clear his head. Somebody yelled at him to use a bathroom. Dirtbag tried to explain his anatomy but gave up.

T.C. paced back and forth. "I'm just glad I looked at that *Raymanac* the other day. I mean, otherwise I wouldn't have known today was the first. Whoa, hold on a second, Dirt. These people don't know about my sword; I bet they think I just stole their money."

"Well, you did," Dirtbag growled.

"I'm sorry, Dirt. I just couldn't sit there and go through another one of these meetings," T.C. said, touching his lips. The skin was already beginning to blister. He took out some burn cream and began applying a generous amount. He grit his teeth angrily. "I mean, that's your daughter we just dragged into—what's been for us—a recurring event."

"Don't you think I know that?" Dirtbag shot back. He breathed to regain his composure.

"Let's face it, Dirt; the odds were never in our favor, no matter how we made the sandwich. I mean, what good is changing the universe when nothing actually changes?"

"It's easy to say people like us are beyond help," Dirtbag thought out loud. "That we exist in our own tier of misery nobody can save us from. But what if it wasn't just the universe that we changed? What if it was us? What if *we* have a chance…and we've been wasting it?"

They heard a commotion outside the room as the deputies regrouped behind the vending machine. T.C. seized the broken window frame and wrenched it out of the wall. Rai drove the Sawstang up beneath the window, engine revving. It whinnied happily. They jumped out the window into the backseat and made their getaway.

"Oh! You look terrible, T.C.!" Rai said, concerned.

T.C. held his head. "We can't do this stuff anymore, Dirt; we just can't."

"Do you want me to heal you?" Rai asked quietly.

"Uh, I dunno. In a moment, Rai," T.C. said, covering his face. "I'm so angry. I mean, about everything. We're on this big mission, and what do we do? We booze up and get arrested. I mean, we can be depressed, but we don't have to live this way. It doesn't help."

"Dad?" Rai asked delicately. "Did we just hit bottom?"

Dirtbag combed his fingers through his grass-hair. "Pumpkin, we're under the floor."

The Sawstang sped across a bridge, over a hill, and far, far, away from the troubles they had created.

CHAPTER 28

———

It was night, warm and starlit. A fluttering campfire spattered an orange glow across the blackish trees that encircled the small glade. The silver enchanted rum bottle lay shattered in the middle of the fire beneath a boiling pot of spaghetti, a large stone dividing its smashed body. Dirtbag raked glowing, hot coals out of the fire to a shallow hole partly covered by bent sheets of metal. It was a crude oven, but it worked well enough for baking cupcakes. He slid two batter-filled trays inside and stoked the coals. Soon a delicious, pleasant aroma poured out, enveloping the glade with uplifting felicity.

T.C. and Rai sat beside one another chatting, leaning their backs against the Sawstang, and frosting cupcakes at a steady but leisurely pace. They carefully stacked the finished desserts upon a large serving platter atop the hood, which was covered over by a sheet of wax paper. The sleepy Sawstang quietly chewed grassaline pellets from a feed bag hanging off the mounted chainsaw.

T.C. dug out another can of frosting from a paper grocery bag and tossed the empty bag into the fire. "OK, then," he casually narrated. "I woke up in the middle of the night—this was right after we saw the marriage counselor—and I caught her trying to shave my toes. And I said, 'Honey, why can't you just accept me for who I am? Why do you keep trying to change me?'"

"Gah!" Rai wrinkled her nose with a smile.

"The way I see it, Rai, what really ended that marriage was when she used my dog as a dish for her charity potluck. I mean, no one even realized what they were eating until she started sharing the recipe. Good ol' Fang. He was just a Winged Chihuahua, too fat to even fly, but he was a competitor."

"Oh no," Rai giggled compassionately.

"The judge ruled the whole thing inadmissible." T.C. swallowed, having run aground on some bitterness. He pushed on. "I dunno, every third divorce I'd have a nervous breakdown. I mean, who knew those things were cumulative? I'm pretty sure that's how the memories got mixed together in my mind. Now, they're just one giant ordeal that I call my life."

Dirtbag checked on the pot of spaghetti. "Well, dinner is almost ready," he said. "That is, if you two haven't filled up with sweets," he added, looking at the colored icing smeared around T.C. and Rai's mouths.

"We should've cooked these after we ate," T.C. said regretfully. "I got talking about exes, and we'd already thrown the rum into the fire. The cupcakes were just there, Dirt, calling to me."

"As long as we have enough for the ninjas," Dirtbag said.

"We only ate a couple, Dad," Rai chirped, drawing a happy face on the cupcake she was frosting. "We have plenty to make it through that ninja town."

"Now, wait just a minute, Rai." T.C. looked at her. "Do you know your ninjas?"

"What? Oh! Red, black, and blue, I guess."

"Simple enough, right?" T.C. grinned. "Trust me; knowing the difference could be life or death. Those aren't just colors they wear; they're three completely different clans that fight in three different styles. I mean, to survive ninjas you need to know the secret behind the colors of their karate-pajamas."

"Karate-pajamas?" Rai frowned.

"Red-cashmere-wearing ninjas love sweets," T.C. elaborated. "I mean, if that town up ahead was infested by blue-suede ninjas, we'd have to fry up some pork cutlets slathered in curry, the spicier the better. Black-leather ninjas prefer bacon-wrapped dates stuffed with mesquite-flavored almonds; they're the hardest ones to please and, therefore, the most dangerous. I mean, as long as you know what each clan likes, you'll have safe passage through any ninja-infested area."

"Unless you do something rash," Dirtbag mentioned.

"Oh, I think I can take a ninja, Dad," Rai said confidently.

"Bullcookies!" T.C. chuckled. "You might think you can handle *a* ninja, but it's never just one. I mean, can you handle fifty? One hundred? Real ninjas swarm like killer bees, Rai. They'll come out of the walls, the ground, the sky, even out of thin air. Big—just huge— swarms, armed with those katana swords and nunchakus, completely silent, except for this low, creepy hiss, like locusts. They don't have much of a sense of humor either. I mean, years ago I told one bad joke and they stole my wallet…and kept it."

Dirtbag added sauce to the spaghetti and served it to T.C. and Rai on paper plates. "Well, how's it taste?" he asked.

T.C. sampled it. "Oats alive, Dirt! I never knew you were such a good chef. You should've shown up sooner, Rai. I mean, you know he only cooks for you."

Rai looked across the dim glade at her father. She smiled warmly. T.C. suddenly stood up. His feet began to slide smoothly across the ground, and he spun. He danced uncontrollably around the campfire. "Dirt, what's in this anyway?"

Dirtbag rubbed the back of his denim neck. "That little grocery store didn't have everything I needed. I had to substitute the tomatoes with a local variety called tangomatoes, so you might feel the sudden urge to dance, but don't worry; they're harmless. You don't have to dance; you can just sit there, but it'll feel like you're being tickled."

T.C. strutted around the camp as he ate, enjoying the combination of dinner and dancing. Rai took a small bite, which caused her to kick her legs out, and being very ticklish, she started to laugh.

CHAPTER 29

———

Ninja architecture defied not only gravity but also the very idea of a sound mind. Configurations of elegant wood beams, fastened together without nails, formed hexagonal rooms stacked on top of one another like trees of honeycomb. Larger buildings were grander in design, with sharp, sweeping angles that jutted outward as if an explosion had been their source of inspiration. All the structures had glossy-black roof tiles and walls covered in a hexagon-patterned white paper material. The entrances were high up, and there were no ladders or stairs anywhere to reach them. Calling the place a town was a misnomer; it was, in actuality, more like a hive.

"Everyone play it casual, big smiles," Dirtbag advised as he lifted the wax-paper cover off the pile of cupcakes, which sat on the serving platter that was duct-taped to the hood of the Sawstang. He looked around at the empty streets and grinned as he cautiously announced, "We mean you no harm."

Having heard that before, T.C. frowned at Dirtbag as he climbed back into the passenger seat, but the blond knight kept his mouth shut about the squid. Beneath an overcast sky, the Sawstang slowly crawled through the tranquil ninja town, deliberately keeping its usual engine growl down to a polite and nonthreatening mumble. They had not seen a single ninja since they entered the town but knew they were surrounded.

"Smell that?" T.C. said in a hushed tone. "The heat from the engine is warming up those cupcakes."

They cruised under the strange buildings at a walking pace that was meant to tell the lurking red-cashmere ninjas they were only passing through and had business elsewhere. They heard a sudden wisp of wind pass overhead.

"Don't look up," Dirtbag warned.

"So, if they don't like people, why is this place in the middle of the road?" Rai asked, cautiously peering over the side of the convertible.

"They're predators, Pumpkin," Dirtbag said, keeping one hand on his holstered shotgun. "Did you put those bumper stickers on?"

"Gah! Come on, Dad; do you really think big-eyed cats and cute kids are going to save us if they start swarming?"

"Trust me, Rai," T.C. whispered. "It's not the pictures; it's the message. All those strange slash marks are supposedly an ancient language only ninjas can read."

"You can't read those?" Rai asked, aghast.

"Can you?" T.C. challenged.

"Yeah, I told you I studied," she reminded them. "Oh, and I bet you thought I was just being difficult when you were buying that gibberish."

"That clerk said they were lucky."

"Oh, yes, the highly qualified grocery clerk. I suppose, 'Can I eat exit?' and, 'Surprise! Whale corn!' are really lucky things that ninjas say all the time."

"Shhh!" Dirtbag said forcefully. "Next time, Pumpkin, don't wait until the moment of crisis to be assertive."

"Fine." Rai lowered her voice. "But just in case, I bought a box of matcha-green-tea brownies as backup."

"Save one for me. I mean, I want to try that," T.C. said.

Dirtbag put his hand on his face, disgusted. "If we're dead, you won't be trying anything."

"I could've found another route from the air," Rai grumbled.

"Pumpkin, we don't have the time to go around, and we have you. You can yell a word if we get into any real trouble."

"Oh, you make it sound so easy," she huffed. "I have a conscience, Dad, unlike Mom."

A red wisp passed by the front of the car. A cupcake was missing.

"Hey, I think it's working," Dirtbag pointed out. "Everyone keep smiling. Think happy thoughts. The red ninja is our friend."

The Sawstang crept into a large, hexagon-shaped courtyard with a massive glass shrine anchored over a reflecting pool. A fountain cascaded upward across the sleek surface, creating the illusion that the entire building was shaped out of moving water.

"That's the ninja equivalent of city hall," Dirtbag said, marveling at the structure.

"Oats alive! Look at that water! I mean, these guys would make excellent plumbers. One time, I was on this high-fiber diet and—" T.C. was suddenly punched hard in the face by a red blur.

"Are you kidding me?" Dirtbag chastised. "You don't compare ninjas to plumbers! Are you trying to start a war?"

T.C. vigorously rubbed his face and let the incident go. The Sawstang's engine thumped nervously. T.C. patted the dashboard and whispered gentle promises to the car. They had wrapped the chainsaw in a zebra-striped shower curtain to make it appear less threatening. They discussed removing the chainsaw altogether but decided it could be an invaluable escape tool, should the ninjas turn against them. More red-cashmere streaks crisscrossed over the hood, taking away cupcakes as they passed.

"They're hungry today," Dirtbag said, worried about how fast their supply was disappearing.

"Oh! Look at that!" Rai whispered excitedly, motioning to a little kiosk shaped like a kitty cat that was rising silently out of the ground. The doors quietly opened, accompanied by a friendly chime. "Cool. It's a ninja gift shop."

"Whoa, that's a new one," T.C. observed suspiciously. "That's just a distraction, Rai. I mean, look how fast they're eating the cupcakes.

They know we don't have enough to make it through. They're tempting us to stop and waste time, so we can't make a run for it."

"That's a bunch of cheap trash anyway," Dirtbag growled. A fist punched him in the face. He shook it off and kept smiling. "I meant if only we weren't in such a rush."

The Sawstang slowly drove past the unmanned kiosk, which was covered in banners that promised deep discounts to visitors. Eerie music played from within, inviting them inside. They continued driving and eventually came to an unexpected fork in the road.

"OK, which way am I turning, Rai?" T.C. asked.

"To the left. That road leads east to the ocean wall, where Jyn, my ex, lives," she said, biting her lip. "It's been a while; I hope she still remembers me."

"Well, people generally don't forget who they've loved," Dirtbag assured.

"I know…" Rai fidgeted. "But the last time I saw her, I sort of burned her house down."

"I'm sure she'll remember you then," T.C. chuckled. A passing red streak dropped something in his lap. "A ninja lost his wallet!" he said in disbelief.

"Gah! Don't touch it!" Rai gasped. "Do they even use money? Or have pockets? It's got to be a trick."

"OK. I'll just give it right back, no problem." T.C. was preparing to throw the wallet out of the car when it fell open in his hand. "Oats alive! This is my wallet! The one they stole years ago."

"That's not a trick," Dirtbag told them. "That's a message telling us we're not leaving here alive."

"It was just one joke. I mean, it wasn't that bad, right?" A fist punched T.C. in the head. "OK, I'm sorry. I was drunk."

A chorus of hissing erupted. They watched the supply of cupcakes dwindle to less than a dozen. A red blur passed through the backseat. "What? They stole my brownies!" Rai folded her arms, annoyed, but then she noticed a pair of wearable cat ears left in their place. "Dad, I think they traded me cat ears for brownies."

Dirtbag was puzzled. "Ninjas don't trade; they kill."

T.C. examined his old wallet for a moment and swiftly put it away, distressed by what he saw. "I dunno, Dirt, aren't we already trading cupcakes? I mean, so they won't attack? I wonder if they didn't give my wallet back. I wonder if they traded it."

"Yeah," Rai said. "Maybe we can trade safe passage for something else before we run out of cupcakes, but I guess we don't really have anything left they'd want."

Dirtbag quickly searched his satchel for anything he could write on and found a leftover scrap from the papercraft ninja. He jotted down a list and then stood up, holding the written paper high. The ninjas began to whisper aggressively; some hissed at him, but none attacked.

"Red-cashmere ninjas," Dirtbag announced boldly. "I know that you enjoy sweets and that you have obviously been enjoying these delicious cupcakes. Well, in my hand is my very own recipe for those cupcakes, which I am willing to trade. All I ask is that in return you grant us safe passage. It's a fair trade. We have no quarrel with you."

"And I promise not to tell any jokes," T.C. added, which was met by an immediate surge of angry hisses and hasty knife sharpening.

"Are you crazy?" Dirtbag growled as the ninjas began pouring out of the shadows. They flowed down from the rooftops like a wave of water, surrounding the Sawstang in such numbers that the traveling trio felt pinned in by hundreds of bodies. Dirtbag quickly pulled back T.C.'s hair to expose his dented forehead. "Don't mind him. As you can see, his brain is wrong."

"I like riding my bicycle at night with some brisket," T.C. improvised, playing along. "My favorite color of the alphabet is bra. My pretzel does loop de loops. Pineapple beans."

Rai dropped her head into her hands to hide her embarrassment. The ninjas were silent, apparently baffled. After a moment, she looked up and added, "Oh, and he also picked out the bumper stickers."

Then the ninjas began making a strange sound. It wasn't quite whispering, but it wasn't hissing either. It was laughing, a sound that biologists thought was physically impossible for ninjas to make. It was a creepy cackle that rolled through the crowd. A red streak snatched the recipe from Dirtbag's hand, and the ninjas cleared a path for the Sawstang to continue on its way. The great swarm bustled about the car in peculiar fluid-like oscillations, similar to breaking waves. Throughout the remainder of the drive, T.C. stayed slumped down in his seat, hiding his face behind his golden-blond hair.

CHAPTER 30

———

The silver pillars of the Grand Barrier gleamed in the distance, catching the light of the late-afternoon sun. Between the pillars, the towering wall of invisibly restrained ocean seemed a brighter blue than usual. The murky depths of the wall diffused the incoming sunlight, exposing the silhouettes of long-forgotten, unreachable things beyond it. Where the land dipped low, it was possible to see mountainous quantities of sediment piled behind the wall. Where the land raised high, the barrier effortlessly cut through the terrain, uninterrupted by varying topography, seemingly tracing the contour of ancient coastlines. The pillars stood apart at a consistent, equal distance, uniform in height, never leaning, never changing—a prevailing monotony that had become an accepted part of the landscape.

Within sight of the Grand Barrier was a large, flat mesa. It was not a naturally occurring plateau. It had once been a small mountain, but the top had been sheared clean off and thrown some distance away. The mountaintop lay on its side where it had landed, the earth still struggling to reclaim it, a relic of an ancient battle of unimaginable forces. The unvaryingly flat mesa had grown over time into a stunning field of wild grass, a choice piece of real estate with an unparalleled view of the surrounding area. It was atop this mesa that Jyn, Rai's ex-wife, lived alone on a sizable ranch.

The Sawstang drove up the solitary paved road to the ranch and turned onto the long driveway extending across the length of the mesa. They decided to slow down because Jyn was not expecting them. The largest structure before them was a luxurious, four-story-tall adobe mansion with a swimming pool in the back. Attached to the mansion was a colossal hangar constructed from the glossy-black skeleton of an ancient war machine. The hangar doors were open on both ends, and the light shone through it, revealing bulky contraptions inside. On the other side of the mansion was a fenced-in corral that took up a quarter of the available space on the mesa. A garage-stable stood adjacent to the mansion, and as they neared they heard the lively honking of Mustangs galloping together.

Rai chewed her lower lip nervously as they pulled up to the mansion. "You guys stay in the car for now, all right?" she asked. "I just need to talk to her first."

The Mustangs in the corral gathered along the fence, honking at the Sawstang. The Sawstang began honking back, excited to see other friendly cars. T.C. gently patted the dashboard to calm the machine.

The commotion drew the attention of Jyn. She stepped out of the garage-stable, sweaty from bailing grassaline. Rai hopped out of the Sawstang and sheepishly waved at her. Jyn wiped her hands clean with a rag and began walking toward them.

"Wow!" T.C. exclaimed, watching Jyn as she approached. "She's just—I mean, look at her. She's refined and mature. You can see it in her face. I mean, that's somebody I could actually talk to, and I don't mean the fluff you have to wade through with young girls. I mean, that's…she's…she's a woman, Dirt."

"I can see. I have eyes—pockets—never mind," Dirtbag growled. He pulled T.C. aside. "We *won't* be going back to old habits, even if we have some downtime here," he whispered.

"We won't, absolutely not," T.C. agreed, keeping his voice low.

"We have to do better," Dirtbag said. They glanced at Rai.

"And we are, in our own way," T.C. asserted. "But, I mean, within reason, Dirt, right?"

"Well, of course. It's us minus the alcohol."

T.C. was relieved. "Got it. Caffeine is much safer anyway."

Rai suddenly hushed them, unaware of what they were discussing.

Jyn gracefully climbed over the corral fence and pulled her dark-blond, sun-highlighted hair back into a loose ponytail. Her skin was aged but well cared for, and she wore no makeup over her naturally beautiful face. She bore the healthy laugh lines of a cheerful person. She was dressed in a white, grease-stained mechanic's jumpsuit that was almost fully unzipped, exposing a pink bikini underneath. Her body was fit, her hands were strong but tender, and her naval was pierced with what appeared to be a wedding ring.

"I had no idea Jyn was so much older than her," Dirtbag said, watching Rai nervously approach her ex. "Sometimes that can be a good thing, but it depends on the couple and what they see in each other."

Jyn stopped walking; she cocked her head to one side, curiously looking over the Sawstang, the occupants within it, and then at Rai. "Nice ears," Jyn's kind voice sang out. "They're cute. They're very you."

Rai reached up to the top of her head and yanked off the cat ears she had gotten from the ninjas. She let out an embarrassed half laugh.

Jyn smiled compassionately. "Oh boy, Rainelle." Jyn exhaled. "The idea that a being as powerful as you is intimidated by me...yikes."

"So, you're not mad at me?" Rai asked, blushing uncontrollably.

Jyn placed her hand on Rai's cheek and lovingly caressed her skin. Rai fell into Jyn's arms. Jyn rubbed the back of Rai's neck and let out a long, deep breath as they embraced. "Oh, Rainelle, I got past what you did a long, long, time ago. I understood why you left. You were scared that I hated you, but I don't, and I never did." Jyn combed Rai's hair back from her face. "I've missed you, Rainelle, you crazy girl. I always thought you'd show up again one day, and I always hoped you'd be a little wiser. I know you must have your own life now, but I sure would like to rekindle what we had, if only for a little bit. I don't think I ever loved anyone as much as you."

Rai went to pieces and cried, "Jyn, I care about you so much, but I can't feel you inside anymore. Mom stole my heart! She took it all away from me!"

"Because of us?"

"Yeah," Rai sniffed.

Jyn held Rai close. "I told you not to go back there."

"I know…I made a mistake, all right?"

"Oh, Rainelle, things will work out somehow."

Dirtbag cleared his throat, interrupting. He and T.C. were standing next to the Sawstang, awkwardly watching the reunion. Rai stepped away from Jyn and wiped her face, smearing her makeup. Jyn quickly searched her many zippers and handed Rai a clean rag to use. Rai dabbed her tears and made introductions. "Jyn, that's my dad, Dirtbag."

"Nice name. It's straightforward," Jyn said.

"And that's T.C. He's a friend of my father."

"Nice hair," Jyn observed.

"Thanks. Your entire body is nice," T.C. said, to the embarrassment of everyone.

"Yikes, is that a dent in your head?" Jyn frowned.

Rai cringed and quickly pointed at the red Sawstang to introduce it.

Jyn scrutinized the beast with concern. "Oh boy, why does that Mustang have a chainsaw?"

"Gah! I know, right?" Rai stammered.

T.C. stepped over and stroked the hood of the Sawstang; it purred affectionately. "Whoa, now, wait just a minute, Jyn. This is not just a Mustang anymore. This is a Sawstang!" The car revved up the chainsaw. "She's my baby!"

Jyn groaned. "That's completely impractical. I should know; I'm an engineer. And what does T.C. stand for? Is your name short for something?"

"Tuna Casserole," T.C. admitted, folding his arms as if expecting to be taken seriously.

Jyn snorted, amused. "I never knew Blitz Knights wore sunglasses."

"Knights? I'm all that's left. Besides, I have my reasons." T.C. took off his aviator sunglasses with an accompanying rip of duct tape. His red eyes glowed brightly in the fading light. "I tell the ladies it's just my love scintillating, like an electric oven of passion."

Jyn snorted again. "Oh boy." She turned to Rai. "This is how you've been spending your time?"

"They're heroes, Jyn, in a way, I guess…sometimes…once in a while."

"Ah, they're no worse than any of my relatives." Jyn smirked. "Don't stand there waiting for me to ask, come on in. We'll have ourselves some piña coladas. Make sure to wipe your feet; I just shampooed the rugs."

As it turned out, Jyn had a knack for finding injured Mustangs and always kept an extra stall open in the garage-stable for unexpected arrivals. After T.C. set the Sawstang free in the corral to frolic, Jyn took her newly arrived guests inside. Construction on the mansion had finished only a few months before, following years of delay. She was still in the process of finding new furniture, but all the bedrooms were set up. She assigned each of them a room as she led them through the house. Rai sneaked off to the kitchen to prepare snacks, giving the others an opportunity to talk without her around. Jyn took Dirtbag and T.C. out to the pool, and they sat down around a patio table.

"Rainelle always made the best smoothies," Jyn said as she angled the table's umbrella to block out the glare of the setting sun. "Did she tell you she burned my old house down? I built this place with the insurance money. I claimed it was a dragon." She let out a sigh, looking at Dirtbag. "Listen to me blab. You must have a million questions for me."

Dirtbag unconsciously fiddled with his stitching. "Well, of course I do; she's my daughter," Dirtbag said, the weight of regret on his shoulders. "I care about her."

"You care?" Jyn exploded. "You know Katvanna really messed her up! You ran off with some princess and left that poor girl alone with that insane woman. What kind of father are you? Katvanna beat her! All that woman wanted was a little clone of herself; she couldn't stand that Rainelle was different. When she found out how different she was—" Jyn paused. "When Katvanna found out about us, Rainelle almost died protecting me. After that our relationship fell apart. She idolized you, and you weren't there for her."

Dirtbag looked down at the table, clenching his denim hands into fists. "Hey, you have no idea how angry I am at Katvanna," Dirtbag fumed. "I've made a lot of mistakes, but Rai—Loranna, is not one of them. It's easy to look back now and see what I should've done, but when I was living through it, I had to leave; that woman was killing me. I never thought she'd turn on Loranna like this and do all these hateful things. You can sit there and say whatever you want, but you will never understand the burden I carry or the guilt."

T.C. leaned forward. "That woman even ruined my first marriage, I mean, the only good one I ever had."

"You're divorced?" Jyn asked.

"Ten times. With a lot of women in between."

Jyn sat back, taking a deep breath. "All three of you have it in for Katvanna, then? Oh boy. So what's the plan? Are you going to just drop in on that witch unannounced and attempt to murder her?

Dirtbag and T.C. looked at one another. "Well," Dirtbag said, "basically, yes."

"I take it Rainelle's leading you to her?"

Dirtbag took out the compass Father Raygun had given him and checked it. "So far."

"You don't even trust her, do you?" Jyn said, disgusted.

"Hey, she flew back into my life out of nowhere," he justified.

"You should trust her," Jyn said, getting worked up. "I probably know your daughter better than you ever will, and I can tell you she loved you and missed you with all her little heart. She knew where you died, but she also understood enough to let you be. I know she loves you more than she ever loved me. That's the way it should be; she's your child. A father and daughter have a special bond; you should cherish that. It's something the rest of us will never know." Jyn calmed herself down. "I care about Rainelle," she said. "I know if you've come this far, you must plan to go all the way." She folded her hands on the table. "How can I help?"

Dirtbag slowly ran a hand through his grass-hair. "Katvanna has some kind of flying upside-down castle, and we need you"—Dirtbag corrected himself—"we'd like to ask if you could convert our Mustang into a dragon."

"So you can fly there?" Jyn paused. "I can do it, but you're going to have to pay for it—at least for the cost of materials. I'd be happy to help, but I have to run a business, too. If you can't pay, I'm sure we can work something out."

"That's fair," Dirtbag said, digging into his chest to pull out a bag of gold coins. "Hey, as long as we don't have to go off questing for dragon parts." He tossed the bag onto the table.

Jyn dusted the dirt off the bag, opened it, and took a stack of coins out. She fiddled with the stack thoughtfully. "I'll need a couple of days to do it."

T.C. pulled out the *Raymanac*. "We have plenty of time, Jyn," he said, checking the date against the moon cycle. He suddenly grinned, excited. "I can't wait to fly a dragon!"

Jyn snorted. "Oh boy. I better explain something. I don't turn the car into a dragon; I just replace the doors with wings and add a tail in the trunk for aerodynamic stability. The most difficult part is ripping out the digestive transmission and replacing it with a more powerful one. She won't run on grassaline anymore; you'll have to feed her ground beef. But she'll be fast, breathe fire, all that stuff."

"Can we keep the chainsaw?" T.C. asked.

"I don't see why not." Jyn chuckled to herself. "If you want, I can change the blades out for real dragon teeth, like the ones around your neck. That would let her cut through just about anything."

T.C. laughed and sat back, dreaming about the potential chaos. Jyn spun one of the gold coins on the table, watching Dirtbag out of the corner of her eye. "Rainelle used to have quite the temper," she told him. "She's powerful, like her mother, and she could be pretty arrogant. She'd use her words all the time to get her way. One day, we had a fight, and she turned on me, held up her little hand, and shouted something that not only destroyed my house—it killed me."

Dirtbag looked at her, shocked.

"Rainelle brought me back, but she couldn't fix everything she destroyed, so she ran away. She'd visit as a bird now and then and sometimes ask me for a favor, but I know that incident changed her. I think for the better."

Rai suddenly walked out to the table with a tray of piña colada smoothies and some little cheese sandwiches she had whipped up. She sat down and noticed they were all staring at her. "What?" she said uncomfortably. "Gah! Jyn didn't tell you about the divorce, did she?"

"No, Pumpkin. But we *were* talking about you," Dirtbag said, taking a sandwich. "Don't worry; it was good things." He smiled.

CHAPTER 31

———

The wild grass shimmered across the airy mesa in undulating waves of serenity. Dirtbag spent a full day walking through the placid landscape, absorbed in thought. He viewed the stars during the night, alone, thinking, and by morning he was back in the house for breakfast.

That afternoon he was opposite the pool, lying spread out on his back as if he had fallen there from a great height. T.C. was at the patio table some distance away. Rai stepped out of the mansion wearing a white jumpsuit she'd borrowed from Jyn. Her hair was held back with pink barrettes, and her bare, makeup-free face glowed with the warmth of happiness. She saw her father lying there and frowned as she walked over to see how he was doing. She sat down beside him and began picking at the many white flowers growing out of the frayed, worn areas of his tattered denim skin.

"Leave them be, Pumpkin," he grumbled.

"Fine, but you look like a flower bed, Dad." She cringed. "Are you even comfortable in that position?"

"I just want to lie here on the ground," he growled. "Don't worry about the flowers. That's just her. They'll disappear after a while."

"Her? Oh, you mean the princess?"

"Yes."

"I guess you never really told me anything about her. I don't even know her name."

"I"—he sat up on his elbows—"I can't talk about it, not even to you, Pumpkin," he tried to explain to her. "That story I tell—I know you've heard it already from T.C., but the end was much worse than what I've told. It's one thing to be in pain and another to see the person you love suffering. It haunts me, like these flowers. My past is always right there, just beneath the surface, and sometimes I wish I'd never known love like that." He lay back down and reached over with a denim hand to pat her knee. "I didn't mean to dampen your spirit, Pumpkin."

"Oh, it's all right, Dad. I understand. I know it's hard to talk about those things. It's hard for me, too. I remember, but I can't feel what I felt without my heart. I just remember it." She picked at some stitching on his hand that had unraveled. "I was afraid to come back here, to see Jyn again, but now I'm glad I did. I really missed her." Her voice faded off as she reflected. She shook her head and perked up. "We're almost finished, Dad."

"You don't have to come with us, Pumpkin." The deep, dark pits that were Dirtbag's eyes looked at her. "We're almost certainly going to be in for the fight of our lives, and we could really use your"—he grinned—"extensive vocabulary, but you're an adult now, and you can decide for yourself."

"Gah! It's so weird to hear you call me an adult," she said. "I feel so lost, like I don't even know what I'm doing anymore, like I'm adrift."

"That's life, Pumpkin," he told her. "There is never a right way, only the way you choose and the consequences thereafter."

She ran her fingers through his overgrown grass-hair, something no one had ever done to him before, causing him to sit very still. She picked out a tiny beetle and flicked it away. "It's weird how you're kind of warm."

"Hey, I'm lucky my rear end isn't a bug farm."

"Thanks, Dad! Way to ruin our moment." She let out a long breath. "Can I ask you something?"

"Of course, Pumpkin."

"Jyn said you just gave her a bag of gold. It was triple what she would've charged, and, I guess, that's not the first time I've seen you do that. I was just wondering where it all comes from."

Dirtbag thought about the answer carefully. "Pumpkin, during wartime, talented soldiers of fortune can amass a treasury that rivals a small kingdom, but sometimes those warriors are wiped out in battle, leaving behind one man. If he is a good man, the value of the money will never replace the friendship of those he lost, and each instance of his generosity will, to some degree, honor their memory."

Rai glanced at T.C. He was sitting too far away to overhear them. "I didn't mean to pry." She could appreciate that sometimes the past was better left ambiguous. "I guess, I really came out here to ask if Jyn and I could airbrush flames on the Sawstang."

"Fire flames? Well, is there any benefit?"

"We won't fly any faster, but it would look cool."

"Will it inspire fear in our enemies?"

"Oh, probably," she snickered.

"Go ahead then," he said. Rai's face surged with joy, and she leaned down to give him a hearty embrace. "Easy there, Pumpkin." He held her tenderly.

She stood up. "I'll be in the hangar, working, if you need me." She smiled.

"I'll be right here, blooming."

She kneeled down and kissed him on the head, right in the middle of his perpetual frown. Dirtbag responded with an affectionate grunt. She bounded away from him, her arms embracing her body.

T.C. saw her from his seat at the patio table. A half-finished game of solitaire was spread out in front of him, next to an uneaten ham sandwich and a cherry cola. He had set his meal aside to go through the old wallet returned by the ninjas. Rai approached him, uncertain if he wanted to discuss the contents with her. He grinned and invited her to join him.

"Oats alive, Rai, I don't think I've ever seen you in any other color but black," he said as she sat.

"I know, right? But I'm still wearing black underwear, so I haven't completely given it up."

T.C. sighed and pushed around the contents of the wallet arranged before him. "Rai," he began with difficulty, "when I look at you, seeing you with Dirt, I mean, just the way you are, as a daughter and not some cute girl I desire, you make me wish I had a family. I've been around. I've been rich. I've been poor. I've been a lot of things, but I've never been a father."

He slid a small, crumpled piece of canvas over to her. It was a tiny, unframed wedding portrait. "Those ninjas," he chuckled. "I just can't believe they held on to this for so long. I mean, that's wife number seven or eight or six. Let's say seven, because that's a lucky number."

Rai gently studied the portrait. "She was really pretty."

"Trust me; they all were, Rai, and that's what got me in trouble." He sipped his soda. "I dunno, Dirt tells his story, saying, 'That's love,' all the time. I've heard it more times than I can count. It's like his creed. I keep thinking…I mean, maybe I did have that with the first wife, but then, what about the rest? I had feelings for them, too. Was it love? Can I call it that? For each of them? Or can't I recognize what that is anymore?"

"You went through ten marriages, and you're telling me that just now you're thinking about these things? You can't go through life as a…a…" She struggled to find the words. "…a serial marrier."

"OK, I admit getting hitched is like going on an adventure: it's a lot of fun, at least in the beginning." He smirked, thinking. "Courting and flirting, I enjoy that, and I mean, I always try to carry that into the marriage, but most of the time women go and get this idea that they're different, that they've changed or have to change, and instead of renewing what brought us together, we grow apart. I think about my first wife: she was beyond comparison and still is, but now I tell myself that relationships are supposed to be transitional and fleeting and that I was just naïve to think it would last forever. It's a lie. I'll never find that again—that innocence, that love. I just wish I'd understood how rare it was when I had it."

Rai folded her arms. He handed her the wallet and asked if she would destroy it for him. She tucked the portrait back inside, and with a word, it was gone. They watched as the ashes were swept away by a breeze. If he was stunned by how casually she had executed his request, he didn't show it, but they both knew the act resolved nothing.

CHAPTER 32

———

The morning sun channeled light through the Grand Barrier as it peeked above the horizon. The rippling surface of unnaturally raised ocean water reflected over the mesa, casting an apparitional web of overlapping light across the ranch, as though it had been submerged. The land became painted in a luminous blue hue that preceded the transition of the sky from night. The wild grass was still, the Mustangs were asleep in their garage-stable, and the only sound was the heavy panting of an approaching paper boy. The boy was a shadow under the dim blue light. His body and the bicycle he rode resembled a strange creature gliding down the driveway. His weekly delivery came to a sudden stop at the sight of a body lying facedown on the front porch. He paused to stare at the unmoving corpse, but it was nothing he wanted to be involved in, so he threw a newspaper at it and sped away.

A series of thumps rolled through the mansion, followed by some griping. After a few minutes, the kitchen light turned on and various cooking noises emanated from the room. The door to the mansion opened just as the sun crossed the horizon and the stars faded into the day. Dirtbag stepped outside, wearing an apron stained with blueberries; he stared down at the body lying on the front porch and growled.

"Did you sleep out here all night, T.C.?" he asked, picking the newspaper out of the wad of tangled blond hair. "T.C.?"

T.C. groaned and lifted himself up. He coughed; a small vole escaped his mouth and darted for the safety of the wild grass. T.C. sat down on the porch, holding his head. Dirtbag parked himself beside his friend. The sky turned a creamy orange.

"My neck!" T.C. said, rubbing his shoulder.

"Your neck? Didn't you hear me fall down the steps?"

"I dunno, Dirt; I heard something. I mean, I'd hoped it was just my body finally imploding. I don't want to worry about dying anymore. I just want to get it done."

"Where is this coming from?"

"I spent all night thinking about my life, Dirt. No booze or cupcakes, just me and all those things I never want to remember." He spit out some vole hairs. "It's been a pretty lousy run."

"Well, so far."

"What do you mean by that?"

"Hey, you're still alive. You have the rest of your life to live better than you've been living. You can take all those lessons and regrets and turn them into wisdom. You have time to be a better man. Giving up is not something you want to do."

"OK. But, Dirt, isn't that what you did?"

Dirtbag combed back his grass-hair. "I did. I gave up, and now I wish I hadn't. I had the strength to keep going, but I didn't. I left Rai alone without a father, and I let Katvanna wreak havoc without a husband. My problems never went away; they just festered and got bigger."

"I think I'm dying, Dirt." T.C. knocked on his hollow chest.

"But are you dead?"

"Nah." He grinned and then looked down at his armored hands. "I'm just scared, Dirt, and I let it get to me."

"That's natural, given our chances." They both remembered the squid, and Dirtbag was amused. "Well, the problem with probability is that it can go either way, and it can't always account for what we decide to do. It can't change the way we feel, and often personal feelings defy common sense. I'm afraid, too." He rolled up the newspaper. "In any case, you have to admit it's going to be fun."

T.C. chuckled. "I dunno, Dirt. When I fought Bloodblivion, I mean, I was scared out of my mind, but Katvanna, I think I hate her. I just want to punish her. Is that right, Dirt?"

"I'm the one that's thinking about killing her. Is that any less right?"

"This is much harder without booze, Dirt. I mean, raging drunkenness was kind of our trademark," T.C. said, his voice peppered with remorse.

"Hey, imagine how they'll react when that crazy thing we do isn't random but intentional, maybe even part of some devious plan."

"It wasn't great planning that saved Trucebell. It was luck," T.C. admitted. "Dragons are allergic to shellfish, and we had some cooking. I mean, I was so drunk I could barely lift my sword. I just flopped myself over a grill as bait, then rolled off a split-second before the beasts struck, giving them a mouthful of barbequed crustaceans. Bravery? Booze just makes it easier to throw your life away, all at once or a piece at a time, and that's courage to cowards."

"We've been sober more often than you think. It wasn't luck that saved Trucebell; it was ingenuity. *You* changed that outcome." Dirtbag instinctively reached for a bottle, but none was there. "Hey, you and I could sit here for the next month, thinking about everything. We need to get up, get moving, and face whatever it will be. I'm not alone on that hill, and you're not dying. We're going to solve our problems together, just like we always have."

"Oats alive, Dirt, this is going to be a long day."

Jyn suddenly stepped outside in a pink robe. "Dirtbag, you left the stove on."

"I'm making blueberry pancakes. I got up early to surprise Rai. I knew you two were together last night, and I didn't want to disturb you. But it was a little dark; I fell down the steps and then found T.C. dead on the front porch, and we got to talking."

Jyn smiled. "Oh boy, you two. I hope you succeed." She offered a hand to T.C. and helped him up. She picked some debris out of his hair. "Rainelle's in the shower. Let me help out with breakfast; I make a killer espresso."

"I think I'll just hit the shower, too." T.C. excused himself.

Jyn looked at Dirtbag. "I thought he couldn't take off his armor."

"He still likes to smell good."

Dirtbag and Jyn cooked together in the kitchen. Dirtbag listened as Jyn recounted the good times she had shared with Rai. He enjoyed hearing about his daughter's life. Once they were done and the pancakes were covered under a dish to stay warm, Jyn reached in her robe pocket and pulled out a small button. Dirtbag recognized it immediately.

"Hey! That's my eye!" he said, connecting Rai to the bird that had pecked it out. "She did that?"

"She did." Jyn handed it to him. "She was mad that you'd given up."

"I was between adventures and drinking. It's hard for us when we don't have a direction."

"I know, and she needed your help, so she came up with this plan to get you involved."

"She could've asked me, Jyn."

"She was afraid."

Dirtbag stared at the button. "I keep wondering how I would've reacted. I was in a rut, and I couldn't see much farther than the next bottle. She had every right to be mad at me. I abandoned her."

Jyn looked at him. "It's not too late to be her father."

Dirtbag squeezed the button in his hand. Nothing mattered more to him than returning her heart, even if that meant killing Katvanna to do it. Something stirred inside him—it was her, the princess—and he knew at once that she supported him. He returned the button to Jyn, and they set the table.

After breakfast, the motley threesome began to prepare for departure. They were nervous about what was ahead, but the one thing that bothered them most was they had no plan.

T.C. sat next to Jyn in the half-furnished living room, telling her about the wedding rings inside the Amber Blade of Divorce. She was fascinated by the creepiness of the weapon. They were waiting on Rai while she did her makeup and hair; all of them had grown accustomed to the extra time a young woman needs to prepare for an outing.

Dirtbag flipped through the morning paper, reading over local news he couldn't care less about. He turned the page and slammed the paper down on the coffee table, disgusted. "I can't believe it! She took out a full-page ad." Dirtbag pointed to the full-color wedding announcement in the paper, featuring Katvanna's smiling face next to a man with bright, sunny eyes, spiked hair, and a business suit of armor.

"That's Van Slice?" T.C. asked, turning the paper toward him to read the text. "His teeth glow, Dirt. Can you imagine waking up to that every morning?"

"Oh boy," Jyn said, reading the paper. "I recognize a few names on the guest list; she must've invited every villain on the planet."

T.C. skimmed the list. "Those aren't just any villains, Jyn; those are our enemies. Oats alive! Dirt, do you know what this means? It's going to be a massacre!"

"We can wrap up all our loose ends at once!" Dirtbag agreed exuberantly.

Jyn looked at them, concerned.

"T.C. and I defeated all these guys before," Dirtbag reassured her. "Most of them are only alive because instead of killing them, we heroically took pity on them, and they promised to reform their ways."

"Looks like they just blew their second chance," T.C. chortled.

Rai entered the room, all set for compliments on her skillfully applied beauty and her updated outfit, which she had stayed up all night sewing pockets on. She was disappointed to see them crowded around the newspaper. Jyn noticed she needed recognition and met her by the doorway with a welcoming, light kiss on the cheek.

"I'm ready, Dad," Rai announced.

"That's nice, Pumpkin," Dirtbag said, not looking up.

"Your daughter needs attention, Dirtbag," Jyn huffed. "Be that good father."

Dirtbag hastily joined them, directing his full concentration to Rai's needs. She showed him the pockets on her legs she'd made to hold her cigarettes. He would have liked to see her give up on smoking altogether—but a pocket was better than having them tucked elsewhere.

T.C. strolled over and unwittingly interrupted. "Oats alive, Dirt! She's even invited our attorneys." He pointed at a list of names. "It says here they're coming by boat but not just any boat. I mean, they're taking my old yacht."

"You owned a yacht?" Rai frowned.

"You can't see me sailing?" T.C. threw back his hair, as though he were riding the wind.

"It's been an interesting morning, Pumpkin." Dirtbag showed her the newspaper. "You look great, by the way."

Rai's mouth dropped open as she read. "She's holding a rehearsal? Gah! There is no way she's that stupid, Dad. There's no way she'd print all that for us to read. She has to know we're coming."

"Or," Dirtbag speculated, "she wants us to know she invited all these people so we're intimidated."

"I know, right?" Rai said breathlessly. "Fighting her is one thing, but that's an army, Dad."

"We've fought armies before, Pumpkin," Dirtbag enthused confidently. "What's interesting is she seems to be gathering the army, but she doesn't have it yet. If we could figure out a way to mix in with all the guests, we might surprise her and take that upside-down flying castle from the inside out."

"Gah! Dad? Did you really just say that? That was planned, right? I hope it was."

T.C. had a brainstorm. "Dirt! Dirt! Rai!" he said ecstatically. "I just had an idea. It's crazy—I mean, it's insane, but hear me out."

They listened, and Jyn decided she needed to lie down.

CHAPTER 33

———

Rai narrowed her eyes and spoke softly. The stern of the luxury yacht, the *Thighlossus*, detonated across the mirrorlike surface of the peaceful cyan ocean, blasting a fine mist of burning fiberglass into the water, accompanied by the deep, clangorous ripping of metal tearing away from the submerged hull on its way to the seafloor far below. Gray ash swirled in the air, the unlucky remains of three paralegals that had jokingly asked Rai for a light and then made fun of her quest to recover her stolen heart. She watched the broken remnants of the hot tub sink beneath the waves with a certain degree of satisfaction. A crooked cigarette, bent from the explosion, hung bitterly from her purple-painted lips, and with a whisper, she lit it.

Before turning the yacht over to his nefarious attorney, T.C. had it emblazoned with an obnoxious bright orange and christened after the only ex-wife whose nickname he could never forget: the Great Thighlossus. As he had hoped, his attorney was too cheap to repaint and reregister the vessel; the mammoth boat was easily spotted from the air as it leisurely cruised through the ancient sea. They had swooped in and attempted to negotiate help from the ship of partying legal professionals, only to be turned down and mocked. The melee that followed had wrecked most of the yacht, causing it to list slightly starboard, but the initial damage paled in comparison to Rai's ensuing outburst.

"That was a little much," Dirtbag said, looking over the completely destroyed stern, impressed, "even if they were bullies."

"Dad," Rai said, blowing smoke through her nose, "words *can* hurt."

"I know they can, Pumpkin." He dragged a jukebox across the deck, scraping the polished hardwood floor. "Can you give me a hand with this?"

"I guess…Where's T.C.? He's super strong," she said, getting behind the jukebox. She began pushing it toward the shattered stern.

"He's below deck, fitting his attorney into a briefcase," Dirtbag said, pulling. "We heard it could be done."

"Oh, and am I supposed to take that seriously?" Rai frowned. She leaned against the jukebox, and together they gave it a good shove, sliding it to the brink, where it wobbled precariously. She heard muffled shouting from inside and jumped back. "Someone's in there!"

Dirtbag shrugged. "That's only my lawyer, Pumpkin." He put a coin into the jukebox and picked a song. Horrible country-western music began to play, and, pleased with the ghastly tune, he kicked the jukebox into the water. Within moments, the floating machine sparked and caught fire. Strangely, the desperate howls of his wretched attorney produced an unexpectedly harmonious rhythm with the music. Dirtbag listened to the begging and pleading as the jukebox sank. He smirked, enjoying the hymnlike quality of the medley as the flaming machine plunged beneath the waves, leaving behind a few bubbles and a blond toupee. He turned toward Rai with a grin. "He's sunk to a new low."

"Yay, disturbing." Rai flicked her cigarette away, rolling her eyes.

"Hey, ridding the world of evil is not always something you can be proud of." Dirtbag explained. "Doing what's needed and justified is never clean or easy, not as long as you have integrity. That's why it's important to enjoy any part you can." He flipped a heavy, marble dining table bottom up and started breaking off the legs. "Give me a hand with this; we've thrown everything else overboard already."

"I know, right? I guess we can always strap people to the anchor," she sneered.

"Hey, that's a good idea, Pumpkin."

"Oh! No! I've done enough, all right? I need a smoke break." She changed into a pied falconet and flew up to the mast.

"Hey!" Dirtbag shouted.

"Screee!" Rai replied.

"Don't you use that tone with me, young lady!" he lectured.

"Oats alive!" T.C. said, emerging from below deck and dragging three whimpering men in business suits by their fancy neckties. He held a book in his hand. "Do you know what this is, Dirt?"

"It looks like the *Guild's Book of Law*."

"I mean, this guy threw it at me." T.C. yanked one of the suited men forward.

"And?"

"He threw the book at me, Dirt!"

Dirtbag groaned.

"Where's Rai?" T.C. asked.

"Something bothered her, and now she's taking a break." Dirtbag gestured to her location high above them as he pulled the heavy marble table over to the edge of the demolished stern.

"She's just under a lot of pressure, Dirt; she understands the power she has," T.C. said, forcing the three men down onto the table. He began duct-taping them to it with a brand-new roll that had a glowing mechanical core. "I can't believe how many of these guys were packed into this boat. I mean, just how many attorneys do you need at a wedding, anyway?"

"It wouldn't be the first time Katvanna hid behind an army of lawyers," Dirtbag grumbled, patting down the three attorneys and looking for anything useful. He opened the suit coat of the one at the end and found a business card. "Another divorce attorney, eh? And a property-distribution specialist, no less? Tell me, scumbag; how do you 'distribute' anything when one side always gets everything?" he snarled. "I better go find some more weights, T.C. I want to make sure this scumbag hits the bottom."

"No! W-wait!" the attorney groveled. "I can tell you Van Slice's plan!"

T.C. continued taping the men down to the table. The other attorneys glared at the talkative one, trying to get him to keep his mouth shut. Dirtbag handed T.C. a cast-iron skillet from the galley.

"Well, speak up, scumbag!" Dirtbag demanded.

T.C. put the skillet inside the attorney's coat.

"It's a real-estate scam! Ow!" the attorney cried between lengths of tape being applied. "Van Slice wants to buy the whole Earth, because it's cheap! It's in a good location for intergalactic yuppies who want space condos. Ow! He can't legally buy the planet, because he's nonterrestrial, so he's going to marry into terrestrialship. Ow! He plans to use his vast wealth to purchase the world and evict anyone who refuses to pay him rent or who would hurt property values."

"Oats alive!" T.C. shouted. "See, Dirt, we *are* saving the world after all."

"Scumbag deluxe!" Dirtbag growled. He grabbed the attorney by his collar and jerked him around the table, tearing arm and leg hairs loose under the bands of tape. "Who's officiating over this travesty?"

"Like a priest? Ow! Ow! They don't have one. They're going to be legally married, not spiritually; these people are so rotten they had to steal a couple of hearts just to comply with the Guild's terms and conditions. Katvanna paid us not to ask where she got them."

Dirtbag fumed. "Who is this Van Slice? Where does he come from?"

"His father, Arch Slice, owns a nebula and manufactures interstellar gas; he wants to marry off his disgraceful son while he's in his prime, before he shrivels up into a white dwarf. Ow! Ow! Ow! Van Slice is a playboy who stumbled upon our planet during a bender and saw an opportunity. That's not even his real name. His real name doesn't even translate into a language; it's a frequency! The whole wedding is just an excuse to find terrestrial investors. The Guild is attending as consultants and as an interested party."

"Now, wait just a minute." T.C. stared angrily. "The Guild of Attorneys is helping to sell our own planet right out from under us?"

"Screee!" Rai yelled from her perch.

Dirtbag nodded. "Exactly, that's bad for the environment. Toss these scumbag traitors over."

"W-wait!" begged the attorney as T.C. slid the dining table past the tipping point. "I thought if I told you some useful information, you'd let me go. Isn't that the deal?"

"What deal?" Dirtbag scoffed. "You didn't negotiate anything, scumbag! You presumed there was an agreement. You're a terrible attorney!"

They flipped the heavy dining table over the side of the yacht and watched as it quickly sank below the surface, leaving behind a few dozen business cards. Rai flew down to the deck and transformed into a young woman. She flicked the butt of her cigarette away and took the glowing duct tape from T.C.

"Whoa! I was using that, Rai," he protested.

"I don't think Jyn gave us never-ending, self-manufacturing duct tape with this in mind, all right?"

"OK, first of all, this is not what you think it is, Rai," T.C. insisted. "I mean, these are attorneys, right? It's not murder; it's something else. I mean, nobody gets upset when you pull weeds out of the ground, right?"

"Or flush the toilet," Dirtbag added.

"Gah!" Rai snarled, conflicted. She returned the roll of tape to T.C.

"Trust me, Rai," T.C. tried to explain. "There is just no way we could've done this without never-ending duct tape. I mean, there must've been sixty attorneys on this boat. Oats alive! I was afraid we were going to run out of furniture to tie them to."

"Fine!" Rai breathed. "I guess it was ugly but had to be done, especially since, in a way, the whole planet is in danger now, or at least the innocent people who live on it."

"And the little animals," T.C. mentioned.

"Oh, I know, right?" Rai wrinkled her nose. "Those poor little animals."

Dirtbag pulled out a flame-patterned key fob from his satchel and clicked it. In the sky above them, the Sawstang honked an acknowledgment. It circled the damaged yacht twice as it descended to make a landing on the limited space of the crumbling deck. It hovered over the yacht, using the small jet turbines embedded in its glossy-black wings, before gracefully touching down on its tires. It roared enthusiastically.

The Sawstang they had known had become an entirely different creature. The newly added, massive dragon wings joined seamlessly at the door hinges, as though they had sprouted out naturally. When on the ground, the wings folded up against the length of the car like extra-long doors. The sleek, scorpion-like dragon tail was able to collapse and tuck away inside the trunk, and the fearsome dragon-toothed chainsaw could retract under a raised bump on the hood to increase aerodynamics. The Sawstang was no longer red; it was now a metallic obsidian, with an intricate flame pattern decorating the front end and the leading edges of the dragon wings. And it breathed fire.

"Good girl!" Dirtbag said, petting the Sawstang. "Rai, why don't you feed her some of the hamburgers those interns were cooking?"

Rai curled her lips, flashing an attitude. She picked through the overturned barbecue buffet. The interns had been stuffed inside a smoker grill and thrown over the side, immediately followed by a meat freezer containing their supervisor. She took a tray of cooked burgers over to the Sawstang. It wagged its dragon tail and revved playfully, causing the stern to grate loudly. Rai tossed a couple of patties into its mouth.

"Hey! Take the cheese off those before you give them to her, Pumpkin," Dirtbag said. "Cheese is bad for cars."

"But, Dad, this could be her last meal." Rai fed the Sawstang a few more cheeseburgers. "She's been so good to us; she deserves a treat."

"Listen to your father, Rai," T.C. sided. "We don't want her to seize up midflight. I mean, we can spoil her afterward, if we survive."

The bow creaked sharply, something buckled below deck, and the yacht began to quickly fill with water. T.C. picked up the pile of belongings they had collected from the attorneys and heaved them into the backseat of the Sawstang. They climbed into the dragon car, and it lifted off, turbines whirling. They watched the empty yacht rapidly submerge from sight and into the shadowy depths of the ocean.

"OK, here's the good news," T.C. said, picking through the heap of business suits. "We have official invitations, badges, and lots of nice things to wear. I mean, I even found lady outfits for Rai."

"And the bad news?" Dirtbag asked, turning the Sawstang to the direction his compass was pointing.

"I couldn't find a time meter anywhere, Dirt."

"Well, that would've been handy," Dirtbag lamented.

Rai sorted through the different business suits. "Dad? How is T.C. supposed to wear any of these? He can't even take off his armor."

"But, Pumpkin," Dirtbag said with a playful smile, "you can sew."

She folded her arms, annoyed.

CHAPTER 34

———

The Sawstang raced over the gently rolling ocean, skimming its surface with glee, dodging sudden swells of sun-sparkling azure. Rai and T.C. sat next to each other in the backseat. She busily sewed his business-suit disguise, a haphazard hodgepodge of dissimilar fabric pieces that happened to fit over sections of his bulky plate armor. His shoulder spaulders were too large to cover, so she had resorted to wrapping sleeves around his arms and fitting together two mismatched suit coats over his chest and back. The Sawstang dove behind a rising wave, and T.C.'s hair whipped into Rai's mouth, causing her to hack.

"Whoops, sorry, Rai," he said, reeling in his hair.

She leaned back and examined her work. "This looks so bad." She cringed. "You look like a hobo, T.C."

Dirtbag turned away from the steering wheel to see. "Hey, you did great, Pumpkin." He smiled.

"Gah! Dad, you're my father; you'd say anything I did was great."

"Trust me, Rai,"T.C. said, tightening his sewn-on false necktie. "It looks like a suit; that's all that matters. I mean, we have official Guild badges, and nobody—I mean, just nobody—questions the Guild of Attorneys."

Rai picked up her Power of Attorney badge and pinned it to the yellow pastel woman's suit she had squeezed over her black leather outfit. The badge was an infuriated golden skull, with white diamond eyes, biting down on a chrome judge's gavel. It was mounted on a miniature replica of the *Book of Law* and weighed quite a lot. Each badge had a unique rank number stamped on the skull's forehead. They had taken badges with the highest ranks they could find.

Dirtbag picked an errant thread off his badge, pleased that he had acquired the emblem from his own attorney. "I still can't believe my guy didn't have a wallet," Dirtbag mused out loud.

"Attorneys don't pay for things, Dirt."T.C. said, affixing his sword to his back as he climbed into the passenger seat. "I mean, you pay *them*—or they take it. That's the power of attorney."

"That's awful." Rai wrinkled her nose.

"That's just the way it is, Rai."T.C. exhaled. "When you want to hurt somebody without breaking the law, you litigate. I mean, you hire the baddest attorney you can find, and you pay him to hate for you. The way I see it, because nobody is actually feeling bodily pain, like you would in warfare, people tend to just hate without restraint."

"Jyn and I never hired attorneys; we filed a no-fault divorce ourselves." Rai bit her lower lip, remembering.

The Sawstang climbed over a wave, revving its engine exuberantly from the thrill of flight. T.C. spread his hair over his shoulders to hide the sewn-together collar. Rai watched him, unconvinced. "So, most attorneys don't have long, beautiful hair, T.C."

"Swell. OK, I know; we can say I'm foreign."

"But from where?" she asked.

"It doesn't matter, Rai. I mean, I'm just not from around here—wherever we are—and nobody knows everywhere."

Dirtbag ran his hand over his denim face. He looked over his brown suit with pink stripes and hoped its near-perfect fit would be enough to distract people from the fact that he had no eyes. He had hidden his shotgun and satchel inside his torso, giving him a brawny appearance.

Rai tried on some thick-rimmed eyeglasses she had found. She squinted, trying to see through the high-powered prescription. Frustrated, she poked out the lenses.

"Hey, you should wear those, Pumpkin," Dirtbag said.

"Oh, so I can look smart?" she chirped.

"No, because you look really cute."

T.C. turned to look at her and agreed. "Whoa! You should wear them with those ninja cat ears," he suggested.

She put the cat ears on over the glasses and looked in the rearview mirror to see what she looked like. "Yay, talk about overkill." Her cat ears twitched downward to match her embarrassment.

"Oats alive! They move!" T.C. laughed. "You definitely need to wear those. I mean, being adorable has a lot of advantages."

"Gah!"

"Well, you are, Pumpkin," Dirtbag said, checking the compass to make sure they were flying in the right direction. "We might fool the morons and a few scumbags for a little while, but as soon as we're discovered, it'll be war. Every little bit helps."

"Fine. Oh, and, thanks, by the way." She pretended to be irritated. "Thanks for the rooting when I kissed Jyn good-bye; way to ruin our little moment," she said, scowling at T.C.

"You were just so shy, Rai," T.C. told her. "I mean, you were standing there, and Jyn just grabbed you by the arms and gave it to you, and I thought it was great. I mean, the last thing that kissed me that passionately was Muffin."

"Last *thing?*" Rai frowned.

"Muffin was a unicorn. She used to be a stable maid, but then my wife found out."

"Dad!" Rai called out.

"I'm sorry, Pumpkin," Dirtbag sighed. "I watched T.C. make out with that horse every night."

"No! Why?" She winced. "Oh, forget it."

A black dot appeared on the horizon, and they all saw it. Anxiety filled their minds, burying their friendly banter under a landslide of inevitability. Dirtbag double-checked the compass just to be sure. It pointed at the approaching dot.

"Well, that's it"—he cleared his throat—"the upside-down flying castle."

"I wish we could do this tomorrow," Rai fretted.

"Trust me." T.C. tried to relax. "When you put off things that need to be done, they just get worse." He shifted in his seat. "I just hope there's a bathroom."

Dirtbag watched the rapidly growing shape on the horizon with suspicion. "I don't think that's a castle," he said. "It looks like a jellyfish."

As the hovering object came into view, he noticed it had an umbrellalike metal dome that could easily be interpreted as the upside-down foundation of a castle, with thick hanging tentacles around a central stalk that resembled conical spires surrounding a towering keep. Yet, it wasn't quite a jellyfish either; it was a spaceship of some kind. The metal dome was white, with strange geometric markings that divided it into quarters. At the very top of the dome, the metal turned transparent, and under it was a small forest of glowing crystal-amethyst trees. The hanging silver spires were irregularly segmented, like collapsed spines with glowing vertebrae, and the central stalk was encircled by rectangular towers interconnected with windowed tubes. Strange petallike landing pads grew from the ends of the outermost towers, permitting different types of flying machines to land on them.

"Now, wait just a minute," T.C. said in disbelief as they circled the dome. "I mean, this is a space jellyfish that happens to look like an upside-down flying castle?"

"What was I supposed to call it? A weird flying thing?" Rai replied, fidgeting. "I said it *looks* like an upside-down flying castle, all right? Which it does, in a way—a really weird way. At least I said it was a spaceship."

"And you've been in there?" Dirtbag asked her.

"Sort of," Rai breathed. "I snuck in a few times to, uh, collect my allowance."

"Well"—he let her thievery go—"what about all my old stuff Katvanna dumped on that bazaar?"

"Oh! That was me, Dad. She moved out of our castle when she met Van Slice. I just hid your things on a balcony and pushed them off every now and then. I was trying to leave a trail for you guys to follow. I wanted to be your mysterious guide, but then…stuff happened."

"Dirt"—T.C. turned, delighted—"you lived in a castle?"

"Well, they don't offer princesses to commoners, do they?" Dirtbag growled. "Pumpkin, what's it like in there? Is it deathtraps and murder machines?"

"Yeah right. You know Mom; she likes the finer things. I guess it looked spacey before she took over, but now it has this total bed-and-breakfast vibe."

"Those attorneys were coming by boat. Pumpkin, how were they going to get up there?"

"Oh! The valets have little balloon things."

"Valets?" T.C. chuckled.

The Sawstang sped around the mountainous dome to the other side, where the sky was full of strange flying machines queued up to follow an approach path marked by hovering lanterns. A red-vested valet whistled at them from a nearby landing petal. He began waving them over, using a pair of glowing magic wands. The valets were pretentious, fresh-faced pretty boys who busily distracted one another by practicing synchronized dance moves. After a craft before them landed, the valets spent five minutes prancing around the tarmac, completely ignoring the threats being hurled their way by those still waiting in line.

"Anybody can dance like that if you drink enough tea," Dirtbag ridiculed, watching the valets gyrate and squat.

He flashed the high beams at the valets to break up their routine. Two attendants, specially trained for parking monsters, began to lure the Sawstang to a prepared dragon-specific landing space by intermittently revealing a freshly made ninety-six-ounce steak from under a sheet of aluminum foil.

As they slowly descended, Dirtbag and T.C. scrutinized the other arriving guests. "That's Lord Cheddar Cheese!" T.C. pointed at a knight clad in golden-orange armor, rolling a ribbon-covered cheese wheel.

"Hey, I slew his brother Baron Brie," Dirtbag said with a shameless grin.

"I heard that guy was lactose intolerant," T.C. casually remarked.

"How do you think I did it?" Dirtbag remembered the irony. "Nobody should take cheese making that seriously."

"I know, right?" Rai sneered sarcastically.

"The man was a tyrant, Pumpkin," Dirtbag elaborated. "Everybody wants a revolution until you give them one. Then they try to prosecute you for the freedom you gave them, because gaining it wasn't as virtuous as they'd hoped. Blaming someone else is the quickest way to a clear conscience."

"Swell. I see three centaurs I know, Dirt," T.C. said, distracted by the half-horse men. "That big one in front with the tan. I mean, that's the guy that—Wait, I don't believe it! Look! Look!" He pointed below them to an arriving woman wearing a business skirt so short it failed to cover the ends of her garters. "That's my marriage counselor."

"So, is she dangerous?" Rai hazarded to ask.

"Just don't let her get those legs wrapped around you."

"Gah! This is going to be the most awkward battle ever!" Rai said, folding her arms. "You can't have a history with *all* these people. What about those ninjas over there?"

A docked, hexagonal-shaped barge was unloading a swarm of three hundred black-leather ninjas wearing sleeveless tuxedo jackets.

"More ninjas?" Dirtbag grumbled as the masked men streamed into the flying jellyfish. "At least they knew what to wear, unlike those centaurs, who could use some pants."

"You're not worried about the ninjas?" Rai asked.

"Rai, I used to wear socks made out of blue-suede karate-pajamas," T.C. boasted, "until a pair of lady ninjas tried to steal them off my feet. I made a peace overture, and they were receptive. I mean, wow, were those two athletic! I wanted to marry the one; the other had really long toes, but then I thought, nah, too many secrets."

"What? Why? Why do you have to be such a womanizer?"

"Now, wait just a minute. What's wrong with womanizing?" T.C. defended. "I mean, most women don't even know who they are until they meet me, and then once they do, they leave; some even run. That's empowerment. I womanize them. You might just say I'm an expert at womanization, that and horrifying divorces."

"But you don't really mean that," Rai said, figuring him out. "You joke about your pain a lot. I guess, in a way, it's like you're punishing yourself, like you don't want to forget your regrets."

T.C. chuckled, barely able to disguise his bitterness. "Spot-on as usual, Rai. I mean, my life has just been a cascading, ever-expanding ruin since that first divorce. OK, I know that. Trust me; I know. I've never been a good husband. I mean, I've never been a good man, but I've been a decent hero." His armored hands clenched as he explained. "Heroes, real ones, are not perfect people. They're like me, Rai: flawed, damaged—I mean, driven by and compelled to do those things that any ordinary person would call foolhardy and stupid. I've got stupid in spades. I've gone and messed up my whole life. I can't fix that. I just can't fix the past, but I can fix you, and I can fix Dirt. I mean, helping you two is the only good thing I have going for me anymore."

The Sawstang touched down on the landing petal, and an obnoxious pretty-boy valet danced his way over to give them a parking stub.

He leaned into the car over T.C., his ear-to-ear grin revealing perfectly spaced teeth. "Welcome to the *Empyrean*! We're overjoyed to have you!" he gushed, placing the stub on the dashboard. He turned. "Madam, if I may, what lovely blond hair."

T.C. punched him right in the mouth.

CHAPTER 35

————

Dirtbag walked through the cavernous, overly decorated maze-like interior of the *Empyrean*, the apparent name of the flying space jellyfish, with T.C. and Rai escorting him like bodyguards. Crowds parted before them, and doorways were cleared without their asking. The eyes of the various invited guests glanced timidly as the three approached, conversations abruptly stopped, and heads turned away, fearing the attorneys might see any second glances. Their true identities went unnoticed; the guests dismissed any passing resemblances the well-dressed trio possessed as coincidental. They were a dread-inspiring force that nobody wanted to question lest they be asked questions themselves, and everyone there was guilty of something in a court of law.

The inside of the spaceship was filled with rich hardwood floors, sporadically covered by vintage rugs and runners made of bamboo. Every other room led into a den with a fireplace or a library. The rooms in between varied and were increasingly unconventional. One featured a sizable fishing pond surrounded by wicker rocking chairs, where ninjas and knights were napping together, apparently waiting for fish to bite. Guests were playing board games in glass-floored rec rooms, where they sat on large couches covered with handmade quilts of precious gems. Occasionally, there was a random ottoman in the hallway, with a slightly ajar storage drawer filled to the top with gold coins, as if daring visitors to steal something and invoke their hostess's wrath. It was a never-ending showroom of ostentatious vulgarity, an interior decorator's worst nightmare, and then there was the indoor golf course.

"Oats alive! We should just crash this thing on a beach somewhere and sell time-shares, Dirt!" T.C. said, crossing the wide-open green and watching villains tee off. "Are we sure the kitchen's this way?"

Dirtbag wasn't listening; he was distracted by the grass fading seamlessly into the hardwood floor as they reached the edge of the golf course. "Astroturf, of course, he's a spaceman."

"Just why are we going to the kitchen anyway?" T.C. asked.

Rai huffed. "It's part of the plan, if we can even call it that. Don't you remember? We came up with it only ten minutes ago, when we stepped into that bathroom together. Gah! As if I wasn't already traumatized enough from everything else in my life! Oh! And I still can't believe you said that valet danced into your fist. His boss even apologized for the inconvenience."

"Nobody wants a lawsuit," T.C. chuckled. "I mean, it's good to have the power of attorney."

"Oh, I know, right?" Rai nodded sarcastically. "At least that bucktoothed rabbit-ogre thing was kind enough to tell us the kitchen is past the golf course and to the left of the horse ranch."

"Horses?" T.C. said excitedly.

"Gah! No! Dad!"

"Hey! Stop it, you two!" Dirtbag growled, taking out the rehearsal schedule they'd been given when they entered. "We're in the middle of a suicide mission here; don't make me separate you two, because I will."

T.C. imitated a sensual horse whinny. Rai pretended to dry heave. Dirtbag scowled at them both and waited for them to straighten up before opening the schedule pamphlet. "Well, we missed the welcome reception, as did most of the guests, apparently. Now it's cocktails and chitchat, then later on a presentation by Katvanna detailing how to kill me, then dinner and a magic show. Rehearsal starts tomorrow, followed by a party precelebrating my death. The actual wedding is in three days, coinciding with the lunar eclipse." The entire back side of the pamphlet was a raffle ticket for a toaster. Dirtbag's brow tightened. "I think we should attack during her presentation. That way all our enemies will be together in one big room."

"Uh, but, Dad. We'll be in there with them," Rai said anxiously, fiddling with the cigarettes in her pocket. "We'll be totally surrounded."

"Now, not necessarily." T.C. grinned cheerfully. "If we sit right in the middle, we can just work our way out like an exploding tumor—I mean, the type you can catch in the tropics."

Rai narrowed her eyes. "Tumors don't explode, T.C."

"Obviously, Rai," T.C. said with authority, "you haven't traveled enough to know."

"Did you even go to school?" she sneered.

Dirtbag stared at the two of them, irritated. "That plan's not as crazy as it sounds, Pumpkin. T.C. and I didn't make it this far without being"—he paused—"smart about things. It's all about orchestrating chaos. If we can just get to the kitchen and speak with Zev Brazier."

"He's dead, Dad," Rai said.

"Why would Katvanna kill the finest personal chef on the planet?" Dirtbag wondered aloud. "Do you know how much trouble we went through to hire that guy?"

"I guess Mom kind of destroyed him because he was somebody you liked," Rai reasoned. "After she found out about you and the princess, she got weird; she started collecting souls in jars and creepy stuff like that. She probably hired some caterers. They'll most likely end up in jars, too. Just like Zev."

"Jars? Swell. What does she do with them?" T.C. asked.

"Once, I saw her sunbathing with an open one." Rai frowned. "There was a straw in it."

"Oats alive! Drinking souls? Does this woman ride a broomstick, too, Dirt?"

"Well, her mother did at our wedding," Dirtbag said, combing back his grass-hair. "My father told me it was a bad sign, but I never listened," he growled. "On one hand, it's terrible she went and drank Zev's soul, but on the other hand, now nobody in the kitchen will recognize us."

"Whoa! Smell that?" T.C. smiled, and they looked at him, disgusted. He took a step back, offended by their unmentionable accusation. "I meant do you smell the pies on sticks baking in the kitchen?"

"Wait. What? How do you know those pies are on sticks?" Rai narrowed her eyes.

"Trust me; it's a wedding. I mean, everything will be on sticks."

Rai wrinkled her nose.

They followed the delicious, warm, buttery-cinnamon scent through the hallways, up two flights of stairs, and into a large kitchen, where hundreds of chefs labored. Upon their arrival, a pastry chef dropped his mixing bowl on the floor, creating a scurry of activity to quickly clean it up. Stew Bolli, the executive chef in charge of the catering operation, rushed out of his office waving a riding crop, determined to run them out of the kitchen. He was a chubby, little snot with a big white cowboy hat and a curly moustache. T.C. whispered he wanted to rip the 'stache off and burn it in a wok. Rai quickly shushed him.

"Holee tornado! That there raspberry pie is done ruined," Stew Bolli proclaimed in a whiney voice with an unusual, vowel-slinging twang.

"Why don't you just scrape that garbage off the floor and cook it anyway?" T.C. ridiculed. "I mean, have you seen the people out there? They won't know the difference. You could serve them whale prostate and tell them it was organic giraffe haggis."

The insult hit Stew like a whipcrack to his hindquarters, causing him to fix his hat. "I've eaten a bowl of beans more polite than you folks. I reckon you better turn yourselves right around and march on out of here before I get surly."

Dirtbag tapped his attorney badge. "Hey, don't be so hasty, unless, of course, you're hiding something."

Stew began to sweat. "The only thing I'm hiding in this here kitchen is Grandma's recipe for heavenly red-velvet java soufflé!"

"Well, are you sure?" Dirtbag pressed. "Because, you know, a lawsuit can put anyone, no matter who he is, right out of business permanently. It would be a shame if we found out you cut corners or used substandard ingredients or that you overlooked the special dietary needs of certain guests."

Stew jumped back. "Listen here; I already have a list of every underhanded coward out there that won't eat meat. I'm a-cooking up a tofu brisket so flavorful it ought to please even their worthless, timid bellies. Don't you tell me there's another bunch of varmints in need of special vittles. I don't care who they are. If they can't consume my delicious undertakings, they may as well excuse themselves from the whole proceedings."

"Well, what if I told you these guests were ninjas?"

"Ninjas?" Stew chuckled. "Why, I better find me a can of antikarate spray!"

Dirtbag didn't laugh. "These are black-leather ninjas, who, as I recall, require bacon-wrapped dates stuffed with mesquite-smoked almonds. You do have those prepared, don't you? It would be a shame if a swarm of three hundred ninjas decided to complain, don't you think?"

"I"—Stew gulped—"I ain't never heard of a ninja complaining."

"I know; neither have I. They tend to just do things. Like come out of the walls at night with knives."

Stew loosened his collar and cleared his throat. "I reckon I hadn't thought about that. Why, I'll cook them karate folks up a feast of dates so scrumptious they'll leap right out of their pajamas. That there crooked magician's demand for steaks on sticks is just going to have to wait. He can feed his tigers both his feet to tide them over, for all I care. I ain't never seen a man dance so badly in my life. Everyone done thought he was having a convulsion."

"Whoa! Did you say tigers?" T.C. asked.

"As big as life." The chef gesticulated as he spoke. "That there magician calls himself Fugue, and I ain't peeling your potatoes about that name. That's what he goes by. He runs these ten white tigers, of varying degrees of invulnerability, back and forth and whatnot. Every night it's the same old thing: fire, ice, acid, explosions. I reckon he might have himself a show if he weren't such a despicable lowlife. Them critters got to be fed twice a day, or they turn sour and start bawling."

"Interesting." Dirtbag considered. "If you'll excuse me for a second, chef, I'd like to discuss with my colleagues the legal ramifications of what you've just told me."

Dirtbag motioned to T.C. and Rai that they should find a quiet spot. Stew noticed Rai for the first time and immediately started to fawn over her. "Holee sweet potato! That adorable young lady is an attorney, too? Mighty fine kitten ears you have there. There a reason why you're wearing them things, or are you just one of them youths that has issues?"

"She's"—Dirtbag smirked—"our employee of the month."

"You don't say?" Stew took his hat off for her. "It's always encouraging to see youths applying themselves, particularly when they're pretty, young things like yourself." He replaced his hat and became more serious. "Don't you be like my wife. She stands in the kitchen all day long, and I tell her to get out, on account she can't fry an egg to save her life. I've been meaning to divorce her; you folks being attorneys and all, maybe we can work something out. What do you say?"

"Trust me. We're lawyers; we can help." T.C. smiled as convincingly as he could.

They excused themselves and huddled in the far corner of the pantry while the kitchen staff looked on nervously.

"Dad," Rai whispered. "What are we doing? I feel like we are dangerously close to things flying out of control."

"Relax, Pumpkin," Dirtbag said quietly. "This is the prelude to chaos. We're just planting the seeds."

"OK, we're starving the tigers to make them angry, right?" T.C. asked, keeping his voice low. "Or is it laxatives for the ninjas?"

"Neither," Dirtbag said, working out the details. "These chef guys love to complain about doing things, but he'll figure out a way to cook for both the tigers and the ninjas if I properly motivate him. I'll offer that scumbag a cut-rate deal for his divorce and a bunch of empty promises on the condition he makes our clients happy."

"Just tell him we represent that whole swarm of ninjas," T.C. told Rai.

"What? Me?" Rai was aghast. "Why me?"

"Because he has a thing for you," T.C. snickered.

"Gah! Did you see when he took his hat off? His hair looked like a greasy bird's nest!"

"Pumpkin," Dirtbag said patiently, "in the bathroom, you reminded us that you studied. I know you're powerful, but can you be subtle?"

"I guess."

"Enchanting the food was a good idea," Dirtbag said, proud of her.

"Whoa, Dirt, are we using magic?" T.C. ribbed.

Dirtbag growled. "That was the plan; I knew you weren't listening as soon as you picked up that magazine."

"It was a swimsuit issue, Dirt."

Rai agitatedly shook her hands to get their attention. "But what am I casting? Please tell me we're not poisoning the tigers!"

Dirtbag grinned. "Just the opposite, I want you to do something so that the tigers and ninjas will see us as their friends. I want you to make them our allies."

Rai's cat ears perked up. She smiled mischievously.

CHAPTER 36

————

Dirtbag followed a lumbering, wheezing, overweight baboon usher through the extravagant amphitheater. It paused for a moment to light up a cigarette, exhausted from the stroll across the plush red carpet. Their seats were somewhere in the floor section of the half-bowl-shaped arena, in front of the elevated stage where a band was currently warming up. Above them, the ceiling twinkled with imitation stars under the distant rim of a synthetic Milky Way shadowed by the ever-approaching Andromeda Galaxy. The baboon startlingly went into a spate of phlegm-laden coughing, inhaling from its cigarette each time it caught a clear breath. Dirtbag vigorously rubbed its back until it had recovered enough to continue; he was grateful the animal had not died in the aisle. The sight of the disease-ridden baboon compelled Rai to throw her cigarettes away.

"Are you sure about that?" Dirtbag asked her. "Cold turkey?"

"That monkey has no teeth, Dad," she whispered, disturbed that another baboon had already picked up her discarded packs.

"Well, you do have a nice smile, Pumpkin."

T.C. trailed behind, sizing up the audience, sipping his dark chocolate macchiato cobbled together from three cans' worth of pureed, roasted coffee beans poured into an unwashed jug that once contained an additive used to degrease stoves. It was the strongest nonalcoholic drink Stew Bolli could muster, but T.C. still missed the comfort of his booze. He drank another mouthful through a wooden straw and watched the long-haired, brightly clothed rock band quietly rehearse various songs on stage, generally keeping people entertained while they were seated.

"Listen to the way that guy's playing; his hand's fake,"T.C. snarled, watching the lead guitarist suspiciously. "That's a mannequin hand; it has to be. I mean, he'd get better sound out of that thing just dragging it across the floor."

The baboon barked and pointed to a group of velvet-upholstered seats.

"Uh, our section is a little empty." Rai cringed.

"About sixty guests went for a swim, Rai. I mean, that opened a few spots."T.C. drank some more coffee, and his eyebrows curled up from the caffeine. "They'll start filling those in when they see no one else is coming."

Dirtbag chuckled. "No one is going to risk taking a seat from an attorney." He tipped the baboon a few gold coins, and it scampered away. "We need the room to maneuver anyway."

"Yay." Rai exhaled nervously, wrapping her cloak around herself as she settled in, sandwiched between Dirtbag and T.C. "Nice planetarium," she observed. "But isn't it weird to have one on a spaceship?"

"Whoa, we got the cheap seats. I mean, check this out." T.C. tore off an armrest. "That's not gold trim; that's just gold paint."

"Well, we're attorneys, not royalty," Dirtbag admitted. "We're feared but not especially liked or considered important enough to be given the best seats."

The VIP section was at the foot of the concert stage, where distinguished people, creatures, and illustrious things that couldn't be categorized sat. In the second-best seats were the black-leather ninjas and a ballet troop of fencing assassins. Dirtbag, T.C., and Rai sat in the middle of the theater, in the third-best seats, right where they wanted to be. Notable guests in the fourth- through seventh-best seats included second-rate wizards who couldn't grow beards, a group of rowdy roller-derby pirates, a few centaurs surrounding a keg of mead, and some bored elementals playing three-card monte against gigantic, radioactive mutant wasps. Isolated in the very back, near the exits, were heavily armed, cog-driven robots; their lawn-mower-like grassaline engines made them too loud to be seated next to anyone.

"So, are we waiting for Mom, then?" Rai wondered, tugging at her uncomfortable yellow suit. "This place is packed. I need a smoke— but I really don't. Actually I know I don't."

"Relax, Pumpkin. Take in the moment," Dirtbag suggested.

"Dirt's right. I mean, there are just so many neat bad guys here." T.C. beamed with caffeinated excitement. "I think that's a hive-mind hornets' nest on that balcony, and that cloud up there, I think that's one of those killer-fog monsters."

"Gah! How can you be so calm?"

"Experience, Rai. I've fought worse monsters in court; trust me."

Rai wrinkled her nose.

"It's hard to see who's sitting up front," Dirtbag grumbled, glaring at the practicing fencing ballerinas blocking their view. T.C. stood up on his chair and threatened to sue the tutus off the dancing men. They stopped immediately and sat down. Dirtbag shielded his face, mortified. "Was that worth it, T.C.? Do you see anything now?"

"I mean, what am I looking for? It's a room full of bad guys."

"Do you see anything from space?" Dirtbag asked, scanning the room.

"I dunno, Dirt; some of these things could be from space. I mean, just look at the size of that guy's forehead."

Rai heard a bellow from the balcony above them. She peered upward, and there sat the lowlife magician, Fugue, with his ten white tigers of varying degrees of invulnerability. He wore a disheveled blue-sequined jumpsuit, with a large, dowdy white collar and a standard, unimaginative black top hat. He lay slumped in his seat, bored, while the tigers busily gnawed on freshly prepared marinated steaks on sticks.

"Oh, I hope this works," Rai said, biting her lower lip.

"So far, so good, Pumpkin." Dirtbag patted her on the shoulder. "Hey, we made it in; we have a plan. We should feel pretty confident about our chances."

"But what if our overconfidence gets us killed?"

"Well, that's why you always find dead explorers with that look of surprise on their faces."

"What?"

"Shhh! Here we go." Dirtbag pointed to the stream of smarmy, red-tuxedo-wearing waiters entering the room with trays of hors d'oeuvres. "I hope that Stew scumbag did a good job making our bacon-wrapped dates; if those ninjas turn on us, I'm going to lead them right into his office."

The seated swarm of ninjas hissed at the advancing waiters, but when the ninjas saw what was on the trays, they began whispering excitedly. The waiters carefully gave one enchanted date to each ninja, using nonthreatening plastic tongs. The whispers of the ninjas quieted as they feasted on the treats. Unfortunately, the neighboring ballerina assassins demanded to know why the ninjas were getting preferential treatment. The waiters, fearing for their lives, served the leftover dates to the assassins.

"Dad, what are they doing?" Rai watched, aghast. "I don't know if my spell will work on those guys."

"Those scumbags," Dirtbag growled. "They could've at least waxed their chests before putting those tights on."

"Oats alive, that reminds me of my ex," T.C. recounted. "She had this condition——"

The theater unexpectedly went dark. The crowd cheered, and the band broke into an expanding melody. Multicolored lights panned over the room as a bright-blue star appeared on stage, pulsing and growing to the escalating song. Pyrotechnics lit up the backdrop in a flurry of impressive fireballs. The bright-blue star launched off the stage and over the crowd and impacted in the back of the amphitheater, outlining a square in the artificial sky. The lead guitarist played a gripping, highly skilled solo. The bassist joined in, and then the drummer. They combined their separate sounds into a thunderous rock-'n'-roll ballad whose lyrics were lost in the resounding adulation of the jubilant crowd.

A platform began lowering from the outlined square in the sky; Katvanna was dancing on it. Two spotlights pointed at her as she strutted back and forth, thrashing her glowing, whitish light-blue hair to the music. She wore a white-leather miniskirt that exposed her athletic midriff; an armored top made of rune-engraved, form-fitting titanium plates that exaggerated her cleavage; and white, knee-high go-go boots that showed off her silky-smooth legs. She teased her figure using a floor-length, hooded white-leather cloak that hung off her scantly armored shoulders. Her every move was augmented by numerous gold bracelets slipping up and down her flawless arms.

"Gah! She stole my outfit!" Rai accused. "I don't believe it!"

"Nah, she forgot the pants…and the underwear," T.C. said, staring. "I mean, that's an entrance I'll never forget."

Dirtbag ran his hand over his face. "She hasn't changed a bit," he said, watching the spectacle.

The platform flew overhead and down toward the stage, leaving a trail of falling pink rose petals behind. Katvanna pranced around the platform, blowing kisses into the crowd and showing off her flirtatious dance moves. The band picked up the tempo as her platform landed on stage. She stepped off it and raised her hands. Silver glitter exploded above her. She threw off the cloak and spun under the falling glitter, letting it stick to her exposed skin. She skipped across the stage to the lead guitarist, who immediately transitioned into another solo as she grinded up against him seductively.

"She's just giving it away!" T.C. bemoaned.

Katvanna then moved on to the lead singer. She put her arms around his hips, pressing her body against him to playfully nibble on his ear while he desperately tried to keep singing. Unsatisfied, she grabbed his head and forcefully began making out with him. The band covered for the singer's vocals while he was occupied, but they seemed increasingly worried about where this was leading.

"I'm so embarrassed!" Rai squealed, making little fists. "What is she doing?"

"I mean, she still plans to marry that guy, right?" T.C. asked as he watched her move on to the bassist.

"This is the last song that band will ever play," Dirtbag assured them.

Katvanna made eye contact with the drummer, indicating he was next. He gulped and messed up the tempo, drawing her ire. She suddenly lost interest in the entire show. She pointed her hand at the band and, with a word, vaporized them into a sparkling cloud of dust, promptly ending the music. Someone in the VIP section complained. She blew him a kiss, and the kingly man, along with his entire royal entourage, burned to death in a flash of fire. She raised her arms. The crowd cheered, and she bowed. A roadie jogged out with a gold-plated microphone. She took it and, with a glance, destroyed him. She began pacing back and forth on the stage, clutching the microphone, breathing heavily from excitement and adrenaline. The crowd cheered for her to kill again.

"You want to know who's next?" she screamed lyrically. "My ex-husband, Dirtbag! *Death to Dirtbag!*" She pumped up the crowd. "*Death to Dirtbag!*"

The crowd repeated her words and began stomping its feet, chanting the phrase over and over with unabashed hostility. Dirtbag sank into his seat, readying his shotgun for battle. Katvanna held her hand up to bring order to the room.

"In three days," she said, with a smooth and beautiful voice unexpected of someone so evil, "I'm getting married to Van Slice, the greatest man in the galaxy. And together, we are going to help all of you rule this puny planet!" The crowd roared, and she continued. "My ex-husband, who is both literally and figuratively a complete dirtbag, is on his way here to stop us. He knows about our plans because my horrible, spoiled brat of a dysfunctional daughter, who was an accident by the way, is helping him."

"An accident?" Rai repeated.

"*I* was an accident." T.C. folded his arms. "If anything, it just motivated me to prove I belonged here. It doesn't matter how you arrive; it matters what you do."

"But is it true?" She turned to her father.

"After your mother and I were married, we had you. You were unexpected but not unwelcomed, and we loved you immediately."

Dirtbag hoped she would never ask again; some aspect of her life had to be stable; she deserved that much.

"She's just being hateful, Rai," T.C. said. "Women tend to change the past based on their present perspectives. I mean, it doesn't matter if it's actually true or not; it's what she wants to be true."

"Gah! Men do that, too, and, in a way; so do entire countries, all right?"

Katvanna yowled animatedly into the microphone, sending the crowd into a frenzy. "Dirtbag!" she screamed. "Who hates him? Every single one of us!" The room clamored with agreement. "Do you know what he's filled with?"

An audience member screamed a description of something that came out of the backside of a particular hairy animal. Katvanna pointed at the man with a smile and an approving nod. "That's who he left me for," she said, pompously walking across the stage. "That powerless little princess! That excrement of a woman! But I got him. Oh, I got him. I sent fifty of the filthiest, cruelest goblins I could find after them. They took her beauty and threw it in the trash, just like he did to our marriage. I was there! I watched her suffer! I listened to her beg them to stop as they painted her body with acid…"

The audience half clapped, and a few people murmured in disapproval, but most of the guests were so villainous that their cheers quickly returned. Dirtbag listened to her, unmoved. He had always known Katvanna was behind what had happened. He had tortured it out of the responsible goblins before he hunted down and slew their entire race. Hearing her confirm and brag about what she had done only fortified his resolve. But T.C. and Rai were horrified by the revelation. T.C. tore off his business suit and unsheathed the Amber Blade of Divorce. Dirtbag stayed his hand.

"Oh, Dad," Rai said caringly.

"The story, Dirt!" T.C. shouted. "That's not love. That story. I'm so sick of hearing you tell it, but now, I just don't think I can stand to hear you tell it again. I mean, not without a proper ending, a happy ending!"

"Hey, you're angry, but I'm excited," Dirtbag said with a grin. "We're here, and she doesn't even know it."

Katvanna jumped up and down on stage, exhilarating the audience. "And now, without further ado, the man from space, the man who fell from the stars and into my heart"—she laughed sarcastically—"my soon-to-be new husband and future owner of planet Earth, Van Slice!"

The lights dimmed, and from out of the stars another platform lowered, with a grand piano on it, the ivory keys being softly tickled by a brightly illuminated man sitting behind them. His playing grew faster and more intense and finally burst into a full-blown cosmic sonata. Van Slice wore a business suit of armor painted flat black and engraved with luminous silver markings that diagramed distant planetary systems and coordinates. His short, spiked hair glowed with soft, golden sunlight, and a pleasant, warm orange radiated from his eyes, ears, and mouth. The platform floated down to the stage, landing gently next to the one Katvanna had ridden. In the middle of the opus, he stood and clapped his hands, and the piano, the band instruments, and the first two rows of guests disappeared in a flash of solar energy.

The lights came up a little, and Katvanna hugged him. The roadie's intern darted out to give Van Slice a microphone and dove off the stage into the audience before he could be executed. Katvanna and Van Slice laughed at the man, reveling in their evil. Behind them a huge projection screen lowered. Van Slice shifted his embrace of Katvanna to one side. He took a remote control out of his pocket and aimed it at the giant screen. The first slide of a presentation appeared, bearing the title "The Classic Planetary Renovation Con in Four Easy Steps."

"Hurrah! Hello, all! How's it going?" Van Slice said in a cheery voice that could've been mistaken for the voice of a politician or motivational speaker. "Um, so who came here for the wedding?" There was laughter in the audience. "Ha! We didn't either." Van Slice leaned over and kissed Katvanna with his winsome, sunlit mouth. The crowd cheered, and he stumbled away from her. "Wow! I'm going to have more of that later, but first, business. No, wait…even before that, we have some unfinished business, don't we?" He clicked the remote, and an exaggerated portrait of Dirtbag appeared on a slide titled "Step 1." The crowd booed and began chanting again.

"Hey, why do I have sideburns?" Dirtbag questioned, confused.

"That's a great look, Dirt." T.C. smirked, enjoying its inaccuracy. "I mean, you should just grow those out and start wearing a bowler hat. Get yourself an accent: ''Ello, gov'nah!'"

Van Slice let the crowd rage for a few minutes then called for calm. "I thought you'd recognize this being. This…man of the earth." He paused to get Katvanna's reaction; they both thought his lame joke was hilarious. "This grotesque bag of dirt is the only thing standing between all of us and wealth beyond our wildest dreams, all because he cannot die. We can't have this walking body bag attacking prospective chumps before we get their money, can we? Ha! Guess what? We won't have to; we found a way to neutralize him."

Katvanna nodded and stepped into the spotlight. "He isn't talking about terrestrial wealth either; this is wealth on a scale beyond what many of you think possible. We're talking about intergalactic-fraud wealth!"

"That's right, Kat." Van Slice grinned, dazzling them with his teeth. "Ha! Imagine owning a yacht that could sail to other worlds, owning beachfront property on a planet made entirely of beaches, or trafficking naïve otherworldly creatures and oppressing them into a lifetime of low-wage manufacturing on a remote moon. All that can be yours! And more! The entire galaxy is begging to be exploited, begging for people like you to help us do it! And we can! It's like my old man always said, 'If you can't make it, just take it.'"

"Let's get rich!" Katvanna shouted.

The crowd was ecstatic. T.C. gripped his sword eagerly. "Dirt, did we just go from revenge to helping your daughter to saving the planet to saving the entire galaxy?"

"Well, I'm still on the first two. The rest is a bonus," Dirtbag said, pumping his shotgun. He removed his suit and took his satchel out from where he had hidden it inside his chest. "Pumpkin, do you have a word ready?"

"Uh, I can't guarantee anything I say will work with Mom in the room. She knows counterwords, Dad."

Dirtbag understood. "That's why we have allies."

"I know." She pulled her hood up over her ninja cat ears; they poked through two tiny slits she had cut. She whispered a word, and her yellow pastel disguise evaporated, along with her glasses.

T.C. giggled impatiently, heavily overcaffeinated. "Oats alive! I just can't wait to see the expression on her face!"

Van Slice clicked the remote, transitioning to the next slide. A diagram of Dirtbag appeared, with blank callouts that were intended to be filled in over the course of Van Slice's presentation. "Let's take a closer look at our common enemy," he said. "Yes, people have made this earthman a hero, but he's not. He's just a dead man, and we've discovered the source of his power…"

"The tigers, Pumpkin," Dirtbag told Rai urgently.

She whispered an activation word. The ten tigers of varying degrees of invulnerability peeked over the edge of the balcony to see what she wanted, their ears curious. Rai's cat ears twitched as she made her request in a manner they could understand. "Rawr!" she commanded.

The tigers stared at the stage, licked their metallic teeth, and leapt from the balcony. Van Slice was rambling through a well-rehearsed analysis when he intuitively sensed the tigers running down the aisle toward him. They pounced, knocking him down before he could react. Katvanna kicked two of them off, not realizing what was happening until Dirtbag waved at her from the audience.

"You!" she shrieked incredulously.

"Me!" Dirtbag shouted with a big grin as he took aim at her head.

He fired a "Special Delivery" round. She easily caught it in her hand and smiled. Then it detonated, completely destroying the stage.

CHAPTER 37

———

The guests' initial shock at the explosion and the apparent death of Katvanna was quickly supplanted by the need for retribution. The whole of the amphitheater rose together to annihilate the foe whose demise they had, only moments earlier, cheered for. Unbeknown to the many villains in attendance, however, the entire swarm of black-leather ninjas was spellbound under a command of absolute loyalty to the three heroic party crashers. Witnessing their allies under attack, the ninjas struck out against the room, a veritable, unstoppable hurricane of slicing swords, nerve-paralyzing darts, and swinging nunchakus. Upon seeing the ninjas' betrayal, any semblance of cooperation among the guests was cast aside, and the room quickly devolved into a suspicion-driven free-for-all.

T.C. barreled through the burning amphitheater, hacking and slashing at anything in his path. The stage had collapsed, and the ceiling was on fire. It was everything he had hoped for. Two baboon ushers leapt onto his back, each yanking on a fistful of his long, blond hair. One put a cigarette out on his forehead. A rock beast elemental folded into a boulder in front of him and began to roll in his direction. Two ballerina assassins were fencing one another nearby. One had eaten a date; the other had not. T.C. led the pursuing boulder their way, squashing them both. A white tiger tackled one of the baboons off of T.C., who skewered the second one with the Amber Blade of Divorce and then tossed it under the trailing boulder for good measure.

"Finally, whew"—he tried to joke, breathing heavily as he hurried—"got that monkey off my back." But the chasing boulder was closing in. "Dirt! Can you just shoot this thing? I mean, it doesn't have any tender areas for stabbing."

Rai shouted something from the other side of the theater, distracting him. He tripped, fell, and braced himself for the weight of the boulder, but instead, a giant marshmallow gently bounced over him. The newly transformed elemental rolled straight out the emergency exit doors, screaming hysterically about what it had become. T.C. had jumped to his feet, ready to thank Rai for the assistance, when he inadvertently bumped into his marriage counselor. There wasn't time to say something witty, so he dragged her over his knee, pulled up her skirt, and spanked her with the flat side of the Amber Blade of Divorce. She howled and kicked, filling him with newfound vigor. She bolted out of the room crying, holding her bruised behind with both hands. T.C. fought his way across the theater and climbed up a pile of broken chairs to where Dirtbag was perched and shooting his shotgun at every opportunity that presented itself.

"Oats alive! It's like a buffet of bad guys! I'm so excited by the variety that it's hard to fixate on just one. I mean, I've got to have a piece of them all!" T.C. hacked off the wing of a passing radioactive mutant wasp and watched as it spun out of control into a wall, where it inexplicably exploded. "Whoa! How about that?"

"Rawr!" Rai bellowed, riding to them on a white tiger. Her ten tigers spread out around the pile of chairs, attacking anything that got close. She climbed up the small hill, shouting a word at an approaching robot, turning it into a vending machine. "I can't believe you took the time to spank that woman, T.C.!" she called. "Oh, I'm sure she deserved it, but really?"

The vending machine gurgled and spat out an acidic cup of coffee. "Hey, nobody drink that!" Dirtbag warned.

"Are those ninjas flying, Dad?" Rai pointed at the black blurs ricocheting through the air. "I didn't know they could do that."

"They're just jumping, Rai," T.C. told her, kicking down an enormous, tattooed Goth-Moth that had been spooked out of the ceiling lights. "I mean, if you watch, they land, but you need to watch."

"Don't watch the ninjas!" Dirtbag shouted, shooting a water elemental behind them that had slipped past the tigers, evaporating it into a fine mineral powder. "Watch your backs!"

"I know, all right?" Rai said, annoyed. "Gah! Why did you even wave us over here, Dad? I thought you needed our help."

"Well, because we should rally," Dirtbag argued.

"Yay! Go team!" Rai wrinkled her nose sarcastically.

"OK, Dirt, we're rallied," T.C. said impatiently, fueled by caffeine. "We should get back out there and press our advantage. I mean, I've only kicked one guy so far."

"Hey!" Dirtbag growled. "Katvanna isn't dead. She's under that mess, and she's going to come out. We need to work together to clear the room before she wakes up. We can't fight her *and* everything else at the same time."

"Oh, right. I'm on it." Rai hissed at the ninjas, issuing them new orders. They whispered back to her. "Cool, the ninjas are going to start driving people out the exits. That should help."

The roadie's intern performed a flying side kick off an adjacent balcony. T.C. caught his leg and wrung him out like a towel, tossing his corpse to the side. "It's about half empty now, Dirt. I mean, the thing is... just what do we do when Katvanna wakes up? Offer her a breath mint?"

"We attack," Dirtbag said plainly. "She's not used to being on the defensive; we have to leverage that while we can."

None of them looked forward to the confrontation.

"I see those three centaurs, Dirt," T.C. said, laughing off his anxiety. "I think I'll just go over there and show them why they should wear pants." He jumped off the pile of chairs and ran back into the fight, beating down a roller-derby pirate in his way.

"Dad, is he going to—"

"Yes, Pumpkin, he's going to 'fix' them," Dirtbag told her. "I think you'd be happier on the other side of the room."

"Gah!" She shuddered. "Let me know if you really need me, Dad." She called for her tigers and reentered the battle.

Dirtbag watched her go, thinking. He detected the swinging rock-hammer hand of a lava elemental plunging down from above and dove out of the way. He twirled the dial on his shotgun and then transformed the creature into ice. A beardless wizard stumbled over to him, opened his book of spells, and started to incompetently cast something, sounding out the words. Dirtbag punched him in the gut and threw him into the frozen elemental. Both exploded into pieces, presumably because of electrostatic discharge. Dirtbag heard slow clapping behind him and turned to see Lord Cheddar Cheese admiring his feats.

"Zounds!" Cheese exclaimed. "You are an impressive warrior."

"I bring home the bacon." Dirtbag shrugged, pumping his shotgun.

"I am Lord Cheddar Cheese." The lord drew an exquisite sword with a strange, milky white blade filled with irregular holes. "I have chosen to personally face you, to avenge my dear brother Duke Ricotta."

Dirtbag laughed at him, not the least bit impressed. They both suddenly glanced upward; the fog monster was hovering overhead, preparing to strike with a poison-gas attack. Dirtbag fired into it, setting it ablaze, and it sailed across the room screaming, incinerating before it could reach a fire extinguisher.

Lord Cheddar Cheese nervously clutched his sword. "I did not know clouds could burn so painfully," he admitted.

Dirtbag scowled. "First of all, I killed your *other* brother, Baron Brie."

"But he was lactose intolerant, the black sheep of the family."

"Second of all, your sword might fit this whole cheese theme, but it's a stupid design." Dirtbag shot the blade, snapping it in half. "What kind of fool models a sword after Swiss cheese?"

"I shall not stand for this insult," Lord Cheddar Cheese swore. "My blade may be broken, but my will—"

"Look, scumbag, I have no problem killing morons. I've been doing it all day." Dirtbag turned and blew away a wizard who'd stopped in the middle of the conflict to tie his shoe. "Ever heard of Velcro?"

"You, sir, are without honor!" Lord Cheddar Cheese said, appalled.

Dirtbag seethed. He opened his mouth to deliver another snappy response but then noticed a shadow on the floor. He looked up. A wood elemental had thrown itself off a balcony, intent on flattening him; he spun the dial on his shotgun and petrified it midair. The dead creature tumbled out of control and landed on Lord Cheddar Cheese instead. Dirtbag brushed himself off.

"Now they can call you Cream Cheese, scumbag!" he shouted. A wizard standing behind him guffawed. Dirtbag turned and blasted him. "You're so worthless I don't even have a line for you!" He angrily kicked the remaining pile of velour lint, trying to grind it into the carpet with his foot. "There!"

A ballerina assassin flew out of a fireball, somersaulting over the petrified wood elemental, and tried to cut Dirtbag with his rapier.

"Are you kidding me?" Dirtbag said, dodging some showy high kicks. He fenced the assassin using his shotgun, until he was able to knock the sword out of the ballerina's hand with one well-placed jab to the funny bone. He grabbed a fistful of exposed chest hair and tossed the ballerina headfirst into a garbage can, which he subsequently shot three times. "You should've waxed!" he yelled.

Nine white tigers scurried past him, and Rai rode up to his side on the tenth, wearing a concerned expression. "Dad? What are you doing? Talking to bad guys?"

"I'm working through some issues, Pumpkin. Part of this is therapeutic."

She heard metallic footsteps behind them and whispered a word that caused the approaching robot to fall apart. Dirtbag turned to see what she'd done, proud of her.

"One of those ballerinas attacked me," he mentioned.

"I guess there weren't enough dates to go around." She smiled, picking a petrified leaf out of his grass-hair. "You all right, Dad?"

"Fantastic, Pumpkin. Best day ever."

They heard sword fighting, a grunt, a scream, then two more screams, followed by loud sobbing, and then T.C. strolled out of a wall of smoke rubbing his jaw, a bright-red horseshoe mark on the side of his face. He waved at them, cheerful. "Room's clear, Dirt."

"Those centaurs give you a hard time?"

"Trust me; they got what was coming to them. I mean, it wasn't easy, but I got them wedged in a doorway, and from there it was just like working on a farm."

"No! Why?" Rai frowned. "I didn't think you'd actually do that!"

"Neither did I, until it happened,"T.C. chuckled.

"Uh, there's a hand on your foot." Rai motioned.

A disembodied dead hand was holding tight to T.C.'s ankle. He picked it off with his sword and tossed it into a fire. He bent down and touched the floor.

"Whoa, this space rug is holding up pretty good. It's even fire resistant, and look, the blood is just pooling on top of it. That's a good carpet. I mean, if it can survive all this, dinner parties are nothing."

The distant sound of people fighting ninjas echoed through the halls as the battle moved into other parts of the *Empyrean*. There was a loud crash from a balcony. T.C. gestured at the tigers with his sword. "Your pets just tore into that hornet's nest, Rai."

She groaned and called to them, but they had already devoured the nest by the time they returned to her. She scratched between their ears, and they nuzzled against her. Dirtbag grinned. The room suddenly shook.

"Katvanna!" he shouted

They rushed toward the destroyed stage and readied themselves for her attack. She shouted a word that vaporized the mound of rubble she had been under. She stood up, seemingly unscathed and elegant, and then she cupped her hand beneath her mouth and spat out a tooth. She screamed with fury. She exploded off the stage, swiftly sprinting over the wrecked theater floor far quicker than any of them could react. She reached Dirtbag first and threw him across the room, as though she was saving him for later. T.C. swung the Amber Blade of Divorce at her. She dodged it, but T.C. anticipated this. He twisted around and met her bare navel with the sword's sharp edge. "Not so hot now, are you?" he said, preparing to run her through.

Katvanna smacked the sword out of his hands; she wrapped her arms around him and whispered a word of seduction as she kissed him. T.C. began to succumb to her charm, but then he heard another word in his ear, a counterword. He reached up to softly run his fingers through Katvanna's hair and instead yanked her head back hard. "Ow!" she shrieked. "Oh, of course, Loranna, you worthless child!"

T.C. grabbed Katvanna by the throat. "You ruined my marriage, you—" He had so many hateful words to say, but all of them would set his lips on fire if he spoke them. "You ruined my life!"

"What?" Katvanna squinted, genuinely confused. "I don't even know who you are!" She broke free of his grasp with such ease he realized she was toying with them.

Rai darted out from behind T.C. Her mouth began to speak a word, but Katvanna countered it, and the space between them ignited in an explosion of energy, knocking them all back. The tigers attacked Katvanna to protect Rai, whom they had bonded with, and she savagely beat them away. She clambered to her feet, outwardly stunned that she had been cut by their claws.

Rai sat up, singed; she staggered a few steps and fell. Dirtbag, who'd finally managed to extract his head from the doorjamb he'd been thrown into, stood up and immediately rushed to Rai's aid. Katvanna raised her hand, furious that her lovely skin had been marred by lowly animals, and took a breath to speak. She heard someone behind her and turned. T.C. was holding the vending machine above his head. He slammed it down on top of her, smashing her into the floor.

"Ha! That is no way to treat a beautiful lady," said Van Slice as he viciously punched T.C. in the back of the head, sending him to his knees. Van Slice confronted the ten white tigers, made a few strange gestures in the air that churned up the debris around him, and unleashed a gravity pulse that flattened the animals dead.

"No!" Rai cried. She held up her hand and shouted a word. A hundred invisible pillars pounded Van Slice from every direction at once.

Dirtbag spun the dial on his shotgun to the "Special Delivery" setting and fired. Van Slice threw up his hands, suspending the shot in the air and trapping it in a magnetic field generated by his suit. He marveled at the yellow, glowing, arrowhead-like projectile.

"Didn't anybody ever tell you it's unwise to wield great power if it can be turned against you?" He shook his head, amused. "Ha! Especially against a spaceman, such as me, who can afford a suit of armor made by the great Van Allen, my uncle, by the way."

The Amber Blade of Divorce suddenly burst through Van Slice's chest, breaking apart the armored suit. "Everyone knows Van Allen only makes belts!" T.C. screamed, twisting the blade.

Van Slice flinched in agony. Having been a bachelor all his life, he was completely unprepared for the pain of ten divorces. He immediately passed out. The damaged business suit of armor malfunctioned, and the magnetic field vanished. The "Special Delivery" round fell to the floor and exploded.

CHAPTER 38

———

Katvanna gradually opened her eyes. The air swirled with ashen cinders, obscuring her view like polluted, muddy water. The vending machine she had been pinned under had shielded her from the brunt of the violent blast. She sat up, holding her pounding head, shocked that Dirtbag possessed such power. She cleared the murkiness around her with a word, revealing that she'd been thrown a good distance by the explosion. Van Slice lay severely injured at the edge of a sizable crater, with bright light escaping a hole in his chest. She quickly made her way over the cluttered terrain and dragged him behind the bulky corpse of the petrified wood elemental. She removed the cracked pieces of Van Slice's shattered armor and held her hands over the gaping, luminous wound, speaking softly in a voice so beautiful that it invited kindhearted presumptions about her character. His injury sluggishly healed, and she sat with him, seemingly alone in the fire-lit ruins of the amphitheater.

Van Slice returned to consciousness with a deep groan. "What did that earthman stab me with?" He winced. "It was a strange pain. I've never felt anything quite like it. It was this emptiness, a sadness inside me, like a feeling, a horrible feeling, that I would never know joy again. It scared me, Kat, and I still feel it."

Katvanna gazed at him coolly, somewhat concerned. She held her hand over his healed injury to diagnose the problem. She quietly exhaled, unsettled. "They've broken your star-heart. I don't know how, but they did."

"Will it heal up?"

"Over time, but it doesn't matter. We have an earth-heart we can replace it with, and it will feel as if this never happened."

"Kat," Van Slice said, looking at her tenderly, "you're missing a tooth."

She frowned at his affection. "I can buy another tooth," she said simply and helped him up. "If we can get upstairs and regroup, we can turn this against them." She shook her head. "They shouldn't stand a chance against us. My ridiculous husband and that kid...oh, I wish I'd never had that kid. Life should be fun, about me."

"About us." Van Slice smirked. "About getting what we want."

"Completely." She giggled briefly. "Just don't forget your place."

Dirtbag pushed over the row of theater seats he had been buried under. "Going somewhere"—he pumped his shotgun—"scumbags?"

"Oh, enough of this!" Katvanna snapped. "You think you're so clever! Van, would you please get that thing for me?"

"But of course, Kat." Van Slice gesticulated some patterns in the air and drew the shotgun away from Dirtbag's grip using the pull of gravity. The weapon flew across the room and into his hands. "Ha! Easy! Here you go, Kat."

Katvanna took the shotgun and examined it. "I see the goblins made this," she said, intrigued by its design. She noticed the mirage ore and played with the settings on the dial. "At least you got something out of her death."

Dirtbag clenched his ragged denim fists. "It's so easy to fall back on hatred. Feeling anything else brings a lot of risk, doesn't it? Only a coward hates so recklessly."

"You're one to talk. You committed genocide," she barbed. "This certainly is a powerful weapon and versatile. The ancients would've been impressed, but science has always been a weak substitute for"—she grinned slyly—"magic." With a word, she vaporized the shotgun and blew the ashes from her hand. "I'm sure you'll find some other means to entertain me."

"You witch!" Dirtbag exploded with anger, but then he breathed. "You're stalling. I think if you could kill me, you would've done it, but you can't, can you?"

"You know nothing." She narrowed her eyes. "I can destroy you with a word, but you…look at all the devastation you've caused, and here I am with a few scratches. You have no hope of defeating me, and you never did. I'll end you at my own leisure."

Dirtbag watched as the two of them strolled out of the theater, arm in arm. They laughed at him as they disappeared through an emergency exit. He pummeled an overturned chair, outraged by Katvanna's self-assured arrogance. He had no way of telling if she was playing games with him or covering a vulnerability. He heard a whimper behind him and hurried to the sound. He uncovered Rai from beneath a velvet-robed, obese wizard's dead body. Her cloak was shredded, and her cat ears had been lost.

"Dad? Are we winning?" she mumbled, sitting up, woozy.

T.C. jumped down from a balcony he had been flung into. Something was protruding from his body. He looked down and saw he'd been impaled by the Amber Blade of Divorce. He calmly examined how the blade had gone through his bulk, finding it interesting but not painful. He figured he had lived with the pain of ten divorces for so long he'd grown accustomed to the emotional anguish and, disturbingly, found the sensation slightly comforting. He walked over to Dirtbag and Rai, who were gawking at him as though he should be dead.

"Can you give me a hand with this, Dirt?" he asked. "It's at a bad angle."

Dirtbag gripped the sword handle and yanked the amber blade out of T.C.'s stomach. Rai quickly put her hand over the gash, expecting an outpouring of blood, but there was nothing. "Dad! Dad!" she cried out, alarmed.

T.C. gingerly touched the open hole in his body. There was still no pain, so he poked his armored hand inside it, feeling how hollow he was.

Rai gasped and turned away.

"That's just superduper," T.C. said, hovering his hand over the opening and noticing light was shining through from the other side. "How bad should something like this hurt? I mean, because it doesn't; it doesn't feel like anything…maybe a little breezy."

"I think we can tape over that for now. Cork it up with some space carpet," Dirtbag said, looking through the hole. "We don't want anything to take up residence, especially from here."

"Unless it paid rent. But, I mean, I'd only sublet my gut to a wolf or a coyote, something I could set loose during a fight. The downside is I'd have to start wearing a girdle-cage."

"Gah! How can you two joke about this?" Rai pointed at the hole. "I can see right through him!"

"Now, wait just a minute, Rai." T.C. managed a smile. "I mean, OK, it's weird for me, too, scary even, but trust me; I feel fine."

"I guess I can try to heal you. I…I've done it before," Rai stammered.

They could see she was unsure. T.C. delicately fixed her messy, singed hair. "It can wait, Rai. Right now we have a job to do, and we're a little pressed for time."

"We have to keep pushing ahead, Pumpkin," Dirtbag told her. "We have some kind of advantage we didn't even know about. I don't think Katvanna can kill me, at least not outright, or she would have already. The two of them said they were going upstairs, and it sounded like they had a plan."

"Dirt? Where's your shotgun?" T.C. asked, seeing his friend's empty holster.

"Katvanna destroyed it."

"Oats alive! That was a pretty good weapon to have."

"Hey, at this point all I need is my two hands," Dirtbag promised him. He turned to Rai. She was petting a flattened tiger.

"They were innocent," she whispered, caressing it.

T.C. kneeled beside her. "I mean, on the bright side, Rai, you got ten high-quality throw rugs there," he said, trying to add some levity. Dirtbag scowled at him. T.C. looked down. "I'm sorry, Rai. I just—I dunno—I don't like seeing you upset."

"I can't bring them back without my heart," she conceded.

"We'll get it back; just don't you worry."

"This is not going to get any easier, Pumpkin," Dirtbag said. "I wish I could tell you otherwise."

"I know…" She let the tiger be. "I guess, with our family—if we can even call it one—things can only get crazier."

Their conversation was interrupted by the approach of growling thunder. They turned toward the sound and prepared for battle as best they could. The Sawstang burst through the theater doors honking wildly, chainsaw blazing, covered with the bodies of dead pretty-boy valets clutching microfiber polishing cloths.

"Hey, looks like somebody rubbed her the wrong way," Dirtbag cracked.

Rai rolled her eyes. "Gah! Dad! Not you, too."

T.C. laughed.

CHAPTER 39

———

The hurtling Sawstang skidded around a sharp corner, leaving scream-ing burnt-tire scuffs across the polished hardwood floor of the ornate hallway. The back end of the car swung wide, straight into a wooden china hutch, shattering the collection of antique dishes within. The powerful engine revved monstrously, and Dirtbag spurred the beast on from the driver's seat, pointing to where it should go next as they chased after Katvanna. The hood-mounted chainsaw tore through impeding furniture clogging the corridor and any guests that had neglected athleticism. The car thumped twice. Dirtbag checked the rearview mirror and saw either a sofa or a wizard lying on the floor behind them. It was hard to tell which, given that either could be covered in the same garish fabric.

Rai watched T.C. as he advanced to confront Fugue, the lowlife magician, on the rumbling trunk of the speeding Sawstang. Fugue was angry that his precious tigers had been taken from him and flattened. Without them, he had no show, no income, and, therefore, no funds to continue his dance lessons. The magician had perched himself atop a wardrobe, intending to ambush the trio of tiger thieves when they passed by, apparently without considering the consequences. Rai feigned disinterest, knowing she could dispatch Fugue with a word, but she was curious to see what T.C. had in mind. A big armored fist punched the magician in the face, and he clutched his mouthful of crooked teeth.

"That hurt!" Fugue cried.

"It was supposed to. I mean, you just can't jump in the backseat of someone else's car and make threats. Don't you know who we are?" T.C. grabbed the magician's top hat off his head, turned it upside down, and, pointing into it, said, "Now, get in!"

"That's not possible!"

"Why not?" T.C. yelled over passing exploding furniture. "I mean, I see you guys pull all kinds of junk out of these things; now it's time to get in one."

"I can't!"

T.C. picked up the magician by his oversized white collar and shook him around as Rai snickered. T.C. threatened to hand him over to her. She whispered a word, and the magician's blue-sequined jump-suit turned inside out.

"Ouch! That burned! Don't do that!" he pleaded, trembling from the painful chafing.

T.C. held the hat down on the vibrating trunk and pointed at the brim. "OK. Now, you're going to get in this hat, and it's going to be the best magic trick I've ever seen!"

Fugue cackled frantically. He gingerly pushed his penny-loafer-wearing big foot inside the small opening. The hat tore, and he looked up at an infuriated T.C., terrified. The Sawstang hit a futon, causing the magician to lose his balance and bend over into a position that T.C. couldn't resist kicking. T.C. drew his leg back and let the villain have the full brunt of his heavy, carbon-fiber-clad boot. Fugue tumbled headlong off the back of the car and was immediately attacked by five black-leather ninjas. T.C. gave a stern salute good-bye and climbed into the passenger seat.

"Oats alive!" he lamented. "I was hoping for something more."

"Like what?" Dirtbag asked, honking at the people running for their lives in front of them. "He fell into a swarm of ninjas; he may as well have fallen into a blender."

"I dunno, Dirt," T.C. said, glancing back briefly to make sure the magician was, in fact, dead. He was. The ninjas dispersed from the scene, leaving behind empty blue-sequined rags. "It was just missing something."

A ninja burst out of the ceiling in front of the Sawstang to attack a roller-derby pirate fleeing the front bumper. Both were sucked under the car with a jolting bang.

"You can't keep running over ninjas, Dad!" Rai scolded. "That's going to break my spell!"

"It was only one, Pumpkin; I'm sure he didn't feel a thing," Dirtbag told her, eyeing the twitching bodies in their wake. A wizard in front of them tripped and fell, going under the car with a stifled wail. "And that's why wizards shouldn't wear robes. If he wanted to be quick, he should've worn a tracksuit. That scumbag didn't even have sneakers on! Stupid flip-flops!"

"They get really lazy, standing around all day," Rai sneered.

"*That's* what was missing,"T.C. said. "Irony."

They turned another corner, and the Sawstang slid to a stop, knocking framed pictures off the wall. They caught a glimpse of Katvanna and Van Slice at the other end of the hallway. The couple glanced back, surprised how close their enemy was. Van Slice made a gripping gesture with his hand and crushed the hallway in on itself, blocking their path.

"Which way?" Dirtbag asked Rai.

"Gah! I don't know; I usually snuck in looking for Mom's purse," she confessed. "I know there's plenty of gold lying around, but I guess it was just more devious to take it from her purse. It's a woman thing; I wanted her to feel violated."

Dirtbag stared at T.C. "I mean, she's a young lady, Dirt," T.C. concluded. "Everything's overly complicated, too slow, and not good enough, right?"

Rai wrinkled her nose. "Oh, you know me so well." She frowned. "Mom's probably going for our hearts; she usually likes a hostage. I think she keeps them up in that weird garden with the crystal trees. That's where she started keeping her purse. I never could get in there."

"Pumpkin, what's the quickest way to the weird garden?"

"Oh, probably from the outside, unless you know how to pick a space-lock."

"I mean, the car does fly, Dirt," T.C. enthusiastically reminded him.

"That it does," Dirtbag agreed. "Let's rough out a quick plan."

T.C. thought it over. "We drive out a window, fly to the top, and crash through the glass roof of that garden while lighting everything on fire as we go."

"Hey, works for me."

"So, that's it?" Rai asked, worried.

"Not quite," T.C. said. "Dirt, do you mind if I drive?"

"Try not to run over any more ninjas," Dirtbag advised. "I think we maxed out our quota."

Dirtbag and T.C. switched seats by confusingly crawling over one another until they managed to get on opposite sides. T.C. shifted the Sawstang into drive and turned the dragon's-breath knob to the highest setting the cataclysmic convertor could handle. Fire breathed out of the front end with each rev of the engine, lighting the fallen pictures aflame. T.C. chuckled as the furniture burned, considering the possibilities. "Hmm. I dunno, Dirt. Do you think it's wise for us to drive into the fire? I mean, we're in a convertible."

"We can always drive backward." Rai stated the obvious.

"Well, that will be slower but more destructive," Dirtbag said, liking the idea. "Plus more bad guys will try to jump in and attack."

T.C.'s stomach growled through his duct-taped-over wound. "OK, I'm getting hungry, and I got this hole. What if I can't eat anymore, Dirt? I mean, what if stuff just falls out? What if I can't have my victory feast? And if I can't fill up on eating, how can I enjoy my celebratory nap? Oats alive! What if this is it and I'm dying, Dirt?"

"You're going to worry about this now?" Dirtbag asked, puzzled. "You're hollow, not dying," he growled. "It's real simple; can you breathe through that hole?"

T.C. tried. "Nah."

"Are you sure?"

"Yeah."

"Then you can eat."

"Swell, so where will the food go, Dirt?"

"Hey! Do I look like a witch doctor? You're cursed. Nobody casts a curse to kill. They want you to suffer. They want you to live with it. That's why food won't fall out, and, yes, I know that's not scientific, but science can't always explain the cruel intentions of other people."

"OK, then what *are* we going to do after this? If we don't all die from Katvanna, I mean."

Rai suddenly understood what T.C. was fishing for. "Oh! You mean you want something to look forward to? I guess Jyn and I have a little surprise."

"I hope it's a prenuptial, for her sake," T.C. ribbed.

"What? No!" Rai huffed, frustrated. "We're not getting remarried…at least, I haven't asked."

"Good, I mean, because it only works the first time; once they know all your charms and have seen you lying facedown in your underwear, half outside the bathtub, with a piece of burnt toast stuck to your back, the romantic aspect of it is gone forever."

"Gah! Seriously?"

"Trust me; women like a man who's easygoing." T.C. beamed.

"You kissed a horse!"

"A unicorn." T.C. corrected.

"What are you two doing?" Dirtbag chided. "Let's go!"

T.C. threw the Sawstang into reverse and turned it around, ripping down a ceiling fan. He hit the gas, and flames shot out the front, lighting everything they left behind on fire as they accelerated backward. He expertly drove the Sawstang in reverse through a coffee lounge and over three couches in an adjoining den. The air filled with the intoxicating smell of burning coffee and varnish as they went. They were speeding through the winding hallways, leaving a gratifying trail of destruction, when Dirtbag suddenly told T.C. to stop. The Sawstang screeched to a halt.

"Well, how convenient," Dirtbag said, stepping out of the car. He walked down an intersecting foyer to a glass door. Behind the door was a circular garage with black and white tiles arranged in a checkered-flag pattern on the floor. The walls of the room were covered with engine parts and tools, all neatly arranged and ready for use. In the middle of the garage was a motorcycle on a raised pedestal, an expensive-looking, custom-painted, red sun spacechopper with a raked-chrome front end and solar-flare-inspired yellow accents.

"Is this it?" Dirtbag questioned, feeling Rai and T.C. standing behind him.

"Yeah. I think he loves that motorcycle more than Mom, if, I guess, you can call what they have love." Rai fidgeted. "It's not alive or anything, not like the Sawstang. It's from space. It's just a soulless machine."

Dirtbag chucked a lamp through the glass door and went inside. He put his foot on the flank of the parked chopper and pushed it over with a loud crunch.

"Help me out with this," he told T.C.

"Just what do you want to do, Dirt? I mean, I'm sure Rai can destroy it with a word."

"No, that's too good for this Van Slice scumbag," Dirtbag said, taking a crowbar off the tool wall. "I want to rip that fancy muffler off, so I can beat him with it."

They messily tore the bike apart and used hammers to pound the chrome exhaust pipe into a club-like shape. Dirtbag shredded the space-leather seat and wrapped the scraps around the crude handle they had fashioned at the base of the muffler.

"I think you just replaced the power of that shotgun with sheer brutality." T.C. grinned.

"Or insanity." Rai frowned.

"Proper vengeance requires some creativity, Pumpkin," Dirtbag said, gripping the muffler like a baseball bat. "It's usually not something that's appreciated in the moment, but it creates an extra layer of trauma your opponent remembers later, after the battle, usually at night while crying."

"Cool. So, can I give it the word now, Dad?"

"Leave it. It's trashed"—Dirtbag kicked the bike—"and emotionally that's worse than completely destroyed."

The Sawstang revved skittishly and honked its horn, calling for them. Whispers filled the air; the ninjas had finally run out of invited guests and were questioning their loyalty.

CHAPTER 40

The late-afternoon sun glinted across the white metal dome of the *Empyrean* as it meandered over a tranquil azure sea. Black smoke billowed from windows that, until they were recently broken, had been hidden from view. A sudden fiery eruption blasted the contents of an elegant living room down the side of the dome, jettisoning the smashed furniture skyward off the curved edge of the spaceship. A raging fireball surged into the open air from the breach, and bursting forth out of the roiling inferno was the Sawstang, tumbling out of control on a disastrous course to the surface of the unforgiving waters below. The car was covered with a writhing pile of angry, hissing black-leather ninjas, who continued their ruthless assault even as the vehicle plunged off the end of the dome to certain death.

The Sawstang entered a terminal descent, spinning end over end, flinging ninjas away in clumps as it toppled through the air. Once all the ninjas had been cleared, it quickly spread out its dragon wings to catch its fall. The small jet turbines screamed to regain control, and the V-8 engine opened up to a deafening roar as the Sawstang fought hard to level out. The dragon wings flapped twice, stabilizing the car into a buoyant hover.

Dirtbag looked over the side at the many ninjas splattering like bugs across the inflexible ocean waves beneath him. "Safety first, scumbags!" he shouted, tightening his seat belt.

"Oats alive! What a ride!" T.C. breathed, gripping the steering wheel tightly. "I mean, whoa, I think I threw up a little."

"You guys are crazy! I'm supposed to be safer inside the car!" Rai squealed, flustered. She pushed her tangled hair out of her eyes and tried to comb it back into place, but her efforts only made it worse. T.C.'s hair appeared perfectly untouched, despite the ninja attack, sudden free fall, and multiple explosions. "Gah! Fine! I give up! What's your secret, T.C.?"

"I mean, it wouldn't be a secret if I told, now would it?" he teased.

Dirtbag turned to Rai. "Pumpkin, I once saw his conditioners evolve into a cycloptic blob that crawled right out of the water he was washing in. I wouldn't even call that blond mane of his hair anymore; it's more like an indestructible wig."

"A wig?" T.C. interjected. "Didn't you see those baboons yanking on my scalp? Trust me; this is no wig. It's a miracle."

Then, without warning, a leftover ninja crawled onto the hood, reached inside his black-leather tuxedo vestment, and pulled out a small bomb shaped like a fist.

"It's a hand grenade!" T.C. said excitedly. "Don't worry; if it goes off, you just get punched in the face real hard."

"But I don't want to get punched in the face!" Rai ducked down.

"It can't be worse than Donny Brooke," Dirtbag said, leaning headfirst to take the explosive beating.

The ninja's eyes darted about, troubled that these enemies were not afraid of his fiendish weapon. Dirtbag asked Rai if she could use a word to destroy the ninja because they didn't have time to mess around with it.

"Oh! But we had time to vandalize a motorcycle?" she complained. "Here's a word for you: 'No.'"

"Fair enough." Dirtbag turned to the ninja. "You've got two choices, scumbag: jump or T.C."

T.C. pounded his hands together. "I like those choices."

The ninja put his finger into the grenade ring, threatening to pull it. T.C. reached under the front seat, fumbling around for something to throw. He pulled out the long-forgotten, uneaten cheeseburger that had previously tumbled underneath the seat and had amazingly been overlooked during the dragon conversion. It was as hard as a rock, and he immediately lobbed it at the ninja's head. The ninja snatched the flying burger out of the air, accidentally tearing the paper wrapper. Toxic gasses that had been building up inside the fermenting burger exploded into the ninja's face, blinding him. He tottered backward and fell onto the hood-mounted chainsaw.

"Whoa! Did you see that, Dirt? I just killed a ninja with a cheeseburger!" T.C. chuckled, cleaning the windshield off with the wipers.

"What a terrible way to go," Rai said, watching the remaining pieces of the ninja flutter down to the ocean.

"Yeah," T.C. said with a grin, "but it makes a great story."

The Sawstang's turbines whirred as it ascended over the *Empyrean*. It was much easier to assess the extent of the damage they'd caused from outside the massive spaceship. Untamed fire licked out of shattered windows on multiple levels of the dome. Volcanic black plumes of thick smoke poured out of the burning interior, drifting far over the horizon. The tentacle spires hanging below the dome were twitching in pain; each jolt knocked countless valets and parked flying machines off the landing petals. The jellyfish seemed to be slowly losing altitude and was likely dying.

"Swell. So much for time-shares," T.C. grumbled.

They soared over the dome to the transparent section at the very top. T.C. revved the Sawstang's engine, aiming the chainsaw at the glowing amethyst trees beneath the glass.

"Well, this is it," Dirtbag said, taking a deep breath to relax. "Pumpkin, you shout a word to weaken that dome, and the Sawstang will ram its way through."

"Gah! I can yell something that might break it—I know one or two good words—but I don't even know what that's made of." She stared anxiously at their destination. "I can't believe we did all that other stuff and survived, and we still have to do this!"

"Rai, Dirt and I...I mean, we've had some tough adventures before." T.C. unsheathed the Amber Blade of Divorce. "I just don't remember them ever being so personal."

"Are we really going to kill her, Dad?" Rai cringed.

"Pumpkin." Dirtbag sighed. "Sometimes to put an end to things, you have to force an end, and that can be some pretty ugly business."

"Everyone ready?" T.C. asked.

"Oh, I guess…" Rai sat forward a little.

"Hit it, T.C.," Dirtbag said, bracing himself.

T.C. turned the steering wheel, and with one great flap of its turbine wings, the Sawstang began a dive. Rai cupped her hands over her mouth and shouted. The dome cracked a little. The Sawstang tucked its wings in tight, spreading the durable, glossy-black airfoils over its passengers to protect them from the suicidal impact. As they closed in on the dome, they saw two figures within run to find cover from the impending crash. Then, at the last second, by chance, the Sawstang noticed an open balcony, turned sharply to the right, then to the left, and flew in through the entrance, completely unscathed, screeching to a stop in the middle of a garden full of crystal trees.

CHAPTER 41

———

Beneath the transparent dome of the *Empyrean* was a large, circular room filled end to end with tightly packed trees of glowing crystal amethyst, a strange, otherworldly garden surrounding a central stone courtyard containing an exquisite celestial mosaic. The trees held within them peculiar, veinlike internal workings that periodically shimmered with soft, white plasmic energy. The branches tapered off into sharp points that met at the tips with neighboring trees, not touching but delicately close, and between the tips blinked faint bursts of purple light, similar to interconnected electric bulbs. The ground at the base of the trees was overspread with shards of unblemished crystal scales that had fallen from the trees' trunks like birch bark or flakes of skin. The shed crystals covered the ground in such quantity that the collective shards had a whitish color, even though they were individually clear. Intricate, winding pathways of polished glass linked the courtyard to the outer perimeter of the forest, creating wide, tree-lined avenues, one of which led to the open balcony the Sawstang had swooped in through.

Rai crouched on the floor behind the Sawstang, with Dirtbag and T.C., waiting for the imminent finale to begin. It was strangely quiet in the room, peaceful and serene, except for the idle, low rumble of the Sawstang's engine. Two shadows were watching through the trees, their malevolent grins caught in the alternating patterns of soft light, like eager moonlit daggers.

"Gah! Why hasn't she attacked us yet?" Rai fretted.

"Because this isn't a garden," Dirtbag said, looking around. "Those 'trees' are giant neurons, and the tips of the branches are synapses. This is the spaceship's brain, and every time you see bright light, that's a thought or feeling."

"But all the trees are lit up," Rai said.

"Well, that's probably because it's in pain from all the destruction we caused."

"Oh…" Rai frowned, conflicted.

"Now, wait just a minute, Dirt." T.C. raised an eyebrow. "If this is the brain and, I mean, we fight like we did downstairs and blow up a bunch of stuff, are we giving it brain damage?"

"Are you kidding me?" Dirtbag quipped. "This is going to be a full-on lobotomy."

"Dad!" Rai whispered urgently. "Here they come."

Katvanna strolled out of the shadows with Van Slice by her side; they were wearing spherical glass lockets around their necks. Encased within the lockets were the lustrous stolen hearts of Dirtbag and Rai. Captured hearts were notoriously fragile things, and exhibiting them so carelessly was meant to deter and complicate any attack.

"Are you hiding? From me?" Katvanna said delightedly as she approached. "And after such an improbable grand entrance through, of all things, an unlocked door." She shook her head, amused. "Surprise only works the first time."

Van Slice unlatched his ruined business suit of armor in layers, tossing the shattered plates aside one at a time, revealing a trim, muscular, tanned body adorned in crudely drawn, amateurish tattoos. The recently healed, jagged gash across his sternum had been filled in by a deep black scab speckled with smoldering orange embers reminiscent of a cooling campfire. "Ha! Why don't you come out from there and let me show you how dangerous I really am?" Van Slice enthused, rubbing his hands together with growing anticipation.

"Perhaps we can talk." Katvanna smiled, brimming with evil. "I have such a way with words."

The Sawstang revved up its chainsaw threateningly and prepared to charge. With no one behind the wheel to control it and the key still in the ignition, it was free to do whatever it wanted. It stampeded full throttle at Katvanna, attacking her with an eruption of dragon fire. She brushed it away with a single word that instantly obliterated the car, reducing it to a mound of coarse black dust. Dirtbag sat, stunned that the Sawstang had been destroyed so effortlessly by her.

"Hey, that's fine," he fumed, positioning himself for battle. "This was our last stop anyway."

"It most certainly is." Katvanna laughed. "I wish I had never met you."

"Then you shouldn't have said hello," Dirtbag growled, with Rai backing him up.

"You earthmen are hilarious! Ha! But tell me...are you smart?" Van Slice flexed his arms and hurled three tattoos off.

"The attack-toos!" T.C. shouted, jumping in front of Dirtbag with the Amber Blade of Divorce.

The tattoos grew into spindly, fluidic, two-dimensional ghostly creatures that moved by distorting and stretching their forms. T.C. faced off with a bat-winged skull covered in barbed wire. He maintained a safe distance, goading it. After all, it was unwise to be hasty with an unfamiliar foe. It attacked, and he cut forward, slicing it in two. The inky innards of the creature drained harmlessly away. "It's a ruse, Dirt!" T.C. said, slashing through a plump, heart-shaped spider. "They're just like real tattoos, good for nothing but a moment of distraction. They should call these things distract-toos!"

Dirtbag swung the bike's chrome exhaust pipe at a thorny rose with butterfly wings, splattering it across the ground. "A distraction?" he repeated, but by the time he realized he'd allowed himself to be tricked, it was too late.

Rai cried out in pain. Katvanna pounded her in the kidney and jammed a knee into her lower spine, bending her backward by the throat. Rai whimpered for help, and Katvanna said a word that gagged her daughter's mouth with a plate of glossy-black metal forged out of the dust residue of the Sawstang. Dirtbag and T.C. rushed to rescue her.

"Don't be afraid, Pumpkin!" Dirtbag shouted. "She went for you first because you're the most powerful. You're a threat. Don't let fear freeze you up. Act deliberately. Don't be rash. Think your way out."

"So much advice!" Katvanna railed. "You have some nerve! Where were you for the tween angst? All the PTA meetings? Do you know how much time I wasted on this brat?" She hammered Rai in the stomach twice and slammed her head down onto the stone floor. Rai's eyes rolled up, dazed from the blow. "I raised this creature while you abandoned her for half her life! I would've given her to you; I never wanted this. You brought this upon me, like a blight, like a curse I can never be rid of because of the title 'mother.' Well, watch now as I end what never should have been in the first place!"

With a word, Katvanna crafted indestructible, glossy-black chains out of the Sawstang dust and cocooned Rai tightly in them, head to toe. With a forceful shout of hatred, she unleashed a sudden tempest that swept Rai out of the garden and through the open balcony, where she fell to her immediate death in the unyielding sea below.

Van Slice applauded zestfully. "Taking out the trash, Kat? Ha!" He shook out his arms and danced about like a boxer. "That girl always lacked the ruthlessness life demands. Victors don't just survive; they fight to win. Tooth and nail. Fist and foot. Ha! Hesitation to destroy, that's true cowardice. Kind hearts are, in themselves, the weakest hearts of all."

"She shared nothing with me," Katvanna snarled as she strode around Dirtbag and T.C.

They stared at her, seething. They voiced no reaction. There were no words, no shouts of revenge, and no clever sayings for what she had done. Their hatred was now absolute, and it no longer mattered if they lived.

Katvanna narrowed her eyes confidently. "I killed a stranger today, a thing born out of me like a cancerous growth. I can always create another child, one in my own image, without the many flaws inherited from her father."

"Where are your jokes, earthmen?" Van Slice mocked, rocking back and forth with his fists up in a cosmic-martial-arts stance. "Where is the wit and banter? Ha! At least say something. I would enjoy this much more if you did."

"Animals!" T.C. screamed.

"That's the spirit!" Van Slice taunted, but a brief glance at Dirtbag drew his attention. "Hold on. What's that? Is that my bike?"

It was enough of an opening for T.C. to move on Van Slice, but as he dashed in to strike, Katvanna shouted a word. T.C. instinctively held his sword up to parry the verbal assault. The ten wedding rings embedded within the amber blade radiated with a golden brilliancy, and the evil word deflected off of it and into the garden, shattering dozens of crystal trees. Katvanna was momentarily shocked that a mere sword had thwarted her attack.

The *Empyrean* shook from the grievous injury, the surrounding trees turning bright white with searing pain. Dirtbag batted at Van Slice with the muffler, but the spaceman dodged it and grabbed Dirtbag by the throat, working his lucent fingernails into a stitched seam, attempting to tear Dirtbag's head off with his bare hands. Katvanna screamed an obscenity at Van Slice to get his attention as T.C. quickly closed in on her.

"What kind of knight wears sunglasses? Indoors, no less?" Van Slice said, bashing Dirtbag to the ground with a fist. With both hands, Van Slice seized the air before him and manipulated gravity. An invisible force lifted T.C. off his feet, and a heavy tension pressed in on his body, as though he were trapped in a vice. The effort demanded Van Slice's attention, and Dirtbag used the opportunity to strike from behind. He swung the bike muffler hard, putting all his strength behind it, and a horrific, bone-shattering crack arose from Van Slice's arm. The spaceman screamed, holding his broken arm in disbelief. T.C. fell to the ground next to the Amber Blade of Divorce, his body noticeably caved in across the right side.

"Noble but futile," Van Slice derided through gritted teeth, swatting Dirtbag away with a wave of gravity, knocking the bike muffler out of his denim grasp.

Katvanna picked up the Amber Blade of Divorce and walked over to where Dirtbag had landed. He saw her coming and stood, ready to fight her. She lunged at him with an unskilled swing. He slapped down her hands, flipping the sword around into his. She opened her mouth to say a word, but the air in her lungs rushed out from the unexpected agony of the blade penetrating her body. She fell forward onto Dirtbag, and he embraced her, driving the blade upward into her torso until it appeared out her back.

"The pain!" she cried out, panicking.

"You deserve so much more! So much more than I can give!" Dirtbag whispered in her ear as he ripped his heart locket from her neck. "This was never yours."

Van Slice tore Dirtbag away from her, infuriated. He violently propelled Dirtbag across the room with a blast of gravity, pushing him into the forest, crashing him through row after row of crystal trees until he became crucified in their knifelike branches, unable to move. Van Slice heard a noise from T.C. and made a gesture that utterly crushed him into the floor with such unrestrained might that the stone mosaic around his body shattered apart.

Katvanna limply removed the blade and collapsed, bleeding out. Van Slice kneeled beside her and grasped her hand tightly. She yanked her hand away from him and pressed it against her wound. She closed her eyes and whispered. The blood drew back inside her body, and within moments, she was healing. She shuddered, swallowing her own sweet blood.

"Did you seriously expect to win?" she shouted breathlessly at Dirtbag, grimacing from the gaping wound he'd inflicted. "Did you think this kind of pain was unfamiliar to me? You left me! You worm! We could've had everything! Anything! The world!"

Van Slice gently lifted her to her feet, entertained by the drama, having heard it all before over sultry pillow talk. "Careful, Kat, that weapon has a way of raising long-forgotten feelings," he cautioned as she paused to heal his broken arm.

"Where is his heart?" Katvanna demanded.

"Beside you," he said, and she turned to see it floating in the air. "I took it from him in the course of my attack. Ha! You know I'm a quick thinker."

"You have all the qualities I desire," she said coldly, even as he assisted her in walking across the courtyard. She used the bloodied Amber Blade of Divorce to steady her uneven balance. The heart followed, and when they reached the tree Dirtbag was suspended in, she plucked it out of the air like ripened fruit, placing it around her neck. "Do you see the engraving?" she asked Dirtbag through bloodstained teeth. "When a heart is taken, the name of who it belongs to appears, the true owner's name. So I ask you again, do you see the engraving? Do you see what's written on your heart?"

Dirtbag remained silent as Van Slice helped Katvanna to sit down in front of the crystal tree. She choked down another mouthful of blood, clearing her throat. She let out a long breath, wincing as her injury continued to heal. Van Slice sat next to her, examining the Amber Blade of Divorce with interest.

"How bizarre!" he proclaimed. "Ha! That deceased earthman placed wedding rings inside the blade. Curious that there are ten; was there a reason for this?" he asked Dirtbag.

Dirtbag hung in the tree, brutally impaled, his threadbare denim skin in tatters and his duct-tapped armor falling apart, dangling above the ground like clothes set out to dry. He glanced at the crater where T.C. lay dead and silently raged, forlorn. "It has the power of ten divorces," he calmly told them.

"What a hateful weapon!" Katvanna gnashed, taking the sword from Van Slice and tossing it away. "What a wasted effort. You never had a chance against me."

Dirtbag chuckled bitterly. "Well, a sudden ketchup migration may have temporally put the odds in your favor." His denim body began to tear under his weight. "You know, good usually triumphs over evil."

"Are you really so naïve?" she admonished him. "There is no morality in life, no good or evil, no right or wrong; you do what you need to do in order to build as much happiness as you can in the time you have. And don't deny what I'm saying as untrue. You, of all people, should know what I'm talking about; those are the very words you spoke when you left me and your late daughter to run off with a little princess half your age."

"You murdered your only child," Dirtbag scolded.

"And it made me happy to do so," Katvanna replied, her strength returning. "I'm glad you left. I never could be myself with you around. You never understood me. You were always so judgmental."

"What now, Kat? Should we kill him?" Van Slice asked.

"We can't." She clenched her fists. "I can't."

"Why not?" Van Slice wondered.

She stood up, fully rejuvenated. "I took Loranna's heart out of spite, but I took his heart for a reason." She held up the locket, revealing two names engraved on it, glaring at Dirtbag. "This is one heart made from two souls. You two didn't just die on that hill, did you? You gave yourselves to one another and turned into this—this walking grave! It sickens me how you loved each other so much you became something else entirely. I doubt you can ever be destroyed. I never knew where you died, but when you became this...thing, I was drawn to its power. You were betrayed by the strength of your heart."

"That's not yours!" Dirtbag shouted.

"For a self-proclaimed scientist, you're an idiot."

She turned to walk away. Van Slice smirked, undeniably pleased with how Dirtbag was trapped. He tested the solidity of the crystal tree with a firm kick. The tree was unmoved.

"She's only using you," Dirtbag told Van Slice.

Katvanna spun around. "Are you actually trying to drive a wedge between us?" She asked, tickled. She looked at Dirtbag as though he were a hideous, ragged dog. "You have nothing left; I've taken everything from you."

Van Slice pressed Dirtbag deeper into the sharp branches of the glowing tree, further ripping his denim skin. The spaceman folded his arms and smiled.

"Ha! Kat and I use each other," he laughed. "That's how we both get what we want."

Katvanna sauntered over and kissed Van Slice lovingly on the mouth. He licked her blood off his sunlit teeth, reacting pleasantly to the taste. They embraced and kissed again, and as their lips met, the stolen hearts around their necks wistfully flickered, bereaved of hope.

CHAPTER 42

Katvanna's voice softly murmured through the garden, a soothing, rhythmically pleasant sound that carried the calming allure of a kindness that could never be experienced, only desired and wished for. She lay across the pulverized celestial mosaic, gently caressing the stone floor of the courtyard as though she were touching a lover, her ear listening to the great spaceship breathe. She whispered healing words, mending the broken crystal trees and taming distant fires burning below, methodically erasing the entire battle. Dirtbag watched as the trees regrew around him, their sharp, glowing branches piercing through his chest with ease, further entangling him in a forest of spears. He hung motionless while his denim body was slowly maimed. He had no plan, and his options seemed few, so he decided to talk to her.

"Hey," he mumbled, but she didn't hear him. He realized his voice was weak from his injuries and tried again. "Hey!"

"Oh, are you still there?" Katvanna rolled over onto her back, annoyed she'd been bothered. She played with the vibrant, illuminated locket around her neck that contained his heart. "Do you have a question? Are you interested in speaking to me now that you have no other choice? Are you hoping that I might reveal my grand plan to you?"

"You mean the real-estate scam?" Dirtbag laughed hard, accidentally bursting a seam.

"Don't you dare laugh at me!" She leaned forward.

"Hey, no need to have a fit. Relax. So, how *do* you kill dirt?"

Katvanna narrowed her eyes. "We found a way to neutralize you, not kill you, fool. Even if I turned you to ash, it would only be a matter of time before you were restored, and time, for you, is eternal."

"Well, how do you 'neutralize' dirt, then?"

Katvanna smirked and lay down once more. "We are going to exile you into space. Do you know much about space? It's vast and unending. You can travel in one direction and never return to where you began. That is your fate, to be marooned in the void between worlds." She sat up abruptly, noticing she had chipped a nail. She picked at it, miffed. "After I removed your heart from that rock, your whereabouts became unimportant to me. I only recently heard about this unstoppable creature, this thing you became, and realized it was you. I couldn't risk you interfering with my grand plan, which you so ignorantly mock. I knew I'd be able to flush you out using your enemies or your daughter. Both were motivated to search for you."

"You couldn't do that yourself?"

"It's a big planet, and you know how I adore cheap labor. Punishment and promises are free, after all. But then you delivered yourself to me. Thank you."

"Hey, you're welcome," Dirtbag replied cynically. "I suppose me killing all those villains was a bonus."

"No," she sighed. "I was looking forward to doing that myself. I promised them everything, and they believed it, as though wealth could be simply provided and not earned."

"Did you ever love me?"

"You spoiled me, and I enjoyed that but only until the next man."

Her answer infuriated Dirtbag, and he knew that was how she wanted him to react, but it was also the truth. She had destroyed her heart and with it the feelings she had once had for him, if she'd had any at all. He hung in the crystal tree, defeated, his body torn, an old, threadbare denim sack of dirt, once a man, once a father, now an eidolon of regret.

Van Slice entered the room with a metal bucket full of chrome ash.

"Your daughter apparently murdered my motorcycle." He set the bucket on the floor next to Katvanna. "Can you undo this? I can't reattach a muffler without a bike."

Dirtbag grinned. Rai must have destroyed the bike when he had his back turned. She was a thief after all, so she knew how to be sneaky.

A tiny white flower suddenly opened out of one of his wounds. He rubbed it off using a nearby sharp branch before they saw, but there was a reason it had appeared. The princess only surfaced to tell him something, but this time he already knew: resilience ran in the family.

Katvanna ran her fingers through the ash, admiring the work of her daughter with diabolical satisfaction. "Loranna used a word," she said, dusting her hands off. "It's permanent."

"It's insured, but they won't believe a word did this. Who would?" Van Slice winced from his injury.

Katvanna hopped to her feet and touched the black scab covering the gash on his chest. "Does this still bother you?" she asked, poking at it.

"Yes, Kat. Ouch! Don't be mean." He stepped away from her. "I still feel bad…inside. I feel really bad."

Katvanna examined the scar from the Amber Blade of Divorce on her own body, unfazed by the sharp pains her curiosity caused her. "What a strange sensation. It's like a shadow I can't grasp." She lost interest in it and put her arms around Van Slice. "No matter; with these hearts we can heal ourselves."

"Ha! Does that mean we're still getting married? Even though the earthmen went and killed all of our guests? Who do you want to use for witnesses? Should we find more ninjas?"

"Ugh." Katvanna rolled her purple eyes. "We could lift a rug and find more ninjas. Let's skip the ceremony and bribe someone in authority to make it cosmically legal. Someone malleable. In fact, I know just the man to do it. He should remember me fondly; I spent a summer at his villa. His name is Bloodblivion. He even has an army."

"With a name like that he should be easy to find." Van Slice combed her luminescent, whitish light-blue hair behind her ear. "What about the hearts? Do we ingest them?"

"No, silly man." She playfully slapped his face with a fussy tap. "First, I must purge them of their memories, so we can imprint them with our own. I wouldn't want you to be contaminated by Loranna's poisoned mind." She pawed the locket around his neck. "We then take ownership of them and allow them to enter us."

"And then?"

"Happily ever after." She slowly and passionately kissed him, keeping one eye on Dirtbag to make sure he was watching.

"Screee!"

Van Slice pulled away from her. "Kat, was that your, uh, dietary problem resurfacing?"

Katvanna ignited with embarrassment. "I warned those chefs not to use red onions! I even showed them the soul jars in the cupboard. I'll just have to have a word with them."

"The ninjas beat you to it. Nothing is alive down there, Kat. Those ninjas even killed the potted plants. We'll never find all the bodies. I'm going to have to completely renovate the entire—"

"Screee!"

"There it is again, Kat." Van Slice puckered his brow, disgusted. "This is why you should rethink the whole underwear thing. That way it won't be so loud. It sounds like there's a bird in here."

Katvanna's eyes darted around the garden until she found it. "That's because there *is* a bird in here, you idiot!"

A pied falconet flew out from the shadows and changed into Rai in a flash of black light and feathers. She yanked a wilted, bent, emergency cigarette out from her cleavage, her hands shaking, and put it in her mouth but left it unlit. She fumed, glaring at them.

"Daddy's little girl!" Dirtbag sang.

Katvanna grinned and opened her mouth, but Rai spoke first. She shouted a word so powerful it incinerated her cigarette and ripped open Katvanna's wound with a ferocity that almost tore the wicked sorceress in half. She shouted again and knocked Katvanna down. Van Slice picked up the Amber Blade of Divorce from the floor and ran over to where Dirtbag was entangled. Without hesitation he stabbed Dirtbag in the chest, turning the blade to bore through his fragmented armor until there was an opening large enough to fit his hand.

"Do your worst, scumbag," Dirtbag growled, immune to the pain but not the fear of serious injury.

Van Slice dropped the sword and punched his hand into Dirtbag's body. He dug out a wad of moist earth and began heating it with solar energy.

"Do you think if I irradiate this soil, you'll die?" Van Slice questioned. Dirtbag watched, worried. Van Slice turned to Rai, steam rising from his clenched fist. "Stop your attack, or I will turn your father into a sterile desert. Then we'll see how alive he truly is."

Van Slice crumbled the dry earth through his fingers. She wavered, unsure.

"Rai," a voice said, "down here, on the floor."

She glanced down and saw that T.C. was moving. "I thought you were dead!" She jumped back.

"I did, too. I mean, I just kept waiting for those silver ponies with the naked ladies to come riding out of the light to collect me, but nothing happened."

"Get up and help!"

"I can't move, Rai, but I'm not dead, so you can heal me, right?"

"Gah! I—I'm not—you're flat!"

"You can do it, girl! I believe in you."

Rai looked up at Van Slice, who'd stepped into the courtyard and away from Dirtbag; flabbergasted that T.C. had somehow survived. She remained calm and acted deliberately. She quickly healed the hole in T.C.'s body with her hands. With a deep breath, she leaned down and pressed her lips against his.

"Hey! *Hey!*" Dirtbag yelled. "I forbid that!"

Rai whispered a word into T.C., and his body inflated, instantaneously returning to shape with a shrill, metallic creak. She helped him up.

"Oats alive!" he said, brushing himself off. "How's my hair?"

"Seriously?"

"That was crazy! I mean, I had no depth!"

"You're just noticing that now?" Rai sneered.

"You taste like candy, Rai, like bubble gum and honey."

"Oh! No! Don't share that, please! Just don't."

T.C. chuckled.

"I'm right here!" Van Slice shouted, frustrated that no one was paying attention to him. "I'm a bad man, and I mean business!"

Katvanna sat up, having healed herself enough to halt the profuse bleeding. "Stop them, you idiot—"

Her voice was cut off by a swift kick to the jaw from T.C.'s armored boot. He leaned down and gleefully duct-taped her mouth shut.

"You even got out the dent, Rai!" T.C. said, thrilled.

"You're still hollow, so be careful."

"Careful? I mean, how do you think a tank like me can move so fast? Besides, we didn't call ourselves Blitz Knights for nothing."

"Go, T.C.!" she snapped. "I'll handle Mom."

T.C. launched into action. Van Slice darted across the room and tossed his handful of dried dirt into T.C.'s face in a vain attempt to blind him.

"OK, whoa, that's low." T.C. wiped his sunglasses off. "I mean, Dirt's my best friend; that's got to be some kind of egregious violation, especially since it got in my mouth. I'll just pretend that came out of your filthy bad-guy pockets while you were looking for bus fare. Don't worry; I'll help you find some."

Van Slice elevated his hands to make some gestures; T.C. grabbed both of them and folded back the spaceman's fingers, breaking them all at once. Van Slice stared at his mangled hands and shrieked. He took off running. T.C. chased after him and viciously tackled him to the floor, sending Rai's heart locket spinning a safe distance away.

"Impossible!" Van Slice shouted, trying to wiggle out of T.C.'s grasp. "You should be dead!"

"It's funny; my exes say the same thing, but here I am." T.C. reeled Van Slice in and pinned him down. "Let's get to know one another." T.C. punched Van Slice hard, slamming his head into the stone floor. He slapped the spaceman's face around, humiliating him, and then punched him again. Van Slice blew out a disoriented breath, and T.C. knew the patient was ready for the operation. He wrestled Van Slice over, tucking his starlight-radiating head under a big armored arm, creating a brawny, unbreakable side headlock. Then, one at a time, T.C. began to pull out teeth with his bare hands.

"*Ahhh!*" Van Slice screamed.

"Oats alive! You have some lungs! I thought there was nothing to breathe in space," T.C. said, holding up the first tooth, fascinated by the way it glowed. "Star teeth? That's just got to be rarer than dragon teeth. I'm going to need enough to make a necklace—and maybe a couple of engagement rings. I mean, with me, you never know."

"*Ahhh!*" Van Slice howled. His body flailed as another tooth was pulled out, roots and all.

"It's like bad opera," T.C. chuckled. "Together now. Ahhhh!"

"*Ahhhh!*"

"Ahhhhhh!"

"No! No! Stop! *Ahhhhhhh!*" Van Slice hollered in agony. He made a mad scramble to escape T.C.'s grip, but T.C. sat there and punched him in the head repeatedly, until Van Slice understood his efforts were useless.

. Dirtbag watched the scene from his tree. "Take your time with that scumbag," he encouraged. "Punish him."

"I almost forgot, Dirt." T.C. took out his trusty hair clippers and indiscriminately shaved off all of the spaceman's luminous hair. He paused to appraise the patchy, bald head and decided to take the eyebrows off, too. "OK, now let's see if I can pull out two teeth at the same time!"

Katvanna shouted a powerful word through her taped mouth, simultaneously blasting the gag off and catapulting Rai across the room. The wicked sorceress stumbled to her feet, healed herself a little more, and raised a hand at T.C., who was immersed in Van Slice's pitiful groveling. Rai flew into her aim as a pied falconet, turned into a young woman, and socked Katvanna in the mouth, splitting her lip.

"You horrid little creature!" Katvanna screeched. "I wish you were never born!"

Rai hardened herself against the hatred. "Oh, I know, right? You hate me! You always have! You never even gave me a chance! You even hated him because of me." She pointed at Dirtbag. "You blamed him for everything! You killed him because he forced you to see who you really are!"

"Stupid child! He killed himself over a girl not much older than you."

"No! You drove him away!"

"Enough! You only came here for that." Katvanna pointed at the dropped locket holding Rai's heart, which was lying on the other side of the room.

"You had no right to take that from me!" Rai shouted, trying to protect it. "I can love whoever I want!"

"I had every right! You were of me; did you think I could allow you to shame me that way?" Katvanna yelled, seizing a fistful of Rai's hair. She pressed her other hand over Rai's mouth, digging in with her nails. Katvanna shouted at the fallen heart, shattering it to pieces. The energy held within the locket burned in the open air for a moment and then evaporated away, without a trace it had ever existed.

Rai bit Katvanna's hand to free herself and ran to the empty remains of her heart. She fell to her knees and cried out, "Daddy!"

Katvanna laughed. "Daddy? What can he do? He was never there for you then, and he can't even be there for you now. You always held him in such high regard, but look at him; look at the weak man he is." Katvanna raised her hand. Dirtbag struggled to free himself from his glowing crystal prison.

Rai stood up, trembling; she clenched her fists and shouted a word she knew Katvanna could not counter. It was a word that was not meant to be used in the manner she had used it. Katvanna dropped her arm and stepped back, stunned that Rai had even said it.

"What have you done?" she gasped. "That word. You've ended me. I hope you're happy." Katvanna turned transparent, her skin became like glass, and she filled with a blue, iridescent liquid as she melted down, shrinking into an exquisitely decorated bottle of designer perfume. Dirtbag's heart locket lay beside it, unscathed.

Rai picked up the bottle; the label read, "Katvanna Dolor: The Scent of Wretchedness." She took a small crystal shard from beneath an amethyst tree and embedded the bottle inside it so it could never be opened. "I'm going to find a really hot volcano and toss you in." She sniffed and placed the bottle inside her purse with her other secrets.

T.C.'s mouth hung open; he was astounded by what he'd just seen. Van Slice struggled a bit, and T.C. punched him exceptionally hard, leaving the spaceman unconscious. Rai carried Dirtbag's heart over to him and freed him from the crystal trees with a gentle whisper that broke the sharp branches. He was weak and needed their help to stand. T.C. hoisted Dirtbag under his arm, and together they walked over to Rai's shattered heart.

"Is there anything we can do?" she wept, picking through the scattered bits.

"I'm afraid not, Pumpkin," Dirtbag said, wiping her tears away with his frayed denim hand, smudging her cheeks. "I'm sorry."

Rai examined her father's heart and began to read the names engraved on it aloud, the names of her father and the princess.

"Don't," he stopped her. "She and I don't exist as separate individuals anymore. Our souls reside adjacent to one another within this body. She whispers, like a conscience, and sometimes I listen, and sometimes I don't...because I miss her. In the end though, all there is is me, whatever I am." Dirtbag took the locket from her hands to inspect it. He closed his deep pocket eyes, contemplating. "Take it," he told her.

"Dad! You just can't give your heart away!" she cried.

"I'm your father, and you're my child. I'd give you everything, because I love you more than anything or anyone else in the world."

"Even her?"

"Even her," Dirtbag said.

Rai wouldn't accept it. Dirtbag carefully opened the locket, and the delicate heart fell into his hand. He pressed it against Rai's chest, where it found a place inside her it belonged.

"Now, that's love," T.C. said with a proud smile. "I tell you, I'd blubber; I mean, if the ex hadn't cursed me. Grapes burst out instead of tears."

Rai laughed through her crying. "Gah! T.C.!" She smiled, holding her hands over her chest. A pleasant warmth returned inside her. "Oh, Dad...you really loved her. I can feel you, and I can feel her. She really loved you, too."

A brilliant white flower bloomed out of a gaping hole in Dirtbag's shoulder, its roots spreading throughout his tattered body, giving him newfound strength. Rai could see the change in him. "Can you survive without a heart, Dad?"

"Pumpkin, I think there comes a point when a man has loved enough, and his time can be better spent living without it, comfortable with the knowledge that he had it."

"I guess, in a way, she never left you," Rai said, gently touching the white flower.

"You would've liked her." He smiled. "She was a seamstress."

Rai hugged him, and T.C. hugged them both.

"Dad," Rai said, smothering under all the affection. "He's making this awkward."

Dirtbag and T.C. chuckled and held her tight.

CHAPTER 43

———

The sky turned a bittersweet orange as the sun set into the horizon, burnishing tea-rose reflections across the rippling black ocean waves far below the floating *Empyrean*. Dirtbag and T.C. sat on the destroyed ledge of a burned-out parlor with Rai between them; they were all eating leftover food they had scrounged from the kitchen. T.C. set his finished plate of picked-clean sticks down on a dead ninja, who was half hanging over the precipice, and wiped his greasy, armored hands off on its ragged, sleeveless tuxedo jacket. He picked up Stew Bolli's big, white cowboy hat and examined the chunk missing out of it. He flung it away, and they watched as it was swept out to sea by a light wind.

"What a day," he sighed, stuffed. He rested an elbow on the ninja, feeling drowsy. "I'm just going to close my eyes for a moment." His head slumped down, and he took a nap.

Rai began to lovingly repair Dirtbag's frayed denim skin. He remained still as she worked. "This thing is looking pretty ratty, Dad," she said, pulling torn ends together.

"It's just old, Pumpkin; that's all. It's been through a lot."

"Oh, I see. Did she make this for you?"

"I buried her in it," he said quietly.

Rai stopped what she was doing. Dirtbag took her hand. "It was all I could afford at the time. We had nothing. Between the attorneys and everything else, this was all I could find."

"Dad, I don't know what to say."

"That's actually the right thing to say, Pumpkin, the honest thing. Sometimes there is nothing you can say; all you can do is be there when someone needs you." He combed back her raveled hair. "I always regretted leaving you behind, and she did, too."

"I...I never knew the princess personally, but I know that, through you, she knew me."

Dirtbag listened to Rai as she sifted through her inner thoughts.

"I can't see any of your memories, but I can feel these vague notions, and one of them was to make me part of your new family." Rai seemed startled by what she'd said. "Gah! Dad!"

"Careful, Pumpkin. That's a big heart you have there."

A minute quietly passed by. "I guess—I guess I could make you a new skin, but would you wear it?" she asked tenderly.

"I'd consider it, Pumpkin, but only after this one has nothing left to give."

She put her arms around him and sighed peacefully. He smiled, tickled by her happiness.

It was well into the evening when T.C. decided he had better find Van Slice to see if the scoundrel was fulfilling his end of the agreement. He wandered the empty, well-lit, debris-ridden hallways of the *Empyrean*, searching for the spaceman. He found him mopping the hardwood floor of a large library, his hands wrapped in casts; he was surrounded by expired villains shrouded with designer bedsheets. T.C. stepped over a pile of blood-soaked books, frightening Van Slice as he entered.

"The ship is taking a little longer than expected to heal on its own, T.C. We should be underway by morning," the spaceman spluttered. "I'm upholding my end. You have six teeth already."

T.C. wore Van Slice's extracted teeth like glowing charms; they dangled from a black, glossy chain on his wrist. Rai had crafted the chain out of dust from the fallen Sawstang, and he displayed it next to the braided cord of Muffin's hair, where he'd remember. He unsheathed the Amber Blade of Divorce, as though he had finally had it with the spaceman.

"Don't try me, Sunshine. Those teeth were just a down payment," T.C. threatened. He waited until Van Slice started to sweat and then put the sword away. "I mean, Katvanna was bad, but you—you enabled that woman to be worse."

"I already apologized, and I've promised to make amends, which is more than she was capable of. She had nothing to lose, whereas I—I could be disbarred for this…or worse."

"Only because it didn't turn out your way, right? Oats alive! You enjoyed every minute of your little rampage! Just because you're from space, you think you're entitled? My attorney acted the same way, but now he's in a briefcase." Van Slice looked at him, confused. T.C. continued. "If you mess up, I'll just find you again. Then I'll wrap your head in aluminum foil and put it in a microwave oven with some popcorn. Trust me; you won't have to leave Earth to see stars. You'll see them all the time. I'm sure Dirt has a few ideas, too, and don't forget Rai. I mean, she studied the ancients and has quite the vocabulary."

Van Slice groaned. "The ancients? If only you earthmen knew."

Dirtbag entered the room, accompanied by Rai, looking for T.C. "Knew what?" he asked.

Van Slice glanced at them, barely hiding his conceit. "I studied a bit, too. You people think you're descendants of the ancients, when you're not. They *created* you. You're their toys they left behind. You're all silicon-based life-forms; your beloved ancients were made of carbon."

"That's ridiculous!" Dirtbag scoffed. "A carbon-based life-form couldn't survive in this environment."

"Not anymore," Van Slice enlightened them. "Your ancients were fragile beings who relentlessly murdered one another until none remained. A mishmash of opposing, long-forgotten armies fought a war driven by such unfathomable, destructive forces and hatred that only the extinction of all life, as it was then known, ended it. This planet became a sterile wasteland. The first thing the ancients did after they moved the oceans was seed the barren land that had once been the seafloor with new life. Life they created. It was their technology that would live on. Eventually, long after the ancients died out, life returned, but not the life of old. This was new life, fashioned to resemble what was lost. This whole planet is a manufactured dream, a memorial of wishes. As barbaric and homicidal as they were, your ancients were still, without a doubt, clever engineers."

Van Slice's arrogance returned to full power. "Ha! And those words? Those ancient words? Those are commands, voice commands. It's not magic. It's science on a subatomic level! It only seems like nothing makes sense on this planet, when everything makes perfect sense. Even your sun was reengineered by the ancients. It should be a red giant by now. Ha! Why do you think I came here? Artificial sun, artificial life-forms. Property can't get much cheaper than this."

None of these revelations bothered Dirtbag. "Hey, everyone knows that Earth has had many eras, and this one is no different than any before. There's no mystery to the true nature of the world. It's always been right in front of us—if we wanted to know, but most people don't care. They're too wrapped up in their own immediate lives to understand the intricacies of super science, especially when the broader, amorphous word 'magic' can explain away anything. But you don't really care either, do you? I think you're one of those insecure scumbags that belittle those around them, because, at the end of the day, you're just another star in the sky."

Rai frowned at Van Slice. "Those shoes you're wearing, they're from space, aren't they?" she asked. Van Slice reluctantly nodded, and with a word, she turned his alien-skin oxfords into loaves of white bread. "We're strong in a way you simply can't understand; make sure you don't forget that."

"Now, wait just a minute," T.C. said, confused. "So you're saying science is magic when we don't understand it, but I mean, magic is science when we do?"

"And neither one can make a decent cup of coffee." Dirtbag grinned.

"I'm never coming back to this planet!" Van Slice seethed, kicking off the loaves. "I hope you know the paper work is just getting started on your little cosmic tryst in the desert. That didn't go unnoticed by the powers that be."

Dirtbag and T.C. were unmoved.

The spaceman turned caustic. "The only thing saving you two is that this is considered the middle of nowhere, the imbecilic back-woods of the entire galaxy!"

"Swell. Just be sure to drop us off before you leave. I mean, do I have to stab you with the Amber Blade of Divorce again?" T.C. warned.

Van Slice winced, clutching his wound. "That shouldn't work the way it does!"

"Funny," T.C. said sharply. "I said the same thing about my first marriage, right before I ruined it."

T.C. walked out of the room, and Dirtbag followed. Rai stood in the doorway, watching Van Slice for a while to make sure he under-stood he was a defeated man. He stared back at her. "I...I really did like your mother."

Rai shrugged. "She didn't care."

Dirtbag, T.C., and Rai spent the night roaming the wrecked hall-ways of the *Empyrean*, filling garbage bags with whatever treasures they could thieve. They discovered an intact tea lounge with an automated shaved-ice machine and made the room their base of operations, filling it with their spoils. Shortly after midnight Rai ambled into the tightly packed room with a sack of wallets. Dirtbag waved her over to the counter where he and T.C. were trying out various colored, syrupy, shaved-ice flavors using shot glasses.

"Yay!" she said excitedly, setting the wallets down. "I can't believe you guys have been skipping all the bodies."

"Pumpkin, you could pick up a communicable curse looting dead bad guys," Dirtbag told her.

"Gah! Why didn't you say something? Look at all the coupons I found!"

"Rai," T.C. said through green, syrup-stained lips, "you defeated Katvanna with a single word. You're now one of the most powerful beings on the planet. I mean, I doubt you can even catch a curse."

"Mom was that powerful?"

"Don't let it go to your head, Pumpkin," Dirtbag cautioned, handing T.C. a napkin. "You need to be a better person than your mother and a much better person than me. You should think about getting back together with Jyn—she seems like a good person—but only if that's what you want."

Rai blushed. "I don't know what I want to do, Dad," she said. "But I want to do good."

"Well, that's better than bad."

"OK," T.C. said, clearing the air. "I mean, are we looting or just trying to melt the place down with gooey feelings?"

"We're looting!" Rai said with a mischievous smirk.

"Oats alive, Dirt! I can't remember the last time we had such a haul. I mean, this is going to take all night."

"Well, maybe we should start breaking some of this down." Dirt-bag rummaged through a garbage bag. "Pumpkin, you've got long fin-gernails; can you help me pry these jewels out of this space portrait?" He punched the picture out and handed the golden frame to her.

"This will only look easy," she promised. "But you have to care to do it right."

She set the frame down and, with a word, divided all the compo-nents into their underpinning elements, creating small piles of gems and precious metals. T.C. blatantly passed Dirtbag a gold coin, and Rai wrinkled her nose at the two of them.

Lying discarded on the floor by their feet was the picture, a half-burnt canvas painting of Katvanna standing next to Van Slice, a pickax in her hands, and behind them, a great rock hunched over a bed of white flowers.

CHAPTER 44

———

A silken, white early morning fog filled the streets of the tiny hamlet of Biscuitdale, sprinkling a fine auroral mist of pleasant-smelling hyacinth essence across the entrance of the Just Good Enough Bakery and Coffee Shop. A pair of dragon cars munched on a bail of grassaline in the modest parking lot outside the front window. The local residents had yet to wake, given that this was a Saturday. The shopkeeper normally opened his doors after he made the doughnuts, but this morning he had been asked, and generously paid, to open early.

Inside, a jukebox played terrible music, but it had enough rhythm for dancing. Jyn spryly moved about T.C., purposely tantalizing the big armored knight. Dirtbag slowly danced with Rai, her head on his shoulder, completely out of step with the fast pace of the song. The music finally ended, and it was time for the women to leave, again. They'd already said good-bye twice.

"Remember, she's a hybrid." Jyn pointed to the metallic sky-blue Sawstang tied up outside the shop. "She's an omnivore, so she may have a few quirks."

"Oats alive! I can't believe our old Sawstang was pregnant!" T.C. said proudly, looking at the new car. "Rai told us you two had a little surprise, but this was a big surprise! I mean, whoa, this one even has dual chainsaws!"

Jyn cringed. "She's still a kid, T.C. Treat her like a daughter."

"OK, but that's not actually my daughter, right?"

"Yikes, you better hope not."

"Dirt! I'm a dad now, too!"

Dirtbag combed back his grass-hair. "That's great…I think." He patted T.C. on the shoulder and turned to Rai. Two months had passed, and she had grown her hair out since he'd last seen her. Dirtbag and T.C. had remained at Jyn's ranch to recover from their adventure for only a few days before departing. When they left, she had stayed behind to experiment with her abilities and rekindle her relationship with Jyn. "You're becoming a beautiful woman," he told her. She smiled warmly and held his hands; she seemed overwhelmed with happiness. "Pumpkin, if you ever need to find me, your heart will lead the way."

"Gah! Dad! Don't make me cry!" She looked away then back at him. "Don't get yourself into too much trouble, all right?"

"Don't worry. I'll be good."

She knew he wouldn't be and liked that they shared that trait. She hugged him good-bye. Jyn walked over to collect her, and they managed to make it out the door without concocting another reason to stay longer. Their yellow Mustang flew off into the morning fog, leaving Dirtbag and T.C. alone. The shopkeeper brought out a tray of freshly baked, glazed doughnuts, but they passed on the confections. They sat down at the brass coffee bar together.

"Did Jyn show you that ring?" T.C. asked, sipping from his dainty espresso cup. "You know, I gave Rai the brightest tooth."

"Yeah, she told me. They seem really intent on making it work this time." Dirtbag ordered some green tea. "I asked Jyn to keep an eye on Pumpkin; she has twice the heart of anyone else now. I think it's affecting her emotions. I can't believe Jyn let her keep all ten of those tigers."

"I dunno, Dirt; that's marriage." T.C. picked a ketchup-flavored biscotti out of a jar. "When it works, you don't get it all, but, I mean, you get more than you expected."

"Hey, they're adults; it's their life. They can live however they want, as long as they're happy." The shopkeeper served the green tea, and Dirtbag produced a generous tip. "Let's focus on us."

"Yes." T.C. nodded, enjoying the rush of caffeine. "We dynamic men of action, of bold tales, and of epic struggles. Do you think we could fit a Gatling cannon on that Sawstang?"

"That's your little girl out there; you need to take care of her," Dirtbag said with a chuckle. "I think Jyn gave her to you to teach you responsibility."

T.C. unconsciously fiddled with the faded blond braid around his wrist. "Trust me, Dirt. Somewhere we're needed, and even if we aren't needed there, that's where we're needed the most."

"And that requires a Gatling cannon?" Dirtbag considered the idea. He called the shopkeeper over. "Hey there, coffeemonger, do you know if there's any trouble in this town?"

"Aye, sir, there is. Are you fellas heroes?"

"Well, we're divorced," Dirtbag assured.

"Good enough," the kindly shopkeeper acknowledged politely. "There not be many men ready to stand up to ol' Mad Harvey Bronco. He runs the flour mill around these parts, but you don't get back what ya give him to grind; he taxes ya grain to feed his varmint army of red squirrels. Aye, last week parents accused him of mixing vanishing powder into the preschool's lunch bread; caused a right panic when the little tots turned invisible during recess."

"Scumbag deluxe!" Dirtbag growled.

"Oats alive!" T.C. beamed with excitement. "My kicking boot just twitched, Dirt!"

The door to the coffee shop suddenly opened, and a man wearing a crimson chain-mail tuxedo with a steel-horned, black Viking helmet waltzed in boldly, announcing to them in a gruff voice that his name was Mad Harvey Bronco and he was engaged as of that morning. He sat down adjacent to Dirtbag and T.C. and told them how the lovely young woman he was going to marry had been convinced to commit to the arrangement after he had laid siege to her family's cottage over three nights. "After all"—Bronco grinned smugly—"a man's got to reproduce somehow."

T.C. glanced outside and saw the street was filled with black-masked red squirrels scampering about, some armed with small switchblades. He noticed the Sawstang was inhaling and loudly eating any that happened to get too close to its mouth. The car coughed to clear an obstruction, and T.C. grew concerned about tiny rodent bones getting caught in the digestive transmission.

Dirtbag listened to the chattering squirrels and calmly stirred his tea with a stick of honey. "That's not love," he told Bronco plainly.

"It sure ain't, mister, but I get what I want out of it anyway. Wedding's gonna be this afternoon, as soon as my attorney rides in. I don't mind inviting strangers. I need me a whole bunch of witnesses."

"Nice teeth," T.C. complimented. "What is that? A diamond?"

"It sure is." Bronco smiled, his incisor gleaming. He flagged down the shopkeeper to order a wedding cake for his critters. "I need me something ironic."

Dirtbag tossed a bag of gold on the counter and told the shopkeeper to take the day off. Bronco spun around, livid, and was alarmed to see the man next to him had no eyes. Dirtbag and T.C. sat back, relaxing at the bar, both amused in a manner that made Bronco uncomfortable. Dirtbag finished his drink and coolly folded his hands.

"Once upon a time, there was a man," he began, "who left behind everything he was and went out into the world to find that one thing he was missing. Wait, I forgot to mention that before any of this, he had a daughter…"

And then, quietly, she laughed.

Thank you for reading.

www.ingramcontent.com/pod-product-compliance
Lightning Source LLC
Chambersburg PA
CBHW070613260626
47161CB00007B/2423